This
I Promise You

Also by Jordon Greene

A Mark on My Soul
Watching for Comets
Every Word You Never Said

Also by Kalob Daniel

The Book of Faerie (A Faerie Tale Novella)
The Nexus of Destiny

This I Promise You

A NOVEL

JORDON GREENE
& KALOB DÀNIEL

FRANKLIN KERR

Published by Franklin/Kerr Press
1040 Dale Earnhardt Blvd. #185
Kannapolis, North Carolina 28083-4476
www.FranklinKerr.com

Edited by Christie Stratos
Cover art and design by Myriam Stasbourg
Interior design by Jordon Greene
Jordon Greene author photograph by Kim Greene
Kalob Daniel author photograph by Kalob Daniel

"A Love Like That" poem used by permission.
Copyright © 2020 by Sabina Laura

Printed in the United States of America

FIRST EDITION

Hardcover ISBN 979-8-9860006-1-9
Paperback ISBN 979-8-9860006-0-2

Library of Congress Control Number: 2022912659

Fiction: New Adult Contemporary
Fiction: Romance
Fiction: LGBT/Gay

To every person who has ever
felt less than because of your past,
your mind or body, or anything else
not within your control.

You are worthy.
You are loved.

the scent of rain lingers

long after the downpour has passed

and I want a love like that.

one that doesn't fade

even after the storm.

- Sabina Laura, *Moonflower*

Easton

WHITE CLAW

I pop the trunk on my dinged-to-hell yellow hatchback. I didn't pack a lot. There's only so much that'll fit in a single-room dorm beyond my roommate and me, so it's good I'm not a clothes freak or hoarder. Around the back of the car, I pull my hands reluctantly from my hoody, instantly regretting it as the biting cold nips at my fingertips. Under one arm, I scoop up a cardboard box holding a few paperbacks from my to-read list—hardbacks are too expensive—a pair of new-to-me black tennis shoes, some pictures, and my meds. With my free hand, I drag one of my suitcases out and then start rolling up the sidewalk.

It's not been a whole day and I already miss Boone and Denver. Hell, I want to get back in my little excuse of a car and drive back to Ahoskie. I like it here, I do, but my dorm doesn't have the cutest little midnight-black Schnoodle, who I left whimpering as I walked out the door this morning, or a regal Belgian Malinois, who was a little more composed, though I'm sure he misses me too. Unfortunately off-campus housing is too expensive and on-campus housing means no pets, so they have to stay home with Dad.

I know they'll be okay without me.

And if I go back I'm going to be a sophomore forever! I don't want that. I scare my brain into believing I did the right thing.

It's never easy leaving them behind.

It can't be warmer than forty degrees out here, which is about thirty less than I want it to be, and some skater-looking dude is still wearing shorts. The wind whips against my thick hunter-green UNC Charlotte hoodie and two layers of sweatpants. A shiver climbs through my bones as I walk past the Resident Life building, a few sort of familiar faces with their hands smartly tucked in their pockets, and across an open courtyard to my home for the next five months, Sandford Hall.

It doesn't matter if it's a move-in day like today or just a regular school day, my eleven-story monolith of a dorm has always given me mixed vibes since my cinnamon-intolerant roommate and I first lived here last semester. It's sort of like a mix between a modern minimalist high-rise and an extra-large bomb shelter. I think it's the white-painted cinder block walls inside that really scream *run for cover*.

Inside, a wall of warmth greets my face and I see Taylor down the hall. She's our overzealous and much too talkative RA, so I duck into the elevator and start tapping the sixth floor button repeatedly. My name whistles between the doors just as they shut, and my face morphs into a skewed victorious grin. When they open I find my way to room 617 and prop my suitcase against the wall. I stop to press my fingers against my temple. My eyes are still tingling. Whatever. I turn the key and push inside.

"What the..." Aidan yells, hands flailing. Something flies into the air and thuds against the wall. "Dammit. It's just you."

"Would you like me to go back out and knock?" I laugh.

"No," Aidan huffs, his hands shooting down to cover his crotch where his pants are undone. "Scared the shit out of me though."

I eye him suspiciously as I fetch my suitcase and he puts himself away. He hurries to pick up his phone off the floor, where

I now hear another voice, and it all makes so much more sense. "I'll call you back, hun."

"Ty?" I ask, and he nods. "Giving him a show?"

"That's between *us*." Aidan pooches his lips and grins, which makes his cheeks bunch up and accentuates all the little freckles across his nose and cheeks. That's definitely a *yes*.

"Uh-huh." I drop my box on the elevated bed along the left side of the room and jump onto the mattress. "I don't want to go back to my car."

"Then don't go back?" Aidan shrugs his little shoulders and lies on his back.

"But the White Claws are in my other suitcase." I drop my head.

"Oh, then get your ass out there!" Aidan jumps up, his big brown eyes even bigger than usual.

I show him my middle finger, and we both burst out laughing.

We've been friends for a bit over a year now. I met him in Children's Lit last year, my first semester here at Charlotte—the class was all about horror stories and children. It was a filler class for me, but Aidan's an up-and-coming author even if he can't see it, so he actually wanted to take the class, which meant he made a great final project partner.

"Where's Ty at anyway?" I change subjects. I know he was just on the phone with him, but I thought he'd be here, helping A unpack.

"He's in Greenville," Aidan says. "He's moving in today too."

That's right. His boyfriend started at Eastern Carolina last semester. I guess the move-in dates are harder to work around over winter break.

"Gotcha." I shrug and then pose for a selfie on my bed. The first three suck ass, but the fourth works. I don't hate everything about the way I look, but I don't like it either. Geeky country guy just isn't the vibe. "He's going to be here for your birthday tomorrow though, right? I mean you're turning twenty."

"He *will* be." Aidan sighs. "Wish he wasn't all the way on the other side of the state though."

"Yeah." I shrug. Me and relationships haven't really had a way of working out, so I don't know what it's like to have what A and Ty have, but they've got it. Makes me jealous sometimes but also sort of gives me a tiny shard of hope that my too-skinny ass might have a chance one day. "Least you got me."

"Now I *really* want that White Claw."

Paul

AND THEY WERE ROOMMATES

Get off my nuts and mind your own fucking business.

That is exactly what I want to say to this woman sitting in front of me. But I don't say it because I need her help. With the amount of times I've bitten my tongue since I moved to North Carolina one week ago, you'd think I'd have bitten it clean through by now. She keeps asking personal questions that have nothing to do with student housing. I've been living in my car since the day after I left Kansas City back in December and I'm over it. School's about to start and I need this apartment. I do not want to live in the dorms again. I can't. But I don't even know what else she wants from me.

"Mr. Acre."

"*Please* stop calling me that. It's Paul. Just Paul."

"My apologies, Paul. Listen, I'm trying to help you. But you don't have enough financial aid to afford single-living housing." Mrs. or maybe Ms. or Miss, hell if I know, Gossard—according to her little nameplate—gives me the bad news. "I'm only asking about your relationship with your parents because if they were to help, then we might be able to make this work. Without them, I'm sorry."

"I told you. They don't like that I'm gay. We don't talk. That's why I moved here." I curl in on myself. I shouldn't be embarrassed to admit that. It's just fucking with my head. And I'm really trying to avoid saying "gay" 'cause I swear she flinches every time. *Gah, I need to get the hell outta here.* I'm sure my sour face isn't helping. I'm itching to get to the gym on campus. I just gotta move in first.

This was a bad idea. How am I supposed to afford living alone when I decided poetry was a viable career?

"If you were open to the dorms—"

"No. No dorms. I already told you that."

"—or a roommate? Perhaps we could find duo-living housing for you." She winces. "Would you at least accept a roommate?"

"Do I have a choice?" I sigh heavily and sit up in my chair for the first time since I sat down in this stuffy shoebox of an office. "For real, if that's it then what the fuck ever. I just can't live in the dorms."

Fuck. I shouldn't have said fuck. I shouldn't lose my temper on the lady that holds my living situation in her hands. I wipe my hands down my face. This whole thing is stressing me out!

"I understand." Her lips stretch into a thin line as she digs through the papers on her desk to staple them together and hand them to me. "Take this. Fill it out in the waiting area. I'll work on finding you a roommate."

"Thanks," I deadpan and leave.

The waiting room is packed full of students and it's far too loud for me to think, and my head is starting to pound. I should have eaten breakfast this morning. I'm getting the worst headache. I cannot with people right now, so I go sit on a bench out in the hall.

"Damnit." I run my hand over my face again.

"You good?" someone asks.

I look up to find a gorgeous African American woman sitting on a bench directly across the wide hall from me. She is slender, impeccably dressed in a wine-colored turtleneck sweater dress and a wool trench coat to match. Her heels are the same glossy wine color with red bottoms and she has long box braids tied perfectly on top of her head. Her celebrity doppelganger is 1,000 percent Zendaya. Holy shit, it's uncanny. It's the whole vibe she's giving off, too. And all she's doing is sitting there.

My solitude is over as quickly as it came. "Uh, yeah. I'm good. This day is just not going the way I want."

"Same." She sets her clipboard next to her and leans back against the wall. "I've been trying to get an apartment for a millennium and these bitches *'can't find my original application'* so now I might have to live in the dorms. Again! I did last semester and I literally cannot anymore. I could live off campus 'cause, like, money isn't an issue, but it's too far away for all the shit I have going on. Whatever. Doesn't even matter to these people that I'm a legacy. Which is incredibly in-fucking-convenient. But again, whatever."

"They told me I can't afford my own apartment. Not enough financial aid." I try to be aloof as I shrug away my problems, but I'm so anxious right now that I'm regretting ever leaving Kansas City to begin with. I have to keep telling myself that this move is good for me. I just wish my brain would believe the words I keep feeding it. But I'm here now. Might as well fill out these forms so I can get to the gym and blow off some steam. Hopefully she'll stop talking to me so I can focus.

"Well isn't this just serendipitous." She looks far too happy. Shit.

Guess we're still conversing. Fine, I'll bite. "Why's that?"

I narrow my eyes at her, hoping she'll take the hint. She doesn't.

"Well, we *both* don't want to live in the dorms and we *both* can't get our own place. Thus it's meant to be!" She's so cool and chill and carefree and gorgeous that I envy her. Like the whole world is her play toy and she can do or say whatever she wants. I'm just some wound-up-tight yo-yo ready to drop into the Grand Canyon and explode.

"What is?" I ask with so much annoyance in my tone. I don't mean to per se. I know she can tell and I kind of feel bad, but I'm just not in the mood right now.

I close my eyes and rub comforting circles into the side of my temple. I really should have eaten something.

"Can you not utilize more of the English language?" She scoffs. "We can just be each other's roommates. Duh!"

I snap my eyes open in bewilderment. This cannot be happening. "I don't know you."

"You will."

"You're kinda bossy, ya know." A statement. Not a question.

"What? Because I'm a woman I can't be assertive and get what I want without being labeled as 'bossy'?" She air quotes "bossy" with her perfectly manicured nails that make her fingers look like they're ten miles long. They are also the same wine color. Seems like a fashion no-no to me, yet she looks amazing. I bet her bag matches too.

"No, no, that's not what I meant—" I try, but she talks over me.

"Is it 'cause I'm black?"

"What? No!"

"It's 'cause I'm an Aries, isn't it?" She snaps her head back.

"What does *that* have to do with anything?"

"Everything and nothing apparently. Listen, this will be good for both of us." She leans forward and smiles. "You clearly just moved here and need someone to be your spirit guide and we *both* could use each other's help with this living situation. Plus, you're hot."

"I'm gay." It comes out like I'm claiming to be a serial killer and she should heavily reconsider.

"I'm bi. So what?" The girl is unfazed.

"Gah, who the fuck even are you?"

"I'm Huxley Davenport. Thank you very much." She tilts her head. "And you are?"

"Paul. Acre."

"So, you in or nah, Paul?"

I relent because at this point, I literally couldn't care less. I just want this conversation to end. "What the fuck ever. Fine. I don't care."

"You do, but that's okay." Huxley's still smiling, the victory hers.

"Are you a psychology major or something?" I squint. She has to be.

"Interior Design, actually. You?"

"That makes sense for you, I guess. English for me."

"English major and yet you are positively the worst at having a conversation. We'll fix that. This is going to be fun." She claps like London Tipton with the relentless smile on her face. She's radiating sunshine.

"Oh shit, I'm going to regret this." I say and rub my temples.

"Oh, never." She winks.

"How did you know I just moved here anyway?"

"It's a gift."

Easton

NO SHOW FOR EASTON

"You brought the drinks in, right?" Aidan asks, shutting the door behind him and Tyler.

"Yeah," I say. *You really think I'm going to forget them?* "I brought 'em in after my run."

We went out for dinner earlier for A's birthday, and then I let him and Ty go off on their own to do I don't want to know what, while I went back to the dorm and finished some reading for class. All I know is Aidan wanted to go stargazing, so they drove like thirty minutes away to get out of the city.

"Nice, you didn't forget." Aidan sticks out his tongue before Tyler pushes him back on his bed and crawls over him to cuddle him like a big body pillow.

Internally, I'm screaming. It's not fair. I want that. I want it so bad. Not Aidan or Tyler, but what they've got. Actually doing the shit to get it? No. Hell, the last time I tried dating was in high school and I still hate the thought of his name: Ryan Cook. It took me a full year to realize he was just using me. I still can't figure out why I was obsessed with his frail freestyle-dancing self. But I was, and it was a rude awakening when I finally realized he was a narcissist. His dancing sucked ass anyway.

"I knew I'd be stuck in here all night with you two. Last thing I want to be is sober," I say, heading for the little mini fridge at the foot of A's bed. I hand them both a can of White Claw and drop onto my bed.

Aidan's side of the room, unlike mine, has life. There are posters—everything from professional soccer players to movie posters to some obscure superhero named Zatara I'd never heard of before—a cute photo collage over his headboard, a slew of books on the stark white school-provided bookshelves, and a strand of color-changing LEDs bordering the skirt of his bed.

On my side, it's a lone *Star Wars* poster, a few of my favorite Dean Koontz novels on my shelf, and a handful of pictures tacked up with some sticky putty—that's it. There's one of my dad and me next to the old shed behind the family home, another of him and my sister, Samantha, trying to throw me in the water at the beach—I think Mom took that one before she left—and a few of Boone and Denver.

Other than that there's a lamp and a stack of books under my nightstand. Sartori's *Theory of Democracy* and, of course, one about Alice Paul and the women's suffrage movement topping off the stack. Riveting stuff. I'm weird. I know. Oh, and there's a white cowboy hat dangling on the chair by my tiny little desk. I rarely wear it, but it helps me remember where I came from.

"You don't want a show?" Tyler jokes.

"I'd rather watch the dogs at the kennel hump each other." I shake my head and crack open my can before taking a generous gulp. The kennel is my main job. It's how I pay for my insurance, food, and gas. But I'm such an animal person, so it's fun.

"No show for Easton." Aidan pops his lips dramatically.

"Thank you!" I blow out a breath. "Y'all want to watch a movie?"

"Eh," Aidan grunts.

"Maybe the new *Don't Breathe* movie?" I shrug.

Tyler takes a drink and squeezes Aidan. "I heard it wasn't near as good as the first one."

"Yeah, and that's some dark shit." Aidan twists around and kisses Tyler.

I look away; it just feels wrong to watch them kiss.

"Coming from the dude who's about to get a gory horror book published." I cock my head and grunt. "I've read your shit. That's disturbing."

"I mean..." Aidan grins and giggles deviously. I think it's partly because he knows it's true and partly because he's getting tipsy. "True. But uh...no one said it's *actually* getting—"

"It is," Tyler interrupts him.

"—published. Stop!" Aidan eyes his boyfriend, head wobbling, and bites at his own lip. "Gotta keep my hopes low."

I shake my head. He finished writing his story before I met him, and he landed his agent last semester, but we still can't get him to believe he's going to make it. He is though. His stuff is good. Scary and bloody as hell, but good.

"No, keep 'em high!" I correct him as I feel the alcohol slowing my speech. We're all lightweights.

"No!" Aidan insists.

"Yes!" Tyler wrestles with him, literally. "My boyfriend is an amazing writer."

Aidan rolls his eyes, and I laugh but it comes out more as a grunt. I'm so damn jealous. I want a man to hold me like that. *Stop it. It's stupid.*

"Let's make a toast," I blurt to get my mind off it. "To A! Newly minted...uh...oh yeah, twenty-year-old, and soon to be best*selling* author." The words drip off my tongue as I raise my white can.

"To A!" Tyler raises his can and we all take a gulp.

"What uh...what were we watching again?" Aidan stutters.

I squint. Hell, what did A say he wanted to watch? Oops. "I don't remember."

"*Star Trek!*" Tyler shoots his pointer finger to the sky like it's some awesome idea.

"No!" Aidan shakes his head.

Was it *Star Trek*? Aidan hates *Star Trek*.

"I mean…we…" I blow out my lips and release a big breath. "Okay."

Paul

FRECKLES

Huxley and her parents spent all weekend moving into and decorating our new place, save for my room. She forced me to meet her parents, and I'm not going to lie, they seemed nice. Rich, but they were pleasant, not really how I expect rich people to act. I'm still not sure why she couldn't just get her own place. Her parents can clearly afford it. I've known her for two seconds and I can already tell she's the type of person to get whatever she wants.

Her parents seem cool though, I guess. I don't know. Parental figures make me uncomfortable. Which makes sense with the parents I have. So I did what I felt obligated to do and left her to do whatever the hell she wanted while I locked myself in my room with the few possessions I took with me.

Gah! Must be nice to have parents to depend on for literally everything. My parents are pretty well off and they gave all five of us a monthly allowance. I tried to get a job as a teenager, but my dad wouldn't let me. He wouldn't let any of us. He said, "If you have time to work, you have time to find your own place and pay your own fucking bills." He wanted to control everything we did. So I just took his money until he stopped giving it.

When I left Missouri I had a good chunk saved up, but I knew it would come to an end, so I lived in my car and showered at any gym I could find on my way to Charlotte.

Until today. This apartment is a godsend.

I still can't believe I actually did it. I moved out of Kansas City. The place I had spent my entire life. The very *center* of hell, though it wasn't always like that. I miss my younger years when life seemed less complex, before puberty. Before I started to notice boys. I had to go though. I couldn't be there anymore with all the bad shit life turned into.

So I found a random school where I could transfer my credits and still graduate on time, filled up my car with anything I could fit into it, and left. There really isn't anything more substantial to it. I didn't give a fuck, I just wanted to go. Now I'm in Charlotte. I could've gone anywhere. Yet I'm here.

Huxley really went all out designing the living room. It's not big but definitely larger than a dorm. Even though I have to share, I'm thankful. We each have our own bedroom with our own bathroom on opposite ends of the house. Her room is toward the front, off the living room, with a balcony. Mine is the smaller room at the back off of the kitchen, no balcony.

I had enough stuff to sort of fill my room, but all the shit in the living room makes my room laughable. She even painted. Peacock blue, she told me. Let me reiterate, *peacock fucking blue*. Who paints their walls peacock blue? I don't hate it, I'm just surprised. It's actually incredibly chic.

Maybe I *should* ask her to help with my room?

"Oh hey, you're home!"

"Shit! You scared me." I jump. Where the *hell* did she come from?

"I tend to do that. My bad," Huxley apologizes.

"So much to look forward to then," I deadpan with an eye roll. She's smiling and I can't help but match it. I just got back from the gym and made a smoothie. I take a swig and gesture to the living room. "How did you do all of this in two days?"

"It's cute, right?" You can tell she isn't really asking. She knows it's cute. She also didn't answer my question. I hate that shit.

"It's amazing. You're a witch or something."

"Damn right I am. Anyway, what are you doing tonight? Wanna go out?"

"What? Why? It's Monday!"

"It's the first week of school and there's shit going on every night. My friends and I go to this little speakeasy to drink and chill and tonight they're having an open mic night. They can't go, so I thought we could go together, yeah?"

"Uhhhhh—"

"I'll take that as a yes. Shower and put on something cute. If you need help, I gotchu. Actually, I might have an oversized striped button-down thing that would fit you nicely. Do you have black skinny jeans? Preferably with holes in the knees?"

"Uh. Pretty sure all of my jeans have holes in them."

"Perf!" Huxley does this shoulder wag thing.

"Are you always like this?" My eyes narrow.

"You'll get used to it. Now go. You stink and we need to leave in thirty."

Thirty minutes? Dammit! I still have no idea who this woman truly is. I've known her for two days and she fucking terrifies me. But also, I think I kind of like her.

* * *

We arrive at Uptown Slam just before the show starts at ten and it's already packed. I let Huxley dress me because I figured it would just be easier than trying to fight it. I'm wearing a white button-down with tan, navy, and cream stripes on it—silk, I think, and it probably cost more than my car—with the top three buttons undone, my black slim-fit jeans, a light-brown suede Chelsea boot that I already owned, and my black leather jacket.

My closet isn't terrible, I just don't have anywhere to wear anything.

It's cold as shit, but according to Huxley these lightweight clothes are "my brand" — I swear she is just like Alexis from *Schitt's Creek* and I love it — so I'm suffering through the January chill. She also lent me some necklaces and a ring that only fits on my pinky finger. My tattoos are on full display.

Oof! I haven't been around this many people in a long-ass time. It is a quaint little place. Totally a Seattle hipster boho vibe. There are a shit ton of plants. The bar sits off to the left and a small stage to the right with an eclectic range of seating that centers around a large leather sofa.

Huxley beelines to the bar where she seems to know a few people. She introduces me as her new BFF. Honestly, it kind of makes me uncomfortable, but I push through my social anxiety. She drove, so I can't just hop in my car and leave whenever I want. *I can do this.* It's just a few hours of pretending with a smile. If I'm good, then maybe we can just go home after this without Huxley dragging me to do something else.

Huxley mentions she's going to the restroom and I crack a joke about her not using the potty before we left. She flips me off, smiling, and she and one of her friends leave. I already forgot that person's name. Maybe I can't do this.

"So, you're Paul, right?" says the other guy Huxley left me with. This better not be on purpose.

"Yep." I could be nicer, but I don't care.

"I'm Pablo." We shake hands. I don't say anything else. It's awkward for a second before he speaks again. "How long have you known Huxley?"

"Two days." Maybe I could lie and say I need to use the bathroom. But he might follow me. Shit.

"No shit? Y'all hookin' up?"

"What the fuck, dude? No."

"Just askin'." He shrugs. Why the hell did I agree to come to this again? "You goin' to perform tonight?"

That piques my interest. "I can do that?"

"Sure. Anyone can. Sign up sheet's at the end of the bar."

I knew it was an open mic, but I didn't know they'd let anyone perform. I feign excitement and leave him because I cannot get away fast enough. My mind is on one-track overload now.

Should I perform one of my poems?

I write. I dabble. I'm an English major because it's the only thing I could even damn well tolerate doing after high school. And it's easy. I haven't picked my emphasis yet, but I do write. This seems like the place to do something like this. It's totally that crowd.

I don't have my notebook, but I have a couple things on my phone. There's this witty one I wrote a while back. It's fun and lighthearted but also complex because it makes no sense. That's something I could do. I should do it. I will. I can do this. I think I'll do it. Should I do it? Oh my holy hell. I don't know why the fuck I'm doing this. Why am I here?

Huxley still isn't back yet, so after I sign up I walk away before I bitch out. People are still conversing, so it isn't hard to find seats. I scroll through my iPhone, and find the piece again. I read through it a couple times and, for the most part, memorize it.

When I look up from my phone I make eye contact with the cutest freckle-faced guy at the bar. He's kinda short—not Huxley short, though, but most everyone is short when you're six-one like me—with a darker olive complexion. His skin looks so smooth. He doesn't seem to be with anyone and he definitely doesn't look old enough to drink. I don't drink, but maybe I could buy him one. He smiles and looks away just as Huxley sits down.

Never mind.

"You good?"

She seems to ask me that a lot. "Do I look like I'm not good?"

"You look flustered and tense. Do you want me to have Pablo give you a neck massage?" I don't like the look of her smile. She definitely left me alone with that prick on purpose. I mean, I'm sure he's fine, but I don't know him. I don't know anyone. I almost tell her what he asked me, but I don't.

"Fuck that guy."

"Alright, well if you really want to I'm sure there's a back room y'all could do it in right quick." She has no filter, and it doesn't stop there. "Everyone loves a good quickie. We stan."

"Huxley," I bite.

"Listen, I saw your name on the sign-up sheet. What are you going to perform?"

"It's...uh." I stop. She'll have to wait like the rest. "A surprise."

"Mysterious. Love that for you. Don't fuck it up in front of all these people."

"Not. Helping," I sputter through gritted teeth.

"Relax, Paul. You'll do great— OMG, yay! Easton's here!" Her eyes shoot by me. "I haven't seen him in forever. You'll meet him after, he's the best."

Huxley keeps talking, but I tune her out. When in the history of someone telling someone to relax has that person actually fucking relaxed? Seriously, I do appreciate her concern, it's not that. It's just been a fat minute since I've even looked at another boy.

I loved—or I thought I loved—my ex, Michael Hernandez, but that dickweed can rot in hell for all I care. Not everyone believes in monogamy anymore and that's fine, but I still do. If you don't, you should communicate that. He had one idea of what our relationship was and I had another. Not to mention he was a dick to me about the whole thing after I found him fucking some other dude in *our* bed. But whatever.

I'm not an idiot, I know people check me out, but I do not engage. I know I have a nice body, all the muscles, but it's not about the aesthetic for me. It's about the function. The gays just don't see it that way. Dating is a hassle and a half that I most certainly do not care to partake in. Call me a bitter, old, cynic, or whatever, I don't care. I don't know about this Easton dude, but Freckles is cute and he smiled that smile at me and now I still don't know what to do with myself. All I can think about, all I can *see* are those damn freckles.

I hope he likes my piece.

I'm gonna throw up.

Easton

GREEN EYES LIKE SEAFOAM

"It's a no-go." Aidan rolls his eyes.

"What did you expect?" I laugh and nod toward a pair of plush-looking seats that resemble living room furniture. This place is different in a cool sort of way. The lights are low and filled with a dull neon blue glow from a hodgepodge of bar lights and beer signs along the walls.

"I'm almost twenty-one." He grins and takes up residence in the chair next to me facing the stage. Somehow Aidan thought they'd sell him a drink.

We ended up at a speakeasy in NoDa — North Davidson; it's the art district, so they can't just call it that. I don't start back at the kennel until Thursday and I finished my Party work earlier, so I can sleep late tomorrow. I'm part of the state Democratic Party's social media team. They hired me after I headed up social media for Nichelle Harrison's successful congressional run against this raging theist named Bob Walters a few cities over. I didn't want to pack up and move to Washington when she offered me the job. Maybe it was stupid to turn it down, but I want to finish school, and I'm already four hours away from my dad and sister. I didn't want to make it farther. Not to mention starting all over finding a doctor, and I doubt there are any country bars in D.C.

"Yeah, but you look sixteen," I remind him. It's because he's so short and can barely grow a beard. All he can manage is a porn stache like a fifteen-year-old going through puberty.

His middle finger pops up, backlit by the blue glow, but he's grinning.

"You going to sign up?" he changes topics. My face skews in confusion. Why the hell would I sign up? "You could bore everyone with one of your depressing monologues on how we're killing the planet or why we need to ban assault rifles. Riveting stuff, you know."

"First, that's important shit." I give him my best faux annoyed look. "And second, fuck you. There's no way I'm getting up in front of everyone."

I'm too anxious in front of crowds. Now give me one or two people to talk to about how they need to require all semitrucks to be electric within the next ten years and that they should make all these smog-blowing small-dick-guy trucks not pass emission inspections and I'm good. Just don't ask me to talk to a group. I can't.

Aidan laughs as a guy takes the stage and the lights brighten around him. Showtime.

Two hours later—and a plethora of musical acts, a few half-decent comedians, and one weird but seriously hot poet dude later—everyone is on their feet talking about their favorite or least favorite act.

"I need that Junaloco group's music," Aidan says again. He was raving the moment he realized they played rock, and I just know I'm going to be hearing their music back in the dorm. "What did you think of them?"

"Eh," I shrug. They were good, not my type, but at least they didn't make me understand why everyone here is drinking, unlike the rest of the acts.

"Huh? That's your type of music though, right?" I can't tell if he's serious or joking. I hope to God he's joking.

"You've known me for, what? Like two years," I remind him. How dare he think I like old '90s covers.

"I know. Swear you're the only gay I know who likes country." He kicks my foot.

"And some indie," I correct him. I'm more than my country music.

"Still weird," he says and I roll my eyes.

Weird my ass. I'll never understand people who go to a concert knowing they're coming out with an ache in their neck from headbanging. It doesn't make sense.

"Uh…hey," someone says to my left. When I look, the first thing I see is an ornate black and white angel on their forearm. Their other forearm is covered in flowers leading up with the bottom half of what looks like a wolf peeking below their sleeve. Part of a butterfly shows on their chest through an unbuttoned shirt. A rose wraps around a dagger pointing up a thick muscular neck leading to the most perfect face, a trimmed beard, and short bleached blonde hair. I noticed the tattoos when he was on stage, but we were too far back to make them out. Now I take them all in, right before my eyes glue to his green eyes. They're like seafoam.

That's when I realize he's not talking to me. His eyes are twitching between Aidan and anything else he can find.

"Hey." Aidan smiles, because unlike me he's nice to everyone. Not to say I'm not, but when some random comes up and interrupts my conversation, a smile isn't what they usually get. Even if they are sort of hot.

There's a pause. Well, this is awkward. His poetry was weird, and I didn't understand it all, but I don't mind looking at him.

"Yeah, so saw you at the bar earlier…and…uh…I…" The guy keeps falling over his own words. It's actually sort of endearing. "I'm Paul."

He puts out his hand and Aidan shakes it. I can see the reservation in A's face, but there's the eternal optimist too. My eyes jump between them, wondering what's about to happen next.

"I'm Aidan," he introduces himself, and I'm about to step in and be like, *hey we need to go, we don't know this guy*, when he keeps going. "And this is my friend, Easton. He's single."

My eyes go wide. What the hell, A? I mean yes, he's hot, and part of me wouldn't mind going down on him, but way to just sacrifice me!

"Pleasure to meet you, and you too, Easton." Paul says my name almost like an afterthought before returning to Aidan. Makes sense. I've got nothing on Aidan. "Could I get you a drink? Maybe we could hang out for a bit," he tries, his eyes still glitching between Aidan and anything but me, "if you have time?"

I lock on Aidan. For the tiniest second I see the gears grinding into overdrive behind his eyes. This guy might be A's way to a drink. But then the gears screech to a stop and a calm smile crosses his face.

"I'm sorry, but I'm taken," is all Aidan says.

God I respect the hell out of you right now, A.

"Oh, I could…still get you a dri—" he tries again.

"Excuse me." I step between them and raise my heels off the ground to get closer to eye level with what's-his-name…Paul. "He said he's taken, dude. Don't be a douchebag."

Like, I don't know where the gall came from. I'm not the type to jump in when things get testy, but it just happened. The words poured out, and it's like I autopiloted straight to Stupidland. My brain didn't finish computing before it decided to jump. Hell, the guy's arms are carved in sculpted muscle and his hand could probably crush my throat. Not that I'm thinking about his hand around my neck.

"Excuse *you*." Paul's voice deepens further, his eyes darken, and the nerves that just a second ago tinted his words are gone. His posture straightens and I lose another inch. "Who are you calling a fucking *douchebag*?"

"You," I blurt. Again, why? I want to coil in on myself and cry, but I can't show weakness now.

"I wasn't talking to your bitch ass. I don't give a fuck who you *think* you are—"

"What the hell is going on here?" Huxley jumps in.

I saw her across the room before the open mic started. I'd meant to say hey—it's been a few months since I've seen her—but I forgot. She pushes her braids back over her shoulder and eyes Paul down. Or up? Their height difference is jarring.

"This asshole won't take no for an answer," I tell her, while Aidan angles his head down and keeps his mouth closed tight.

"Paul?" She looks at him again, but there's confusion painted across her face.

Wait, what? She knows him?

I don't know Huxley well, but she doesn't seem the type to hang around assholes. And this guy is one hundred percent asshole.

"I was only offering to get him a drink." Paul nods toward Aidan.

"Well he's taken, and he told you that, so beat it." I keep up my bravado even though I don't know where it's coming from.

"If you say one more word to me I'll *beat* your ass." Paul lurches forward in a false start, and it scares the hell out of me.

I jump back as Huxley throws herself between us, pushing Paul back as he reaches around her to get to me. I freeze. I don't know what to do. I'm never in this type of situation and apparently I have no flight response, because I'm just staring at him like a paralyzed antelope ready to be devoured by a lion.

"What's going on over here?" a voice yells from the counter, and then there are men rushing over and yelling for us to get out. It's all a blur until we're outside on the sidewalk. Then the fact that I about got my face beat in for opening my stupid mouth sinks in. My pulse races. I take a deep breath. We're not out of deep shit yet. The Paul guy is still here.

I turn to Aidan. His eyes are wide and annoyed, and his mouth is moving, and slowly the words take form in my ears.

" —a grip, man."

But I missed the rest.

"Sorry, I didn't mean to—" Paul, otherwise known as the douchey hot guy, starts to apologize, but I'm not having it.

"Just fuck off, man." I show him my middle finger and then turn to Huxley as she's holding him back. "Take your *friend* home."

"Don't worry, we're going *now*." Huxley eyes Paul. "*Right*?"

He practically growls at me before huffing and turning.

I smack my lips and look at Aidan. "That was something."

"Yeah, he's definitely your type."

"Excuse me?" I jerk my head back in surprise.

He looks at me like I'm insane but doesn't say more.

"Okay, okay." I roll my eyes.

Fine, I might have a history of sketchy narcissistic guys. And he was hot.

Paul

ON A FUCKING MONDAY

We round the corner from Uptown Slam to head back to the parking lot. "Seriously, what *the hell* was that about, Paul? It was pretty fucking petty if you ask me."

Huxley's brow is furrowed and she's walking fifty miles an hour. I struggle to keep up while simultaneously trying to put on my leather jacket. She's pissed. It's cold as shit and I'm pissed, too. More at myself than anything. When that shithead called me a douchebag, it just set me off. She's probably trying to figure out how she can get out of living with me now. Wouldn't be too hard since the apartment is pretty much hers anyway. Maybe I should just pack my shit back up and go.

"I'm sorry. I'm so sorry. I—" It's all I can say because I don't even know who I am right now. I never fight. I've never actually hit anyone before. Having muscles is still a new development for me to wrap my mind around. I've been a six-foot-one skinny white boy my whole life. But now that I have muscles I...I, what? Want to fight someone?

No.

And the look on his face. Dammit, I shouldn't have done that. But he didn't need to call me a douche! How was I to know Freckles had a boyfriend? I finally put myself out there and I get fucked in the process. *This* is why I don't do this shit. AND ON

A FUCKING MONDAY!

Huxley doesn't say anything else for the rest of the night. She blasts Demi Lovato all the way home and then goes straight to her room.

I guess she knew that dude? I can't even remember his name now. It's like I blacked out. I can't do this. I just moved here, started *one day* of school and I'm already in over my head. Moving here was a bad idea. I should have just stayed my ass in Kansas City, Missouri. I could have figured it out. I could have. But I didn't and now I'm in North Carolina picking fights with bad-mouthed *children*.

I can't do this.

I stomp into my room, curl up in bed, and grab my notebook. I start to write manically. It's all so terrible. I know the words I'm pouring out are not good, but it's the pain I'm feeling right now. It's my loneliness and every moment where I've fucked up my own life.

Once I'm done I feel empty and raw. But at least these feelings are no longer inside of me for the moment. And then I am able to fall asleep.

Easton

THERE IS NO MAYBE, ONLY DO

"I can't tell if you hate or love this Paul guy," Cameron says. He's Aidan's former roommate, this tall, slim, pale boy, with short messy brown hair and a voice that is so much deeper than you'd expect from a cute guy like him.

"Like, really?" Aidan laughs.

We're taking a short break between classes for a quick catch-up in the little cafe in Fretwell. My egg and cheese croissant is half eaten on my plate, and a surprisingly good mocha frappe is in my hand.

"Come on. Nothing wrong with admiring the bad guy a little." I shrug and look at Aidan. "I mean, you saw him. He *was* hot. A major asshole, but *hot*."

"Eh, I don't know. Being an asshole sort of makes people unattractive to me. Plus," Aidan pauses, then continues, "he was a *little* too built."

"Yeah, yeah." I roll my eyes and take a sip of my frozen treat. It's not like I want to date him. Sex? Sure, but that's it. He's a total douche. No question about it.

"So how are things with Quinton?" Aidan asks Cameron.

I don't have a clue who that is, so I sit back and listen, while the douche's face keeps scrolling through my mind. I can't get the image of him wrapping his hands around my neck out of my mind, and it's got me all worked up.

"I don't know." Cameron smirks. That doesn't sound good. "I think maybe we're just too different."

"Oh." A's lips form a tiny O. "Sorry, Cam. That sucks. He seemed really nice."

I zone out for a moment. I don't know who Quinton is and it doesn't sound like it's going that well. All I catch between more flashes of the Paul-sized-douche is something about there being too much of an age gap and wanting different things, and Cam's thinking about calling it off. Then Cameron gets up.

"I gotta get going. Can't be late for Chemistry again." Cameron rolls his eyes. "Hat looks good by the way."

Cam's looking at me and nods toward my cowboy hat. I finally decided to wear it today, and my cowboy boots to match. I might be in Charlotte, and I might be gay, but I'm still country. That'll never change.

"Thanks." I smile and we say our goodbyes before he heads off.

"It actually does look good," Aidan says.

"Of course it does." I put on a little fake confidence. I mean it is a cowboy hat, of course it looks good. It has nothing to do with me though.

Aidan shakes his head. "You've really got—"

My phone rings on the table, serenading the room with Kane Brown's "Heaven" and saving me from whatever pep talk I'm sure A was about to give me. I check the screen. "It's Dad."

I accept the call and put it on speakerphone. Dad loves A. The music fades as the line opens.

"Hey, Dad, what's up?" I answer.

"Hey, bud—" Dad's voice comes over the line before Aidan yells.

"Hey, Dad!" Aidan always calls him that. It's weird, but I don't say anything about it.

THIS I PROMISE YOU

"Is that Aidan?" Dad laughs.

"Yep, it's me!"

"Hey there, Aidan," Dad says. "Just thought I'd check in."

"It's only been four days," I remind him, laughing and shaking my head for Aidan. "And aren't you at work?"

"I'm sitting in the parking lot," he says. I have to bring the phone closer to hear over the chatter in the cafe. "Got another ten before I have to go in and just thought I'd see how your classes are going. You too, Aidan."

Before I can respond, Aidan scoots his chair right against mine and starts up. "Classes are exhausting, Mr. Belle. I'm in my first actual nursing class and ugh. It's going to kill me, I swear."

"Nursing's a hard major," Dad says.

Before Aidan can reply I speak up, eyeing A jokingly. "Classes are good so far. This class on the planets is going to be hard though."

"But so much fun," Aidan tails my sentence.

"Sounds difficult," Dad laughs, and then his tone changes. It gets quieter. "How've your eyes been?"

"They're okay." I tell him while Aidan shrinks a little and eyes me caringly. There's still a small tingle behind them, but it's barely noticeable. The week before last my vision got all blurry and oh my God my eyes hurt. It was a relapse. I have multiple sclerosis. Didn't know until junior year when the very same thing happened and I thought I was going blind.

I don't like thinking about it.

The line goes quiet for a moment. Dad knows it's not my favorite topic, but he wouldn't be Dad if he didn't ask, I guess. I hear him cough on the other end.

"Well that's good. Make sure you let me know if it gets worse, okay?" Dad says more than asks. "And don't forget to take your meds."

"Okay, Dad. I will, don't worry about me." I tell him. "I'm

good. Promise."

"So, met any guys?" Dad's voice morphs into excitement. It's weird. Like I knew growing up that he'd always be there for me, but I never expected him to ask if I found a guy. But he does, a lot, and it's honestly sort of awesome.

"Nah, it's a drought so far," I laugh, telling myself not to say anything about last night's hot asshole. Of course, I also fail to mention I'm not looking, and that even if I did, none of the guys I find attractive are going to want a chronically ill guy like me. He'd have something to say about that.

"What about Aidan? You two get along." Dad refuses to let it go. And while I did have a crush on him when we first met—and made the mistake of telling Dad—he does have a boyfriend, plus he's sitting right here, eyes wide and biting at his lip like he's about to burst out laughing. Why me?

"Dad! He's right here!" I remind him.

"Oh, darn it. Sorry, Aidan," Dad apologizes. "Old man brain."

"It's all good, but yeah, I've got a boyfriend," Aidan reminds him. It's the second time in less than twenty-four hours he's had to say it.

"Which I've *told* you before," I remind Dad.

"I'll try to find him someone, Mr. Belle." Aidan eyes me down, trying not to laugh.

"Sorry." Dad huffs again. "Well, there's got to be someone out there. It's Charlotte. Aren't there supposed to be lots of gays there?"

"Yeah, but…" I shrug even though he can't see, guess it's more for A. My cheeks are burning up. A knows I don't like him like that, but it's still embarrassing. "Maybe one day."

"No. There is no *maybe*, only do." Dad even makes his voice sound like Yoda, and I cringe inside for him even though A seems to be eating it up. The impersonation wasn't even close.

"Please no," I giggle.

"Alright. I gotta go anyway," he laughs. "Love ya, bud. You too, Aidan."

"Love you, Mr. Belle!" Aidan nearly screams, and I roll my eyes.

"Love you too, Dad."

Paul

FUCKING GOOSE

Waking up at six a.m. is always easy for me. No matter what time I go to bed, my body wakes me up bright and early. I used to hate it, but now it works in my favor. Working out early is so much better for my body and my mood. And let's be honest, anything to boost my mood is *insanely* welcome. Especially lately.

Wednesday is cardio and it's time for a five-mile run around campus.

I shuffle my Boys Like Girls/All Time Low running playlist and start running.

The squirrels here are larger than the ones at UMKC, which I didn't think was possible, and there are geese everywhere! I'm just passing Panda Express when I almost run right into one. I keep running, but I see another just ahead and I *swear* that it's staring me down. If I have to fight a goose today I will burn this entire campus to the ground. Oh shit, and now it's coming closer. It's moving fast toward the sidewalk. Surely the little shit can't be coming for me. They're everywhere, so surely they're used to having people around. I pick up my pace to get past it, but it's not enough. Its wings flare and it jumps me, it literally jumps me. I scream and leap away…right into another person.

Well shit! I think as we both fall hard into the grass. Limbs flailing everywhere, trying to get the upper hand. We land with me on my back and them in my arms on top of me. Their face is a blur, inches from mine, and I can feel their minty breath on my face. I lick my lips subconsciously and then I panic and throw them off of me to stand.

The killer goose is gone, deciding I'm no longer a threat, or so it seems, as it waddles off.

"Shit, shit, shit! Oh no! I'm so sorry, man. I didn't mean to run into you. That fucking goose got in my way. I was just— *You!*" It's him. The dude from open mic night. Out of the thirty-something *thousand* students on this campus I just *had* to run into him? And over a damn bird.

"You've got to be shitting me," he says as he rounds on me. He's pissed, but I'm more pissed 'cause I have to look at his face...again! He better not try me because today's not the day. I just barely started my run.

"Like I said," I start while I pick up my AirPods off the ground. My phone is strapped to my arm and I put my music on pause. This child isn't worth me missing "The Great Escape" over. I'm taking my time on purpose and I can tell it's making him even angrier. This is actually so fun. "I didn't fucking mean to knock you over, *dude*. I was running and that goose— I shouldn't have to explain myself. It is was a fucking accident. Get over it." I try to keep my cool, but my blood starts to boil just from looking at him.

"Like hell it was!"

At this point I completely lose my shit. Petty doesn't even begin to describe what is about to come out of my mouth. The nerve of this guy, the audacity, the gumption! "Yeah fucking right. Get over yourself, man. No one is fucking coming for you like that. You're an idiot. Now move along back to Mommy."

He steps closer to me. He's shorter but not by much. Maybe five-eight if I had to guess. Either way he has to look up at me, which makes me chuckle. Pure, unadulterated anger flashes in his eyes at the same time that I smell something citrusy yet spicy. It actually smells good. Maybe his cologne? Either way, that just tells me he's way too damn close. But I'm not backing away now. His puny ass doesn't scare me.

"What did you say?" he asks. His brows are nearly lost in his eyes with shock and bewilderment and...fury.

I step close enough that he is obscured by my shadow and whisper, "I said back the *fuck* up and get outta here before you *deeply* regret it."

The lump in his throat drops and rises again. Not so tough after all, huh?

"Don't worry. I'm gone." He sneers and shoots around me, never looking back.

I follow him with my eyes and say, "Good."

"Good!" he yells back without turning around and flips me off, again.

I watch him leave before I remove my phone from its arm strap to text Huxley.

PAUL: *ur friend from uptown slam is a fucking dick wad!!!!!*
HUXLEY: *Easton?*
PAUL: *idk his name but i can't stand his bitch ass*
HUXLEY: *What did he do?*
PAUL: *he's just an asshole! does he have to do anything to be an asshole?*
HUXLEY: *Generally, yeah.*
PAUL: *he's rude and disrespectful and so mf full of himself. he's cute and he knows it and he thinks he's better than everyone else. i don't know why, but he just fucking pisses me tf off. just looking at him makes me want to VOM*
HUXLEY: *Drama queen, you are.*
HUXLEY: *So you think he's cute?*
HUXLEY: *You sure YOU weren't the asshole?*
HUXLEY: *Cause you're kinda an asshole, Paul.*

PAUL: fuck you too then
HUXLEY: Love you!

Easton

2 ON 2

"Oh! I almost forgot." Aidan's eyes go wide and he points at me. "This idea just hit me today. So, like, hear me out now."

"O-kay." I'm worried now. No conversation started like that has ever gone well, like ever. Especially in the middle of the Student Union over bagels. "Why not?"

"So, my mamá's single, right?" He waves his hands at me until I nod and squint. "And your dad is single, too, right?"

Is he seriously going where I think he is? "Yeah." Again.

"So we should hook them up. We'd be brothers!"

"Okay, first off, ew." I shiver. It's just weird. "And second, ew."

"What's wrong with my mamá?" Aidan slumps his shoulders but keeps his grin.

"Nothing!" I throw my hands up, then shove my face in my palms. "It just…seems weird playing matchmaker with our parents. Plus, isn't your mom like thirty or something? My dad's forty-two!"

"She's thirty-six…I think." Aidan doesn't look convincing. "But we'd be brothers!"

"Stepbrothers," I correct him.

"Same thing."

I roll my eyes and laugh. This isn't the first time he's come up with the idea. Not sure why he acts like it's this exciting new thing every time. Guess that's just A. It would give me a mom though, like a real one. Not the bitch that couldn't stand looking at me after I came out.

"But…" I stop, bagel almost touching my lips before I put it down. Maybe there's a positive in there somewhere. "If we were stepbrothers, maybe my dad would stop trying to set us up with each other."

"See! Win-win!" Aidan laughs.

"Still weird," I tell him and down the rest of my bagel before getting up. We came to have a little brunch-like snack and play pool in the Union's game room.

"Such a prude." Aidan tags along.

"You know, it's not fair," I blurt.

"That's what I've been saying. They should totally hook up." Aidan glances at me.

Oh my God, that's so not what I meant.

"Not that, just that, uh…" Think, Easton. Ah! I take it in a similar yet better direction. "Just that I swear you managed to pull the only non-total-asshole gay dude that exists. Like, what are the rest of us supposed to do?"

It's not a lie. I've thought about it a few times. Just never really said it.

"You saying you want my boyfriend?" Aidan's eyes become slits, and he crinkles his nose.

"I mean…" I drag it out with a big smile. "Nah. Just, I swear all the rest are assholes."

"Who've you been talking to *again*?" He shakes his head.

"No one. That's the problem. They're all *ugh*," I remind him as we enter the game room.

"Sure, no one." The skew of his mouth says it all. He's not buying it. "Spill the tea. What asshole have you been messaging on Grindr?"

"I'm not spilling no tea," I say back. "Plus, it's nothing. No

Grindr shit. Just a general thing."

"Uh-huh." He doesn't believe me, but I guess he decides to give me this one while he takes a pool stick from the wall. "Most guys are trash."

"Right?" I sigh.

"And who said Ty wasn't a whore?" Aidan laughs.

"Excuse-a-me? What?" My words are garbled. It's not at all what I expected.

"Just with me of course, but if you only knew."

"Oh my God, did I tell you what happened this morning with—" I start.

Aidan's eyes widen. "Don't look now, but Douchebag is approaching."

"Douchebag?" I question.

"Huxley, do *not* make me do this," an annoyingly husky voice whispers from behind me.

I slouch. Dammit.

"Shut up, Paul. Heeeeey, Easton!" Huxley comes over to me and gives me a big bear hug. "Easton's friend." She hugs Aidan too. It's very Huxley. But her hair has changed since the last time I saw her. She's a long, wavy blonde now.

"It's Aidan," Aidan fills her in.

"Well, nice to meet you, Easton's friend Aidan."

And then I see Paul. "Come to plow me over again?"

"That was a fucking accident and you know it. I told you the goose—"

"Plow?" Aidan asks like he's about to burst out laughing at the same time Huxley says, "Paul, grab a cue. We're playing pool."

"We are?" Paul and I ask at the same time.

"Yes, we are. Paul and Easton against Aidan and me. Loser buys drinks this weekend. So get your shit together. You're breaking."

Paul scrunches his eyebrows. "I have no idea what the fuck

that means."

Goddammit he's sexy.

"It means you hit the balls first, Paul. Isn't that how it works?" Huxley asks, rubbing the little chalk cube on her cue.

I feel like I'm missing something here, but I'm not about to ask. I mean it's pool, it's pretty simple, besides the fact that I have to play with Paul. It's been a few years since I've done this, but I'm not going to lose, not with him here.

"Think your dream just came true," Aidan whispers behind me, and I swat him off.

"Yeah, you go first." I nod at Paul, hoping it comes off equally sarcastic and nonchalant.

"Fine. Whatever. Let's just get this over with." I swear Paul's whining, but it's sort of hot the way his voice drops even lower.

Huxley finishes setting the balls in their little triangle at the other end of the table and in pure Huxley fashion pulls away the triangle border with a, "Ta-da. It's all you, boo."

"Uh..." Paul looks at me. "Do you know how to do this?"

How do you not know how to play pool? is the first thing that rolls through my head, but I keep it to myself. I shake my head and hold back a laugh.

"You break the balls." I fling my hand toward the green felt table as if it's the most obvious thing in the world.

"Right. Break the balls. Like I'm supposed to know what the fuck that means." Paul shrugs.

"You just...break the balls, like it's that simple," I try again. How else do I explain it?

"I don't know what 'break the balls' means, dipshit." Paul sounds really irritated. That didn't take long.

"It means to break the balls." My hands are moving about, trying to think of another way to say it, but I'm failing. "Like I don't know what else you want from me. You—"

"Say 'break the balls' one more time. I dare you." Paul

narrows his eyes at me.

"OMG this is like watching a car crash," Huxley says. "I love it."

"Damn right." Aidan shakes his head.

"You just—" I'm about to say again, this time on purpose, but Paul isn't having it.

"You fucking do it then. You do it!" Paul throws his hands up and relents, moving to stand next to Huxley. Who has the *biggest* smile on her face.

"Don't. Do not say any-fucking-thing to me right now." Paul stops Huxley before she can even try.

"Gotta do everything for you." I shake my entire body like I'm about to have a fit. It's overkill, but I'm not letting him upstage me right now. Douchebags never win. Or they shouldn't. "Move then."

Once he gets out of my way, I get into position. I aim my pool stick down the table toward the perfectly placed set of balls and lean over the table. But it feels so weird. Like this is normal, leaning over the table to take my shot, but I feel like everyone is staring at my ass, at least whatever little ass that's back there.

Just play pool.

* * *

Only the eight ball is left on the table, thanks mostly to Aidan and me. I think Huxley might have gotten two in, but the only ball Paul managed to get in, I had to set him up with a little baby shot.

It's on me. If I get this, Paul and I win. If I don't, and Aidan manages it, we lose. And I do not want to hear about losing *with* Paul from my best friend for the next month.

"You got this, dude! Don't fuck it up. We can't let them win."

You'd think this was a super tense game of basketball the way Paul's been into the last few shots. And his "hyping" isn't helping; like for one I need to be able to hate this guy, but it's so endearing.

"I've got it, would you shut up?" I eye him and then turn back to the table and line up my shot. "I'm calling the left edge pocket."

"Corner pocket." Paul corrects.

"Who made you the expert?" I huff, losing concentration. "Let me focus."

I set up again. I wish I could say it was one of those moments when everything slows down and the people around me go quiet, but none of that nonsense happens, because this is a goddamn game of pool. But I'm ready. I'm going to make this shot. I breathe and go for it. The white ball jolts forward and clanks against the eight ball. It shoots off and falls perfectly in the left *corner* pocket.

"Yes!" I yell, a little too loud for the middle of the Student Union.

"YEEEEES! You fucking did it! WE WIN!"

"Hell yes!" I'm jumping and shouting. Then I grab the closest person to me and hug them and we're both jumping. "We did it! Take that, A!"

That's when I realize it's Paul's arms around my waist as we're jumping in celebration.

"Uhhhh…" he says at the same time I realize what we're doing. He lets go of me.

"Oh shit, sorry." I jump away, dropping my pool stick and trying not to look at him. But I can't help it.

"It's cool. Whatever. Um, yeah. Cool, cool, cool." Paul's nodding his head quickly and looking at his feet.

"Yeah, of course." I nod as I realize how nice his arms felt now that they're gone. I try to remind myself he's an asshole. "Totally cool."

"I think my work here is done."

My eyes dart to Huxley and I let out a defeated breath. Seriously?

Paul

GIRLS NIGHT IN

"How long are you going to keep this up?"

"What the — Holy shit! Keep what up?" I'm sitting at *my* desk in *my* room, vibing to Blake Rose and working on homework. Huxley just showed up outta nowhere. She's leaning against the doorframe with her arms folded all aloof and chill like she didn't just scare the shit outta me. Guess she was right, she does do that a lot.

She looks good today. But then again, she always looks good. Her hair is big and curly and her makeup is flawless. I'm wearing black short shorts and a white wife beater, but she's wearing a matching violet velvet sweatsuit. Probably something from boohoo. boohooMAN makes up 75 percent of my closet, so I know the brand well. Or it's Gucci. What do I know? If I wasn't gay with trauma, I would probably try to date her. She's gorg. "I haven't done anything, Huxley."

"That is exactly my point, Paul. You've done nothing since we moved in. The last time we had a decent conversation was when we first met and —"

"I'd hardly call that decent."

"Point. Again. We're roommates now and I'd like for us to be friends, too. You're stuck with me and I don't even for real know you outside of your lack of communication skills — even though you're an English major — and your anger issues. So spill."

"Uhhhhh…" I don't know what to say, so I change the subject back to her. "Well, don't get fucking mad at me for not talking when all you do is *not* go to class and read your damn books."

She leaves her perch and moves to stand behind me and looks over my shoulder to see what I'm working on. "First of all, I go to class. I have to if I wanna be in the musical. We just had auditions for *RENT* so I've been preparing for that as well. Not to mention I'm always in the art center until late working. Artistry never sleeps. We just run on different internal schedules." She moves to sit on my bed. "And second of all, don't come for my books. It's a dope-ass book and you'd do well to read something *modern* now and again. My bookstagram friends would be so disappointed. Though if you need a book rec, let me know. I gotchu. Actually I have the perfect series you should read that'll go with your wolf tat."

I turn around to face her. "Booksta-what?"

"Nothing. Now, order a pizza and meet me in the living room in fifteen. I'll find something to watch. It's gonna be a long night for both of us. We *will* be friends by the end of it." She stands and saunters out.

"You don't have better things to do on a Friday night?"

She turns around, aghast, feigning a wounded heart. "Ouch. Consider yourself lucky I'm gracing you with my presence. Thank you so much for me being here." And then she does the one thing I never would have expected… She fucking curtsies. This woman is batshit. And I'm dead!

I laugh so hard I can't breathe. Huxley is laughing because I'm laughing and I laugh harder because she sounds like a goose. And then I think about the goose attacking me the other day and I fall out of my chair.

I needed this. I really fucking needed this. Huxley's determined, I'll give her that. No harm in making friends, I guess. It would be nice to have someone in my corner for once. When I finally get my shit together, I agree to her terms. "Fine. But if it's not *Schitt's Creek*, I don't want it."

"Oof. He has great taste. Okay, I see you. *Schitt's Creek* coming up."

* * *

An hour later, Huxley is sitting on the floor facing the pizza on the coffee table. She throws her crust into the box and turns down the volume. "So, tell me, Paul Acre, who are you? Where did you come from? Why are you here?"

I sit up from where I was lying on the couch, place my elbow on my knee, and run my hands over my face. "Uh. Well. Um. I guess I'll start with the basics. I was born and raised in Leawood, Kansas. It's a suburb, kinda, of Kansas City, Missouri. Went to college at UMKC, University of Missouri - Kansas City. But it wasn't for me. I needed to get out of there, so I picked a random school with decent weather and bounced. What else is there to tell?"

I legit don't know what I'm supposed to say. I don't like small talk. I don't like getting to know new people. It's all too much of a hassle, and since no one sure as shit actually sticks around, what's the point learning all this shit about them? It just takes up space in my brain that I could use for something else. I don't know what else I would use it for, but that's not the point.

"Firstly, the weather here is complete trash. Like literally, the whole thing needs to be thrown away. And secondly, that's all great, grand, and glorious, but it still doesn't tell me *who* you are, Paul."

"I don't know what you want me to say."

"Okay, let's start with this." Huxley closes the pizza box and sets it on the floor under the coffee table. "We'll do some rapid-fire questions and you just say whatever comes to mind first. Okay?"

I throw myself back as dramatically as I can with the biggest this-is-such-an-inconvenience sigh that I can muster and slide down the couch like I'm made of slime. "Sure, I guess."

Huxley ignores my tantrum. Smart girl, she is.

"Okay, favorite animal?"

I flash my tattoo. "Wolf. Duh."

And just like that, Huxley and I spend the night getting to know each other. By the time we're two large pizzas and one empty wine bottle in—Huxley's doing, not mine—I think we might actually be friends now. She fires off question after question like she's Alex Trebek. And it's fun! I never thought I could have this. It's weird, me having a friend like this.

"Biggest fear?"

"Time." I sigh. Always the biggest fear question.

"Huh?" She cocks her head like a dog and moves her curls to fall over her right shoulder.

"T-time," I stutter. "I'm afraid of…time. Gah, I know it's fucking weird and irrational. But like… It's a losing battle, yet I'm always trying to win anyway, ya know? Getting ahead of it is impossible. Falling behind is too easy. You can't get back any time once it's lost. Time steals and never gives anything back. It takes your youth. It can take your mind. Time literally kills people, everyone. It brings life, sure, if people give it the correct tools by having sex, but it will *always* kill. Time is a bitch and a half."

Damn. I need to write that down.

Huxley is silent for a while after I finish my explanation. She's playing with one of her curls. It's either a nervous tick or something that she does while she's thinking. Probably both. "I've never heard it explained like that. Whoa. I mean you're right. But who even thinks of something like that? Interesting. I'll need *time* to process that one. Ha! See what I did there?"

I'm shaking my head and chuckling because that was actually a funny pun. She's ridiculous! "Ha ha. Good one."

She pauses to check her phone and goes to the kitchen to get herself another bottle of wine. So I pick up my phone too, to see if I've gotten any new messages.

Nothing.

I haven't heard from my brothers in weeks and I'm actually kinda hurt by it. Trevor is the oldest and then Jace and then me. Then there's Dani and Felix, but both are too young to really have a relationship with. Though my brothers and I were always close.

Jace and I were born in the same year, nine months apart. I was premature. I felt like we were twins and he was my best friend. Or the closest thing to one anyway. He had other friends, but he always made time for me as a kid.

I tried texting them both for New Year's and Jace for his birthday, but neither of them responded. I'm sure they're mad — I just up and left without a goodbye. I knew that if I talked to them they'd convince me to stay, and that was completely out of the question.

She throws her phone on the couch, fills up her wine glass, and sits back down on the floor. "Anyway, why English?"

I put my phone and my disappointment aside.

"I like words." I shrug. It's the most honest answer I can give, but it still feels like bearing my soul. "Like, individually. I mean, I know I'm not good with my words, but I like…words. Putting them together is fun but challenging. They can be beauty. They can be danger. I…" I cut myself off because this just feels like too much. I've given her enough about me already.

But she's not having it.

"Oh no you don't! Keep talking."

I sigh. This shit sucks. Trusting someone with my thoughts,

my emotions, it's only left me hurt and bleeding. But for some reason, I feel like I can trust her. I guess? I don't know. It's whatever. So I bite the bullet and open up to Huxley as much as I know how.

"Words can change a person's life, ya know? Like, 'I do'. They're two simple words, and yet they mean everything. But they don't mean the same thing to everyone. They are consent in their most basic form. They can be freedom to another world or they can be torture, a ball and chain. Love is a four-letter word. Singular. But it holds so much weight. Hate is also a four-letter word, but hate can be a release. Fuck is another four-letter word, the most universal word. Yes and no are also each one word. They can both make complete sentences even though they have polar opposite meanings. When you string words together you can create magic, like your book or music. Words can be healing, but words can also cause someone to commit suicide. They are beauty. They are danger."

Her eyes are wide, but I can't read her. She hasn't moved at all while I've just been rambling about *words*. I'm such a nerd. I probably said too much.

Damn it, Paul!

"Whoa. Okay. Wasn't expecting that. Seems there's more to you than meets the eye."

Oh. So, okay. Um. Huh? "Wait. Is that a good thing?"

"Uh, yeah!" Huxley squints and does this sassy head sway. "Paul, you're so smart and wise. I would have never guessed all these tattoos and anger issues actually held a soul. It's beautiful."

Thanks, Huxley. But I don't say it. All I can do is blush. That might simultaneously be the nicest and most sarcastic thing anyone's ever said to me about me.

"Mind if we go deeper?"

"Uh, sure. Why the hell not."

"Switching gears." She lays back down on the floor. "What

does love mean to you then? Earlier you talked about it like it was a curse or something."

"Isn't it?" I'm sitting cross-legged now, facing her.

"Elaborate."

"It's just... Love is nothing but a promise left to time, a sentencing. A trap. I don't do promises and I don't do love because love is a lie. People use 'love' too frequently and rarely ever mean it. Sure, not everyone. But the masses for sure." I pause. "You... You can't fucking go through what I've been through and believe in all that sappy lovey-dovey bullshit. It may be real for other people, but it's — Fuck. It's just not real for me, okay?"

"And what have you been through?" she asks reluctantly. But I can tell she wants to know. I'm sure she's been dying to know since we met.

"Huxley. Don't."

She moves to sit across from me. "Come on, Paulie. You were doing so well—"

No. No! I can't fucking do this. "Don't call me that! Don't you ever fucking call me that again." I'm on my feet before I can stop myself. My hands are in fists at my side as my nails dig into my palm. I'm fuming. I can't. I can't, I can't, I can't. My arms are flexed, tense. My knees locked. "Never again. Don't ever fucking call me that. Ever. Do you hear me?"

Huxley jumps up and wants to touch me, I know, but I give her a look to stay away. "Shit. Paul, I'm sorry. I'm sorry, I won't. I hear you."

"Whatever. I'm going to bed."

"Yeah. Okay. Get some res—" But I'm in my room and slamming the door before she can finish. I sink to the floor and try to even out my breathing. I can't leave to go to the gym now and work off this anger, so I need to get my shit together before hearing that fucking name causes a full-fledged panic attack. My heart is racing. I start counting back from one thousand to focus my mind, and I lay back on the floor at the foot of my bed while I force myself to stop shaking.

Paulie.

Easton

DLSTRAIGHT92

I drive by the house again. Its black wrought-iron door and white trim stares back at me with each pass, and the glow of fake lantern light bathes the house in flinching yellow hues.

"Just do it," I whisper under the twang of Reba's voice over my car speakers, and I make myself turn into his driveway. I take a deep breath, eyes locked on the front door.

I asked for this. Why am I so worked up about it? It's been months since I've had something real inside me. Halloween actually. I still remember it, even if I don't remember the dude's name — a lot like right now. He was dressed up as Thor, I was the Playboy Bunny, and I swear it felt like he was using his hammer inside me and I loved every last minute of it. But it feels like it's been forever.

So here I am at DLStraight92's house a few miles from school. I'm hoping it'll do the job. I'm in control at least, unlike everything else in my life. It's my choice.

Finally I get out of the car and walk up the path. Before I can knock, the door opens and the face I saw online comes into view. He's tall, like over six feet tall, with broad shoulders, thick arms, and thick thighs in baggy pajama bottoms, and a full beard and mustache under dull gray eyes.

"Come in," he says, and I do. I walk through the door, and

suddenly his hand clamps my left ass cheek. "God, you really are fucking hot."

"Thanks," is all I get out before he shuts the door and squeezes harder. "You like it, Daddy?"

I start to play the part. He wanted a toy, and as messed up as it might sound, I like being the toy, I like being used. I *need* to be used. It's weird to most, but I don't know. I just love it.

"Yes, Daddy likes. Follow me," he says and starts off down a hallway, motioning me through a door on the left.

I should be horrified. Like, I know this is stupid, and every part of me says I'm going to die one day doing this, but it's like that part of me goes silent when my boy parts decide they need some action and that's all that matters. So I go where I'm told. In my defense, I did tell Aidan where I was going. He didn't like it and tried to get me not to come, but I'm here all the same.

The room opens to what I assume is his bedroom, complete with a floor scattered in piles of clothes and an overflowing trash can. Okay, maybe he is straight.

He grabs my hand and I spin around next to the bed, and his body presses against mine.

"You ready to be my little whore?"

"Yes, Daddy," I say quietly. "Make me yours."

In response his mouth presses against mine, and our lips part. As his tongue slips inside my mouth, I'm inundated by the taste of pepperoni and cheese, and it's all I can do not to retch. I kiss him back, willing away the taste, and try to feel the texture of his mouth and tongue as his hands slink around my body.

I remind myself that I'm in control. This only goes as far as I want it to. His hands make an abrupt change of direction and I gulp as his fingers slip under my pants and clutch my ass. He squeezes and squeezes while our mouths play a fake game of passion. I seriously expected this to be better.

"Let's get you naked." He leans back long enough to pull up

my shirt. I lift my arms and let him remove it, and without the tiniest delay he's unbuttoning my pants, and suddenly they're on the floor in a pile of their own.

It feels colder as his eyes devour me. I guess he's determining whether I meet his wants. I'm just hoping he's better at fucking than washing his mouth out after he eats. Hell, I washed my ass out for this.

Then out of nowhere he grabs my crotch and feels around. It doesn't matter that he's not that amazing, it still works. I grow under my briefs and my breathing gets heavier.

"What are you waiting for, make me hard," he demands.

I break out of my stupor and put my hand to his pants. It doesn't take long to find what I'm looking for. It's obviously as big as he claimed and he's at least half hard already.

"Yeah, you like that, boy?"

I suck my bottom lip in to look pouty and nod vigorously. I *am* at least looking forward to this. As if he knows it, Mr. No Name uses his free hand to push down on his PJs, but I take over, pulling them to the ground. Woah. His dick bobs in front of my face as I'm bent over helping him get his feet out of his pants. That's a lot of dick.

"Suck it." He puts his hand on the back of my head and pushes.

I drop to my knees as my face smothers into the hairy mess of his thigh and he slaps my cheek with his cock. I moan; it's reflex. He slaps it on my face again, and I grab it and swallow it whole. If it weren't for the fact that I really like dick inside me, I'd be giving up right now. It literally stinks down here, like actually stinks.

Focus on what you're doing. Try to enjoy it.

He must be really ready for more because suddenly his hands are under my armpits and throwing me onto the bed. My body bounces on the soft sheets and I give him a fake grin as he yanks my briefs off my body and flips me over.

"Arch that back, you fucking little slut," he barks at me, and before I have a chance to comply, a palm strikes my ass cheek.

I yelp in surprise, but a moan escapes directly after. If he weren't total trash I'd like it. Part of me wants to turn back over and just be like, *Hey, sorry, I'm just not feeling this. Let's call it quits*, but I feel like the moment I walked in the door I committed, so I don't. Instead, I arch my back and he grabs my ass.

I tighten up when his mouth makes contact and his tongue slathers against me. My mouth gapes open and my eyes roll back into my skull. I enjoy it for the whole ten seconds it lasts before he gets up on the bed and rubs lube on my ass. That's when I feel bare skin on me.

"Woah, hold up." I crane my neck around. "Condom, big boy."

"Seriously?" he huffs. "I'm fucking clean."

"Condom or I'm out." I put a little force in my voice. Sure, I like to be used, but I'm not stupid.

"Whatever," he huffs again, and the bed jumps as he gets off to fetch the condom that apparently was lying on his nightstand the entire time. Like, how hard was that?

A moment later he's behind me again and I feel his dick brush against my ass.

"Give it to me, Daddy." I roll my eyes since he can't see and grab the sheets around me.

A few minutes later my body aches in the best way possible and he releases deep inside me. "Fuck yeah." He breathes hard and proudly shows me the result in his condom before slapping my ass again. He gets off the bed and starts dressing. "Swear you've got one of the roundest asses and tightest holes I've ever used."

I smile like it means the world to me, while inside I'm screaming, *Why would I ever do this? What is my problem?* "Glad you liked it."

"Hell yeah, I'll have to have you over again soon." He grins and throws my clothes next to me on the bed. "Time to go."

And just like that, I'm putting my clothes back on and doing the walk of shame back to my car.

Easton

THERE'S JUST SOMETHING ABOUT A MAN WITH TATTOOS

Not going to lie, this class is already way more boring than I thought it'd be. If it weren't for Aidan I'd be dropping it right now.

I figured a nursing major would want to take some physiology class, or maybe another biology or nutrition science class, but no. Not Aidan. He wanted an astronomy class. So here I am, and have no doubt I'm going to complain about it. Hell, I'm a political science major with a minor in history. This isn't what I'd call fun.

It's one of those big auditorium classrooms where the professor doesn't give a shit if you're paying attention, which I'm not. Sure I'm looking down at the platform, but I'm not seeing any of it.

Instead my head is filled with a movie-like reel of that Paul dude from this morning. I saw him on campus again, but I don't think he saw me. He must have been on a run, because he was dressed in tight spandex, long sleeves, really short shorts, and his forehead was glistening with sweat despite the cold. His headphones were in, muscular thighs pumping, and oh my, I love the tattoos. There's just something about a man with tattoos, and I swear every thick sinew of his left arm is covered with them.

In my mind he's running in slow motion, and instead of not noticing me, his head turns and we lock eyes. God, he's pretty. I have to remind myself that I hate him. He's a brute, an egotistical ass. But douches can be hot too, right? I just—

"Hey." A whisper and poke on my shoulder knocks me from my daydream.

"Huh? What did I miss?" I jump and say a little too loudly. I turn to see what's going on and slink lower in my chair with an awkward grin.

"You totally zoned out," Aidan says. "Please tell me you're not thinking about what's-his-face."

I might have mentioned to A that he'd been on my mind yesterday. He wasn't exactly excited about it, and for good reason. I don't blame him, but I can still fantasize, right?

"No," I lie, mouth skewing stiffly. He raises his brow and cocks his head. "Okay, yeah."

"You know he's bad news, East." Aidan leans in and punches my shoulder playfully.

"But he's such *hot* bad news." Let me dream.

"Ugh, God. He's not even that hot."

"Excuse me?" I lean back, trying to keep my voice low. Why am I defending this asshole?

"Really?" Aidan frowns at me.

"Would you two shut up?" some girl behind us whispers.

"Sorry," Aidan and I apologize simultaneously.

I grin at A. Looks like we're causing trouble. He sucks his lips in trying not to laugh and nods.

"But maybe he's not *that* bad," I keep going, just quieter.

Maybe he's not. Maybe he's just not very social and comes off as a total dick until you get to know him. I know it's a lot of imagining and theorizing, but hell, I'm also in a class on the planets right now, and that's not me.

"We're talking about the same guy, right?" Aidan squints.

"Yes." I nod. "Paul."

"Nah, he's a total fuckboy." Aidan shakes his head.

Ugh. He's right.

Paul

THE INVITATION

I've been doing two-a-days at the gym lately to make up for all the pizza and aggression I consumed during the movie night I had with Huxley.

I did end up apologizing to her…after three days of not being able to calm myself down. That weekend was rough for me. We didn't talk, but I eventually explained where my head was at without actually telling her why that nickname is a trigger for me. I'm just not ready yet. Maybe I never will be. Gah, I need therapy.

Huxley said there was nothing to apologize for, but I think she understands. She and I have hung out a lot since then. It's been about a week and a half and she hasn't really gone out like she normally did. Aside from her rehearsals, she's always at the apartment. I try to finish up my homework in the library so she doesn't distract me, but I've been finding myself rushing to get home to hang out and eat dinner with her.

Getting home after a busy-as-shit school/gym/homework day is by far one of the best feelings in the entire world. I just want a protein shake, some fruit, and to binge *Superstore* tonight. Anything to let my mind go numb.

I discard my shit in my room. Not messily. Everything has a place and every place has a thing. Even if it's bland as hell. Yeah,

I still haven't asked Huxley to help with my room. I have a low platform bed and white desk—Huxley helped me pick them out from Amazon—my TV and some books. The bedding is all white. The walls are white. Could be considered an insane asylum or minimalistic. The jury is still out.

Huxley did buy me a palm tree to put in the corner and a small lightly stained wood nightstand. Well shit. Maybe she did help me without me having to ask. Typical of her. My closet is full of shit though. And it's color coordinated because duh. Though a quarter of it is gym clothes. My shoes are organized on the floor. Guess I have more shit than I thought.

I go to the kitchen to make my protein shake when my phone buzzes. It's Huxley.

HUXLEY: *Whachya doooooin?*

PAUL: *just got home. u?*

HUXLEY: *I'm home. In my room.*

PAUL: *then whyyyyy r u texting me? u HEARD me come in. u couldn't just come to my room?*

HUXLEY: *It's late. I'm tired. Didn't wanna move.*

I feel. I finish making my shake, grab a banana, and go back to my room.

PAUL: *fair. what can i do you for, m'lady?*

HUXLEY: *Gym?*

PAUL: *nah. homework. lost track of time.*

HUXLEY: *Cool.*

HUXLEY: *Sooooo, I saw Easton today.*

Oh hell no. I jump off my bed and walk swiftly over to her room. I throw open the door without knocking.

"Fuck if I care," I declare.

She smiles and sits up in her bed cross-legged.

Her room is the exact opposite of mine. The walls are still white, but it looks like color threw up in here. She has her bed against one wall, the bedding a colorful ikat pattern, I think. A *line* of tall bookshelves sits on the opposite wall. They're color-coded like my closet. Her closet door is closed, though I'm sure it's full of Prada and Balmain. Gorg silk curtains adorn the window. Art and photos and plants are all over the place. So many plants.

"He told me about this pre-Valentine's Day party this weekend some frat is throwing for all singles. Queers welcome."

I roll my eyes, lean against the doorframe, and take a swig of my shake. "How inclusive. Still, you know I don't party."

"*Still*," she mocks me. "Could be fun."

"I'm sure y'all will have a blast. Give *Easton* my regards."

"You really don't like him, do you?" She leans against her headboard and folds her arms.

"You're damn right I don't. And I wouldn't give a shit if I never saw him again. He's a fucking douche canoe."

Huxley laughs. "How elegant."

I start fussing with the hem of my shorts. There's a thread there and I want to pull it so badly, but I also don't wanna mess up my $70 Lululemon shorts. I don't even know why that shit is so damned expensive. "He's your friend, not mine."

"Well, if I can befriend you, then anyone can. You gotta put yourself out there more, Paul. Everyone needs friends. Or more…"

I tap my head back against the doorframe. "I'm not everyone. I don't care and I sure as fuck don't want Easton to be my friend. *Or more*. Fuck all if he smells good." I say the last bit as a mumbled whisper. I didn't mean to say it at all and I thought I caught myself and changed my volume so she didn't hear me, but I failed. Her smile is too big.

"So you think he's cute *and* smells good?" She wiggles her eyebrows.

"Huxley. Lay off."

"Fine, fine," she surrenders.

I push myself off the doorframe and head back to my room.

"Ya know, you should still come!" she yells after me.

"Not coming!" I yell back.

"That's what he said," she yells back.

"I hate you," I yell again.

"I hate you more," she yells again.

That pretty much sums up our friendship.

Easton

YEP, THOSE ARE GREEK LETTERS

I keep telling myself this is more fun than sitting in my little jail cell of a dorm room all by myself tonight, but do I really believe it? Eh. I mean I could be watching some B-grade horror flick or maybe rewatching one of the *Star Wars* movies for the umpteenth time, but no. I'm here under the flashing glow of red and white lights with bad pop music blaring in my ears at some girl's house I barely know with way too many people I definitely don't know.

I'm beginning to wish I hadn't come, but tonight isn't one I want to spend all by my lonesome. Especially with my anxiety pulsing on high alert and my best friend absent. But it's the day before Valentine's Day, and of course Aidan left for Greenville last night to spend the weekend with Tyler. So I'm all by myself. Cool.

The house is small for a party, but that didn't keep Kylie from inviting so many people that I'm literally squeezing between jumping bodies to get from the front door to the little drinks and snack table. The only place that really matters at a party. And so far I've not seen a familiar face yet, which isn't helping my nerves. I swipe a cold beer from the open ice bucket and pop the top. My only rule tonight is not to get drunk.

I walked here, and it's less than a mile off campus, but I ain't walking home at eleven at night drunk off my ass, trying to cross

University Blvd. Frogger isn't a game I want to play in real life. I'm also not calling an Uber while nineteen and drunk. A little buzzed is fine for the walk home, but that's it. On top of that my MS meds don't play well with blackout drunk me, so go me!

I take a sip, hoping it'll make me not regret coming. It doesn't help. Like, I know none of these people, and dancing? Nah. I know a few TikTok dances and how to line dance, but that's it. Period. This shit they're all doing, grinding up on each other — I'd feel like a fool.

I take a deep breath, like I'm about to go into battle, and start across the room. I duck below sloshing, explosive cups of alcohol, wind through a trench of girls trying to twerk up on me, and dodge some dangerously slinging arms. On the other side, I work my way into the next room, hoping it'll be a little less crowded. Maybe I can find some cute guy to talk to without it looking like I'm trying to flirt. I mean, chances are, in a party this size, there are at least one or two more gays or bis hanging around, maybe some pan guys. Not like that's going to help me, because I'm not going to ask, but you know.

The next room is about the same, a tiny bit less crowded, but still more people than I like. I scan the crowd and find a few possibles right off the bat. Closest is a Rudy Pankow look-alike — I love OBX — with swooping blonde hair and all, then along the edge of the room is a more brooding figure, taller and thicker. Like Paul. No, not like Paul. That's not what I mean. Whatever. I start toward blondie, trying to ignore the god-awful music. But the moment he looks my way I divert my gaze and slide right.

That was an utter failure. Just once, I need that to work. Hell, he might have actually been an option, but I'm *never* going to know because I'm a pathetic loser who can't even walk up to a guy, let alone start a conversation without a damn app.

"Easton?" A voice pulls me out of my thoughts with an excited soprano.

I turn and a smile lifts my lips.

"Huxley!"

But does that mean... I do a quick check to see if Paul's here — he's been with her every other time I've seen her lately. I'm half relieved he isn't and half irritated when I don't find him tagging along. It's better like this. I know she's a decent person, which is why Paul can't be *that* bad. She wouldn't have brought him to play pool if he were. That was actually a lot of fun, but it's been a few weeks since then.

"I didn't think you'd actually come by yourself." She pulls me in for a hug.

I'd usually shrink from such, but it's Huxley. You don't say no to a hug from the Amazing Huxley.

"Yeah." I roll my eyes.

"I could barely get you to come to the library for study sessions," she reminds me.

"But I did," I remind her back. "That's why you passed, remember?"

"I mean it's *part* of why I passed." Huxley shrugs.

We had a great time in political philosophy last year... well, at least I did. As I remember it, she hated it, and I helped her pass.

"Not how I remember it." I smile.

I definitely recall her in desperate need of help the last half of the semester. It's not like I just volunteered my tutoring services, despite us already being friends at that point.

"How about more you, less me." Huxley bounces her shoulders and takes a drink from her bottle. I do the same and finish mine off. "*After* we get another drink."

"Uh..." I start to say no, but what the hell. "That I can agree with," I say and follow her to the corner where there's a random bucket filled with ice and bottles. We both take another and pop the tops.

"So, where's your boyfriend?" she asks.

"My boyfriend?" I squint and take a drink.

"Yeah, Aidan. Or is it Tyler? Tyler *and* Aidan? Are you in a throuple situation?" There's a slur to her words. "I always see you with the one. I remember you mentioned them both. I think? Could be wrong."

I nearly choke on my beer. I cough to keep it from going down the wrong pipe. I'm beginning to wish I *were* drunk.

"Oh shit, you okay?" She steps back so I don't spit on her.

"Good, good." I swallow and clear my throat. Aidan? My boyfriend? Where the hell did she get that from? "And no! Definitely not. Aidan's my *friend*, not my *boy*friend. Ty's Aidan's boyfriend. And a throuple?"

"It's 2021. Why not?" She doesn't miss a beat.

"Uh...nah." You do you, boo, but that's just not for me. *If* I ever do manage to find my guy, I'm a selfish bitch. "Not for me."

"Fair. So, Paul." My heart lurches at his name and I think, for a split second, that maybe he did show up after all. Huxley moves closer like she's about to divulge a huge secret. "Cute, right?"

"Ye..." I start to agree but stop myself. I do *not* need her telling Paul I said he was cute. Plus, he'd probably not want to be called cute anyway. So instead I give her a sort-of answer. "Uh...I...sure, I guess." I gulp. Why am I suddenly twice as nervous? "Uh...no. Is he here?"

"Maybe. He might be here. But he doesn't really party. He does, however, spend a lot of time in the gym." Her shoulders raise and she squints suggestively at me. "Which, I mean, come on, right? Like, he's hot, but not for me. He's, like, super gay. Did you know that? I'm bi, myself. Are there any other queer people here, you think?"

She doesn't give me enough time to answer her questions. It's seriously one after the other after the other without a breath between them. I just grab the last one and go.

"I don't know. I don't usually come to these things alone.

Love to party, but you know me, socially anxious and shit." Still not sure I made the right decision. "Although right before you caught me, there was this one guy…maybe…"

"Ooooh, gotcha. Interesting. Another guy, hmmm?" She skews her lips and pops her hip out, like it's some deep thing she has to figure out. She always did have a flare for the dramatic. "Well, he probably wasn't queer. I mean, it's a frat party after all. Right? It is, right? I mean, not that frat guys can't be qu—"

"Wait, what? A frat party?" Excuse me! Unless I'm the center of attention in one of those crazy *Frat Bros Gone Wild* videos I've watched, I'm not so sure I want to be at an *actual* frat party. "I thought Kylie was throwing it."

"E. Look." Huxley waves her hand around the room, and my eyes start to connect with the things I'd missed coming in. "There are frat symbols all over this bitch. *If* they weren't the ones throwing it then, like, set me on fire and call me Sandy."

"Dammit." I throw my head back and then take a massive gulp from my bottle. "You definitely ain't Sandy. I would end up at a damn *frat* party when A leaves me by myself."

"Could be worse. I could not have shown up to save your ass. Yes, I know, I'm a literal goddess. You're welcome."

"Goddess might be—"

"Anyway, we're probably the only queer people here, you and I. We gotta stick together. Anything could happen, after all. And then what? It's V-Day! No hate crimes tonight, amiright?" She's rambling and drunk, so that makes total sense. Then her eyes light up like she just remembered the coolest fact. "OMG! I almost forgot. Here, gimme your phone."

"Uh," I say and get my phone out. Before I can hand it over, she's yanking it out of my hand. "Okay."

"It's locked," Huxley sings to me and holds my phone up to my face.

"Usually is." I smile, not thinking, and it unlocks with my

Face ID. Damn she's good even when she's drunk.

I wait while she does who knows what with *my* phone, hoping to God she doesn't open my photo gallery. To get my mind off it, I let my eyes wander around the room. Yep, frat party. Those are definitely Greek letters. Not sure about the first one, but that's definitely Sigma and Lambda.

"Okay. There. I got a new number." She hands my phone back to me with her new contact card still open on the screen. That's when I realize I'm a little buzzed already. I have to squint to see it. Too late now though. "Oh! Let's do lunch tomorrow. I'll be alone on V-Day too. But you gotta call me. I'll be passed the fuck out 'cause I plan on getting druuunk."

"Yeah, okay. That sounds great." I smile. It's been a while, so lunch could be good. Then she starts to head off. "You leaving or something?"

"Leaving to get *more shots*! You're not nearly drunk enough. You need to get on my level."

That won't take long. I'm a lightweight.

"Oh, I..." I start to protest. I need to be able to walk home, and my doctor is really going to get on my case, but then I remember it's just going to be me when I get back. Alone. "You know what? Fuck it. Let's do this."

* * *

"Hey East, what's up?" Aidan's voice comes to life over the line.

"I love you, man," isn't what I intend to say, but it's the first thing to come out. "Not like I want to fuck you, I love you, not saying I wouldn't, but you know that'd be weird, but, like, you're the best friend ever. Like ever."

"O-kay," he stretches it out. "You drunk?"

"Maybe a little. Just a little," I assure him. I nod to my right as if he can see the girl sitting next to me. "This girl thinks I need a ride home. Can you come get me?"

"I'm in Greenville, Easton" he reminds me. Dammit. That's right. "I'm like three hours away!"

"I can wait," I blurt.

"Easton, you gotta call someone else," he tells me. He's starting to sound real concerned. "Where are you at?"

"Uh, Kylie's party. Although I think it might actually be a frat party. My bad," I apologize. "That's what Huxley thinks, anyway."

"Huxley? Is she with you?"

"Nah, she left," I tell him. "She wasn't drunk though, so she's good. I'm not even that drunk really."

"Yeah you are!" the girl yells loud enough for Aidan to hear.

"Okay, so could you call her—Huxley? See if she can give you a ride," Aidan suggests, and dammit if he isn't smart *and* cute.

"That's a great idea, A! You're so smart. I should do that." I'm about to hang up but remember I should say bye. "See you tomorrow, right?"

"Yeah, late, but yeah," he says. "Let me know when you get a ride, okay?"

"Okay," I assure him. "Bye, best friend."

I end the call, and look at the girl who told me to call him. She's so nice.

"He can't. He's with his boyfriend. Yeah. He's got a boyfriend," I tell her. "I want a boyfriend. I really want a boyfriend. There's this guy—"

"That's wonderful, but maybe you should call that girl he was talking about," she says.

"Were you listening to my call?" I make a big O with my lips. "So rude."

"You really need to call your friend," she urges.

"Ugh!" I grunt and find the contact for Huxley after stumbling through the alphabet. It rings and rings and rings.

"Come on. Answer or this girl isn't going to leave me alone."

The ringing stops and a voice comes on the other end. She sounds hoarse, but I yell into the phone anyway.

"Hey, Huxley. It's me again!"

Paul

I WISH YOU WERE SOBER

My eyes snap open at the sound of my phone buzzing on my nightstand. Who in the actual fuck would be calling me this late at night? I check the clock. It's two a.m.!

I dig my fists into my eyes to wake myself up.

I answer and immediately my ears are assaulted with the bass of a song I can't make out. Now I'm pissed. "Who the fuck is this?"

"It's me!"

Ummmm. Huxley? "Who's me?"

"Me. Like, me. Duh," they practically sing. "It's *me*."

Is this a prank call? No. Their voice sounds familiar even though they're very clearly shit-faced. And they know Huxley. It better not be who I think it is. "Right. Who the fuck is *me*?!"

"E.A.S.T.O.N. Duh."

Shit. It is. And did he actually just spell his name? I try not to laugh. "Easton."

"Ding, ding, ding!"

"How the hell did you get my number and…are you drunk? Is Huxley with you?" I run my hands down my face in frustration.

"*Yooooou're* Huxley! Oh hey, Huxley?" There's a pause and I think he's talking to someone else. His voice comes back through my phone. "Can you give me a ride home? You left and I can't find you and I might be a *little* tipsy."

Shit. I knew it. "Where are you?"

"Frat party. They're the WORST! Sending my location nooooow."

What the flying fuck is going on? My phone pings as I get an iMessage saying he shared his location. I'm honestly impressed since he sounds completely shit-faced. Wait… How'd he get my number? What is going on?!

"Don't you dare move. I'll be right there."

"Okay. See ya. Bye. Love you. Think I'll have another drink." But the last part sounds like he's talking to someone else again. Is he with someone else?

And he hangs up. Shit. Love you? *Love you?!* Whatever. I don't have time for this shit. He's drunk. I pull on a pair of running shorts and my oversized *LAKERS* shirt, tennis shoes, grab my keys and my wallet, and drag myself to the door.

* * *

Upon arriving all I can think is, *fuck this, and fuck this party*. I literally wish I were anywhere else but here right now. Like, I don't know, *my bed*. There are people spilling out onto the front porch and into the lawn. The lights inside are off, music is *blaring*, and party lights flashing through the windows make it look like a rave. What. The. Fuck.

Easton could be anywhere. People are making out on the stairs and on the couch, even against the wall. A couple dudes are passed out in the corner leaning on each other. A girl is even *sucking her spilled drink out of the living room rug*. Others are dancing and yelling and playing beer pong and doing keg stands. Seriously! What. The. Fuck. This is definitely not my thing. I've never been into shit like this, and a fraternity is *not* my kinda crowd.

That little pain in my ass bastard could be anywhere!

I walk into the kitchen.

"PAAAAAUL!"

Yep, it's Easton and he's *fucked.*

"Paul, the grumpy love of my life! What are *you* doing here?"

"*You* called *me.* I came to get you." I grab his wrist and start pulling him to the door. "We're leaving. Right now."

Shit. It's too late for there to be this many people still here. Maybe I can escape out of the window? I don't like this many people so close to me. It feels like everything is threatening to close in on me. Every sound is spikes to my brain and I feel like I'm being steamrolled. Like, physically flattened. My heart is racing at warp speed and I'm sweating already. I can't do this, but I suppress it as best I can while I try to find the best way to exit. Gotta get the hell outta here. Maybe if I make a run for it, Easton will follow me out.

"Where's Huxley?" I ask. "Is she with you?"

He shrugs. "We danced, then she puked. It was sooooo gross." He starts up. "Wait, I called Huxley. Now you're here. You weren't and *now you are*! You're *sort of* hot, so it's okay. I accept."

I take a glance at him, ignoring what he just said and the little hiccup. So Huxley was here, but she puked. She might be in the bathroom? I tried calling her phone before I got here, but she didn't answer. I can't just leave Easton while I look for her. Shit, I don't know what to do. Maybe she found a ride home already?

Somehow Easton's managed to get another drink in his hands, but he decides he doesn't like it and trades it with a random chick.

"Do you know her?" I try to say, but my voice is drowned out by the music. I pull Easton into me as a group of girls runs by.

And...

Then…

Everything slows down. Everyone is on pause as Easton and I are looking at each other.

He's far too close.

We're nearly nose to nose now. Well, my nose to his forehead, but he's looking up at me like he wants to kiss me. And hold on a fat fucking minute, he might be drunk, but I feel like I'm seeing him for the first time because he's actually insanely attractive. His brown eyes are warm like honey; his full pink lips are parted…for me. Even his ears match his cheeks, all peachy colored and cute. Are those…freckles lightly speckled across his nose? His hair is a mess, but his body fits nicely against me and I can feel—

No.

Nope.

FUCK THIS.

Everything speeds back up to normal.

"We are leaving *now*. Don't take a hit, don't drink any more. No more for you. You're done. We are leaving even if I have to carry you out myself. Do you hear me?"

"Aye aye, Captain." And then he salutes, he literally salutes me. He's what, eighteen? Maybe nineteen, acting and drinking like he's fucking twenty-five or some shit. This would be so much easier if he were sober.

Gah! And I'm trapped in a Conan Gray lyric.

"Let's go!" I say again, only he doesn't move. Fine. *Fine*. But he asked for this.

I bend and throw him over my shoulder. His feet are forward and he's facing backward yelling for help and his hands pounding on my back. I don't care as long as we get out of this fucking overcrowded house right the fuck now.

We finally make it outside and down the steps of the front porch when some dude stops me.

"Whoa, whoa, whoa." And whoever it is grabs Easton and I jolt to a stop. "Do you know him?"

Before I can respond Easton says, "Oh yeah, he's my boooyfriennnd. We're just role-playing. Can'tchya tell? Isn't he hot?" It all comes out in a slur and much deeper than his regular voice.

"You're his boyfriend?" the random dude asks, his face painted in the same disbelief I feel in my chest.

"Ye-yeah." I set Easton down and wrap my arm around his waist to support 99 percent of his weight. "What the fuck of it? Got a problem with it?"

"No problem. Just get out. He looks like he's about to puke."

"Gone." And I drag Easton toward my car.

He can't even walk on his own without tripping down the road and I'm so far beyond annoyed.

"Where do you live, Easton?" I ask.

"Duh. We live together. You're my boyfriend, rememberrr?" He trips down the road and I grab him tighter to balance him. "And you're really strong."

I stop and face him so I can get his attention. "Focus." I hate drunk people so damn much. "Easton, focus. Where. Do. You. Live?"

"Okay, but, like, could you please be my real boyfriend? Would you please ask me on a date? You're so hot. The hottest. Like, *theee* hottest guy I've ever seen. Even if you are a prick." And then he crosses his arms, sticks out his bottom lip, and pouts.

First, I never noticed he had *such* a country accent until tonight. Like, it's *very* apparent in his drunken stupor. Second, this is useless.

We finally make it to my car and I settle him into the back seat so he can lie down while I drive. And the first thing he does is vomit. All. Over. Everything.

"Thanks. You're a doll," he says when he's done puking. He

wipes his mouth and falls right the fuck to sleep. He's so damn adorable all curled up against the seat with his head propped up on the window. If he wasn't covered in puke I—

No.

Nope.

No, Paul!

Shit.

"I fucking hate you," I say and slam the door.

Easton

YOU CALLED ME

The light stings when I open my eyes. I bring my fingers to my temple and massage the pressure points, trying to ease the thud in my head. And my mouth is so damn dry.

"Ugh," I groan and maneuver onto my side.

My entire body aches and whines. Why the hell do I do this? Where was I even at?

"Kylie's party, *frat* party," I tell myself. "Yep. Oh my!"

My eyes jump open despite the sunlight streaming in through the windows. I'm going to throw up. God no. The bathroom's down the hall. I don't have time to make it. No. No. No. I jump from the bed and race toward the door, but my feet stop before I get a few steps. I grip my stomach. Woah.

This isn't my room.

"Where the hell am I?" My eyes widen even more while I will back the junk in my throat. I'm standing next to a short platform bed I've never seen in my life. There's a desk on the opposite wall with a stack of classic books: *Wuthering Heights*, *Little Women*, and…*Death on the Nile* by Agatha Christie. Huh? Damn, there's a lot of Agatha Christie. Two end tables free from clutter flank the bed. In fact, the whole room is free of clutter, and any color apparently. It's a lot of black, but mostly white and, like, a sand accent color. The bedding is probably 10,000 thread count or something. This is so much nicer than my dorm room.

Where the hell am I?!

My stomach churns again. I need a toilet or a trash can or a sink. I don't care which.

There are two doors. Dammit! I make a quick judgment call and I rush toward the door to my left. Relief floods through my body as a toilet comes into view. I rush in and retch into it. I swear I'm never getting drunk again.

Once my stomach is done, I get up and wipe my mouth with some toilet paper and check to make sure I didn't get anything on my... Wait. This isn't my shirt. I had on a white tee and a red plaid button-up when I left for the party last night, but that's not what I'm wearing now. I've never seen this shirt in my life. It's this oversized — at least for me — retro-looking yellow t-shirt with *LAKERS* written across it and a basketball. It's hideous.

Who the hell did I go home with last night? Please at least have been hot...and have used a condom. *Your shirt, Easton. Just find your shirt.*

I find the closet, and it's impeccably organized. Like a serial killer, and the bathroom was as clean as the bedroom. Ed Kemper's mug shot blares behind my eyes and I can hear Samantha's voice telling me how he kidnapped and killed six college students that night she made me stay up to watch some murder special before I left for college. For a second, worry coats my stomach and I think I'm going to vomit, but I push it back. It isn't a first for me.

I give up looking for my shirt. It's not here. Fuck the shirt, I'll keep this one. It's time to get out of here.

I start toward the second door and carefully twist the handle. *Please let them be out. I don't want to know who it was.* But what if they're here? I stop twisting the knob. Why do I do this?

"This is not good," I whisper and slowly twist and push. I peek through the crack. Looks like a kitchen directly ahead, and maybe a living room. Maybe.

Please don't be home.

I ease the door open and slip through. I head straight for what looks like the living room. Whoever I let fuck me last night at least has style. The room is well kept and dotted with splashes of color and art. It's actually inviting.

Then I find my goal. The door. I think that's the exit. I squint, struggling to see past the sunlight blaring through the window blinds. Hangovers suck. My knee slaps something hard, and I almost double over onto the floor.

"Shit!" I yelp, my eyes landing on the end table I just kneed. Then my eyes catch movement and I freeze.

Someone's on the couch! "What the hell!" the person yells.

"Who are—" My words catch in the back of my throat. Paul? What the hell am I doing at Paul's? Wait! Did I? "Did we?"

"What? Did we *fuck*?" He throws his hands up like *I'm* crazy, but I'm the one in someone else's house. "Fuck no!"

His response hits differently than I expect, and it doesn't help that my eyes catch on his naked chest. Oh. My. God. Now I'm wishing we had and I hadn't been drunk.

Focus, Easton. Like, that's the best answer, right? I should be glad he didn't—as long as he isn't lying—because he's a dick, but my brain shoots a drop of sadness in my veins. It's the way he said it, like he wouldn't ever want to be with me.

What the hell, Easton. Get a grip.

"Then why am I here?" I yell back, willing myself to keep my eyes locked on his instead of trailing south with his tattoos where a little trail of hair disappears beneath his pants.

"You were absolutely wasted last night and you called *me* to come pick you up." Paul shrugs as if it's the most sensible thing in the world, but why the hell would I call him? "I don't know where you fucking live, and you wouldn't tell me, so I had to bring you here. And you're welcome for washing your puke-drenched shirt, by the way."

He reaches to a table next to the couch and grabs a plaid button-up and t-shirt and throws them at me. I catch them. They're mine, and they smell freshly laundered. Oh.

"You even threw up in the back of my car. The *entire* back seat. So fuck you very much because I had to clean that shit up before I could go to bed at three in the morning," he goes on, but he's not done. "And you're welcome for the bed. *I* slept out *here* instead. You didn't puke on it did you?"

"Uh…no." I drop my head and glance away. "But how did I call you? I don't have your number."

"I sure as shit don't know, but you did. And let me tell you, you're a wild drunk. Very handsy." Paul shakes his head, but there's a hint of a smile under those wide eyes. I have to look away again. He's looking hot again. Then he laughs, "You still want me to take you on a date?"

"Excuse me?" I blurt. "Why the hell would I want that?"

It's not what I want to say after the words come out, but that didn't stop them from spewing with all the disgust in the pits of Hades.

"Hey, *you're* the one who said," and he smiles way too big, "and I quote, 'Would you please ask me on a date? You're so hot.' But don't get your hopes up. I wouldn't fucking date you anyway."

"What? Wait. No. There's no way I said that," I bite back. "I'm getting out of here."

"You're welcome for picking you up," Paul yells after me as I make for the door. "You want a ride to your place?"

"I'll walk!"

Paul

HAPPY FUCKING VALENTINE'S DAY

"I'll walk!" he yells, but I get up and race him to the door.

"Come on. At least have breakfast first. I can make you that omelet you wanted so badly last night before you went comatose."

There is no fucking way that this shithead standing in front of me can look this good wearing my clothes, but he does. Even hungover as fuck.

He really should eat something.

Shit. I can't stop looking at him. Like, really *looking*.

Last night I thought it was all in my head. That maybe I was second-hand drunk from the party. That I most certainly could not have thought he was cute. Like, actually cute. But…he is. I've been blind this whole time. Holy shit, I've been such an asshole. I guess I didn't want to see it. I guess I couldn't. That's the funny thing about trauma, isn't it? It can alter your reality.

He looks so confused and ready to bolt. He's like a scared baby deer. It's kinda cute.

Shit.

What the hell would I even do? Huh? Like, obviously he's into me. Drunk people are the most honest people in the world. He was honest with me. Maybe he just wants to fuck, maybe he wants more? I wouldn't know what to do with either. I don't hook up for…reasons. And I certainly don't date. Not after my one and only ex cheated on me freshman year of college. So no. I can't do this.

We're just standing here, staring at each other and I can't read his face, but it *is* cute to watch him squirm.

"Huxley?" His eyes shift from me to Huxley coming out of her bedroom.

I turn around and suddenly everything clicks. I look at her the way Miranda Priestly looks at Andrea in *The Devil Wears Prada* when she goes up the stairs in her townhouse.

"Oof. Never mind. Y'all have fun." And then she turns right back around and shuts her bedroom door.

What did she do?

My anger flares something fierce.

Easton must see it on my face because he turns toward the door and pulls it open. "Just— I've got to go. Bye."

He slips out and I don't stop him this time. I have someone else I need to fucking deal with right now.

Huxley reemerges from her room and oh so very casually says, "Oh hey, Paul."

"No you don't! Don't 'Oh hey, Paul' me. What the hell did you do? How did Easton get my number? And where were you last night? You just got drunk and left him *alone*? Anything could have happened to him! What the hell, Huxley?"

Huxley puts her nose in the air and marches toward the kitchen to start her morning coffee routine. "I have absolutely no idea what you're talking about. And I didn't just 'get drunk and leave', I was puking my guts out, then I couldn't find him so I Ubered home."

"The fuck you don't know what I'm talking about." I follow her. "What are you playing at here, Huxley? What the shit do you think is going to happen?"

"Okay *fine*! I gave him your number by pretending I got a

new one. But I honestly didn't think he'd call you *last night*. I only meant for him to call you and invite you for a V-Day lunch or something. I don't know."

"You had no right." I say through gritted teeth. My jaw is so tight I can taste blood.

"Wait, did you sleep on the couch?" she asks.

"You know I did," I answer.

"Interesting," she comments. "I need coffee."

"Huxley!" I yell.

"Paul!" She dramatically throws her hands around like *I'm* the crazy one and stops making her coffee. "He clearly likes you. And you like him. You may not have known it, but I saw you two playing pool. I hear the way you talk about him. And by the way you were watching him just now, I'd say you finally pulled your head out of your ass and *noticed* him. All thanks to me. You're welcome."

"Huxley. I don't want this. I can't. We can never be a thing."

"And why not? If I've learned anything from all the enemies-to-lovers books I've read, the best, *most epic* love stories — or tragedies — all start out with a hate-hate relationship. And now that's changed. You need this and I think he needs this too. Y'all would actually be so perfect together. So stop *deflecting* like you always do and go after that man so y'all can fall in love and get married and adopt cute little babies. Again I say, you're welcome." She's in the kitchen starting a pot of coffee all nonchalant like none of this is fucked up.

Well, *it is*!

"What? So we can fit into the heteronormative bullshit storybook idea of what it means to love and be happy and lead a fulfilling life? No thanks. I got enough of that from my parents before they knew I was gay and I sure as *fuck* don't need that from my *queer* supposed friend. I told you to stay out of it and you didn't fucking listen. You never do." I'm fuming. "You just do whatever the hell you want like you always do. I was perfectly fine hating the dude and now I have to deal with him looking too fucking adorable in my clothes? Nah, I'm good on all that. *And* if I ever wanna see that shirt again, which I do 'cause I really like that shirt, then I *have* to see him again. I. Don't. Want. That. You fucked up, Huxley. So instead of standing there looking all smug and happy about whatever you think is going to happen, you'd do well to mind your own *fucking business.*"

And then I do the only possible thing that could follow my monologue without a rebuttal: I storm out of the kitchen into my bedroom and slam the door.

I don't want her to be right, but fuck. And why can't I just talk like a normal person instead of exploding all the time? I don't want to hurt people around me just because I'm hurt, just because this monster inside of me is tearing me apart. *And* I hate that I might be falling for someone and she can see it. This is the last thing I need. I'm clearly too fucked up to be loved.

Easton

THEY ALL JUST WANT ONE THING

"I say trash the shirt and never see him again." Aidan shrugs on my phone's screen, sitting in Tyler's dorm room.

The thought crossed my mind, but the shirt's not technically mine, so it seems sort of wrong. Even if Paul is a douche, he did come to the party when I was absolutely wasted and made sure I got home — well to *a* home — safely. Still, I've been dealing with damage control all morning. Aidan isn't a fan, and when I didn't text him back last night it sort of scared him. He thought I was in a ditch dead or something.

He's calmed down, a little. Now we're Facetiming and he's going on about where I was. He absolutely lost it when I told him, and I might have yelled back that he was getting too involved in my love life — and I use the word *love* lightly. I apologized though, and I think we're good now, he gets that I didn't mean to end up at Paul's house at least.

"Maybe he's not *that* bad," I say, fully knowing the response I'm going to get.

"Not that bad? We are talking about the same asshole, right?" Aidan turns and resettles himself. He must have turned toward a window; sunlight stripes his tanned skin.

"Yeah," I drag it out. There's just something else there, like, yeah he comes off this brash asshole, but maybe we're reading him wrong. "I mean, would a real asshole have picked me up?"

"Uh, yeah. To get in your pants." Aidan's eyes go wide like it should be obvious.

"Yeah, but he didn't," I remind Aidan for what's probably the sixth time since this call started. "And would it really have been so bad if he had?"

The look on A's face tells me it wasn't the right response. But would it have been that bad? I mean how can you not just drool over that thick neck, and oh my, those abs. I didn't need to see that, but God am I glad I did.

"Really? Yes. You have to stop falling for the bad guys!" Aidan rolls his eyes. "You are so much better than that, Easton! So much better. You've got a warm heart and you deserve someone who's going to understand that and care for that. Not just have their way with you and leave you. You deserve love too, ya know."

A few seconds pass and I can't think of what to say to that. It makes something deep in my chest stir, but A just doesn't get it. He's got Tyler. He has it made. Guys like that don't want me. They want cuties, or the hot twinks, not…whatever I am.

"Would a real asshole have cleaned my shirt for me? The one I puked on, by the way," is what comes out instead. "Or hell, asked me to stay for breakfast? Like really?"

I don't know why I'm trying to convince him. I have been mulling over that last bit all morning though. He asked me to stay for breakfast after I popped off at him. Who does that? And for a second, before Huxley came walking out and it all became clear what happened, I almost said yes.

My phone vibrates. Huxley.

HUXLEY: *Could I treat you to Waffle House soon? My apology tour?*

She's been apologizing all morning, and rightfully so. When she came walking out at Paul's place — actually, their place — I knew exactly what had happened. She'd given me his number during the party, not hers. Sneaky bitch. She says she didn't mean for me to call him drunk off my face to pick me up. Something about hoping I'd try calling her later in the week and maybe it leading to Paul and me going out. Fat chance on that. Like, I want it, but it's such a stupid idea. Aidan's right even if I don't want to admit it.

"But he's still bad news!" Aidan complains. "You always go for the bad boys, East, like the really bad boys. They all just want one thing. *One thing*."

I release all the air in my lungs with a massive sigh. He's not wrong.

"Yeah," I say right as my phone vibrates again.

HUXLEY: Oh! And maybe bring Paul's shirt? Please!

HUXLEY: Wednesday, say 9:30pm?

The text pops up and I frown at it. She wants me to wait until Wednesday to give this damn shirt back? Whatever. I send a quick text back and make a mental note not to forget.

"Huxley wants to meet Wednesday to get his shirt back," I tell A.

"Just get the shirt to her and be done with him, okay? Please," Aidan pleads.

"Okay."

Paul

PANCAKES AND WAFFLES AND SYRUP

"Fuck," I huff, pulling into the farthest parking space I can find from the entrance. I turn off my car.

Huxley asked me to meet her here but didn't give any context. I'm still pissed at her for what she pulled this past weekend, but I can't avoid her forever. I mean, I could. But I know I shouldn't.

I open my door to head inside Waffle House and Huxley is sitting in a corner booth fiddling with the table condiments. She actually looks nervous and my heart softens a little. She's wearing sweatpants and a hoodie today. It's far too big for her, but the juxtaposition of her Ariana pony and forever flawless makeup is a nice touch. And she's wearing heels. Of course.

I slide into the seat in front of her. "What am I doing here, Huxley?"

She startles and I bite back a smile. "I thought maybe we could call a truce…over some carbs."

"Is this you deciding what I *need* again even though you know I try to avoid carbs?" I really don't know why I have to be a dick sometimes. It just comes out. "Shit. I'm sorry. I didn't mean that."

"Shit. No, *I'm* sorry. It's okay. I deserved that. I wasn't thinking. I just thought… When I was a little girl and I had a...bad day, my parents would take me to Waffle House because they said, 'Waffles and pancakes and syrup always make everything better.' I know that's obviously not the truth because life is a bitch and waffles and pancakes can't actually fix...well, anything really. But I like to try at least. They're — "

"They can fix an empty stomach?" I offer.

She smiles her perfect toothy smile. "Yeah, they can. They're comforting, ya know? But you don't have to eat them. I just wanted to talk...and apologize."

The past month has been wild. We have truly become like family. We've had a blast. We've laughed and joked and watched far too much *Schitt's Creek*. We've made dinner together and played games. We've gone on drives around town to blare music and sing at the top of our lungs. I've even gotten her to come to the gym with me a few times. We've had so much fun, but we haven't really gone much deeper than that. Not outside that one night. But I sense that is about to change. Things are about to change, and I think it's needed. So I don't say anything. I let her talk.

"My whole life, I've always been looked at as 'too much'. Too dramatic, too over-the-top. I've had friendships and relationships fall apart because I can be...a lot. I know I'm a lot. I know this. And I don't mean to be and sometimes I can't control it. I'm an Aries, a triple fire sign. I'm fiery and passionate and opinionated. I love strongly and deeply. And it all can come off as...selfish or self-righteous or self-indulgent? I don't know. That's what I've always been told. But that's not *me*. I'm misunderstood."

Huxley pauses, not looking at me. She glances at the table, fidgeting with her hair. Then she finally meets my eyes. "You have no idea what it's like being a mixed *and* bisexual woman. I'm not white enough for white people or black enough for the black community. I'm not gay enough for the LGBTQ+

community and not straight enough for the straights. I have mild ADHD and Type II Bipolar Disorder. I've been on medication and have gone to therapy my whole life. Everything about me shouldn't work, shouldn't make sense.

"But I promise you, Paul, I was just trying to help. I know I overstep sometimes, but I've grown very fond of you. Contrary to popular belief, I don't have a lot of friends. Actually, my last BFF and I just went through a really bad friend breakup over winter break. It was really messy and it's been a bitch to get over."

"I...I didn't know that. I'm sorry, Huxley." How did I miss all of this?

"It's cool. I have my theater friends and my art friends but we're not close. I just saw you that day in the hall and...I don't know, there was something about you. And now you're kinda my best friend even though we aren't exactly on that level yet... But...I want to be. You're cool as hell and dress so much better than I originally thought. You're smart and insightful. You're a thinker and it's nice to know someone who's deep, ya know? We're kindred spirits, you and I. I can sense your soul and...I-I don't know. I like it. Just...please forgive me, Paul? Please? Because I... I can't lose you too."

I let Huxley finish saying what she needed to say. I feel like it's important for her to get it all out without being interrupted. But I honestly don't know how to respond or what I should say. She's amazing. Clearly. And I would never judge her. For any-fucking-thing. But what do I say?

She's waiting for an answer, expectant. I move to stand and her face falls. She thinks I've given up, but really I just want to hug her.

"Come here," I say before she gets the wrong idea. Tears fall as she exhales. She stands and I wrap her in the warmest, biggest hug I can muster. I may not know what to say, but I can show her. She hugs me back and, to be honest, I can't even remember the last time I've been held like this. I didn't know it was something *I* needed.

I've never been a lovey-dovey kinda guy, but I think she may give the best hugs.

"Thank you, Paul. Thank you for being my friend."

"You don't have to thank me, Huxley. But you're welcome."

"Now, let's eat. Or I'll eat and you can have an apple or something."

"Ha. You're funny," I deadpan as we sit back down. "Nah, I'm already here. Might as well eat some waffles. 'Cause let's be honest, waffles are 1,000 percent better than bullshit pancakes."

"Don't you dare! I will fight you right here, right now. Pancakes over waffles any day."

"Ha! I beg to differ as we sit here in a *Waffle* House."

"Semantics," she pffts.

* * *

At least an hour goes by and we're back on our regular bullshit. I don't think I've laughed or cried this much in my entire life. My abs and my cheeks hurt. Maybe she's on to something with the whole "waffles and pancakes and syrup make everything better" thing.

"Oh, hey, what time is it? My phone died," Huxley sobers and asks.

"Uhhhhh…" I pull my phone out of my pocket and check the time, "It's 9:27. Why? Hot date?" I wiggle my eyebrows at her.

She looks out the window behind me, then drops her head. "Shit."

"What?" I look too, but I don't see anything. It's too dark outside.

"Remember when you forgave me two seconds go?" She

cringes and ducks her head.

I narrow my eyes. "Huxley. We *just* fucking talked about this shit."

"I know, I know. But I technically did this before we talked. Don't hate me," she pleads with puppy-dog eyes.

Just then, the bell to the front door rings and I look to find Easton standing there. He's in his typical attire: jeans, t-shirt, and colored flannel button-down. His hair looks…combed? And his cheeks are pink from the cold.

He squints and waves like something is off.

Damn it all to hell, he's adorable.

I look back at Huxley. "What the fuck?"

She leans over the table and whispers quickly, "Just talk to him. If you still want nothing to do with him after tonight, then fine. But at least talk to him, like, a real conversation. And I told him to bring your shirt."

"Oh, that's good at least," I say with so much sarcasm dripping from my lips.

"Hey, Huxley. Paul." Easton's voice is hesitant.

"Hey!"

"Hey, dude," I say without rolling my eyes. I really want to roll my eyes.

Huxley gives me a look that says, *behave*. "It's so good to see you, love. But I gotta run. I have a…rehearsal thing. Playing Maureen in *RENT* is tough business." She gives Easton a hug and a kiss on the cheek and leans down to me and whispers, "*Be nice*."

She kisses me on the cheek, too, and I fucking growl because I was not prepared for this today.

I'm not mad. Not really. Just irritated by the surprise attack. But I gotta get my shit together so I don't scare off the cute baby deer.

Easton

I THINK I HATE YOU

I'm left standing in the middle of Waffle House as the entrance door swings shut behind Huxley. What the hell was that?

I turn around and Paul is sitting in the booth, looking at me with aggravation painting his face. She did it again.

"Uh…" I struggle for what to say now that it's just Paul and me. Well, and the staff and this old gray-haired guy in a black leather motorcycle jacket — the type without the sleeves — a few booths from the door. "So she did it again, eh?"

He gives a long sigh and leans his head back.

"Yeah… It appears she has."

"So… Uh…" I don't know what to do now. I was coming here to meet Huxley to give her Paul's shirt. Oh! Right! The shirt I'm literally holding in my hands. I shake my head and hold it out to him. "Your shirt."

"Oh. Yeah. Thanks. Did you wash it?" There's a smirk on Paul's face that I simultaneously want to kiss and punch right off. The conflict. But wash it? Seriously?

"I'm sorry, did I what?" I jerk my head back. "Did I wash it?"

"Yeah." Paul motions with his hands. I guess he's opening the washing machine or something, and I'm seriously about to walk out right now. "Like washer, dryer? Did you wash it?"

"No. Unlike you and Hux, I have to pay to wash clothes."

Sure, it's only like a dollar or something, but that's a dollar too much to do something just for him. "I think you'll be okay."

"Actually that works out perfectly because I don't like other people washing my clothes." Paul's grin intensifies, pulling at his cheeks in this annoyingly hot way. "I'm pretty particular."

"Then why ask?" He's at least right about the pretty part, but he's just trying to get under my skin. That's it. It's how he operates. *Just ignore it.*

"Had to make sure you didn't mess my shit up," he keeps it going, and I'm about to *lose* my shit. "Duh."

"Maybe Aidan was right," I mumble under my breath, then look him in the eye. "Funny. You're a real piece of work, you know that, right?"

I think that, of all the things I could have said, *that* got under *his* skin. He fidgets in his seat and rolls his eyes. I'll take it.

"Okay, fuck you." His voice is colder, but I don't care. "I'm just—"

"Could I get you anything?" An older waitress comes to the table, acting like we weren't in the middle of a heated convo.

"Uh, no. I'm not staying," I tell her.

She leaves and Paul picks back up. "I'm just trying to make conversation. This is...awkward."

"Awkward? For you? How do you think it is for me?" Like what is his deal? "I come to Waffle House, of all the places Hux could have chosen, to give *her* your shirt, and now I'm stuck here with you trying to act like you're not a prick."

He raises his hand and flicks his fingers toward the door. "No one's keeping you here, dude."

The heat rises in my cheeks. I know I should just go, just leave and be done with this asshole, but I don't. I stand there, staring him down like I'd actually try fighting him, as if that were even an option. Bluffing. It's a good half-minute before either of us speaks again.

"You got your shirt," I tell him, giving him my best annoyed look before I start to turn around. "So —"

"Wait." Paul throws his hand up. "Don't go. Just...wait."

"Uh..." For some reason, I listen. I don't know if it's just my inner submissiveness or because I sort of want to stay no matter how stupid it is, but either way, I stop and stand next to the table.

Paul's eyes drop to the tabletop. "So...do you...um... How are classes going so far...for you?"

"Uh...they're..." I pooch my lips out and blow a poof of air through them. "I mean, they're okay."

"What's your major?" Then his tone changes to annoyance, "Also, please sit. You're making this worse."

"Sure." I take a seat opposite him. At least Huxley partially warmed the bench, it's truly the least she could do. Please don't let there be any syrup on it. "Poli sci and history...well, if I can get through three levels of Spanish." I chuckle lightly and look down at my hands, then back up at Paul. "You?"

"Political science, right?" Paul furrows his brow and tilts his head.

"What else could it stand for?" Okay, now who's being an ass? *Come on, Easton!*

Paul rolls his eyes again and leans forward against the table. "I don't fucking know. Anyway, I'm a boring ol' English major. Do you speak Spanish?"

"English, huh? A..." I'm about to mention Aidan because he's a writer, so it connects with English, right? I stop myself just as his name is trying to slip from my tongue. Probably not the best idea right now. "Me? Speak Spanish? I've only taken the first class, and let's just say it's a struggle."

"Probably no more than me." Paul huffs. "I couldn't learn another language if my fucking life depended on it."

"You're an English major." I make sure I say it as dryly as possible. Like how can you not learn another language when you

THIS I PROMISE YOU

literally study a language? "How is another language hard for you? And you really like to say fuck, like a lot."

Believe me I don't mind one bit, but I'm thinking the glares the kitchen staff keep giving us might have something to do with that.

"Damn fucking right I do. What the fuck of it?" Paul drops back against the cheap booth and laughs. If I didn't know any better, I'd think he was about to throw his feet up on the table. "English is easy. It makes sense. I like words. I tried taking German in high school, but I just couldn't wrap my brain around it. I don't know."

"Seriously?" I'm still surprised. "I was going to be a German minor when I got here as a freshman, but I took my first German class that semester and well, hell no."

"And Spanish is easier?"

"Well, a little. At least these instructors don't refuse to speak in English the entire class." It brings back those days when my dream of speaking German in that guttural scary way went out the door. "My German professor wouldn't utter a single English word from the very first day. We were expected to understand from what he was doing, I guess. Stupid if you ask me. I dropped it after the second class."

"They do say the best way to learn a language is complete immersion." The look on Paul's face says he thinks it's quite obvious. I beg to differ. "My German teacher did the same thing."

"Eh. Nope. Not happening here."

"Well, I hope Spanish goes better for you then," he says, and it actually sounds genuine.

"Me too." Then I move the attention off my shoulders; I hate talking about me. "So you write or something?"

"Ha! I guess. Poetry, yeah. I try, but I can't seem to actually finish anything. Or at least nothing feels finished. I have notebooks full of unfinished shit. But I like my classes here and

I'm hoping I can learn something that'll help me pull my head outta my ass. My last school kinda sucked."

"That's actually sort of cool still." And yeah, pulling his head out of his pretentious ass would be a great idea. "I can write, but not stories. Just academic shit or political stuff."

"Hard fucking pass on politics. Nope."

"I mean yeah, it's not for everyone, but, like, it's important." Yeah, you don't say you hate politics around me. I get it's not everyone's cup of tea, but it means something. "If people don't say something, we're not even going to have a damn planet in the next fifty years because of global warming. So like, it sort of matters."

"Easier said than done, but I guess you're not totally wrong." He backtracks. "I get it's important though."

"So what do you *care* about?" I say as sarcastically as possible.

"Like I said, I like words—"

"You already said that," I interrupt. If I'm going to sit here in the middle of a Waffle House with him, I'm getting answers. It's not like I'll be seeing him much after this, so it's my best chance to find out more about this beautiful brute. "But that's not caring about something."

I don't think he liked me interrupting him, at least not by the way he sighs and his eyes latch onto me.

"How else can we communicate?" Paul leans across the table. I want to go the opposite way, but I don't. "First it was pictures, right? Caveman shit. But eventually we evolved when pictures and drawings weren't enough. Words are important. Even sign language is a series of *words*, just communicated differently. You think your political people, whatever bullshit, could do what they do without someone writing their speeches? Not a fucking chance. They make a difference *through* words, *with* words. Whether it's Spanish or German, Japanese, Zulu, or

ASL, words are used to make a difference."

Okay. I wasn't expecting that. I hope it doesn't sound pathetic that words being that important has never crossed my mind. I mean, they're just words, but he sort of has a point. I try to think of what to say, how to come back from *that*, but nothing's coming to mind. It was deeper than I expected from...him.

"I...well...yeah," I stutter as I try anyway. "Yeah, you're right. Sorry? I just didn't—"

"What, 'cause I'm all muscle and tattoos I can't have a brain?" The look in his eyes says it all.

"Not *exactly* what I was thinking. Uh...more like...like..." Goddammit, Easton, stop stuttering. "You know what, forget it. Just forget I opened my mouth. Words are important, and I obviously suck at them."

"Don't do that, dude." Paul shakes his head and puts his hands on the table, much too close to mine. Think I just pissed him off. Again. "Don't degrade yourself like that. You don't have to be good at words to speak. What were you going to say? Don't hold back now."

Hell no. I will definitely be holding back, because my reasoning wasn't that he was brainless because he's muscled and tattooed. No, it was because he's a muscled, tattooed douchebag. I pull my hands off the table and grip them tight. God I'm being judgmental as hell. *Remember, he did come get you at the party. A little grace, Easton.*

"I was...I just... Can we just not?" I try.

Paul cocks his head to the right and pooches his lips before opening his mouth.

"Think whatever you want of me, but you don't fucking know me. Maybe if *you* weren't such a dick you could see through the name-calling."

"Oh, now hold up!" I lurch forward, the tabletop pushing into my stomach. "Who's calling who a dick now? You're the asshat that tried getting in my friend's pants, and about took me out running on campus. Oh, and have we forgotten the stunt in the Student Union?"

"I let you talk. Will you hear me out now?" he says plainly. The angered response I was expecting doesn't come, and honestly I'm shook.

"Uh...sure." I don't know what else to say.

Paul takes a few deliberate breaths and repositions himself in the booth before giving me this grin that screams, *I'm trying real hard not to lose my shit.*

"Good. Now, first of all, the 'stunt' in the Student Union was Huxley, but I did go along. I admit." He pauses to nod. "Secondly, the fucking geese here are monsters and I will not apologize for being attacked. Fuck them. Lastly, I was nervous *as shit* and misread the situation with your friend —"

"Misread?" I mumble without moving my lips.

"—but...you didn't have to call me a douchebag, dude. *Words matter* and that was fucked up."

"What'd you think it looked like when you kept hitting on him after we *told* you he was taken?" I say, but something about Paul's demeanor shrinks and I actually feel bad for it.

"Y'all are clearly under-fucking-age." His voice raises in defense. "I...I was just trying to be a nice guy and offer my *legal* I.D. to help y'all, to make up for it. Like I said, I was nervous."

"You, nervous?" I say it quietly and with a grin, trying to make sure he knows I'm not being hateful. "Didn't take you for the type."

Paul shrugs, but that's all he gives me.

"Your friend is cute. And before you chop my head off, *he is.* I didn't know he was taken or with anyone at the open mic night for that matter, so I tried to put myself out there. I won't fucking apologize for that."

When he puts it that way it does seem like nothing big, and

definitely nothing bad. Suddenly he doesn't come off as the douchebag I'd nailed him as at the open mic, and honestly my stomach drops a notch thinking how I've acted. So to make up for it, I do the only thing I know how. I joke.

"You really *do* like to say the F *word*."

"Fuck you," he says, but a tooth-filled grin reaches across his lips, and the flecks of brown in his seafoam-green eyes seem to glitter.

We both laugh. Which feels weird and good at the same time.

"Yeah, well, fuck you too," I mimic him. "I don't know. Maybe, just *maybe*, I pegged you wrong."

"Oof. Pegging. Not my thing." Immediately Paul's hand comes up and he throws his face in his palm. "Sorry, bad joke. *Anyway…*"

"That's more my thing." I shy away and mutter it just quietly enough. But that is a useful piece of information, it means my late-night fantasies weren't too far off at least. "But sorry."

"It's cool, man. Shit happens." He shrugs. "Guess we both made our mistakes. Truce?"

"Truce," I repeat warily. Not because I don't mean it, but because it seems like something I'd have done back in fifth grade with my middle school bully Ben, not in college. "I really should be going though."

"Alright. No worries," he says, but his shoulders slump. "Do what you gotta do. I need to pay my bill and head home too, I guess."

"Ugh. Bills." I slip out of the booth and get to my feet. He pays, then follows me outside, and suddenly it hits me that now I'm the douche who never thanked him for not leaving me at the party. "So, you got your shirt back. And…uh…I guess I never really said thanks for picking me up from that party. So…uh…thanks."

He laughs, stopping in the middle of the parking lot. "I'm

not a monster, dude. If only you could have heard yourself. You *desperately* needed someone to rescue you."

"Oh, so now we're saying you rescued me?" I shake my head and allow a little laugh before waving my hands in the air in this exaggerated motion. "My knight in shining armor. Nah. But still, thanks. And of course you're not a monster. Sorry."

"You're welcome," he says. "And don't worry about it."

"Well, uh…bye."

"Yeah. Bye." And he turns around and walks off.

As I unlock my car and get in it hits hard how this isn't how I expected tonight to go. Hell, I didn't even expect to see him. But damn.

I turn the ignition and all I hear are clicks under the hood. Hold up now!

I try again, but it's just more clicking.

"Oh, come on! Not this!" I look around the car and notice I left the overhead light on. Dammit! It's not the first time, and yeah, Dad told me I need to watch it before I left a few weeks ago, but well, I didn't. I try again, but nothing changes.

"What the hell!" I punch the stupid steering wheel as headlights blare to life a few parking spaces over against the building.

Paul! But do I really want to ask him for help? I throw my head back, but I've only a second to spare before he's gone.

His car starts moving, and I make my decision. I swing my door open and jump out, waving for him to stop. Part of me expects him to just keep going, but that's the stupid part that still hasn't let go of Douche Paul, because he stops and rolls down his window.

"Uh…hi?" He squints at me in confusion.

"Yeah, hey. Uh…my car won't start." It sounds so pathetic as the words roll awkwardly off my tongue. "Think I left the interior light on. You wouldn't maybe jump-start me, would you? I have the cables."

A smile creeps across Paul's face and he shakes his head. "Oh, well I might require some sort of compensation for saving your ass twice now."

"Excuse me? I'm not a whore." What the hell? I thought we'd just got done establishing he *might* not be a total dick, and then this. "I'll just—"

"Stop! Just stop." Paul holds his hand up, obviously restraining his temper. His words come deliberately and slowly. "I only meant... Listen, they are having a poetry slam tomorrow night at Uptown Slam. Join me?"

"Oh..." I want to cave in on myself and cease to exist. "Sorry. So that's it? Go to this poetry thing with you, and you'll jump-start my car?"

"You got it!" He nods and shrugs.

"So you won't if I don't promise to go?" I ask. I can't say I really want to go to a poetry slam. Don't get me wrong, I like poetry, but it's sure to be a bunch of locals.

"So perceptive of you."

"You wouldn't leave me stranded here." I let my mouth pooch and tilt my head knowingly.

"The fuck I wouldn't. Try me." And with that his car starts moving forward and his window buzzes upward.

"Okay, okay! Fine." I wave my hands in a panic. Like seriously, man! "I'll go with you to your poetry thing. Fine!"

"Cool. Then just call me your knight in shining armor. Again."

"I think I hate you," I say, but I can't hold back the grin that swallows my face whole. How is he so hot and annoying at the same time?

Paul grins and rolls his eyes. "The feeling's mutual."

Paul

LOVE IS...

What the fuck did I do?

I haven't been on a date in two years. I haven't so much as looked at another guy since…whatever. Then Easton's friend — I still can't remember his name — and now Easton. I've done too much. I thought this might be a cute idea. I already planned on coming to the poetry slam. There's a piece I want to test on an audience. Inviting Easton though? I shouldn't have done that. I'm in way over my head. But I'm here now and I just gotta get through this.

Outside of my anxiety, it hasn't been all that bad. Dinner was awkward. It wasn't easy conversation like last night at Waffle House. Yesterday was so nice. It was really nice, but this is torture. How are our interactions so all over the fucking place like this?

It's probably me. It's always me. I don't know how to human.

And Easton's already had two drinks since we got to Uptown Slam. I bought them, even though he protested at first. I've paid for everything tonight. It was my idea, so I gotta pay and I wanna be nice, but I'm not made of money either. I'm going to need a job soon. But I just really wanna show that I'm a nice guy. Because I am.

Easton said he was going to the bathroom and came back

with a third drink and I don't even know how he got it. Now I feel like he actually hates this *more* than I hate the anxiety this bullshit is causing me. I just *really* hope we don't have a repeat of him puking in my car again.

If I open my mouth right now, I might throw up. So I chicken out on my performance as we've just been sitting here...not talking.

We're side by side facing the small stage. Easton finishes his drink, gets up to throw it away in between acts, then comes back and leans into me. Just shoulder to shoulder, but I immediately go stiff.

PDA has never been my thing. When I was a kid we did a project in class involving our initials. My full name is Paul Donavan Acre...PDA. I never lived it down until graduation day when I could fuck off. Like it was my fault. Like I picked my own name. It's not like my initials spelled out TIT or STD or some shit. PDA for initials is mild, in my opinion. I actually like my name, but I was still the butt of everyone's joke because of it. So I put off displaying public affection at all for fear of further scrutiny. Years of bullying and anxiety don't go well together. It's like mixing Coke and Mentos. I'm the explosive foam that follows.

So Easton leaning into me sets me off a little. But I suppress it as best I can because I really don't want to mess this up. I mean, come on. This is our first unofficial date, it's awkward as hell, Easton's on his way to being shit-faced again, and I have pit stains from anxiety. I doubt this'll ever happen again.

Do I want it to happen again?

What the fuck did I do?

"Did you understand anything that guy was talking about?" Easton leans over and asks me as the crowd snaps and the dude walks off stage, Easton's hand on my forearm.

It's like my mind is hyperaware of every point of contact our bodies have. I don't think I like it.

"I don't know. I wasn't really paying attention." I give him a shy smile. "Sorry."

"You okay?"

"Uh-huh. Yep. I'm cool."

He nods and turns back to the stage. His hand back in his lap.

The show ends, we stand, and Easton puts his hand in mine. Oh my holy fuck. I can't take this shit. I can't do it. So I rush us directly back to the car.

We both get in and before I can even start it Easton says, "Uh, hey. Would you maybe want to come back to my place? We could hang…maybe watch a movie or something?"

I pause. He wants…to keep hanging out? I'm confused. I thought this whole night was a mess. But maybe I'm reading the situation wrong? Can I handle a movie night with potential hand holding and possible cuddling? We'd be alone, though I suppose his roommate could be there. I could deal with it, I think. Maybe I could avoid the cuddling…for now. But he might think I'm avoiding him. I don't think…I want to avoid him… Shit, *I don't know*.

My jaw is clenched so hard my teeth hurt.

"Sure," I say as I try to relax a bit. I start my car, turn on my Why Don't We playlist, and head back to campus.

Turns out Easton doesn't live that far from Huxley and me. We park in the visitors' lot near his complex because I really don't want to get my shit towed tonight, or ever, and we make our way inside. Easton stumbles a bit, but I'm unsure if it's the alcohol or just because he can't even walk.

Maybe this is a bad idea too.

We get into his dorm and it's so damn small that I really have nowhere to go besides stand by the door or sit on his bed. I'd rather not sit on his bed right now, so I opt to stand where I am. He closes the door, hangs up his coat, toes off his shoes, and stares at me.

He steps closer. "Can I help you with that?" he asks as he reaches up to unzip my jacket. I swallow hard and barely nod my head.

He helps me out of my jacket and throws it on the footboard of his bed.

"Shoes?"

"Oh…I'm…I'm good."

"Okay."

We're nose to forehead again like we were at the party. I can smell the alcohol on his breath, but it's lightly mixed with the amazing spicy citrus scent of his cologne. He's looking up at me *that* way again, lips parted, and I realize I have two choices: I can kiss him or I can leave.

FUCK.

I kiss him. Just like that, I kiss him.

His lips are warm and wet. He wastes no time to tongue me down and pushes me back to the bed. I stumble, but since it's a matchbox in here I land softly on his mattress. He straddles me and makes quick work of finding my tongue again. I wrap my arms around his waist and pull him as close as I can. His hands are cupping my face and he lets out a light moan and I completely lose my shit because *damn* that's hot.

His dick is already hard against my stomach. I'm…not. But I'm sure I'll get there. I mean, I haven't masturbated since I was a teen. It's been *years*. Maybe my dick is broken?

My anxiety from the night fades to a dull roar as I try to tell my brain to live in the moment. This is actually kinda…nice. I don't know. I haven't kissed anyone for real for real since my ex, and he certainly didn't kiss me like this.

Easton is messy and quick with his kisses and he refuses to let go of my face. I try to help him find a rhythm, but I keep my hands wrapped around his lower back so he doesn't get the wrong idea. This kissing is nice, but if this escalates I won't be able to continue. I hope he knows that. I really hope he can sense that.

Then he takes off his shirt.

Oh no. Then he's back on me and his hands rest on my pecs in the extremely slim space between us. He slowly moves his way down to my abs and finds the hem of my shirt.

He lifts it and starts undoing my pants

And I freeze. He does want more. A "more" that I can't give him. Fuck. My brain flares with scenarios and I really don't know what to fucking do.

But I don't have to decide because there are keys in a lock and a door is being pushed open.

We break apart.

"What the hell are you doing here?" someone calls out. I can't figure out who while my adrenaline spikes and everything becomes hazy.

I need to get out of here right the fuck now. I can't think of anything else. My body chooses flight over fight as I throw Easton off of me onto his bed, grab my jacket, and run. I run, I run, I run. I don't even notice who was in the doorway, I just push past them. Fuck the elevators, I run down six flights of stairs at warp speed. I race through the lobby with someone yelling my name. Or maybe it's in my head?

I don't know and I don't care.

I burst through the door and fumble for my keys. I can barely see my hands. My face is wet, but my brain can't compute why. I just need to go.

Footsteps rush up behind me and Easton stops near the trunk of my car. "Paul? Paul, what's wrong?"

My eyes snap to his. "I—" is all I can get out through my dry, hoarse throat.

"Paul, what the hell is wrong with you?" Easton asks.

"Please just talk to me."

I bite my lip and squeeze my keys so tight I think they might draw blood. "I just can't. I can't. So just...leave me alone."

"What do you mean you can't? What are we even doing here then? I thought... First you're a giant asshole, then you're actually kind of nice and I thought— Goddammit, I don't know what I thought!" Easton says. His face is red and he's yelling. I keep my eyes down, not wanting to know if people are staring.

I can't look at him. I just can't.

"Look, I'm sorry. You're cute. Really fucking cute. And a bit of an asshole, too, but not really. I'm just not worth it, okay? It's best we stop before we hurt each other. I'm sorry."

I'm frantic, but I finally get the key in the hole, open my door, turn on my car, and throw it in reverse before I can even get my door shut.

Fuck all traffic, anything. Speed limits and stop signs don't exist right now. I jump a curb and a horn blares. I almost get hit as I whip into my apartment complex parking lot. I throw my car into two spaces, put it in park and scream.

I scream and scream until I can't scream anymore. I pound the steering wheel again and again and again until my hands hurt. I cry and I cry. I can't stop crying. I crawl into the back seat and curl into a ball while I try to catch my breath. But I can't breathe, I can't.

Someone help, I can't breathe.

Someone...help, I...can't...

Someone help.

Someone.

Anyone.

What do I do?

I kissed him. He kissed me. I liked it? He *really* liked it. He likes me. I like him? But...

I can't. I can't like him. I can't go through this again. I can't.

I won't. Liking means loving and loving means pain. Love is always pain. Love isn't real in the way people think it is.

Love is forced compliments and required time. Love is gaslighting and lies. Love is unwanted soft touches that wake you up in the middle of the night. Love is someone you trust coming into your room and pulling back your Winnie the Pooh sheets and pressing close to you. Love is them forcing you to stay quiet while they press into you and you feel the pain of them taking up space inside you where you know they don't belong but think it must be okay because they say it is. Love is thinking you can't say anything because doing so would ruin everyone's life. Love happened over and over and over again for *years* no matter how many times I *begged* and I *pleaded* for it to stop. Love pounded me in the chest, told me to "Shhhhhut up, Paulie. You'll wake everyone up."

Love is the idea of a reprieve that's only followed by betrayal. Because *love* is being blindsided while showering before school, and calling in sick as blood's running down your leg and you're only the husk of a soul.

Alcohol. Love is the bitter smell of alcohol.

Love is weakness. Love is shame. Love is pain.

Love is…sleep.

I let my lungs fill, hold for seven seconds, then exhale.

I let my lungs fill, hold for six seconds, then exhale.

I let my lungs fill, hold for five seconds, then exhale.

And then four…

And three…

Two…

One.

My heart rate slows as my breathing evens out. I close my eyes and give in to fatigue while I rest my face against the knees that I'm holding tight to my chest for dear life.

DOGS > HUMANS

Dogs are so much simpler than humans. They either like you or
don't like you, and hell, nine times out of ten even if they don't
like you at first, it doesn't take long for them to warm up. People
on the other hand. Shit. They're so hard to understand.

"So he's an ass or he's not an ass?" Melanie asks. She's my
boss at the pet kennel. She's lathering up Ivy, one of our repeat
clients, a beautiful black and gray Cocker Spaniel.

"He is, but at the same time, there's something…" I struggle
for the word. I don't want to say he's sweet, because that might
be a stretch. Maybe he is, but it's too soon to say that.

"Less assish?" Melanie makes up her own word in her
trademark high-pitched voice.

"Yeah!" I nod quickly. "That. Sometimes he's less assish."

"You know I pulled that right out of thin air, right? That's
not a word." She shakes her head. "And you're in college."

"You're the one who said it." I hold Ivy still while Melanie
rinses the soap out of her thick coat. "But yeah. It's hard to
explain. Like I swore he was just an egotistical douche, but I think
maybe he's a little more."

Melanie huffs. She's been a party to these conversations a
few times since the semester started and I had my first encounter
with the enigma known as Paul. She sided with Aidan early on,

but now she doesn't seem to be as anti-Paul anymore, even if Aidan still is, especially after last night.

"Aren't most people?"

"Huh? Aren't most people what?" I ask. I think I zoned out for a second, but a splash of water brings me back when Ivy shakes her head. I give her a little pat.

"A little more. Like aren't most people more than just one thing? That's sort of the whole human thing. We're complex." She gives me wide eyes, sounding like one of my philosophy professors, or hell, sort of like Paul when he went into that spiel about words.

I've thought about that a bit too. He was right. We don't think about it because they're so normal to us, it's the everyday, it's expected. But that doesn't change their importance. Of course, I can't put it as eloquently as he did but, yeah, he was right.

"I guess so. I'm pretty simple I think, but maybe," I say.

"You? Simple?" Melanie scoffs and I let it roll off my back with a grin.

We let Ivy go after a quick blow dry and follow her outside to the fenced-in play area. The sound of cars buzzes over the fence and the wind whips at my exposed cheeks. I pull my green hoodie tighter around my chest and glance around at the dogs. Tall and short, loud and quiet. Mostly loud, especially Milo.

As I've been doing all morning, my mind throws me back to last night. The sweetness of his lips, the scent of leather and sage the closer I got, especially when I kissed his neck. My body felt so right against him. And then how he jumped and ran and kept running as I yelled his name. I stood in the parking lot and watched his tail lights dim to nothing around the corner.

The crazy part is that I don't think it was all just the alcohol. I felt something burning in my chest all evening. Something that made me nervous in a way other guys don't do to me. A feeling that burrowed deeper and tugged my chest downward when his car disappeared, and every time I texted to ask what happened and he didn't respond. He still hasn't. Unworthy is the word that keeps flashing in my mind. *Unworthy.*

"So are you two dating?" Melanie leans around to get my attention.

"Huh? Dating?" I straighten. "Definitely not."

"So why you so worked up about him not texting back?" she asks as we sit down at a table outside. I told her about that when I got to work an hour ago after classes. I might have triple texted him this morning.

"I don't know. I mean he came to my room, and then...gone." I wave my hand in the air.

Melanie chuckles and I join her. It's silly. It really is. It wasn't a week ago I couldn't stand the thought of Paul beyond his beautiful physique, and now? Now I'm fretting over something that never was.

"One-night stand?"

"More like half a night and just kissing," I correct her.

"Same thing." She shrugs.

It still just hits so weird though. Like, things seemed pretty great. Sure, I was awkward all evening and I drank more than I should because I didn't know why I liked being there with him so much and just knew he hated every moment of it. The poetry was horrible and I didn't talk much. I thought with a few drinks I'd loosen up and talk, but I didn't. I might have gotten quieter, until we got back to the dorm, and I sort of went full horny on him. But he did ask me to go in the first place, or did I read his intentions wrong? Oh my God, does he just want a friend?! I drop my face into my palm.

"What?" Melanie's surprised.

"Maybe I read him wrong. Maybe it wasn't a date." I'm reeling. I thought it was a date. That's why I was so nervous, but if it wasn't... Oh my God. And I even cussed Aidan out for scaring him off when I got back upstairs last night. I had to apologize for that this morning. One more reason he doesn't like Paul.

"So you're all worried about a boy that just wants to be friends?" Melanie nods and pats the table between us. "You're crushing so hard."

"No I'm not!" I blurt back and straighten.

I let my head fall against the back of my chair and stare into the cloudless blue sky, letting the breeze chill my nose. I knew we weren't *dating*, but I thought it was a *date*.

Paul

THE INTERVIEW

Huxley and I walk into Uptown Slam, her to drink, me for a job interview.

I've been looking around the past few days for something part-time. I still want to make sure I'm focusing on school and working out, but a part-time job would be a nice distraction and Uptown Slam is looking for a barback/bartender and I wanna give it a shot. Huxley came with me because she knows the owner because of course she does. She said her being there would "totally land you the job." I figured I'd take all the help I can get.

Huxley orders a drink and I sit down next to her at the bar, waiting.

"So, Paul. How are you? It's been too long. We can't let this happen again."

I order a water. "Um. It's been two days and we've both been busy."

She huffs. "And that's three days too long in my opinion."

"Yeah, okay."

We're silent for a moment before she says, "Heard from E?"

I told Huxley about what happened. She doesn't know all the details about why I had a panic attack, only that I had one and I let her come to her own conclusions.

"Yeah. He's texted a few times. Even left me a voicemail like it's 2008."

"Oh please," she says, waving me off, "you were barely out of diapers in 2008. You have *zero* room to talk."

"Still."

"Still."

I fiddle with the condensation running down my glass. "I don't know what to say. I fully freaked the fuck out on him. He probably thinks I'm batshit."

"Would someone who thinks you're batshit keep trying to contact you though?" Huxley's eyes go all wise Buddha on me.

"No, probably not."

She pats my shoulder. "I know this is hard for you. But you like him—don't give me that look, you know you do and I'm not wrong about these things. We've already established that. Just...when you're ready, talk to him. I know E. He's, like, so easy to read. Super deep, lots of layers. But you gotta put in the licks to get to the center of his Tootsie Pop—"

"I fucking hate you."

"—and you can tell he's been through some shit, *so* y'all already have so much in common! Look, nothing can get done unless you com...mun...i...cate. Whether it's good or bad or somewhere in between, *at least* communicate."

"No, I know. You're right." I relent and drop my head. "I'm trying. I'm working on it."

Huxley rubs circles on my back. "I know, babe. Just don't give up on him."

"I don't know what to do," I tell her, eyes glued to my glass. "I don't know what I want."

"It's simple: do you like him?"

"Yes, but it's definitely not fucking simple."

She sighs. "You like him, it's simple. *Tell him you like him.* Things always have a way of working themselves out, but nothing can be done unless you *communicate*. Wait, I believe I just said that. Didn't I just say that?"

"Yes, Huxley…" I groan.

"Then stop making me repeat myself. E's a catch. Don't let him get away."

"Who even are *you* seeing right now? Hmmm?" I change the subject. "You're all up my ass about Easton, you've got to be practicing your own advice, yeah?"

"If you *must* know" — she rolls her eyes and takes a generous gulp from her glass — "I was talking to this guy, but I don't think it's going to work out. The dick was good, like really good. But the rest? Meh. *However*, I did meet this girl the other day that I wouldn't mind pursuing. Her name is Devina and she was cute and bubbly. Her parents came here from South Korea back in the '90s. They apparently have a cute little Korean restaurant that we *have* to check out. My mom is going to love them!"

"Do you even know if she's gay? Or bi/pan?"

"Ugh, I don't know. Girls are so much harder to tell if they're queer because, like, we girls always compliment each other. It's how we roll. So yeah, I'm not sure. I did get her number though. Just gotta bide my time to crack this mystery. I mean her jeans were cuffed and her phone case was clear so that's a good sign, right?"

"I wouldn't know, but I'm pretty sure anyone can cuff their jeans and buy clear phone cases — "

"Not likely."

"Y'all bisexuals are on another level, speaking your own damn language and shit."

Huxley nods vigorously. "You right, you right."

"Huxley?" A man steps out of the back room. "Huxley the-motha-fuckin'-G.O.A.T. Davenport, is that you?"

"OMG! Jeremy *the*-fucking-V.V.I.P. Blitz!" Huxley squeals. "This is my roommate, Paul Acre. Paul, Jeremy. He owns this dumpster fire."

"And I will kick your ass right the fuck out." Jeremy pulls her in for a big hug.

"You wouldn't dare." Huxley hugs him back, then straight up punches him in the arm.

"Try me." He smiles, then turns to me.

I hold out my hand. "Nice to meet you, sir."

"Oof." He smacks my hand away playfully. "Cut the fuckin' shit. No. No 'sir'. Just Jeremy or Jer."

"Sorry, Jeremy." I refuse to call this man *Jer*. No nicknames.

"You good, my dude. So about this job…"

Easton

WHY DO I DO THIS?

The door eases shut with a light touch from my hand and the light from the hall disappears. I'm left in shades of gray cast from the singular window between our beds.

I gulp and let out a long slow breath.

Aidan's asleep, so I step gently and undress for the second time tonight. I don't bother folding my clothes before sliding into bed and pulling the covers tight.

Why do I do this?

I close my eyes and try not to think about it. My breath stutters from my lips and I clench my teeth. I push the thoughts away, but they're replaced by him.

It's his fault.

Those green eyes, that hard chin, the tattoos. It's been six days since he ran from this very room, but I keep thinking about him. No matter how many times I tell myself it's just a stupid crush, a child thing, I can't seem to rid him from my thoughts.

My phone dings quietly outside my sheets. Maybe. Maybe it's him. Maybe he's decided he messed up and wants to talk. I throw the covers back and scoop my phone from the shared makeshift nightstand of plastic storage drawers. I deflate when it comes to life. It's Sam, my sister.

SAMANTHA: *You home yet?*

A huff escapes my lips. I don't want to answer. I don't want to think about this, but if I don't answer she's liable to get the entire Charlotte-Mecklenburg police force out looking for me. I didn't want to tell Aidan where I was going. Rebound sex isn't a cool look and I know it worries him and he has class early tomorrow. So I told my sis instead. I might be stupid for loaning my body out, but I'm not stupid enough to do it without telling someone where I'll be.

EASTON: Yeah.

In my defense, I hadn't planned on it. DLStraight92 sent me a message yesterday and I ignored it. I did good. But the more I thought about Paul, the way he ran out of the dorm when I kissed him, how it's like I don't exist to him anymore, and how much for some goddamn reason I give a fuck, the lower I sank. It's one of those things your brain doesn't fully process in the moment, then it waits for you to fuck up before it pulls everything in and lets you reexamine your choices in full HD. So I messaged DLStraight92 back and I went over. Again.

Why did I go over again? My body aches, and I feel like a piece of rebar was thrust up my ass and pounded by a jack hammer. The way he threw me around and degraded me. And the entire time I felt like I deserved it, like it's all I'll ever deserve. But now it's all crashing down.

I drop my phone back on the cabinets and curl into my blankets, covering my face and bringing my knees up into my stomach. I want to disappear, to not feel, to not be. I'd rather be numb, feel nothing at all than this grating guilt and the shit playing out in my head, the memories of being violated, but asking for it. What the hell is wrong with me?

I'd thought it was just a kink, a little fetish with being dominated and demeaned I'd discovered with Ryan my junior year in high school, but it's become so much more than that. In the moment, I feel like I deserve it, like it appeases this guilty part of me that applauds who I am. It's like punishment for all the things I couldn't be *and* that I am. If I'm honest, and I'm no therapist, part of me wants to blame my mom, that bitch who left when I was only fourteen, only months after I came out, and it was no coincidence. She made it clear she wouldn't have a gay son and if that was who I *chose* to be, she didn't know me.

I remember the day she walked out the door, the day Dad gave her his ultimatum. It was either accept and love me or pack her bags. I can still picture the jean jacket she was wearing that day, the red-and-white plaid scarf over her shoulder as I watched her walk away without ever looking back, without ever saying goodbye. That was November 12, 2014, just two weeks before Thanksgiving, over six years ago.

I pull myself back to the present and I don't want to be here either. Why is who I am always a battle? If it's not the literal person I was born and who I love, it's the things battling in my head for dominance, and if it's not that it's a boy who can't really see me, and if it's not that it's the disease that's slowly wreaking havoc on my body.

I clench my eyes tight, willing myself into the darkness. I wrap my fists around the covers and squeeze. Tears slip between my eyelids and cross the bridge of my nose, dripping onto my sheets. I pull into myself and bury my face in my pillow as I let it all out.

Paul

I'LL REMEMBER THIS FOREVER

I started masturbating again.

I don't want to be scared of sex. Not anymore. I like sex, I do. Or I used to and I want to again. But I have to work my way up to it.

Baby steps.

Well, that is if he ever wants to see me again. He's texted a few times. Even left me a couple more voicemails. I do really like him…I think? I'm not too sure since we haven't really gotten to know each other past the bullshit. I'd be willing to. I'm pretty sure I want to. But I'm just… I don't know what to do right now.

So I started masturbating again. I was on the verge of another panic attack after the first time, but I was able to work through it. The first time jerking off after three years going without was nothing short of glorious. Panic attack be damned. Since then I've tried to do it at least once a day with no panic attacks in sight.

Today, though, I just finished my *second* session, and I'm very proud of that, thank you very much. No porn though. Porn is too addicting and I don't want to go down that road. So I guess I'm working on this in the hope that Easton will still want me after I finally get my shit together.

I towel-clean myself and head to the bathroom to touch up my hair. I pull the forty-volume developer out from underneath the sink and get to work. Once my hair is freshly bleached I grab my clippers and give myself a clean new buzz, then hop in the shower.

I was able to land that job. I don't start until next week, but I'm pretty stoked. Before I transferred schools and moved to North Carolina I was never allowed to have a job. My dad was well off, I think. But he was so incredibly controlling that we never really did anything fun as a family. The only extracurriculars he let us do were sports, but no jobs. So he gave us older kids an allowance "out of the kindness of his heart" once we each started high school. It didn't feel like much at the time, but I saved and saved and eventually I bought my car from my parents and got my own phone plan "to show I was being responsible". After that I just kept saving until the moment my dad decided to cut me off. I left Kansas City shortly after that. Gah! I hated how controlling he was. I could never do anything I wanted. Like, ever. Though I sure the fuck did take all I could outta him while I had the chance. I knew it would end eventually anyway.

Moving took a good chunk though, and I've been kinda reckless since I've been here.

So this is my first job. Part-time, but still a job.

I throw on some sweats—I don't think Huxley is home, but in case she comes back I don't wanna be flouncing around the house buck naked—and head to the kitchen to start making dinner.

I'm just about to finish up and fill my plate when there's a knock on the door. Huxley wouldn't knock unless she forgot her keys again, and I sure as hell wasn't expecting anyone. I don't know anyone here.

I go to my room and put on a shirt, then head back out to answer the door. I open it to find Easton. My chest hitches with the loss of breath. Damn he's cute. But fuck, I've been avoiding him and now he's here. He's *here*.

"Hey," I say surprised. I can't trust my voice right now because I'm nervous and excited and *holy shit* I think I actually missed him?

"Uh... Hey, Paul..." he stutters like he does and it's so cute I might die.

What is this shithead doing to me?

"I... Sorry for just showing up but...you haven't responded to my texts...or my calls." He pauses and looks anywhere but at me. I can't look anywhere but at *him*. "I was worried, is all. I swear I don't just show up like this normally."

He blushes that peachy color I like that reaches his ears, and I surprise both of us by asking, "You hungry?"

All he does is nod. I let him in and tell him to sit at the table, then I go to make him a plate. I didn't really make enough for two, but I think I can split the chicken and broccoli evenly so there's enough for both of us. I might have to make more for myself later.

I set the plate in front of him and move to sit across from him. I'm nervous because *he's here* and I have some apologizing to do. I'm not sure where to start, but his presence is calming while we eat.

"Listen, I —" I say at the same time he says, "So, how —"

We both say, "Sorry" in unison. Then, "You go first."

We laugh together.

Once we both calm down he asks, "Did I do something wrong?" and it breaks my fucking heart. He legit thought all of that was his fault?

"No, Easton. No. You did nothing wrong. I swear. It's...me." I hang my head.

His head drops too, and his eyes close. "That's what they all say."

"No, it's not like that. I'm truly so sorry, dude. I was...I was on edge all day that day. I have..." I pause, close my eyes, and rub my hands down my face. Then I look him directly in the eye. "...anxiety and I wanted our date to go well. But I fucked it up with my issues. I don't do well with PDA, and then your roommate showed up, and then I've been ignoring you and avoiding you. Gah! I'm so sorry. I just...didn't know how to do this. Not after... Not after you saw me... Not after you saw me like that. I should never have treated you like that. Hell, I shouldn't have treated you the way I have since we first met. My...attitude has been inexcusable and I'm so very sorry. I've just been...um...going through a lot, but that's no excuse for my behavior. I'm...um. I'm so...so sorry, Easton."

Now I'm the one who's fucking stuttering.

Get your shit together, Paul.

"You didn't fuck it up. I was nervous too. You're uh...well." His focus darts away from me. "It's hard to believe that someone like *you* would want to go out with me."

"Wh-what?" I stammer, surprised.

"Yeah, you know. You're all..." Easton shies away again. "Uh. You're sexy as hell. And I'm not. Like there's no —"

"Are you serious? Easton, come on. I may not know you very well yet and we definitely didn't get off on the right foot, but you're fucking adorable, dude. I...I like you. And I liked kissing you. Like I said, I just have issues."

"We all do, I guess." His eyes twitch. "I liked kissing you too. So much. And I'm sorry you're going through so much. Same honestly."

I wasn't expecting him to show up here. I wasn't expecting to have this conversation with him, but now that it's all out there I feel like we really could figure this out. Just gotta take the leap.

After a brief silence Easton speaks up again without looking at me. "Sorry if I came on too strong. I...uh..."

He stops and throws his head back in frustration.

"You don't ha —" I lean forward with my hand out to try to

stop him, but he doesn't let me.

"No, I do." Easton puts his hand up and takes a breath. "I'm not used to guys actually seeing *me*, and I just assumed you wanted to fuck. I wasn't even sure if it was a date. Sorry."

He looks away, his cheeks pink and cute as shit, but the hurt in his eyes is too much.

"We could...try again," I suggest. "All I ask is for patience and grace. I'm far from perfect, but I hope I can make it up to you. I definitely want to try. If you want to, that is."

"Okay," Easton jumps in the moment my lips stop moving.

"Yeah?" I can't stop smiling.

"Yeah."

I get up from my seat, circle the table, and hold out my hand to him. I need to make this real or I might chicken out. He grabs my hand in earnest and stands in front of me. I waste no time leaning in and placing a long sweet kiss on his pink lips. He doesn't part them this time and I know I'll always remember this moment. The gratitude I feel for such a simple, sweet gesture. A moment left to time. A moment I want to have again and again with him, with Easton.

I pull back and place my forehead against his. "I think I want this."

"You think?" Easton jests, and I want to melt into him because he's just so damn adorable, his eyes alight with infinite stars.

Like, how could I have freaked out on him? Why have I been ignoring him? I mean, I know *why*, but now that he's here in my arms I kinda feel like there might be a possibility to overcome my bullshit past. He does that to me, for me.

"No, yeah. I do. You and all the flannel that comes along with it. I'd like to see where this goes between...us." I raise my head and look into his *gorgeous* honey-brown eyes. And just then I realize I don't think I really knew what my favorite color was before this moment, before I looked into his eyes. In this lighting they almost glow, a rich golden yellow around his irises, and I nearly buckle at the knees. "Okay?"

"I almost gave up on you, you know?" He doesn't break eye contact. "You didn't respond and I didn't know what to do. And then I thought maybe it wasn't supposed to be a date and somehow I read the situation wrong and thought you only wanted a friend. I've been really confused. I don't normally show up at guys' doors by the way. But…I can't get you out of my head."

"I don't want you to." I grab the back of his neck in earnest and kiss him again. Deeper this time. I can handle it, I'm okay. I'm in control and oh my holy *hell* he tastes so good. Like seasoned chicken. I kiss his cheek, his jaw, his neck, then back to his lips.

He kisses the tip of my nose. "Can we try again?"

"Again? I mean, I *guess* I could kiss you again. I guess." I smile and roll my eyes playfully.

"Yes. No. I mean, yes, I want to kiss you again. No, stop distracting me." He laughs. "I only mean a date. Can we try a date again? Like, officially this time."

"I'd like that."

"And you only said 'fuck' a few times, by the way." Something about the way he smiles is so serene and playful at the same time.

"You're never going to let me fucking live that down, are you?" I smile wide because dammit, I never want him to stop giving me a hard time.

"Well now you've just crossed the line." And oh how he smiles. "And not a chance. I'll pick you up tomorrow at noon?"

"Wait, *that's it*?" I ask.

"Yeah. Tomorrow," he says.

"So you just eat my food and leave? You could at least help me with the dishes." I smile and bite my lip so he knows that I'm joking. I just don't want him to leave yet.

He smiles back and rolls his eyes. "Fine."

Easton

LEATHER AND SAGE

My brakes squeal to a stop in front of Paul's apartment. If he didn't hear that, he sure will in a second. They've been screeching the past two days, but I keep putting it off. It's always something.

Please keep working, I don't have the money to deal with this shit right now.

I get out and start up the sidewalk. Paul said to text him when I got here and he'd come out, but forget that. I'm going to be a gentleman. At his door I knock and wait for a full two seconds before the latch clicks and out comes Paul. My eyes immediately jump up and down his body, not to examine those thick thighs this time but because of how he's dressed. I admit I'm the tacky, no-sense-of-style type of gay, one of an unfortunate rare breed, but now I feel so overdressed.

Paul's standing in the doorway looking perfect in a white oversized, long-sleeve shirt under a black tee with the words *PRETTYMUCH* plastered across the front, and skinny light-blue jeans with holes all down the knees and legs. I mean, he looks hot in it, plus the pink ball cap is a nice touch.

Then there's me. I rushed back to the dorm after work to take a shower and change into "date" clothes. Which to me meant a blue and yellow plaid button-down tucked into my slim-fit jeans with the bottoms cuffed twice. Hell, I even put on my blue suede dress shoes, no socks — I do get that at least — and a denim jacket.

"Hey." Paul grins.

"Uh, hi!" I do my best not to jump out of my stupor.

"You good?" he asks, his eyes looking *me* over now, and internally I'm screaming. "Where you going? The neighborhood hog-tie or a frat meeting?"

"Uh..." I skew my cheek. "Frat meeting? Really?"

"I mean, I did have to rescue you from one," he grunts.

"I overdid it, didn't I?" I roll my eyes, but he's not done.

"You got a shirt on under that?"

"Yeah, why?" Seems like a weird question to me.

"Untuck and unbutton. You look like you're going to church to meet a pretty girl."

I do as he says, even though it sort of feels like I'm undressing in front of him. If he says it's better, then it's better. I don't know.

"I mean, maybe not for a pretty girl, but a pretty boy."

"Oh, so you're taking me to church?" Paul eyes me.

"I... That could..." My mind goes to that Hozier song that's all about sex called "Take Me to Church", but I decide it's best to keep my mouth shut. "Never mind. You ready?"

But I'm glad I mentioned how great he looks because my nerves ease a bit. He does look hot.

"Love the hat by the way," I say after he nods and we start back down the sidewalk to my car. "Just ignore the brakes squealing. It's fine, I promise."

Is it a lie? I don't honestly know, but I think we're good.

* * *

I wish I'd worn a heavier jacket. I don't know how he's dealing in only a long-sleeve shirt, unless he's got a few extra under it.

Despite the cold I think things are going better this time. I'm not scared out of my mind and Paul seems less tense too. Maybe the farmers market in Kannapolis wasn't a bad idea after all. I mean who can hate locally sourced produce and area crafters?

We walk past a booth stocked entirely with carrots and onions, then another with an arrangement of cabbage, peas, spinach, and a few things I don't recognize. I honestly didn't think the market was open during the winter months, but in my haste yesterday to find somewhere to take Paul, this popped up in my search. I hadn't planned that far ahead when I decided to knock on his door unannounced, another thing I can't believe I did.

"Ooh, I love homemade soaps." I point at an enclosed booth just ahead with a banner out front that proclaims *Rub-a-Dub Soaps*. "Come on." I take off for it.

He jogs after me and into the booth where a lady around our age is standing behind a quaintly decorated table covered in an assortment of soaps and bath products. There are so many scents. Midnight Sea, Pink Blossom — I bet that one's really sweet — Thunder Clash, Peppermint Mocha, and the list goes on.

"How about this one?" Paul says, picking up a yellow and pink bar.

"Citrus Lemonade?" I ask, slightly confused.

"Yeah, I thought you'd like this smell. It's like the cologne you use. Spicy citrus, kinda. Maybe? I don't know." Paul blushes and my mind empties. He smells me? He knows how I smell?

"Uh yeah, I do." I gulp back the sudden nerves in the back of my throat. And now I don't know what to say, so I pick up one called Whipped Mocha and give the bar a whiff. Not bad. Not sure I want to smell like a Mocha Frappuccino every time I bathe, but not bad. I offer it to Paul and he leans in and smells it. His nose crinkles but he smiles. "This isn't bad."

"What about this one?" Paul shrugs and shows me one called Fireside. He smells it first and gives an approving grin. "Kinda woodsy. Kinda fitting with all the flannel country vibes."

I step closer, letting my free hand brush his, trying to ignore

THIS I PROMISE YOU

the spark that races up my arm, and take a deep breath of the bar's scent. Fireside is accurate. It brings back memories of sitting around a fire on Bertie Beach with Dad and Sam and Shane — my high school best friend — back when things were a little simpler and it didn't feel like my body could break down at any moment.

I grin and nod, but in the same instant I'm overtaken by a sense of dread. I look Paul in the eyes for a brief moment and wonder if he could see me the same way he does now if he knew that at some point I could end up on the ground seizing if my MS got that bad, or that I might have to use a walker, or that I might not be able to…perform in bed all the time.

I'm not an idiot. I know I've been reckless with my sex life, but it's just terrifying knowing that one day my body might take over and I won't have any control. I already get a small taste of it, but…I don't know. I just want to have as much control as I can before it's gone. Even if it isn't real.

No, stop. Stop it, Easton. That's all a long way down the road, and you're doing everything you need to to avoid it.

That's why I always have my morning run and stretches. It's why despite the amount of alcohol I might have I still try to eat mostly healthy. I don't plan on letting it mess up my life, but a part of me still wonders if it would matter to Paul.

"This one's not bad." He lifts a bar to my nose and I smile for him as I smell it. Woah. Lemon. There's definitely lemon in that.

"Ew." I shrug. "It's not *the* worst."

"You don't like it?"

I shake my head and crinkle my nose. His shoulders slump a little, but I'm not going to lie to him.

"So lemon's a no go," he says.

"Yeah, no. Not really into the strong fruity smells despite my *citrus* cologne, I guess," I tell him. I'm more into the deep musky scents, like the way Paul made my car smell when he got in it, that combination of leather and sage I can't get out of my nose, and don't want to. "I'm more…woodsy?"

"Woodsy." Paul points at me and nods, like he's committing it to memory.

"And ocean scents."

"Got it."

"Come on." I nod out of the tent, and before I can get a few steps, Paul's hand grasps my forearm.

"Funnel cakes!" There's an excitement in his voice, like a kid who just saw Santa for the first time.

I meet his eyes. They're open wide, excited, an ocean of roiling sea-green waves. In that moment he's not just hot and handsome, he's adorable and I want to pull him close and breathe him in so badly.

"Oooh." I make a little O with my lips.

"Come on, we've gotta." He drags me along by my arm.

Paul

FUNNEL CAKES AND DIRTY THOUGHTS

I grab his arm — it's not his hand, but it's the next best thing. It's like, now that our first "unofficial" date is out of the way, there's something about him that relaxes me. Like...like I feel at home. I don't know, but I'm really enjoying his company. So I grab his arm and drag him to the funnel cakes.

"*Please* tell me you have a sweet tooth?" I do try to eat healthy, but fuck it. I trade a ten for a funnel cake for us to share. "I can*not* resist a good funnel cake. Or corn dogs. Or Red Vine licorice."

"Hell yes! Peanut butter and chocolate. Anything strawberry."

"Powdered sugar?" I swipe my finger along the top of our newly acquired dessert treat and hold out a finger of powdered sugar for him to taste.

His eyes go wide for a millisecond and I realize what I'm asking him to do, but I'm not about to show him I didn't think it through.

"My hands are clean, promise," I say, and that's apparently enough. He leans in and takes my finger into his mouth, never breaking eye contact the entire time.

"Definitely powdered sugar."

"I—" Okay, I really didn't mean for that to be sexual. It was supposed to be a cute gesture, but the way he just licked my finger? Oof. I don't know what to— Um... "Wanna sit and split it?"

"Sure."

It's weird because I remember his country accent from when he was drunk, but it's so subtle in his day-to-day I can hardly tell it's there. But when he said "sure" just now it was very much there and it makes me weak. He's the exact opposite of me, yet I say y'all more than him. Balance, I guess.

We move to a nearby picnic table and sit across from each other. Easton looks like he's cold even with his jacket and I wish there was something I could do to help, but I'm not wearing a jacket. I'm fine because I normally run hot, so the cold doesn't really bother me. I'd wrap him in a hug if I could trust my anxiety not to be a bitch, but it is.

"So...do you like...sports?" Easton asks, and I have no idea where *that* came from.

"Ew, the hell. What makes you think I like sports?"

"Your Lakers t-shirt." Easton angles his head. "The one you...the one I borrowed."

"Oh, that! No, that's just for style. I liked the look of the shirt so I bought it." I shrug while I rip another piece from the funnel cake. I stuff it in my mouth and wipe my hands together to get off the powder. "I don't give a shit about sports. My two older brothers played. Trevor was into baseball, Jace soccer. My little sister is in gymnastics, but me and my little brother, Felix, could *not* care less."

He shifts uncomfortably in his seat, nibbling on a piece of funnel cake. "So you have four siblings?"

"Yep. Lucky me for being the middle child."

"Are you close to any of them?"

I guess we're just going in for the kill then. He asked, so I might as well be honest. "I used to be, yeah. Though the two

younger ones are too far apart from me to really have any kind
of relationship with them. Do you have any siblings?"

Easton smiles. It's a good smile. He has a little powder on his
nose and now I feel like I'm in a gay *Hallmark* rom-com. Do I tell
him? Do I lick it off? I have no idea what the edict is in these
situations and now all I can think about is licking his —

Easton pulls my mind out of the gutter. "I have an older
sister, Samantha. Sam. We're, like, four years apart, but we're
pretty close. Other than her it's just Dad. Our mom, she…she left
when I was fourteen."

Shit. "Oh. I'm sorry, Easton."

Silence follows, but now I'm curious. Since we're on the
topic, I might as well get it over now so I don't have to awkwardly
bring it up again. "Mind if I ask why?"

"She, um. She— Well, my dad gave her an ultimatum after
I came out."

And holy hell the look on his face makes me want to dig
myself a hole and bury myself alive. "Shit. Now I'm doubly
sorry. I shouldn't have pushed."

"It's okay." He waves it off and wipes the end of his nose.
The powder is gone now and thank fuck because now I don't
have to embarrass him. "It was a long time ago. It's funny that
you bring her up though. I was thinking about her earlier."

"Dude, seriously. I'm sorry. We don't have to talk about it."

"What about you?" He unknowingly goes for my jugular.
"Are you close with your parents?"

I really don't want to talk about this right now. I should never
have brought up my family. My heart starts beating quickly and
fuck this I'm not going to let my dickhead of a sperm donor ruin
this date for me. No, nope, nada. No panic attacks today!

"Unfortunately, no," I say quickly. "And if it's all the same
to you I'd rather not talk about it. It's cool, it's just not important.
Don't wanna ruin our date with my family drama."

"Yeah, okay. Sorry." Easton grins sheepishly.

"No need, it's cool. You done with this?"

He nods and I get up to throw the remains of the funnel cake away. Then without another thought, Easton heads off toward a booth full of paintings that I assume are by a local artist. They're pretty. They remind me of Jackson Pollack and Leonardo da Vinci, like, if they had a baby or something. I like it, but he doesn't seem interested since he's already on his way to the next booth.

I want to hold his hand and walk with him. I really want it, it's just so awkward for me. So I stay behind and follow him around. Easton looks back at me and smiles kindly. He slows down, and as if he knows the very thoughts in my head, he offers his hand. I meet his smile and step into him as our fingers interlock. I stiffen a little because PDA, but I'm out here trying to do better. I have to relax, so I kiss his temple. He leans into my shoulder and hums.

"So then...why did you move to NC?" he asks. "Huxley mentioned something about you not being from here."

"Of course she did." I chuckle. "Guess I just needed a change of scenery. Kansas City is alright, but I was over it a long time ago. UNCC seemed like a good school, so I transferred."

"One of the best in the state." Easton's cheesy grin switches to an amused smile. "Or at least one of the biggest. One of those."

"I made the right choice then." I unlock our hands and throw my arm around his neck.

"I think so." He grins, diverting his eyes and sucking his lips in nervously.

We keep walking, though neither of us are interested in the booths anymore.

"And you're from North Carolina, right?" I ask.

"Yeah. Ahoskie. It's a small town near the coast. Nothing special." He shrugs under my arm.

"You were born there?" I stop walking and turn into him.

"Yeah," he nearly whispers.

"Then it's special." I smile and wiggle my eyebrows at him.

His eyes narrow. "Is this you flirting with me?"

"So! What's on the agenda next?"

* * *

We're back in Easton's car and I gotta say that it's a piece of shit, but it's kinda charming in a way, too. He's embarrassed by it, I can tell, but I think it'd fit him more if it were to get fixed up a bit. I can sense money is an issue and I don't want to comment on anything that might be a trigger. So I keep my thoughts and opinions to myself.

I'm having a really good time, I actually am. As far as dates go, this is pretty mild. Nothing crazy has really happened, but he planned this and I'd follow him anywhere today. He seemed to really like the farmers market deal or whatever the hell it was. Can't say I've ever been to one myself, though it did remind me of First Fridays back in Kansas City, where all kinds of vendors and artists would set up booths in the Crossroads Arts District and sell their work. Maybe I'll go back next week and get him some of those soaps.

"What are you looking at?"

Shit. I guess I have been staring at him. But fuck me sideways, I can't stop looking. His profile might be cuter than his front and that's a tall order. His nose is small and peachy from the cold. I just want to bite it—

What the actual hell, Paul?! I sit back in my seat and stare straight ahead without answering Easton. Who even am I right now, this is not me. This is not who I am. I don't think gross cutesy things like that. He just, he just *does something* to me. First holding hands and *canoodling* in public, now this.

But also...I feel like my head hasn't been clearer. Like an intense shift happened after the panic attack and masturbating again and spending *good* time with Easton. I can feel it. I haven't felt so calm, so peaceful as I am when he's around. It's been less than twenty-four hours since we "made up" and now—fuck, now I'm thinking about kissing him again. It seems that's all I want to do now. To just be…close to him.

I look over at Easton again and he's gripping the steering wheel so tight his knuckles have gone white. I decide to lean over and peck him on the cheek. I don't pull away as he snaps his head in my direction and I kiss him full on the lips.

"What—" Easton starts.

"Eyes on the road Mr… Shit, I don't actually know your last name."

Wow. I'm on a date with the boy and I don't even know his last name.

"Belle. Easton Nicholas Belle. But—"

"Nice to meet you. Paul Donovan Acre here." I touch my chest.

"Paul—"

I place my finger on his jaw and move his attention back to driving. "Eyes on the road, Mr. Belle." Then I kiss him on the cheek once more before I sit back in my seat.

"Fine! But what was that for?" he asks with surprise drawn all over his face. But he's relaxed and smiling and I'm puffed up with pride because mission accomplished.

I shrug. "I wanted to kiss you. So I did. You got a problem with that, Belle?"

"Uh, no. No problem." He smiles big, like really big. "Not at all."

"Good."

He's silent for a second before we come to a stop at a traffic light. "Do it again."

The biggest smile stretches across my face to match his and I waste no time doing as he requested. It's a little more teeth than lips because neither of us can seem to stop smiling, but I don't mind. I like his teeth too.

"Another one," he says, mirth eclipsing his entire demeanor. So I do.

I've become a different person. Stay tuned on whether it's a good thing or a bad thing. The jury's still out.

Mr. Belle pulls into the only empty parking spot on the side of this building, but I'm so confused. Where are we and what are we doing?

"Uh, when are you going to grace me with the oh so very coveted explanation as to what the fuck is going on?" I place my elbow on the center console and lean into him. I truly, honestly have never been the touchy-feely one, but I can't help it.

He leans closer to me. "Trivia Night."

"Gesundheit," I say and laugh because him saying "Trivia Night" is about as foreign to me as if I'm supposed to decode a sneeze.

"It's Trivia Night." The confused look in his eyes says it all. "And was that German?"

"Hmmm, yes, yes it was. And you said Trivia Night, but I still have no idea what the hell that means."

"Uh... Trivia. Like questions about stuff. They do it once or twice a month with different themes. Tonight is Modern Comedy," he says matter-of-factly, like I'm supposed to know what any of that means too. I mean, I don't live under a damn rock, I know what trivia is, but I've never heard of anyone *actually* doing a Trivia Night.

Easton shrugs then chuckles. "I thought it'd be a good laugh to watch you lose."

Oh wow. He's joking, obviously. He has to be. So I jab back and feign being offended. "Oh, *I'm* gonna lose?"

"I mean, you're not going to win."

This little shit is looking at me with so much pleasure set into his features. He legit thinks I'm not going to be good at this and he finds it so damn funny. I still don't know what it'll entail exactly, but I might have to *actually* be bad just to hear him laugh. Wait, I've never for real heard him laugh before. Little chuckles and near silent giggles, but nothing substantial, and now I will stop at *nothing* to hear a full belly laugh from him.

Oh, it's on!

"Them are fighting words, Belle, and I will wipe your *ass* with this so-called trivia. Prepare to get fucked."

"Prepare to get— What?!" He leans away from me with wide eyes again.

"Come on, dude." I shake my head, then chase him down for a kiss and win. "Do they have iced coffee?" I ask, then hop out of the car.

Easton

WHY DO MOMENTS LIKE THIS HAVE TO END?

I've only been here a handful of times since my freshman year, but it's one of those little places where you automatically feel cozy and welcome. I don't know if it's the smell of coffee and books swirling together or the mix of art and crafts scattered about the store. Either way, it's pretty great.

We're on the ninth round of trivia. Each one has been around a single TV show, and so far, it isn't looking good for us. Oh, and we're on the same team. I misunderstood that part when I read about it online, and now I'm wishing I wasn't right about Paul losing. I know I got them all right for the *It's Always Sunny in Philadelphia* round, but that doesn't make up for the other seven rounds. I've only watched a handful of the others so far, *Seinfield* and *Shameless*, and today was the first I've ever heard of *The IT Crowd*. But hey, I'm doing better than Paul. I think he's gotten maybe one question right so far.

He's sitting across from me smiling, holding his second vanilla iced coffee with a splash of cinnamon, in the middle of winter no less. I can't say anything. I'm drinking an iced chai latte, but I still gave him hell when I made him order first. The look on his face when I ordered next was priceless.

"Alright, quiet down. Time for the last round." Scott, a heavyset man with a keen wit and the greatest side commentary, and also the gamemaster, settles us. I smile at Paul, ready to continue dominating, even if I sort of feel bad he's not doing so amazing. In my defense, we're a team. So if I win, so does he. Plus, I didn't know what shows the trivia was on tonight and I didn't think I'd do this well. "This round is on the award-winning hit Canadian show —"

He hasn't even said the name of the show yet and I see Paul's eyes light up. Huh?

" — *Schitt's Creek*."

"Yes!" Paul jumps in his seat and almost spills his drink.

"Uh… You like *Schitt's Creek*?"

"Do I like… I fu…" He lowers his voice to a whisper and tries again when he remembers where we're at. "I fucking love *Schitt's Creek*!"

"Guess we'll do pretty good this round then." Maybe this is our shot at third place out of four.

"Hell yeah!"

I laugh. His sudden enthusiasm is intoxicating. I want to lean across the table and kiss him, but that just seems a bit much in the middle of a little coffee shop. Is it weird that I actually miss his lips already?

"Okay. Cell phones away, remember to keep it quiet so other teams don't hear your answers, *Laura*." Scott eyes a pretty brunette a few tables down. She's been so enthusiastic the entire night, and she might have yelled a few answers by accident. I'm assuming she's a regular based on their banter. "First question."

Paul leans over the table and swipes up one of the pencils. Our faces are close, hovering over the answer sheet. I wonder if he's thinking the same thing I am, if he wants to kiss me again too.

Focus. Trivia. Not his lips. Trivia.

"What was the date of David and Patrick's wedding? Don't need a year, but a month *and* a day at least."

Before I have time to think about it, Paul's writing. I spy *September 3* in his sort of messy but somehow elegant handwriting. How'd he know that? Like, I've watched the show. Love it actually, but the date of their wedding? All I know is that they got married and Moira officiated.

"Are you sure?" I crinkle my brow.

"One hundred percent!" He wiggles in his chair. This boy's excited.

"You *do* like *Schitt's Creek*," I say as Scott repeats the question.

"That's the understatement of the century." Paul giggles. "I might be obsessed. I've watched all the seasons at least ten times. Maybe more. September third is also my birthday, so that'd be sad if I couldn't remember that."

My eyes pop open. "Damn. I mean I like it, but I think I might have seen them all twice, maybe?" I don't comment on his birthday, but I do make a mental note to remember it.

"So sad."

"Question number two," Scott starts and I shut up.

There is no way I'm messing up the excitement in this boy's eyes. I love it. Something about it is infectious. The way he sits up and his head tilts toward the sound of Scott's voice, and he keeps wiggling in his chair. It's making my heart happy, but, like, how? And he keeps glancing at me, and it's not just a regular glance. There's something cutesy, something wanting in his eyes, and I can't get over it. Today's been amazing, and I kind of want to tell Aidan I told him so.

"Oooh, radish," Paul whispers and starts writing down the word.

"Huh? Oh! The answer." I nod like I have a clue. I didn't even hear the question.

"It's the flavor of wine David says they should make for Moira Rosé when he's drunk," Paul fills me in. Despite his obvious love of the show he doesn't seem to mind that I zoned out looking at him.

"Ah, yeah. I think I remember that." Maybe.

Eight questions later, our answer sheet is filled out with not a single blank and the confidence in Paul's face tells me we — well, *he* — dominated that round. I did know the name of David and Patrick's shop though. *Rose Apothecary*. We blurted that one a little loud at the same time.

I lean back in my chair and hand our answer sheet off to the gamemaster to be scored. I'm feeling a little more confident about our chances now. Maybe third. But I never expected to win, that's not why I brought him here. I wanted to show him a cute little place that I like, even if I don't come often enough. I don't know, it's like opening up some I guess, and welcoming him in, just a little.

"I was no help until the very end," Paul laughs and wraps his hands around his cup.

"Not like I did that great, but you damn well ruled the last round," I tell him.

"Not like we won."

"I mean don't be stupid." I giggle and stretch my arm across the table, putting my hand over his as if it's something I do all the time. Is it bad I want to touch him?

Part of me recoils inside myself and wants to pull back. Surely he can't want this, but I push that side of me down and focus on the smile on his face and the softness of his hand.

Just enjoy the moment, Easton.

A few minutes later, after finding out we did manage to pull off third place, and a little mock victory cheer, we're browsing the books together. I drag him to the horror section first, where all my favorites are, and watch him silently judge my book selection. Guess he's not a horror gay.

"I'm beginning to think you don't like horror." I let the back of my hand graze his.

"More into the classics," he answers. "But there is a book Huxley told me I had to read. Wonder if they have it here?"

The interest in his eyes returns, and inside I fight back the feeling that I was boring him. "What book?"

"She mentioned it was new adult. I think? It's queer, too," he tells me, and I immediately start off toward the general fiction section. "I'll text her real quick."

"This way."

"Called Wolf-something — oh, it's *Wolfsong*. By T.J. Klune," Paul reads the text he just got from Hux.

Oh, fantasy. I redirect us down the neighboring aisle. I've heard of the author but never read them. We stop in the fantasy section and start browsing.

"Ks…" Paul squints, index finger wagging along the shelf under the spines.

"Uh…" I'm in the Ks now, and —

"Found it!" Paul grabs a thick black book off the shelf. "*Wolfsong*. Yes!"

He looks so excited. It's adorable, and in that moment I do a quick glance behind me. The room seems clear. I jump forward and kiss his cheek like he had mine in the car.

"Ooh." Paul coos, but his eyes drift around the shop.

Maybe I shouldn't have, but I couldn't wait any longer.

"How about we get out of here," he suggests.

"Sure." I nod when his smile rises higher than usual. "You getting that?"

"Oh yeah. Huxley would fuck me up if she knew I went to a bookstore and left without it."

"True." I nod as if I'm sorry for him.

We check out and start outside and down the ramp to my car. God my piece of shit car is so embarrassing, but I try to focus on him instead. I don't have to try hard because he grabs my hand in his and squeezes before we get a few steps outside. I glance in his direction and smile. He's already looking at me, but neither of us say a thing. I don't think we could say anything that would make this any better to be honest.

At the car I get in and lean across to unlock his door. My electronic locks are totally broken and manual now. He gets in and stows his bag on the floor.

The urge to kiss him again has me all out of sorts, but I don't do it. I don't need to be that guy who only thinks about that. I don't want Paul thinking it's just about that.

I start the ignition and my car burps to life in the most inharmonious way. I tighten my hands around the steering wheel. *Just let me get him home safely.* My hand goes to the gearshift, but before I can pull it into reverse, Paul's hand lands on top of mine.

"Hey." Paul's voice comes soft, deep and smooth.

I turn to face him and he's already leaning toward me. Our faces are so close I can smell the leather and sage of his cologne radiating from his body.

How are you here and so beautiful at the same time? I think.

Paul leans in. Our closed lips connect, and my eyes close. I can't place the taste of his lips, but the feeling is wonderful. He pulls away, and my eyes slowly open, my lips already missing his touch. Neither of us speak, but our eyes lock together and I can see the longing in them, the same longing I feel down deep in my chest.

I swallow the lump building in my throat and practically leap forward, lips parting, and kiss him. He kisses back, lips matching mine, his tongue invading my mouth. My entire body quakes in ecstasy at just his kiss, and I push closer. His hand brushes my cheek and then cups my chin, pulling me in.

The heat of his mouth seeps into mine and radiates through my entire body. I want this to last forever. I want this.

Why do moments like this have to end?

Paul

HE'S A CAT

I was anxious about my first day at work all day until I actually got here. My anxiety has been so much more manageable lately and it's been the reprieve I needed. Panic attacks are the worst, but it's like the last one I had was an awakening and now I feel so fresh and new and ready and in control. Huxley is amazing, Easton is the greatest, I'm doing well in all of my classes. I really think this job will be a nice little cherry on top.

Jeremy is a no-nonsense, no-bullshit kinda guy, but also he's not. He's a lot of fun and probably swears more than I do, kinda makes me think I might swear too much. It's a weird dynamic he has, but I think he's going to make for a great boss. He's not that much older than me — twenty-nine I think Huxley mentioned. So he gets it.

Easton and I have spent nearly every day together outside of classes and I honestly can't get enough. I never could have anticipated this, this intense building affection I have for another human.

"What the flying fuck type of lovebug bullshit crawled up your ass?" Jeremy *rudely* interrupts my thoughts.

"Excuse me?" I clap back.

"You look like you're best buds with cupid, fuckshit. Got it bad, huh? Who's the lucky lady, person, or dude? Yeah, I think you're more into dudes, aren't you? I can tell." He nods to me like the dude bro that he is. At least he's not an ass.

"Bingo." I raise my hands in surrender. "Flaming homo here."

"Figured. Hux keeps good company." He's putting the chairs up on the tables so he can sweep and mop. I'm organizing bottles and dusting. "I'm pan and poly. Been married to my wife for six years, but each of us also has someone else. I have a boyfriend and she has a non-binary partner. It works for us. You poly or mono?"

"Oh, cool." Damn, I wasn't expecting that from him. He seems so…straight? But then again, people think I am too. Guess we all need to learn not to judge people at face value. "I'm mono. Guess I'm too selfish of a person not to be monogamous."

"That's wassup. Jealousy is dope shit. It's a natural human emotion, you know? I've never been the jealous type, so jealous bitches make me curious. I'd love to dissect that more." He grabs the broom from the back closet. "Plus, it's kinda hot."

Now I'm curious. "How do you get around being polyamorous in North Carolina? Isn't this place, like, *extremely* conservative?"

"That's the entire fucking south for you, sweet cheeks. You just have to find your tribe, your people. And it just depends on what part of North Carolina. It's more progressive than you think. But the queer community can be just as fucking toxic as anyone else, especially out here, but there's still good out there. Huxley is a good start, my dude. Keep that chick around." He's sweeping and talking while not looking at me. My back is toward him and I smile.

I'm so glad I found Huxley. Or she found me, really. "Yeah, she's pretty great."

"Good." He sets his broom against the bar and goes into the back. He comes back out with a huge crate of clean glassware.

"Now, while you're daydreaming about getting your dick wet, polish these glasses."

"Uh, sure. Yeah."

Damn. I mean it's not like I *haven't* thought about "getting my dick wet" as Jeremy so eloquently put it, because, like, I have. Though in my mind it's much more romantic. I just...sex usually is the farthest thing from my mind. I've trained it out of my head and so it's not what I think about...mostly. I just like being around Easton. And with Easton, sex seems much more...tangible? Like I'll actually be able to enjoy it again and it'll finally *mean* something. And I want to, I really want to.

I feel something special for him. The more time we spend together the stronger it gets. Our date was kinda perfect. He's always watching me, but I don't think he knows that I see him. But I notice everything about him when he's around. My senses are hyperaware of his touch, his smell, the entire universe in his eyes. It's a craving I can never satisfy. Sometimes I get the urge to bite him randomly, to mark him as my own.

Not like that, more like...making it official? I don't really care about labels, I guess, but maybe he does and he's waiting for me to make a move.

He's not shy with me. On the contrary, I feel like he's his most authentic self when he's with me. I see him out in public and I see him when we're alone and it's not the same. With me his attitude is calmer and his demeanor is more relaxed; there's an edge to him that softens when he looks into my eyes, and when we're close he rubs on me like we're magnetic. I don't think he notices he does that either, but I do. When we kiss he melts and when I touch him he hums. Oh my holy hell. He's a cat. I'm dating a cat.

Are we dating though? Damn it all to hell, I don't know what I'm doing here. I should plan something. I'm going to plan something.

Easton

DON'T PANIC

I came out of Dr. Vale's Citizenship lecture this morning with a raging headache. It started slow, just a tiny tingle, and then it bloomed in the last ten minutes of class. Now I'm trying to blink away the pain behind my eyes in my Poli Sci Methods lecture, but it's not helping.

If this gets much worse I'm going home and making the rest of the day one big nap. A nice nap never hurt anyone, right?

"You good?" Oliver leans over, his bright red hair inflaming my vision.

"Just a headache," I whisper and nod. Dr. Adams is very particular about being interrupted during class.

Oliver doesn't question it. You'd think in a class full of political science majors it'd be a bunch of nerds, like some IT class, but nah. It's literally like someone took a random sampling of the entire United States and dropped them in the same classroom and said, *study yourselves.*

Not only do we have the usual cliques, the talkative popular ones, talkative annoying ones, quiet nerds that everyone knows would destroy them with information if they were willing to open their mouths, the ambiverts, the Guccis and Walmarts, we also have the leftists and liberals — I'm somewhere in there — the middle of the roaders, the "original intent" people who wouldn't know the Constitution if it bit them in their ass, the conservatives, and then the scary ones, the far-righters. The issue and philosophy classes can get really interesting, we've all got strong opinions.

I try to pay attention to the professor droning on about the reliability of poll data and causation versus correlation. Normally I'd be all into this. Digging into data to understand how people are thinking, how the public views an issue to understand how to phrase a message or policy, but not today. Right now, I just want this damn headache to bite the dust. I'd rather be thinking about Paul, how excited he was when we hit the *Schitt's Creek* round and the answers flowed like they were asking questions about him. Instead I'm focusing on the pressure in my head, and…

I blink. Wait. The edges of my vision begin to blur. I shake my head. Hold up. No. Not this. I take a deep breath and close my eyes.

It's just in your head. That's it. That's all it is. I loosen my eyelids and the world comes into view under a light haze. No. No. No. I blink furiously. Please no. I clench my fists and keep blinking, willing the blurriness to go away. But it doesn't. It stays, and it's getting worse.

What should I do? This is how it started. This is how I found out I had MS, and it scares the hell out of me every time it happens. My heart beats hard, and I grip my desk. I can't call Dad, he's four hours away. So is Sam. Paul? No! He's not going to find out like this. Uh… Aidan. I pick up my phone and squint at the screen, making out enough to find our text thread. Thank God for pinned messages.

EASTON: Don't panic, but can you take me to the doctor? Like now!

He's in class too, but I know he'll answer. Sure enough something moves at the bottom of the screen, I guess it's the little bubbles, and a message pops up.

 AIDAN: *Where U at?*
 EASTON: *Fretwell. Vision's blurring.*
 AIDAN: *Oh! OMW! Meet you on the first floor?*
 EASTON: *K.*

* * *

"You scared me, bitch!" Aidan nudges me on our way out of my doctor's office a few blocks off campus.

That was one of the first things I did when I got accepted at Charlotte. I found a local doctor to be my primary physician in the area for shit like this. I've only had to go a few times since freshman year, but it's helped. When I'm panicking the last thing I want is to have to explain everything, my entire medical history to a new doctor in the Emergency Department.

"Sorry." I drag my feet, feeling stupid. "It seemed like before."

My head is still killing me, but it wasn't a relapse. It was just a migraine. I've had them before, but never enough to blur my vision. But apparently that's why it didn't get that bad. Still sucks though.

"I bet that's scary." Aidan frowns, unlocking his car. We both get in and he starts it up.

"Uh, yeah. A little." It is. Like every time I have the slightest symptom my mind goes into hyperdrive. It's not like MS is fatal, not exactly at least. It's basically a guarantee I'll kick the bucket a few years before my alternate healthier self in another universe, but that's not what scares me. What really unnerves me is that I'll end up with chronic ongoing pain or need a cane or walker to stay mobile at some point. It's the lack of independence.

"Have you told, you know, him?" Aidan still refuses to say Paul's name.

It's a good question. One I've thought about a lot the last few days, and now I'm one hundred percent not bringing it up. Paul even texted while I was with the doctor, asking how class was, and I told him it was great. I lied.

"No." I wince. Mostly from the lie, but also the splitting headache.

"Why not?" A gives me the side-eye, pulling onto the main road and back to the dorm.

"Just too early," I lie again.

TONIGHT IS GOING TO BE PERFECT

Okay. I got everything for the picnic: bread, condiments, an assortment of meats, chips, some peanut butter and chocolate chip cookies for Easton, a couple protein bars for me, a coffee thermos, a small cooler full of ice, water, and this drink I've never heard about before called Cheerwine. He said he likes it and I don't think it's alcohol. We'll see. Then I got all the extra blankets and pillows from Huxley's closet to make lounging, and possible cuddling, comfortable in the back of the pick-up truck I rented. I'm taking him stargazing with a cute little picnic. Nothing crazy.

I rented the truck right before they closed and went back to the apartment to pack everything up before I drove up here to make sure it was all perfect. I even bought some fairy lights and an adapter thing for the cigarette lighter to be able to plug them in. Then I strung them around the edge of the truck bed and turned them on low.

I'm going to ask him if he wants to be my boyfriend. I like him, he likes me. Why wait? I think I'm ready. No, I know I'm ready.

You can do this. I breathe in and out slowly. *Deep breaths, Paul.*

Now I wait. I told Easton to meet me here after I shared my location with him. I realized that when he shared his location with me that night when he was completely shit-faced that he shared it indefinitely, so I went ahead and did the same thing. I also shared it with Huxley and told her the plan just in case we die up here in the mountains from some crazy ax murderer and she needs to know how to track us. She'll be at home finishing reading her faerie book, waiting for my arrival. It just makes sense.

I told Easton to meet me here at ten p.m. It's 9:53 and I think I see headlights.

Yep, it's him. Shit. I'm so nervous.

He pulls next to the truck with the *biggest* smile on his face and I think my heart just stopped beating. I really like him. Like, really, really like him.

And I— Ope, he's wearing skinny jeans and a flannel with the same denim jacket from our date. Oh wow, his ass looks amazing. I mean, I've noticed it before, but *hot damn*!

I'm sitting in the truck bed and he stops at the edge of the tailgate. "What's all this? And when did you get a truck?"

"It's for you. I wanted to do something cute for you. And I rented it—"

"You *rented a truck* for...*a date*?!" I think he's excited.

"Yes, Belle. I rented a truck. For you. Now will you shut up and come up here and kiss me."

"Shutting up." He climbs into the truck bed and nearly attacks me with kisses.

Fucking hell. I'm so happy right now.

After getting my fair share of his taste I lean against the back of the truck and fish through the picnic basket.

"Okay, I got a variety of things because I wasn't sure what you'd want and I didn't want to ask because I didn't want you to know what I was doing. I did get your fav drink and I also got water and coffee and some snacks for later. I know it's late, so you don't have to eat anything if you don't want to. Are you hungry?" I'm rambling but his hand is in mine and my entire body oozes tranquility.

"It's perfect, babe. I've never... I mean, no one's ever done something like this for me before. It's, uh..." He pauses.

"Babe's a new one. I like it," I say and lean over and kiss him. "I'm glad I'm the first because no one else deserves moments like this with you. In that, I will be 1,000 percent selfish."

"Be very selfish," he smiles at me. "Babe."

After we make our sandwiches, eat, drink, joke, and laugh with each other over the course of the next hour, I clean up and help us get in the perfect cuddling position with my back against the cabin of the pickup truck and him between my legs. Pillows prop us up and blankets wrap around us. I turned off the fairy lights so we can see the stars. It is perfectly clear out tonight, and a little nippy.

Now, right here in this moment, I feel an immense amount of peace.

"Belle?" I ask while I lace my fingers through his.

"Yeah, Acre?" he responds but starts acting like he ate a bug. "You know you have a weird last name, right? I'm never calling you that again."

"What? You think it's weird? I like it. It's fun and unique. Never met anyone outside of my own family who has it." I've always liked it, but it is kinda strange. "Um. So anyway. I have a question. And feel free to not respond immediately, like, take your time. I don't need an answer right away, okay?"

"Uh...okay." He pauses, but I can feel his body stiffen. "What is it?"

"Will you...um...shit, I'm so nervous. Um...will you do me the honor of...being my boyfriend?"

He sits up so quickly his head almost knocks into my chin, and he turns and faces me. "What?"

"Will you be my boyfriend?" I ask again, a little more tentatively. Shit. Maybe this is too fast. Maybe this is too soon.

Shit!

"Wait, you're serious?"

"Of course I am. Why wouldn't I be serious?" I'm not sure what else to say.

"You want *me* to be your boyfriend?"

"Yes, silly goose." And then I say, "Please?" like I'm a damn child. I mentally repeatedly facepalm.

"YES! Of course I will!" he yells, then falls forward and takes my face in his hands and kisses me with a ferocity I can't help but match.

I scoot down so we're lying flat with him on top of me. This is the first time we've truly been this alone and intimate with each other since my last panic attack. I've worked on myself mentally and physically to get ready for the moment this happened again, and I want it.

His hands rest on my chest tentatively, waiting. I feel them twitch, wanting to move, to explore, but he remains where he is until I give him permission. It's so touching that I deepen our kiss and move my hands down to grab his ass. I can feel his dick harden, so I grab his ass again and press him tighter into me. He moans in my mouth but doesn't break contact.

He breaks away and breathes heavy into my ear. "Paul, you sure this is okay?"

I turn my head into him and bite his neck lightly. I'm rewarded with another moan in my ear. "I'm sure."

"I want you," he says, and that's all I need.

I move my right arm across his back for support and flip him over so he's on his back. I brace my hands on either side of his head and look down at him.

"I...I brought condoms. And lube."

His jaw drops. "*You did*? You planned this?"

"I wasn't sure. But I wanted to be prepared just in case. I've been fussing over the details for days."

"Aw, Paul."

Suddenly I'm self-conscious. "I don't want to presume, but just so you know, I'm a top. Only."

"Good." He smiles, wrapping his hands around my back. "Because I'd be lying if I said I wasn't a bottom. Only."

I smile and kiss him lightly. "I'm nervous. I haven't slept with anyone in—"

"It's okay. I'm nervous, too," he says as he reaches up behind my neck and guides my mouth to his again.

I lay most of my weight on top of him and grind into him. He moans again, and holy shit it might be the best sound I've ever heard.

So I do it again.

And again.

And again.

"Fuck." He drags out the word in a whisper. I bite his neck, his collarbone. He grabs the hem of my shirt and helps it off of me. The cold stings my skin, but his palms bring the warmth back. He sits up and I do the same for him. His hands immediately go to my abs, but all I can do is look at him. He's not muscular, but he's lean, on the skinny side. No chest, but he has a tight stomach and the most *perfect* v-cut I've ever seen. I waste no time showing him just how I feel about his body with my tongue and teeth.

His torso is pink in splotches as I make my way back up to his mouth. His hands map out my shoulders and back with gentle fingers and rough fingernails. He moves his way down to grab my ass and push me into him.

"Don't! Please," I yelp, startling him.

"What? What is it? What did I do?"

"Just— Don't touch my ass." No. Fuck, fuck, fuck. We were doing so well. I should have said something. I should have *said something.*

"It's okay. I'm sorry. I won't." He's worried and nervous, but I don't want to keep talking about it, so I kiss him again and get to work on taking off his pants. Fuck it all, I'm getting him naked.

His skinny jeans might as well have been painted on, but I manage to peel them off and toss them aside. Holy shit, his dick looks amazing. I think it's…bigger than mine? That's interesting, but I have heard that the smaller, skinner guys can have the biggest dicks. Lucky me.

I bend down and take him into my mouth. My chest tightness internally and I'm starting to feel like this is too much. My thoughts are running rampant and I'm having a hard time calming myself down. Easton's enjoying what I'm doing, but he has no idea what's going on inside my head. Thank fuck for that. So I suck and suck until he grabs my jaw. "Wait, wait. You're going to make me come."

"Sorry. Grab the condoms and lube. They're behind that pillow."

He makes quick work of it, hands me a condom, and gets to work with the lube. And dammit, I don't think I want to do this anymore. But he's just lying there on his side, naked and swollen and pink in the moonlight while the fresh air causes goosebumps to eclipse his skin. He's sexy and this is exactly how I've pictured him during my jerk-off sessions, I just don't know if I can do this.

But I'm in *this* deep, so I might as well finish quickly before I have a completely heinous meltdown in front of him. I don't want him to think he's done anything wrong, I don't want him to think he doesn't turn me on and that I don't like him. I just asked him to be my boyfriend. I don't want to mess this up.

So I do the only thing I can at this moment. I pull my pants down to my thighs and put on the condom. He's done lubing up and grabs my dick with his lubed hand so that I match.

Oh fuck.

I take a thick throw pillow, lift his lower half up and place the pillow under him. He wipes off his hands and lies back down comfortably.

I move to finger him to get him ready for me. I learned this trick with my ex where while you're fingering someone, if you press your finger to the side of their opening and hold, they'll open up the quickest. Like you're tricking that muscle to ease up. So I do that and I can feel that he's ready.

I remove my finger with a pop and he moans. His head is back and it's a good thing his eyes are closed because I'm on the verge of freaking out. *I'm in control.* I think. I can do this, I just don't want him to see my face right now. I hope he keeps his eyes closed.

I place my tip at his edge and thrust forward slowly.

"Tell me if you need me to stop or slow."

"You're good. Keep goi— *Fuck, Paul,*" he drags out in a moan. I'm halfway in without any trouble. "Just go," he whispers. So I do.

This should feel good, right? I should be enjoying this, right? He is. I can tell he is, but I can't shake the feeling of what happened the last time I —

No! No, Paul. I just need to hurry up and finish. But I can already feel myself going soft and I'm thrusting into him and I can tell I'm doing too much, being too aggressive. I can't stop it. I can't. My mind is going back to *him* and what *he* did to me and my body is reacting. I'm on autopilot as my body moves the way *he* moved. Holy shit what am I doing? Am I hurting him? Is there blood? What am I doing to Easton?! No. No no no.

"STOP! Stop, stop, stop. I can't. Just stop." I pull out of him and move as far away as I can.

"What? Paul? What…happened?" He's disoriented as he quickly comes down from his euphoric high.

"Get dressed. Get fucking dressed." I pick up his pants and throw them at his chest. But he doesn't move, he's just staring at me like he... Is he about to cry?

Fury courses through my veins. At him, at myself, at the situation, I don't know. I just can't deal with him crying right now. "Don't cry. Just *get dressed*!" I button up my pants and hop out of the truck.

"Paul. What's going on? What the hell happened?" He's pleading, asking over and over again, but I can't answer him. I can't tell him. It's too humiliating, I can't say it aloud. He'll look at me differently. I just need him to go.

I'm frantic and I can't breathe. I'm taking everything out of the truck bed as quickly as I can and throwing it into the back seat. He's dressed and trying to get me to stop, to talk to him. He keeps grabbing my arm or standing in front of me, but I shove him off or move around him. My face is wet, but I can't understand why. And he's crying, I think? But I'm not sure because all I can picture is being trapped in the shower, wet and...bleeding.

"Fuck, stop! LEAVE ME THE FUCK ALONE!" I scream at him until my throat is sore. "Go home, Easton. Forget me, forget this ever happened. Just go home!"

"No! Fuck you! Talk to me, tell me what the fuck is going on."

"I WAS RAPED! I WAS RAPED AND I CAN'T FUCKING DO THIS SHIT!" I jump into the truck, start it, and race away from the scene as if I can race away from my horrifying past.

* * *

I pull into a guest spot since this isn't my fucking truck and run until I get into my apartment. I bang through the door and slam it shut and keep running into my room.

"Paul? Paul what the hell— OMG Paul, what's the matter? Where's your shirt?"

I'm pacing. I'm pacing and pacing and crying and screaming

and pacing and crying and *holy shit* I can't breathe. I can't breathe, I can't breathe, I can't breathe.

Huxley slowly moves toward me. "Paul. Take off your shoes. Do it now."

I don't have it in me to argue, so I do as she says.

"Now." She's standing right in front of me and takes my face in her hands. My eyes are closed because I just can't look at her right now. "Breathe with me." I do. "Now, tell me what's going on. What happened? Where's Easton?"

I try to breathe. I try to center myself, but everything is boiling to the surface and I'm about to spill over. I can't fucking do this shit.

"We fucked, Huxley!" I push myself out of her reach and start pacing again, wringing my hands. "We fucking fucked, and I can't fucking do this because it wasn't me fucking him, it was *him*! I wasn't fucking Easton, he was. It was him! And I let him. I let him into my head and I let *him* rape Easton the way —" My voice cracks and hitches from yelling.

"Um," Huxley starts. She moves a little closer again, only this time I cower. I still can't look at her. "I'm sorry, Paul. I'm so confused. Someone...raped...E?"

How does she not understand! "No, *he raped me*! He raped me, Huxley, and there was nothing I could do to stop him. I couldn't stop him. I wasn't like I am now. I was skinny and scrawny and *weak*! I was so weak and I couldn't fight back. I just...I just let him do that to me. And it *hurt*!"

I'm crying, my hands are as frantic as my heart as I talk, and she's just standing there. Her hands are in fists by her side and I can't look at her.

"It hurt so badly I couldn't move. I was bleeding and I could smell it and I couldn't move! He cornered me, and he hit me." I can't sit still. I try, but then I stand and start pacing again. My mind is on fire and my chest is as tight as a rag being wrung. I feel like I'm going to implode.

"He wanted more and I said no and he hit me. He raped me. I was *raped* after…my dad, he…" I drop on the ground hard against the wall by my closet and Huxley kneels in front of me. Her hands are on my shoulders, slow and soothing. I finally look into her eyes. "He called me," my voice hitches, "Paulie."

Understanding crosses her face. Tears fuck up her makeup and I feel so bad because she's so pretty and doesn't deserve to have her makeup fucked up. And it's my fault. It's all my fault.

So I cry. I can't finish my words or my thoughts because I cry and I cry and I cry while Huxley holds me and cries with me. Then I feel someone else on my other side holding me and crying too. And they rock me and let me cry until I can't breathe, until I'm struggling. Someone rubs my back. Someone else whispers in my ear.

They say, "*You're safe.*"

They say, "*You're loved.*"

They say, "*I promise that you're safe.*"

Once I get my breathing under control I look up into Easton's wet eyes and it finally registers in my brain that these are my people. These two gorgeous human beings sitting in front of me, taking care of me, crying with me are mine and I'm theirs and Easton is my *boyfriend* and I say, "I'm so sorry, Easton. Please forgive me. I'm so fucking sorry."

"There's nothing to forgive, babe," Easton says.

"When did you get here? How much did you hear?" I ask.

"All of it…I think." He nods past my bedroom door. "The door was open and I could hear you screaming, so I let myself in."

"My dad, he…when I was nine he…touched me. He—"

"Paul, you don't have to do this. It's okay," Huxley says.

"No, please. I need to say it. I need someone to know. We're already here, might as well." I shrug as another tear rolls down my cheek. It itches and tickles, but I don't move to wipe it away. I don't because Easton does.

"Okay," she says, "get it out. But please stop if it's too much."

I nod. "It happened when I was seven. But it didn't happen again until I was nine. I thought it was just a bad dream the first few times. I didn't know what was going on. I was *nine*. But the smell of the beer on his breath was too real. He touched me for years. He'd hit my chest hard with his fist and would tell me to shut up. He would tell me to be quiet and to stop crying so I didn't wake anyone up. I never said anything. He said he would hurt me if I did.

"It went on for years, until my brother Jace walked in on him. It never happened again, but no one ever talked about it. I thought I was fine. I thought I was *fine*. And then I was seventeen getting ready for school and my dad came into my bathroom, and he—"

"Shhhhh, you don't have to say it again," Easton whispers in my ear and kisses my temple.

Huxley is shaking her head. I can tell she has something to say but doesn't know how.

"Just say it, Huxley."

"Have you been to someone about this?" she asks, eyes glassy. "You were sexually abused by your *father* for *years*. Please tell me you've sought help."

There it is again, the shame. I know she's right. Coming forward just wasn't an option. I wanted to but…I couldn't. "I've wanted to. I really have. I'm just—I've been so scared. I thought I could deal with it myself. I tried. I really tried. I started going to the gym and threw myself into that. I never wanted to be so weak, so helpless again. I want to be able to fight back…in case…in case— Easton, *I'm so fucking sorry*. I should have never tried to have sex with you before I got my shit together, but I truly thought I was okay. I thought I was okay…I've had sex before.

With my ex. But not since…ya know."

"Don't apologize, Paul." Easton hugs me tighter. "It's okay."

"Paul?"

"Yeah, Huxley?"

She takes my face in her hands again and forces me to look her in the eye this time. "Can I call someone? For you, can I call someone? I've been in therapy my whole life. Can I please call someone for you?"

My throat closes and I can't speak. I've never been more grateful to have a best friend in my entire life. I swear she's a literal angel. I'll never be able to repay her. I'm scared shitless. I'm so scared and I can't speak, so I do all I can do: nod and cry.

Easton

NUMB

My phone says it's 2:06 a.m. when I sneak into the room, which is pointless because Aidan is still up.

"Easton!" He looks away from his phone briefly enough to smile at me. "Ty got that promotion I was telling you about a few weeks ago."

"It's nothing, really," Tyler's voice says from Aidan's phone.

"That's great." I try to sound happy for him, but it comes out dull and sad.

"Uh…" Aidan doesn't seem to know what to say to that.

Our eyes meet and I shrug.

"Ty, let me call you back, okay?" Aidan doesn't miss a beat.

"Yeah, sure. Bye, East," Tyler yells happily from Greenville into our room. "Te amo, A."

"Yo también te amo."

Aidan ends the call and throws his feet over the edge of his mattress. He aims his body square at me. His eyes narrow, but his face is concerned.

"What's wrong?"

Everything. Everything feels wrong, but at the same time it all feels so right. Like, how do those two things go together? They can't, right? But they are. Up until the moment Paul's past jumped into his head, everything was perfect. I felt wanted. I felt

THIS I PROMISE YOU   **167**

needed in a way that wasn't just for my body, not just for how someone could use me for their own pleasure, but for *me*, for me as a person. And it was wonderful. It was perfect and surreal and exciting. Those few moments meant more to me than all the guys I've ever known combined. It felt right.

But then it felt wrong.

I exhale deeply and drop my ass onto my bed, eyes flitting to the green cheaply carpeted floor. *We need to vacuum.* That's what comes to mind first, but it's quickly replaced by the words that keep running through my head in Paul's voice.

"He raped me. He raped me."

I clench my fist around a handful of bedsheets and let out a stuttered breath. I don't know what it's like living with that. It's bad no matter who it is that's dealing with that aftermath, but Paul. My Paul. My *boyfriend*. Why him?

For me, it feels like it just happened. It's this sudden blow. I wasn't around to stop it, but I wish I could have been. I should have been there to protect him, but I wasn't. I couldn't have been. I didn't even know him then. It's stupid to feel like this, but I still do.

It hit like a freight train when he said those words out by the truck. I couldn't move for a solid minute as he sped away while my mind processed what he'd said, and how what we did in the back of that truck must have been for him.

Once I broke my stupor, I got in my car and raced after him and got the whole story, and honestly I wasn't ready for it. I don't think you can be. But I like him and he doesn't need to carry that alone.

"Paul," I utter, and before I can get myself to keep going, Aidan is on his feet.

"That bastard! What the *hell* did he do to you?" He rushes over. "Are you—"

"Of course *I'm* okay!" I yell in his face, which I know in an instant is the wrong thing to do. I slump, tears starting to stain my cheeks. He doesn't know. "I'm sorry. I didn't mean to yell."

"Uh. It's okay." Aidan stands his ground, but his shoulders relax.

"Paul... He was, uh..." I try to find the words, but they're not coming, and I'm not sure if I should even say it. Is it alright for me to tell Aidan? I feel like it isn't. It's Paul's story to tell unless he says otherwise. So I think a moment on how to explain why I can't quite form a smile. "Paul went through a lot before he got here, and when he was younger. *A lot.*"

I bore my eyes into Aidan on those last two words to make certain they hit home. Aidan steps back and gently sits across from me.

"Oh," is all he says at first.

"We, uh... I mean he took me on a picnic." I decide to start there instead. I clasp my hands over my knees. "It was great, actually. Clear sky. The stars. All of it. You would have loved it. And uh... Then we started having sex, and he panicked. I thought I'd done something wrong. He just jumped up and left."

Aidan doesn't stop me. He doesn't interrupt to say, "Again?" or any of the smartassery he would have pulled before.

"I'm so sorry," is what comes out of his mouth instead. "I didn't realize."

"Neither did I."

For a long moment we just sit. Aidan on his bed. Me on mine, with my mind wandering in every direction. I don't want to lose Paul. And I'll be there for him, but how? How do I support him? How do I know what to do?

"What do I do, A?" I ask.

"What do you mean?" Aidan looks at me, confusion clouding his eyes.

"I don't want to lose him. I've never had anyone see *me* like *he* sees me," I admit.

Aidan's cheeks bunch up into this adorable little smile that's both kind and sad.

"You really do like him, don't you?"

I simply nod. I do.

He thinks about it a moment, skewing his lips from one side of his face to the other and scanning our ugly carpet.

"Take things a little slower," he suggests, and he giggles the tiniest little bit. "Make it simple. Why don't you take him on a date tomorrow after class? Show him that none of that is going to stop you, and that you can go as slow as he needs."

That's a great idea, actually. And I can. I have to. I'm not losing this.

"Okay." I give him a faint grin. "Thanks, A."

Paul

DR. ORLEEN

Four days later and I still feel hollowed out. Being vulnerable on such a monumental scale has...never happened to me before. Huxley has given me space, though she still makes sure she stays close by. Easton has spent as much of his free time with me as possible. We even went on a date.

He took me to one of his favorite parks where we just walked in silence, taking in the scenery, talking here and there. It was nice to be able to enjoy the peace of another being. After what happened on Friday I honestly thought I'd want nothing to do with him. But he chased me, he fought for me, he comforted me and never judged me. I feel connected to Easton now. I want him around and our bond just seems to keep growing.

Huxley held to her promise and called her therapist, Dr. Orleen, who was able to move her schedule around to meet with me on Tuesday, today.

After finishing my classes, I met Huxley back at the apartment and we drove over here together. They had me fill out some forms and Huxley dropped her credit card on the counter — which made a *ting*, by the way — and now we're sitting here waiting. She told me not to worry about the money. That she already spoke with her parents and it was their idea to cover the costs until I can figure out a way to pay for it myself. She called me family and I didn't want to argue. I'm grateful, but I also feel useless and not worthy of their kindness. I'm holding her hand because I'm scared shitless. I've never done anything like this before.

"Paul Acre," a woman calls out.

I look up to see a tall slender woman with long, graying blonde hair. She's dressed in a business casual suit, high heels, and a gorgeous bulky necklace.

"Yeah, uh, that's me." I halfway raise my hand and stand to shake hers.

"Mr. Acre. It's great to meet you."

"Oh, Paul. Please. Not Mr. Acre," I insist.

"My apologies, Paul. Huxley, good to see you again." She gives her a hug and gestures from me to the hallway. "Shall we?"

Huxley pulls me into a hug. "I'll be right here when you're done. If you need me for anything just text, okay?"

I nod, then follow Dr. Orleen back to her office.

It's a nice office. Not stuffy or pretentious like I imagined. There's a desk toward the back of the room by the large window. The far left wall is a large built-in bookshelf full of books and accessories. A green velvet sofa/chaise combo butts against the far right wall with an acrylic coffee table. Two chairs complete the living room-style staging.

"Have a seat." Dr. Orleen points to the sofa.

I sit down as she retrieves a notepad and pen from her desk and sits in the wingback chair across from me.

"Sooooo…" I drag out, rubbing my sweaty palms on my thighs. "How exactly does this thing work?"

"How would you like it to work, Paul?" she asks.

"Uh, well." My hands are in my lap and I'm nervously picking at my cuticles. I feel so stupid and awkward and just…empty. I guess I have nothing to lose here though, right? Might as well be as open and honest as I can. Feelings and emotions be damned. "I have some shit I need to work through. Not sure what Huxley told you, but it's...not good. I want to work through it, I do. I'm just...I don't know what I'm doing."

Dr. Orleen places her notepad and pen on the small table next to her chair, crosses her legs, and rests her hands in her lap. *She looks like a princess,* is my first thought. Second is, *I can now tell why Huxley likes her, trusts her.* She gives off a very demure but educated, motherly vibe. The type of mother I never had.

"First, I would have you know Huxley has not mentioned why you are here. She understands the importance of speaking for oneself. What is going on with you is strictly between us unless you say otherwise. I very much value my patients' confidentiality and will do nothing to break that trust with you. Secondly, I appreciate your transparency. For therapy to work, it is ultimately up to you. Having the mindset you have expresses your willingness to evolve and your innate self-awareness. These are all good things. Lastly, I'm here to help *you*, to guide you. Together we will get to the bottom of what burdens you, dissect it, and create a firm foundation to build upon. How does that sound?"

I nod vigorously. "I like that, yeah. I need that. I want that. I'm tired of...feeling like this. I'm exhausted."

"I understand." She picks up her pen and pad and scribbles something down. "Now, let's start from the beginning. I think that will be easiest for us both."

So we do.

Easton

STUDY DATE

Midterms are on Thursday and Friday and I'm 100 percent not ready for them. If I was lucky like Paul here, I'd only have two, but no. I have five!

"What were the significant contributing factors to the Nazi Party's success in the 1930 election?" Paul reads off the next question. "Motherfuck. I feel dirty even saying Nazi."

He reads off the choices and I narrow it down. Two deal with economics, and this type of thing is usually always economic in a way, but the right answer is clear.

"Economic insecurity after the Great Depression and the Party's massive voter campaign leading up to the election," I answer, and Paul nods. "They actually gained power democratically at first. Did you know that?"

"Uh... No."

It's one of those crazy things you never think about growing up hearing about the Nazis, that it wasn't just some government overthrow by a dictator and his goons. No. He used the electoral system, fear, and his oratory skills to persuade the masses, who suffered from woes he blamed on outsiders, and some within.

"Yeah." I nod. "Next question."

"This shit is depressing." Paul huffs but starts reading the next one anyway.

He ain't wrong, but it's important history. Sort of like the history we're making. Okay, maybe that's not the best comparison. We're not making *that* type of history, but we *are* making a history of our own. I think. I hope.

We went canoeing at the Whitewater Center over the weekend. I was really tired after, but the rush of the wind, the spray of the water gushing against us, the canoe tumbling about with just me and him. It was fun, even if Paul did keep threatening to tip us over. I threatened to smack him if he tried, and he joked back that he might like it. At first I wasn't sure what to say, but then he laughed and said no, he very much would not like that. And before I let my brain catch up I'd already said, "That's more a me thing I guess." I swear his cheeks turned pink and his eyes bloomed. I changed the subject so fast. That's how we started talking about books.

In the moment, which book I brought up didn't matter, anything to avoid that conversation, so I bored him for like twenty minutes about how most people don't understand what democracy really means, and how in its truest form a real, lasting democracy isn't direct democracy but a representative democracy, a republic, and how it bugs me when conservatives whine that we aren't a democracy and all that shit. In my defense, I'd been reading some excerpts the night before from Sartori's *Theory of Democracy Revisited* and it was on my mind. Sorry, Paul.

We did manage to get to normal books eventually, and I found out that despite him being an English major, his reading history is lacking. It's not that he doesn't read, he just has a narrow palette. Apparently it was *Frankenstein* and *The Canterbury Tales* that got him into literature, and then it was the classics like *Beowulf* and *Little Women* he read in his first British Lit class that got him into writing. I'm more of a modern horror guy myself, but he hadn't heard of any of my favorites.

We wrap up the Third Reich practice questions and decide

to take a break. Classes are done for the day, and I took most of this week off from the kennel to focus on studying…and Paul.

I'm lying on my bed, legs draped over Paul's lap as he sits with his back against the white-painted cinder block wall. I huff. Part of me wants a nap but the other part wants food.

"Fuck this shit, can we make out already? Isn't that what study dates are for?" Paul sets *our* studying aside and crawls on top of me.

"Why do you cuss so much?" I look him in the eyes. It doesn't bother me, it really doesn't. I've just wondered because he does it a lot, and yeah, I'd like to make out too, but I'm not sure he's really ready for that. But that's not my call.

Paul shrugs. "I don't know. I guess I was never allowed to. My dad…he was pretty strict. More on me than anything. I would get spanked if I did so much as say God's name in vain, which is pretty weird if you think about it 'cause my parents aren't religious. Like, at all. So I don't know. I don't say 'Oh my God' or 'goddamn' out of respect 'cause it's ingrained in me. But I guess I say fuck a lot 'cause I don't know what else to say, and then it just became habit." He pauses long enough to kiss my cheek and pecks a path up to my forehead. Apparently he likes my few freckles. It's become a thing. "Do you not like it? Want me to stop?"

"No, I'm fine with it! I promise. I was just wondering. That's all. You know what? I'm hung—" I say as the door creaks open and in comes Aidan. "—ry. Hey, A!"

"Hey…" Aidan pauses when he sees Paul, but he doesn't let it hang. He's doing better. "Guys."

"Hey." Paul waves carefully, sitting up.

The last time the two saw each other Paul was rushing out of our room with me on his heels. Aidan's still not terribly fond of him, but at least now he knows he didn't see the whole picture before, even if he still doesn't see it all, and he's being a good friend about it.

"How was class?" I sigh. I don't want to study anymore. I hate it. Or maybe I just hate school.

"Ugh. Chemistry sucks balls." Aidan drops onto his bed and falls flat in dramatic fashion.

"Just like all of us," Paul laughs.

I snicker. I think it catches Aidan off guard, or maybe he still can't get the image he has of Paul out of his head. Finally he grants us a little laugh and sits back up.

"What are y'all up to?"

"Study session," I tell him and pat Paul's sinewy arm.

"Uh-huh." Aidan grins.

I don't know whether to be proud that he'd smile at that or offended that he thinks sex is all I think about. It only occupies like 60 to 70 percent of my brain. That's all!

Instead of giving him the satisfaction of a response, I switch topics. "So A here writes fiction."

"Huh?" Aidan pops back up.

"No shit, really? You're an author?" Paul's attention piques. He sits forward, laying his hands over my legs.

I like it like this. It's not too close or suffocating for him, but it's still contact. He's had two therapy sessions, one this morning, since his last panic attack and he's doing better already, but I'm still trying to be careful while not making it obvious. I don't want him to feel like anything is rushed or expected. I do have a right hand after all.

"Yeah, I guess." Aidan shrugs as if it's not a big deal that he's written a *literal book* and has an agent and all that. "It's not published yet though, so…"

"You guess?" Paul almost seems offended. "You wrote a book, right?"

"Yeah."

"Then you're an author." Paul bounces his shoulder, like

with that simple motion he's made it so.

"That's what I keep trying to tell him, but he's always got something negative to say," I explain.

"I do not," Aidan comes back quickly.

"Yeah you do," I laugh.

"Maybe."

"Sounds like you do." Paul smirks, and I think that might be pushing it. Aidan's not quite ready to adore him like I am.

I shake my head and huff. "He's a great writer. I've read his book. One of only two people in the world to get to."

"Well, technically that's not true." Aidan puts up a finger.

"Huh?" I gasp. "Other than Ty, I thought it was just me." I pooch my lips like it hurts.

"My agent's read it, you know that's sort of how I got her," he says, and now I feel stupid. "Plus all the publishers that rejected me."

"Ah, yeah. And there's the negativity again."

Aidan rolls his eyes.

"Not so special after all?" Paul smiles at me and puts his hand in my thick hair and tousles it.

"I'm not special?" I pout.

He told me I was on the way to our canoeing trip, that there was something special about me. So of course I'm going to eat that up.

"Uh…of course you are," Paul rebounds. "Just not to him."

"Excuse me!" Aidan's head jolts back. "He's—"

Oh my. This is devolving.

"He's just joking." I put my hands up and slide off the bed. "How about we get dinner?"

That was already the plan. Study session then dinner, but originally we—meaning me—were going to study for at least one more class before leaving. Not now though. I think they'd be alright in the same room for a little longer, but I'm not chancing it this early.

"Sure." Paul shrugs and comes off the bed after me. "But no carbs."

I laugh and roll my eyes. "See ya later, A."

In the hallway once we're out of earshot Paul pops his lips and asks me a question. "So, what's his name? I can't for the life of me remember and you pretty much only call him A."

IT IS TIME

I am mentally exhausted. Between work and therapy and school and Huxley and Easton always asking how I'm doing, I'm spent. Though therapy is going great! I'm loving it. It's hard, but it's good. It's really good. And I like Dr. Orleen. She's been extremely helpful with everything and I'm so blessed to have Hux—

"Hiya, bestie! How was therapy?"

See, always asking questions. But I adore that about her even if it can be annoying AF at times.

"Wait, no rehearsal today?" I counter.

"Nah, since spring break is coming up and with midterms this week, the theater professors decided to give us today and tomorrow off to focus on school."

"Damn! That's nice as shit! How's that going anyway, rehearsal?"

"Rehearsal is good! I've always been obsessed with *RENT*, as you know, and portraying Maureen is *such* a dream come true." She's in the kitchen cooking, packing ingredients in a pan and adding seasonings. And cheese. So much damn cheese. None of us are going to be able to shit for a week. "Once we get back from spring break we'll have like a month-ish of rehearsals left until we open."

"Well, I'm excited to see it! I'm sure you'll be amazing." I drop my school stuff off in my room and go back to sit on a bar stool at the kitchen island.

"Thanks, boo! *Anyway*, stop deflecting—therapy, how was it?"

"It was really good actually." I nod. Huxley's putting the finishing touches on her infamous homemade four-cheese twice-baked mac and cheese I've heard so much about. After weeks of me begging, she's finally making it and it looks like Huxley has completely torn the kitchen apart in the process. My diet is fucked.

"Dr. Orleen is brilliant," I continue. "She's really helped me see things from new perspectives. We've talked through every bit of my life and have been combing through...situations to work through the trauma. She's great."

"That's great! Toldja she's amazing. Truly the best therapist I've ever had." She takes some store-bought bread crumbs and sprinkles them over the entire dish.

"Yeah, well, there's still a lot to work through, but I feel like these past two weeks with her have been sort of monumental. Never in my life have I felt like this. She even gave me some homework outside of the self-reflective journaling she has me doing."

"Oh yeah? What kinda homework?" she says, distracted.

"Uh—"

Her head snaps to look up at me. "Obvi you do *not* have to tell me if you don't want to. Whatever you're comfortable with."

I shrug. "Well, it's...like, sexual homework. Like, *with* Easton. Nothing too heavy, just what I'm up for is all. I know she and I haven't met much, but I sort of brought it up and she gave me some ideas to think about."

"That's fair. You think you're up for it?"

"I honestly don't know." I shrug again and look down at my hands, forever fucking with my cuticles. "Maybe? I think so. Like

I said, I feel like I've grown a lot these past two weeks. I've been really trying to get my shit together. For me, for Easton, for you. I don't know. But she gave me things to do in case it doesn't work out. Best case, it works. Middle ground, it's a little awkward and we stop and move on. Worst case, I call her."

Huxley puts the dish of mac and cheese in the oven, takes off her oven mitts, and turns to me. "Paul, first, time isn't real. Ever since you told me about your biggest fear being 'time' I've done some research and I honestly believe that time is just a human thing we've created to understand things better. So it doesn't matter if it's been two weeks or two years, go at whatever pace works for you. You're smart. You are very self-aware and I think that you should give it a try. Never know if it'll work if you don't try it. Secondly, Easton and I are here for you. We get it. I'm not sure if he's ever been in therapy before, but I know I have and no matter what happens, you'll be okay. Though, please be careful. I don't want you to do more than you're ready for, ya know? But, if you need anything, I gotchu, boo." She leans over the island and grabs my hands. "No matter what, I gotchu."

"Thank you, Huxley. I know. It means a lot." I chuckle. "It's actually funny you brought up the 'time' thing. The piece I'm performing tonight is about time. Also, Dr. Orleen said I was self-aware as well. So that's comforting even if I feel like my brain's broken. It's nothing but unorganized chaos with absolutely no chill."

"OMG! You're performing tonight?" She starts cleaning her mess and I hop up to help her. "You haven't done that since the first week of school."

"I'm going to try, yeah. I wrote this piece for my realism poetry class—well, it's my midterm actually—and I feel like it'll do well in front of a crowd. I even have it memorized. I think. I hope."

"OMG, look at you!" I knew she'd be excited about that.

"I fucking knowwwww. I'm trying. Thought you'd be proud of that, Little Miss Theater Geek."

"I most certainly am." She starts shooing me out of the kitchen. "Now hit the gym like I know you want to—but no longer than half an hour to do, like, cardio or something, young man—and then wash up. By the time you're done, dinner will be ready. Easton and Devina will be here at six to eat before we head to Uptown Slam. Oh shit, and before I forget, I'm having a dinner party tomorrow. I have a proposition for everyone." She claps like London Tipton, then adds, "It's going to be so exciting! I can't wait! Keep your spring break opeeeeen."

Oh hell.

* * *

I've only worked a handful of times at Uptown Slam since I started. They're training me to be a bartender, but Jeremy doesn't think I'm ready yet. Once he gives me the green light I'll be able to work Thursday nights, and fuck yeah do I want to. It's packed in here tonight for their monthly poetry slam. Can you imagine the tips?

Their monthly slams are pretty well known. Not like the open mic we went to before. It's so much more intense than that. I had to sign up a week ahead of time even though I work here. It's intense and I'm so fucking nervous I might piss myself stupid.

Now might be a great time to start drinking.

Easton finds a table toward the far right of the stage—stage left is what Huxley calls it—at the back of the building. I take the seat against the wall so I can ground myself. Grounding is something Dr. Orleen taught me to do when I'm feeling anxious, overwhelmed, or nervous. Easton's at my side holding my hand. He squeezes it and kisses me on the cheek and I just want to burst into tears from cuteness. He's distracting me and it's working.

"Your kisses are the perfect distraction, Belle." I breathe out.

He gives me one of those cute skewed grins. "You okay? Your hands are clammy."

"I thought I smelled something fishy," Huxley chimes in, and Devina bursts out laughing. Devina has been a nice addition to our little group. She and Huxley are officially together as of last week. She's like this dope as shit '90s grunge K-pop/e-girl. She has *long* dark hair and only wears black and it suits her. She and Huxley together look like the ultimate bisexual power couple and I fucking stan. She's about as tall as Easton. Huxley's five foot flat without the heels, but even their height difference gives power couple vibes. She's even been teaching Huxley some Korean. It's cute.

"Okay, screw you," I say and I flip her off. "Both of you."

"'Alright, alright, alright,' in the great words of Matthew McConaughey. Everyone sit your asses down, the show is about to begin, like, *now*." Jeremy's voice blares through the mic. He pauses a brief moment to let everyone settle. "Dope. Okay. So! Welcome, everyone, to our monthly poetry slam at the most *iconic* bar in *all* of North Carolina — actually, fuck it, in all of North *and* South Carolina!" He finishes and everyone screams and claps and snaps and hollers at him. He lives for this shit.

"In case you live under a fucking rock and don't know shit, everyone who entered will be drawn at random. You have ten seconds to get your ass to the stage or we move on. Y'all better not bitch out either. Paul, I'm looking at you." Jeremy points to me and I want to duck and roll out of here because fuck you very much, Jeremy, and please shut the hell up. I flip him off. He gives me a cheeky grin and continues, "Votes will be determined by how loud the audience gets and the top three will go head-to-head. Get it? Got it? Good. Ret, set, go!"

Why did I do this to myself?

"Up first…" He leans over and takes his beanie off his head, then digs around inside. Jeremy pulls out a piece of paper and unfolds it. "Alejandro Chaplin. Let's get it."

One by one each of the contestants are called. Easton, Huxley, and Devina all huddle together so they can talk about each act, but every time Jeremy takes off his hat I want to explode into fairy dust. This was a bad idea. What if I forget everything? I mean, I can have my phone, but what if I go blind? What if I throw up all over everyone in the front row?

And then, "Paul Acre. You're up!"

"Shit," I say.

"You'll do great, babe," my boyfriend says.

"Just breathe through it." Huxley slaps my back.

"You got this," Devina says.

I make my way up to the stage and take out my phone just in case. I look directly at the light of my life and say, "This one is for my gorgeous boyfriend, who inspires me every day to do better, to be better."

"What about your best friend, asshole?" Huxley yells and everyone erupts in laughter.

"Fine. You too. I guess." I roll my eyes and smile. "Anyway, this is called, *It Is Time*." I close my eyes, take a deep breath for stability, and begin.

"Time.

Once upon a time

I was asked,

'What's your greatest fear?'

To which I replied,

'It's time.'

Time

is an elevator

with a mirror.

I am a human

with a phone.

Obvi."

I pause. I'm so nervous I feel like I'm going to vomit. My hands are shaking and so far, I haven't needed to look at my phone, so I put it in my pocket and look over at Easton. He's sitting there all astute and expecting. He's really into this. Maybe it's because it's me or maybe it's because he likes what I'm saying, I don't know. But he gives me a small smile and that's just enough motivation for me to continue.

"Hashtag tbt
to a different time
and place,
through time and space
it went.
I went.
I *am*.
It seems strange
to me that
once was then
and then was
once upon a time.
Ages ago it seems,
and yet
it seems...
it *seemed* like only
yesterday
was here.
Today is now.
Today was yesterday.
Tomorrow is today.
But it's gone.
I'm standing in an elevator now
and then,
holding my phone,

taking a picture of myself from yesterday.
Who was —
I was —
then.
I am *now*.
I am
still relevant tomorrow
and ages to come.
Time flies
and yet I feel like nothing has changed.
Except everything has changed
and I'm not the same person
I was back then
today.
Yet
I still am me, going backwards in time as it flies by me and I
see nothing but memories from tomorrow that turn into
yesterday.
Was it a lifetime ago?
Like these memories don't belong to my mind
but only to the memories of the mind of *time itself*.
It seemed like ages ago
and yet
it is now.
Now is the time to begin.
To begin
is the end of what once was
and the end of what is
is to begin what is to come.
To come together as one
separate and alone,
but together alone with myself
standing in front of a mirror

in an elevator
taking a picture
of myself yesterday
to archive myself tomorrow.
For tomorrow
is not guaranteed.
A *guarantee* is a promise left to time.
They say only time will tell.
They say time heals all wounds,
but *I* can tell time,
not what to do or how to be
but *where* to be.
I put my clock on the wall.
I put a watch on my wrist.
That is where I put time
and time is now where I say it is.
And yet
I am a human chained by time
on my wrist,
on my wall.
Time.
It's a losing battle, but I'm always trying to win anyway.
Getting ahead of it is impossible.
Falling behind is easy.
Too easy.
I'm easy,
uneasy with this
time
testing my patience to the umpteenth degree.
It takes me over.
Overtakes me
like the waves in the sea.
Like the waves of

my thoughts,
and I'm running out of air.
They're drowning me.
No matter what I do I can never speed it up in
time
or slow it down.
Time,
it haunts me.
The scent of you
wrapped around me
time
and time again,
like the sheets we lost ourselves in the night before...
or was it tomorrow?
Tomorrow,
whispering in my ear
like your 'I love yous' I want to hear,
my 'I love yous' I want to tell.
The 'I love yous' I want to believe are real.
This is unreal.
Time.
Oh, how I want to control it in those moments
but never can,
even in my mind.
We are always
trying to get more of time,
trying to turn yesterday into tomorrow.
Can we,
can I
rewind
back to those moments
because my time is running out.
My time is in a drought,

and I'm afraid that if I stay here,
in this elevator
holding my phone
taking a picture of myself
here and
now
for too long
I'll never get out.
It
is
time."

Oh my holy *shit* that was amazing. I'm a little out of breath, but I was able to get through the whole thing without needing my phone. It just came out. But…no one is saying anything. Uhhhhh? Should I just return to my seat? Everyone else at least got some claps and screams of approval from their friends. Everyone is just…staring at me. Shit. What the hell do I do? Was it bad? Where's Jeremy?

"Uh, that's it," I say into the mic. And then it happens: the claps and cheers, the screaming and whistling. It's so loud that I feel like I'm at a concert standing right next to the speakers at the front of the stage. I look over to find Huxley and Devina and — where's Easton?

I take an awkward bow and make my way back to my seat. Halfway there I spot Easton standing in the hall by the bathrooms. Somehow I missed him getting up.

Next thing I know he flings himself into my arms and starts kissing me on the mouth. My mind is all over the place as I'm trying to process what the hell is going on.

"That was *amazing*, Paul. Holy shit."

I'm beaming. "You liked it?"

He bites his lip and nods, then kisses me again. I pull back and see Easton's honey-brown eyes looking back at me with so much sparkle. He smiles and I can't help but match it. He kisses me again. I kiss him back.

The cheering gets louder. How is it still going?

"Well, fuck me!" I hear Jeremy say into the mic. He's on stage waving his arms in front of him to get everyone to settle down, but I only have eyes for Easton. Eventually, the cheering dies out like blowing out a candle. "I'm utterly shooketh, my dude. Paul! Get your sexy ass back up here." I look back to the stage and see he's waiting for me. So I grab Easton's hand and bring him with me. He tries to get away, but I think he forgets I'm stronger than him.

We hit the stage and Jeremy claps his hand on my shoulder as I snake my arm around Easton's waist. "This is my fucking bar and I'll do whatever the fuck I want, ya hear? And I think we have a *clear* winner." Jeremy takes my hand and hoists it into the air like I'm a damn MMA fighter who just won a match. It's awkward, but also…feels pretty damn good, too. "Paul Acre!"

The cheering commences again and I'm smiling harder than I ever have in my entire life. With Easton by my side and Huxley in my corner, I feel like I'm on top of the world.

HOMEWORK

"Strawberries & Cigarettes" by Troye Sivan is blaring through my shower Bluetooth as I step out into my room and —

"Holy shit!" I scream. Easton's sitting on my bed. Huxley must have let him in.

He scared the ever-loving *hell* outta me! I double over, hands on my knees, breathing hard. I'm completely naked except for the towel wrapped around my waist. I feel a bit out of sorts at first, but oddly, I'm relaxed about it. I want to be naked with Easton and…um…tonight I want to work on the homework Dr. Orleen gave me. Stay tuned for that.

"Damn, babe. Didn't mean to scare you," he says, but he's laughing and it makes me chuckle. He doesn't think I notice, but he takes a quick glance south of my stomach and I so badly want to pick him up and pin him against the wall. But not yet.

"It's cool, Belle. I could get used to getting out of the shower to you." I wink. He blushes that gorgeous shade of peach that I like so much. He's propped up on his elbow in my bed, so I sort of crawl up to him to give him all the kisses.

"I could get used to this, too," he murmurs into my mouth.

"Hmm, good. Now, get out so I can get dressed."

Easton huffs, then hurries off the bed. "Well, hurry up then. I need my Paul time. Oh, and Aidan's here, too. Huxley told me to bring him. I know you two aren't exactly friends, but I'd like you to be at some point—"

"Don't worry. I'm not going to hit on him again." I peck him on the lips. "Lesson learned. Ya know, like that Carrie Underwood song you *forced* me to listen to the other day."

"What? I didn't *force* you to—"

I shut him up with a kiss. "I'm kidding, babe. Now *go* so I can get dressed."

He rolls his eyes and turns to leave. I slap his ass on the way out the door and he yelps. Playing with him like this is so comfortable for me now. I live for these moments.

* * *

I swear, Huxley is so extra. Where did these dishes even come from? There's a million forks and spoons with like seven plates and whatever the fuck even is a charger plate.

Placemats. There are placemats. And a centerpiece with real flowers.

We even have assigned seating.

"Hux, this is *beautiful*," Easton says as Huxley finishes setting the table with all the food.

"Yeah, I didn't even know our table could fit this much shit on it. When did you have the time to do all of this?"

"Paul. Shut your shitty ass up. And I skipped my last two classes. Shhh, don't tell my parents. I can make up whatever we did later." Huxley glares at me, then smiles sweetly at Easton. "And *thank you*, E. Anyway, dinner is served."

"Uh, and what are we eating?" I ask.

Huxley stands up and goes full-on Vanna White with the food closest to her. "I'm so glad you asked, thank you, Paul. For our first dish we have red and yellow tomatoes layered with fresh mozzarella cheese, fresh basil, and zesty balsamic vinaigrette." She pauses and moves to the other end of the table.

"For our second dish, arugula greens and feta cheese, toasted pecans and sliced fresh peaches drizzled with white wine vinegar and honey." Huxley steps to the center of the table and gestures around her amazing floral centerpiece. "For our main dish, we will be having a garlic herb-crusted rack of lamb with rosemary smashed potatoes and asparagus. I didn't have time to make dessert, so later on, we will be fawning over the everly delicious caramel apple cupcakes Dev picked up from Copain in Uptown."

We all stare at Huxley in awe.

"Whoa," Aidan says.

"This might be the best meal I'll have in my entire life," Easton says.

"*You* did all of this?" I ask.

Huxley shrugs. "You damn right. My mom's a chef and I spent most of the time on Facetime as she walked me through it—*after* I was supposed to be in class obvi—but yes, I did this." Devina clears her throat. "With Devina's help, of course."

"Holy shit, how did I not know that?" I ask.

She shrugs again. I smile at her. And oh how proud she is. She knew she did the damn thing and I will surely never doubt her again. Not that I ever did before, but still. That woman is a beast and she could take over the world. With tonight and her mac and cheese last night, I never want to eat at the dining halls on campus ever again.

"Dig in!"

Easton was right, this has to be the best meal I've ever had in my entire life. Aidan and I have been talking while Easton gabs with Huxley and Devina. He's told me about his book and I told him about my unfinished poems and, I gotta say, he's actually pretty cool. We just got off on the wrong foot, I guess, big time. I can see why he and Easton are such good friends.

"Okay!" Huxley clinks her wine glass with a fork. "The time

has come…"

She doesn't continue. She just pauses like the dramatic bitch she is. I almost burst out laughing when everyone kinda just looks at each other for what to do next.

"…for the main event."

"Wow! The drama. The suspense," Devina pipes up.

"Don't let her fool you. She's probably about to tell us she farted or something." I can't help it.

Easton and Aidan laugh and Devina joins in. I'm not too far behind because the look on Huxley's face is priceless. She is shook and speechless and now we're all in tears. I'm dying! I finally got her!

"OMG the look on your face," I manage to say between breaths.

Easton has his head on my shoulder while we all calm down. Huxley is just sitting there waiting for us to stop, but even she can't help but laugh with us.

"Anywaaaaay, what I was *going* to say waaaaas… My parents have a beach house in Myrtle Beach and they have agreed to let us use it for the *entire* week of spring break! And I want you all there. Aidan, Tyler included. I've already reached out and arranged everything with him. Isn't that wonderful?"

Devina squeals and claps her hands.

Easton and I look at each other with surprise.

"You asked Ty? How?" Aidan asks, flabbergasted.

"There's this new thing, maybe you haven't heard of it, but it's called *social media*. It's a glorious invention. Makes it super easy to contact people."

"But how?" he asks again.

"You tagged him in a post and I went to his page and asked."

"Stalker much?" I whisper for only Easton to hear. He shakes his head and giggles.

"He's down! He said he'll meet us down there. I sent him my

parents' address and everything. He awaits your call. You in?"

Everyone's looking at Aidan.

"Uh, of course!" The look of surprise on his face is so sweet. "So that's why he couldn't come back up the mountain!"

"Paulston, you in? Actually, Paul doesn't have a choice since he's never been to the beach."

"Paulston?"

"Your ship name."

"Wait, you've never been to the beach?" Easton asks me.

"You gave us a ship name?" I eye her and she just shrugs.

Easton's shocked. I mean, I get it. I'm twenty-one and haven't really been outside of the Midwest until moving here. Going to Austin, Texas, for my aunt's wedding a few years back was probably the closest I've ever been to a large body of water. But I still have never been to a beach. Lake of the Ozarks 1,000 percent does not count. I told Huxley this a few weeks ago during one of our *Schitt's Creek* game nights. That little shit set this whole thing up. Damn, she's good.

I shake my head slowly. "Nope. Never been."

"Then yes! We're totally going," he tells me. Then turns to Huxley. "We're totally going, Hux."

"Yes. Perf. Lovely. This is going to be *ah-maze-ing*! Spring break here we come! Oh, and I need everyone to text me their fav artists so Dev and I can create a road-trip playlist." Her eyes lock on me. "I will not stand for fighting over music in my car."

We all agree, then Aidan slips out to Facetime Tyler while Devina and Huxley turn on some music and dance around the apartment.

I lean over to Easton. "We?"

"Uh...yeah?"

"I like when you refer to us as a we." I kiss him.

We've kissed since my big meltdown, but we've kept it pretty PG-ish. It's only been two weeks but fuck it. I don't care anymore. I may not be ready to have sex with him right now, but there are plenty of other things we can do until then. Like Dr. Orleen told me yesterday, if I think I'm ready, I should try to do things outside of my triggers. And it's happening. Tonight.

* * *

Aidan left shortly after his call with Tyler so they could...*finish* their call. But we all know what that means. And since Huxley — and partly Devina — cooked, I volunteered Easton and myself to clean up.

He's wiping down the table while I put the last of the dishes in the dishwasher.

"Done," I declare to him triumphantly.

"Me too." He smiles and I wrap my arms around his waist.

"Good. Go brush your teeth."

"Damn. Yes, Daddy," Easton says with sarcasm dripping from his words.

I swear I immediately get a hard-on. Didn't know I liked being called daddy until this very moment. I kinda would have expected the opposite. After everything, "daddy" wouldn't seem like a turn on. But...surprisingly, it is. There's no...anger or anxiety, etcetera. This is strange, for me to feel anything positive toward that word. And yet, from Easton, I'm so into it.

I smirk devilishly. "Do. Not. Call me. That. Or you *will* pay."

Easton wraps his arms around my neck and whispers in my ear, "Will I? I've seen the way you've been looking at me tonight."

"Oh yeah?"

He pulls back to look me in the eyes. "You sure, Paul? I'd be lying if I said I don't want it. 'Cause I do. Like, really badly. But are you sure?"

"Brush your teeth and meet me in bed, silly goose."

His eyes go wide. "Is that supposed to be a joke about—"

"The goose that attacked me and caused me to run into you and then you proceeded to yell at me like it was *my fault*? Nah, just a coincidence." I wink. "But the geese here are the literal spawns of Satan. You can't change my mind."

"You're not wrong."

We brush our teeth together like we're some gag-me-with-a-spoon cute AF Instagram couple. Ew. But also, I'm blushing. I really could get used to this.

We finish up and head back to the bedroom. Easton goes to turn off the light and I waste no time pinning him against the wall in the dark. I put my hand behind his head so he doesn't bang it against the wall and find his mouth quickly. He parts his lips and lets my tongue find his in a familiar greeting. He tastes like spearmint and...well, Easton.

My taste buds explode with ecstasy.

"I want you," I say into his mouth. "I really, really fucking want you."

"Then," he says in between kisses, "have me. But don't...do more...than you're able."

"I won't." I slide my hands to his ass and lift him up. He follows my command and wraps his legs around me. I spin around and guide us back to my bed, never breaking contact.

I'm so grateful for all the time I've spent at the gym. My muscles might be screaming at me from my workout earlier, but lowering him to the bed is a piece of cake. I crawl on top of him and move to take off his shirt and throw it to the floor. I kiss down his neck to his collarbone and on to his nipples. I lick and suck and bite while he moans and moans and moans. I kiss him back up to his lips, then step back so he's lying on the bed and I'm standing over him.

"You okay?" Easton asks as he props himself up on his elbows.

"Better than. Can you see me?"

"Yeah, but only kinda."

"Good," I say, then slowly take off my shirt. I have his attention now as I toss it on top of his and move my hands to my waistline. Easton parts his lips and lets out a small sigh. I unbutton my jeans and slide them off until they hit the floor, then kick them aside. I'm standing in my boxer briefs, completely hard and I know he can see it since his eyes keep looking at it and then my face, back and forth, over and over. He licks his lips then bites the bottom one. I move my thumbs behind my underwear waistline and pull them off too.

Easton's eyes go wide with excitement since this is technically the first time he's actually seen me naked.

"Come here," he begs, scooting to the edge of the bed to be in front of me. He comes close but makes sure not to touch. He raises his eyebrows in question and I smile. His pants are gone in two seconds flat.

I put my hand to his chest and urge him to sit at the edge of the bed. He opens his legs and I step closer to stand between them. He doesn't break eye contact. He's looking at me in earnest with swollen kissed lips and a slight hickey already forming along his collarbone.

"Can I?" he begs.

I know what he's asking. No one's sucked me off since my ex, so I think this is safe territory. My heart is racing and my adrenaline is high, but I don't think it's anxiety. I think I'm...actually excited? This is all so new to me, but I feel...I feel safe.

I nod.

"I need you to say it, Paul. Yes or no?"

"Yes. You can."

"Tell me if you need me to stop, okay?"

"Okay."

While keeping eye contact, Easton takes me into his hand

and licks the tip. I lace my fingers through his hair so that I can see his face. He slowly goes deeper and deeper until he gags a little. He eventually closes his eyes and I do the same. Easton wraps one hand around my thigh as he uses his other hand to help. It's wet and sloppy and I swear my eyes roll so far back into my head that I see my own soul. A soul that is slowly opening up to another human being. A soul that is brighter and more at peace with its path than it's ever been. A soul that finally feels seen and heard.

Time escapes me in a bubble of euphoria. Easton hasn't stopped and I don't want him to, but if something doesn't change soon I'm going to bust.

"Easton. Easton." I grab a handful of his hair to pull him back so he's looking up at me. "I'm close," I whisper breathlessly.

"I want it."

I hum, "Where?"

"In my mouth."

"Okay. Come with me?"

"Always."

Easton

ROAD TRIP

"Don't forget to pack sunscreen."

"Duh." Aidan pulls the can out of his suitcase and shows it to me.

"Wouldn't want your boyfriend going up in smoke," I giggle. It's an ongoing joke.

Tyler is meeting us at the beach house. It didn't make sense for him to drive over three hours to get here, just to drive another three hours to the beach, when he could literally get to the beach from his college in the same three hours.

Something solid hits my arm and then topples onto the floor. I look to find a wadded-up pair of socks. Aidan's socks.

"He's not *that* pale." Aidan groans and picks up the socks.

"Did you throw your nasty socks at me?" I try to act offended, but I can't do it.

"They're clean, bitch."

"Sure." I put on an exaggerated grin. "I still can't believe you're older than him."

It just looks the opposite. Ty is taller by a few inches, nothing massive, but it's there, and I guess Aidan just puts off this younger vibe. I don't know if it's the wildness of his hair or something about his dark brown eyes. They're adorable honestly. Maybe it's the freckles.

"Just because I'm shorter doesn't mean I'm younger." Aidan stuffs another pair of pants and trunks in his case.

I convinced him to take his swimming trunks. Sure, it's not going to be warm. I think the weather is calling for a max of sixty-five degrees this week, so I can only imagine how cold the water is going to be, but I'm so stoked about swimming in the ocean. I don't care if I freeze my ass off, and I'm making A get in with me.

"Yeah, yeah, I know. You've said it a hundred times." I put the last of my toiletries in a little bag and stuff it near the top, above my t-shirts and flannels.

Aidan's all excited about the miniature golf places. Apparently that's what his mom and grandparents do when they go down, hit up every single one throughout the week. I mean, that's sort of like my family in a way. Sure, we live literally half an hour from *a* beach, and less than two hours from the OBX, but it's still not somewhere we go a lot. But for us, instead of hitting up all the mini golf places, we stop at every single beach merch store. They're all basically the same, but you never know what little thing you might find in one.

"Promise me you're not going to work on your book while we're down there." I turn and look him right in the eye.

"But..."

I put my hand up, index finger in the air. "No but. Just yes. That's it. Period. Full stop."

He giggles at that, and I lose my stoic composure. Aidan has a tendency to not know when to stop working, especially when it's about his book. So the reminder is key and not totally selfish.

"I'm sure Ty would prefer you pay attention to him," I remind him.

"I know, but I *am* taking my computer." Aidan pats the front compartment on his single suitcase. "Just in case I need it."

"You're not going to *need* it, but okay. I'll be watching you."

He snickers but doesn't bother saying anything back.

A few minutes later we walk out into the cool air toward Huxley's little Prius. Crazily enough she has the biggest car of the four of us. Mine is tiny, plus I'm scared it might not make it to the coast with us all in it. Paul's isn't much bigger, and Aidan's Mustang definitely isn't made for five *and* luggage. And come to think of it, I don't know what Devina drives, but it must not be big for us to be packing five people in this thing.

"Belle!" Paul pops out of the back seat and rushes me in a hug.

It's weird to think just a few weeks ago the idea of him touching me would have sent me into a rage, and now it's basically all I want. He grabs my suitcase and leads me to the car.

"Babe." I peck him on the cheek.

"Want to help with mine, too?" Aidan holds his suitcase out and Paul's face skews into amusement, but he doesn't take it. "Okay. Fine."

"You'll have your man at the beach," I tell him.

"Yeah, yeah." He waits behind Paul as he literally stuffs my suitcase in the trunk like a game of Tetris.

"Y'all ready for this?" Huxley yells out her window.

"Hell yeah!" I hoot, while Aidan throws his hand up with a mock grin and feigns excitement.

He's excited to see Ty, not for the trip down. Can't say I blame him. The two of us are going to be packed in Huxley's back seat like sardines with Paul. It doesn't matter that none of us are big, the back seat is tiny. I swear if I get a cramp in my leg I'm going to hurt someone.

Aidan gets in on the driver's side, and I open the passenger door to slide in, but Paul stops me and kisses me on the cheek. I smile and look into his eyes for a short second before pecking him on the lips.

Patience, Easton. There will be plenty of time for more when we get to the beach.

We slide in and scrunch up close together. I'm stuck between Aidan and Paul, my legs spread around this big blue cooler with a white lid that better be filled with cold drinks and snacks. That was Paul's job, so I will have words if it isn't. Huxley cranes her neck around her seat and looks at each of us in turn, and then her girl, Devina.

"So I've decided by my own royal decree that we shall begin the drive playlist with, drumroll please..." And Devina actually starts one while the entire back seat stares blankly. "Seriously, y'all are no fun. It's Easton's. We're starting with Easton's."

"Yes!" I fist pump the air, as she taps her phone and a Kacey Musgraves song, "Space Cowboy", comes on. It's not my favorite but it works.

All at once everyone in the car, besides me, says a simultaneous, "Ugh!"

"Oh, come on!" I roll my eyes.

"This is going to be a long-ass three hours." Paul shakes his head.

"But you...like me, so it's okay." Ooh! I almost slipped.

Not going to lie, I've thought about it a lot, but no. I'm not there. I adore him, I absolutely adore him, but that's a step I'm a little horrified to make.

I tuck the thought in the back of my mind and focus on the twang in the song they all hate.

"Yeah, yeah," Paul says.

"What about us?" Huxley says, pulling out of the school.

"Too bad."

Paul

FRIENDS AND FAMILY

I wake up in a beach-themed room with light spilling through mahogany shutters. A light breeze creeps in through an open window. My arms snake around Easton's waist to pull him closer. He stirs and stretches, grinding his ass back into me.

"Oh shit, I'm sorry! I didn't mean to—"

"It's okay," I whisper into his ear and grind into him. My already deep voice is deeper from disuse. I clear my throat. "Good morning, Belle. Sleep well?"

"Of course, babe. I had you to keep me warm."

"Bullshit." I stifle a yawn. "You hogged the entire bed all night. I had to get up and find another blanket in the hall closet. *And* you wouldn't let me touch you because I'm, and I quote, 'a human heater'. You're a monster."

Easton quickly flips to face me. We're nose to nose, dick to dick, and I can't help but flex. He does that to me.

"If I'm such a monster," he starts, rubbing his hand down my shirtless torso to my underwear line, "then you wouldn't be so…" he looks down, "excited right now, right?"

"You wish. I just woke up, Belle."

"I beg to differ." His lips are hovering mere centimeters from mine without getting any closer. This little shit likes to tease and it's driving me *mad*.

I want to kiss him. I try to kiss him, but he moves out of the way.

I huff. "I hate you."

We're quiet for a while. It's not uncomfortable or annoying. It's nice. Two people being able to just exist with each other is really nice.

"I've been meaning to ask about your tattoos," he says, "but I keep forgetting."

"Ask away, Belle."

He lightly traces my right forearm with his fingers. "This one?"

"I read this book a while back, *The Song of Achilles*, that reminded me of those ancient marble statues of Greek gods. In the book the main character, Patroclus, is just as much of a god as Achilles is, in my opinion. I got this tattoo of Patroclus with wings, hiding most of his face with his arm to symbolize that not all heroes are gods. The basic, normal human boy can be just as strong, just as important. It reminds me of potential. The rest around him are just pretty embellishments."

Easton switches to my left hand as his fingers trace around the koi fish on the inside of my wrist. "This?" he whispers.

"Two koi fish. Yin and Yang. Balance."

"These?" His fingers trace up my forearm.

"Three moon phases. To symbolize death and rebirth."

He flips my hand over to show the flowers and a geometric ten-sided star.

"I got these first. To show the beauty and interconnectivity of life." His fingers move to my bicep. "Then I finished my sleeve with the wolf, which is my soul animal. Out of every mammal on the planet, I feel like I connect with the wolf the most. I'm glad I got it too, because that book I bought on our first date, do you remember?"

"*Wolfsong*?"

"Yeah. It's all about werewolves and family and pack. It's fitting 'cause I feel like that's what we have with our group. I feel like I finally belong and it's all because of you and Huxley. Maybe Aidan too? I don't know. I feel like he still hates me."

"He doesn't hate you, babe. Just give him time to warm up," Easton assures me, but I'm still not so certain. "Ty being here will help."

We fall silent. Easton slowly and lightly tickles my tattoo sleeve. Up and down, up and down, like a metronome.

Then he presses his hand to the middle of my bare chest.

"And the butterfly?"

"Again, rebirth. I was hoping it'd bring me luck when I moved to Charlotte. I got it right before I left Missouri."

I tell him about the word tattoos on each of my thighs just above my knees and how they're Italian for peace and paradise. I tell him about the tattoo on the right side of my neck, a dagger with flowers wrapped around it, and how it's for my favorite Shakespeare play, *Romeo and Juliet*. I tell him about the tattoo on my ribs that reads, "Work hard in silence. Let your success be your noise". I even tell him about the small tattoo I have on my lower hip by my crotch of the Playboy bunny I got on a dare back in my senior year of high school.

"Just when I couldn't be more amazed by you, Paul Donovan Acre, you go and surprise me again."

I hum, nestling into him, kissing his neck.

He smiles. "Can I?" He's tracing his fingers along my waistline, awaiting my reply.

"Sure."

Waking up to a half-naked, half-sleepy horny Easton might just be the highlight of my entire existence. His hand creeps into my underwear and grabs ahold of me. I groan, eyes rolling back into my head.

"Wake up, bitches! It's beach day!" Huxley yells, busting into the room with her hands covering her eyes. "Y'all better not be fucking."

"Ha ha," I deadpan and Easton scoots away from me. I'm going to kill her.

"Are you decent?"

"Yes, Huxley. We are clothed." I roll my eyes.

"Kinda." Easton follows it up and grins at me.

I kiss him on the forehead and move to sit up, making sure to keep the blanket over my hips.

"Good." She uncovers her eyes just as Devina comes in with an iced coffee for me and a sugar-free Monster for Easton.

"Joh-eun achim-ieyo!" Devina says, what I've learned to be "good morning" in Korean.

"Oof, cinnamon?" I ask, grabbing for it like a child.

"Duh," Devina says, feigning offense and hands each of us our drinks.

"You *trying* to kill A?" Easton gives me the side-eye.

"No—" I try, but Huxley barges over to me. I completely forgot Aidan is allergic to cinnamon.

"Make sure you keep the cinnamon away from Aidan." Easton looks at Huxley. "He's allergic."

"Got it." Huxley nods and keeps on without losing a beat. "Well, drink up, bitches. It's beach day and I don't want to waste a single second of sunlight. Mom and Dad will be in tonight to cook for us and then we have a bonfire after that. Lots to do. Chop-chop!" And then she's gone with Devina trailing after.

After Easton and I both shower and shave—him shave, me trim since I refuse to shave my beard completely on account of looking like a twelve-year-old with tattoos, plus Easton seems to like it—we make our way down to the kitchen. It smells of bacon and biscuits and gravy and various other breakfast items I'm not familiar with. I could have a protein smoothie or I can have a good ol' Southern breakfast with a little Korean flare. I'm going to have to hit the gym hard AF when we get back to school. Maybe I can find a local gym here and get a one-week pass or something.

We sit and eat, waiting for Aidan and Tyler to get down here. The house gives off *Grace and Frankie* beach house vibes. It's so homey and cozy. I could live here till I die if they'd let me.

Aidan and Tyler finally grace us with their presence and holy shit that dude looks like a vampire. He's taller than Aidan, skinny with dark shaggy hair. He's cute though, and he and Aidan look great together. Easton told me they've been dating since high school. I'm sure Aidan has told him about me and all that shit that went down when we first met. I hope he doesn't hate me. I really don't want to make this vacation awkward.

Easton jumps up first. "Ty! I'm so happy you came."

"Hey East!"

Easton gives him a quick hug and turns to me. "Ty, this is my boyfriend, Paul. Paul, Aidan's boyfriend, Tyler."

I stand and offer my hand. He takes it, beaming. "Hey, Paul! Good to finally meet you. I've heard a lot about you."

"Uh-oh," I say, stealing a glance at Aidan and then Easton. He gives me a "yikes" face, then looks away. I look back to Tyler. "Uh, I'm really sorry. I didn't know Aidan had a boyfriend when—"

"Dude, it's okay." He chuckles and shrugs. "Shit happens."

"Okay." I nod quickly. "Okay, cool. Good."

"Awwwww," Huxley and Devina chime in in unison. Their elbows are resting on the island counter, their hands cupping their adoring faces.

"So cute," Devina says.

"All's right in Gay World," Huxley says, winking at me.

"Anyway," Aidan pipes up, "what's the plan for today, Hux?"

"To the beach!"

* * *

The waves of my mind syncopate to the ocean's rhythm
  as I'm floating on Her travesty.
  Calming tranquility
  washes over me like the music of the sea.
  It washes over me like the emotions of a first love,
  like the feelings of a forever love,
  but lingers like a soulmate love.
  Two souls diving, drowning, sinking into Her abyss.
  Light snuffed out like a candle, like a phantom kiss
  as the waves of my mind syncopate to the pounding of your bliss.
  To the —

"Whachya writin'?" Easton plops down next to me, his country accent on full display, interrupting my thoughts. Sand sprays across my writing notebook, and water drips from his thick dark hair. The sun has kissed his skin, pronouncing his freckles even more, like constellations in the night sky. He needs to put more sunscreen on before it turns for the worse. But right here, at this moment, I don't think I've ever...loved him more.

Shit.

Excuse me, *what*?! What just happened to my brain? What *is* happening in my head? My heart clearly hasn't gotten the memo and my facial expressions are gone for good.

I snap my notebook shut and bury my face in the crook of my elbow, hiding. "Nothing. Just felt inspired by the ocean."

"Yeah, it'll do that I suppo— Are you okay?"

"Yeah, yeah. Fuck yeah. All good here." I look back up at Easton, but the sun is directly above him, so I have to squint to see. "It's just so...big! The ocean, that is. Like, how fucking terrifying, ya know?" I bury my face again.

I look back up at Easton and he's eyeing me like I'm in trouble. Then he smiles and laughs. "You seriously love that word."

"Huh?"

"Fuck. You *love* to say that word." Easton shakes his head.

"You know, fuck is an extremely universal word, maybe even *the* most universal word in every single language. You can throw it anywhere in any sentence and it would still make sense. It can be a noun, adjective, blah, blah, blah. But there *are* other words and I've been having fun exploring those options. And I think it's helped my writing, too."

"Yeah, that makes sense. Words are important to you blah, blah, blah," he playfully mocks me. He rubs his hands in my short needs-to-be-bleached-again hair. "I'm just giving you shit 'cause I think it's funny how flustered you get. It's cute."

I lean up for a kiss. "I know."

Tyler and Aidan are walking back to us from their romantic beach stroll. Tyler's fully dressed and probably for the best since he would burn the easiest. Aidan is in shorts and a tank top. Huxley and Devina are back up at the house helping her parents. They said they wouldn't be long, so I'm surprised they're not back yet.

"Hey, guys, how was your walk?" Easton asks Aidan as he sits down on the large blanket we have sprawled out.

"It was good."

"Jacob? Jacob!" Tyler yells, waving at someone in the distance that I can't quite make out. "Skylar! What the hell are you two doing here?" He runs off.

"Jacob and Sky are *here*?" Aidan gets back up to chase after Tyler.

"What? No *way*!" Easton's up in a flash.

Everyone jogs away and I'm so confused. We're three hours from Charlotte, how can all three of them know these people? I put my sunglasses on and make my way to Easton's side. There's a taller guy in a hoodie and shorts with hair somehow more pale than Tyler's skin and a much, much shorter guy wearing a beach dress similar to the one Huxley has on.

The one in the dress is signing something and the tall one is translating it.

"He said, 'I can't believe we ran into y'all all the way out here.' Oh, who's this?"

"Oh my God, sorry! This is my boyfriend, Paul." Easton motions to me.

"Hey, y'all. Nice to meet you," I offer.

"Yeah, nice to meet you, too. I'm Jacob. This is my boyfriend, Skylar."

Skylar, the one in the dress, signs something to me. I don't know what he said, but I can only assume it was "nice to meet you too" by the way his mouth moved with his hand motions.

"He said, 'Nice to meet you too.'"

"Pleasure. So…how do y'all know each other?" I ask anyone willing to answer.

"Well, Tyler and Jacob met through some video game," Easton explains, "and then Aidan and Skylar met because they're dating them, and then I met them all when I started on the Harrison campaign last year. She was running against Jacob's dad."

"Your dad, huh?"

"It's a long story." Jacob shrugs it off.

"Yeah," Easton continues, "and I met Skylar through Jacob while we worked on the campaign. We'd hang out every so often at Editions — you know, the place we went to Trivia Night. That's where they live. Not the shop, but Kannapolis."

Skylar starts signing something again, making Jacob laugh. "He said, 'Us gays have to stick together.'"

We all join in a chorus of laughter.

"So, what are you two doing here, anyway?" Aidan asks.

Jacob shrugs. "Spring break. Florida's too far, so the Big

Brown Wet Thing had to do."

"Big Brown Wet Thing?" Easton squints.

"It's an inside joke." Jacob laughs. "Oh! Imani's here too, but she stayed at the Airbnb to Facetime Seth. He couldn't get the time off work to come too."

Skylar's signing again.

"'What brings you all here?'" Jacob translates.

It's weird because I've noticed Skylar signing, but no one is signing back. "How come—" I start.

Easton laces his fingers into mine and smiles. "He doesn't have a voice, babe. But his ears work just fine."

Skylar laughs.

"Oh shit. I'm sorry! I didn't mean to assume anything."

Skylar signs while Jacob translates. "'It's okay, you didn't know. Don't worry about it.' I'm his voice and he's the brains and beauty." Skylar hits Jacob, mouthing "shut up" playfully.

"That dress does look amazing on you, not gonna lie," I say.

Thank you, Skylar mouths.

"Anyway," Easton cuts in, "yeah, we're here for spring break too. Our friend's—Paul's roommate—parents have a beach house."

"Oh my God, we're having dinner and a bonfire tonight! Y'all should join us. Imani too!" Tyler says.

"Yes! That would be so much fun. You don't think Hux would mind, do you, babe?" Easton says.

"Nah, she would *love* more guests! Seriously, y'all should join," I say.

Skylar is smiling wide, nodding his head quickly.

Jacob speaks for both of them. "Yes! We'd love to! Im would be down too. She's always up for a good party."

* * *

Dinner was *chaotic* to say the least. A house full of queers, not to mention Huxley with her sister, Luana, and Imani is just *insane*. The three of them are the funniest people I've ever met. Whoever's idea this was is crazy and I'm so grateful. I have a large family. With four other siblings plus all my aunts, uncles, and cousins, let's just say holidays are beyond deafening. But I've never felt anything like this. So safe or wanted, I've never felt so...loved. To have Huxley's parents be as welcoming and accepting as they have been is new for me. It's a little awkward though, so I've tried to avoid them even though it's fucked up because they're paying for my therapy, which I'm sure isn't cheap. It isn't personal, I just have a hard time with father figures for...reasons. Dr. Orleen is aware and has been helping me work through it. I don't think they've noticed though, as I've kept to Easton's side most of the night.

Huxley's mom is a first-generation immigrant from Italy, which explains why she's such an amazing cook. She told us her whole backstory over dessert. She has her own restaurant in Burbank — a suburb of Atlanta. Huxley's dad's African American, born and raised in Georgia. He's a family/child lawyer, which would explain the beach house.

To have a family like Huxley's...I don't even know what I would do. But I have my own version of a family in Huxley and Easton. I don't know the others well. Hell, I just met most of them today, but I can *feel* the depths of their souls and it's good. It's all so very good.

Skylar, Devina, Luana, and Mr. Davenport clean up the kitchen. Mrs. Davenport, Aidan, Tyler, Jacob, Easton, and Huxley are all drinking wine and talking and laughing in the living room. I'm standing out on the balcony watching the man I...love have the time of his life. He's the most relaxed and carefree I've seen him since we met. He looks a little exhausted, but who isn't after spending all day in the sun?

Huxley glances my way and I smile and wave awkwardly,

but my smile falters. I turn away from her to look out at the near-black ocean. Its music and aroma wafting around me in a gentle, cool breeze as the waves lap at the sand below.

I hear the sliding door open and close, footsteps approaching. It's probably Huxley. Easton sounds like an elephant when he walks and no one else would come out here with me.

"You've been avoiding us, child," a woman's voice says through a thick Italian accent.

I grimace and turn toward Mrs. Davenport. "I'm sorry, ma'am. I mean no offense."

"No need for apologies. Huxley has told me enough. We have a close relationship, she and I. I've put the rest together myself."

"Regardless," I say, looking her in the eye kindly, "I'm sorry."

"Yes, I can see that." She smiles and pats my cheek, then leans against the railing to look out into the darkness.

I mimic her. "You have a beautiful home. I've never been to the beach before and it's been a wonderful trip already. Thank you for hosting us." She looks at me and I smile, even though I don't feel like it.

"What troubles you, Paul? I have yet to see a genuine smile on that gorgeous youthful face since we first met."

"My..." I pause. "My parents wouldn't be so kind."

"Why are you not close with them, if you don't mind me asking?"

"I don't want to be. They've...hurt me...in unforgivable ways. I'm better off without them." I turn around and lean my butt against the railing. Easton and Tyler are talking about something, then they both bend over laughing. "Just because they're my family doesn't mean I have to choose them though, right?"

THIS I PROMISE YOU

Mrs. Davenport follows my line of vision. "Not many your age could come to that conclusion. But you miss them?"

"I miss my siblings, yeah." I look at her. "I worry the two young ones are being treated the same way I was. I couldn't…" I pause and bow my head in shame, my voice barely above a whisper. "I can't save them. I could barely save myself."

"And the regret you feel for leaving eats away at you."

"Something like that."

"Paul. Paul, look at me," she demands with kindness and grace, so I do. "You mustn't let the *good decision* to rid your life of toxic, hurtful people burden you. You have a responsibility to yourself first and foremost, to look out for *you*, and only *you* can decide that for yourself."

"But what if—"

"*Child*, you cannot control the actions of others." She smiles thoughtfully. "Our actions are our own and we will each be held accountable for them, including your parents."

My lip trembles slightly and I'm fighting back tears. She's right.

"I'm scared," I admit.

"I know. Take that fear and turn it into action. Good relationships, regardless of the type, take work. You left, but you can still show your siblings that you are not gone. Do not wait to tell the ones you love how you feel. If you feel it, speak it. Simple as that."

My eyes immediately dart to Easton, who's in a heavy discussion with Skylar. His arms are flailing and Skylar is doubled over laughing. That makes me smile.

Mrs. Davenport follows my eyes. "That's a good boy you have. His eyes hardly ever leave you."

"He's the best person I've ever known. He's intelligent and cares so intensely and deeply about the world…and animals. He loves his dad and sister so much, even though his mom left him at a young age, but it hasn't deterred him from his ideals, from his family. He wears basically the same things day after day, but I love it. It's...it's just *him*." A deep chuckle rumbles in my chest. "He's kinda messy and hates cleaning, but he would do anything for his friends. He's sensitive and wears his heart on his sleeve. He even does this thing when he's nervous or when he's thinking where he rubs his top teeth back and forth along his bottom lip, but I don't think he realizes that he does it. It's cute..." I pause. "He's honest even when words fail him," I tell her, my eyes never leaving him. "He's beautiful."

"You love him." A statement, not a question.

I hum, "I do."

"Waste not." Her voice is smooth and kind but filled with urgency. "Tomorrow is a new day, but do not delay because tomorrow is not guaranteed. *If you feel it —*"

My eyes finally leave Easton and look back to Mrs. Davenport. "Speak it."

"Ah, there's a good boy." She pats my cheek. "That's enough emotion for tonight. Tomorrow morning we'll make some pancakes and waffles for us all. For now, I think it's time for some s'mores and camaraderie. Don't you?"

Easton

I FEEL WEIRD

Aren't vacations supposed to be relaxing? Well, I'm not relaxed. I swear I'm not complaining. This week has been epic. We've been all over the place: an amusement park on the beach, the zip line—which Tyler refused to get on—some big hedge maze that took us like two hours to get out of. We've had little mini us-only house parties every night—I've woken up with a hangover most the week—and we've been on the beach every day.

It's really been great, but I'm exhausted.

The temperature hasn't topped sixty once, but I still made Aidan get in the ocean. Tyler and Paul even helped. It was great. I took his legs while Paul and Ty hoisted him up by his waist with him trying to kick free. People probably thought we were kidnapping him at first, but we did let him go once we were in the water.

I wish I could take a day to recoup. Like, I swear I need a long-ass nap, but I can't do that to them. They're having so much fun, and Paul's been amazing. We haven't had sex, and I'm not pushing it, but the number of blow jobs that have happened...yeah. It's a lot. That sort of makes up for how drained I feel.

Plus, it's loud as shit in here.

The crowd cheers as two men on horses, dressed straight out

of the dark ages with massive lances, rush from either end of the dirt-filled arena. I can't remember their names, but one is the blue knight and the other is the green knight. There's a yellow and red one too, but they already jousted. Yellow ended up tumbling awkwardly to the ground, giving Red the victory.

"Go Blue!" Paul yells, a chicken leg gripped in his hand. He's really getting into this.

We're at a dinner show, Medieval Times to be exact. It's this massive arena that looks like a bona fide castle inside and out. Every seat is set behind a small table and served a multi-course meal that includes roast chicken and garlic bread with a cup of mead, aka a water for me—they IDed me. Oh, and there's no silverware either, none. You have to use your hands for everything.

The knights rush forward. The rumble of the crowd screaming shakes the arena. They lower their long slender lances, each aiming for the other, and lean forward, bracing. The noise intensifies, louder and louder as the crowd grows more excited.

My fingers twitch and my hand closes into a fist, but I didn't do it. I look down and try to unclench, but I can't for a moment. Finally my fingers let loose.

Weird.

There's a clash, and the blue lance bangs into the green knight's chest plate and he goes flying off his horse. It looks like it hurts, even though it's an act. It looked really real. I flinch. The crowd on our side erupts into cheers while the rest of the arena boos. The blue knight is ours.

"Yes! He did it!" Paul is out of his seat again, jumping. I didn't think he'd get this excited. He hates sports.

"Hell yeah!" Tyler joins in a chair over. Aidan's between us, and Paul's on my left.

"This is so cool, Easton." Paul finally takes his seat again.

"I told you it was." I try to laugh.

"You okay?" He grins caringly at me.

"Yeah, just tired." I grin big for him.

While the blue and red knights get ready for the next match I dig back into my chicken. They don't skimp on this shit. It's good, really good. But something just feels off.

The corner of my vision blurs in my left eye and I freeze up. No. Please no. Not on vacation. But then it's gone as quickly as it came. Okay. All good.

The announcer calls out the next match, riling up the blue and red sections. My friends are yelling and screaming, and I join them when he calls out the blue knight. They ride their horses up to the marks and lift their lances.

I reach forward, but I don't know why. I do it again, and my eye starts to blur again. What the hell?

"You okay?" Paul takes my hand, the one not reaching into nowhere.

"Uh…" I start, but I don't know. My vision isn't getting worse, but my body just feels off. "I feel weird."

"What?" Aidan's attention snaps from the field and he leans in. "Easton, you okay?"

That's when my entire body seizes up. My arms and legs start to shake, but I can't speak. I can't stop the shaking, and I'm scared. What the fuck is happening? I can't even move my eyes. But I hear the crowd yelling around me, screaming, but not for me.

"Belle!" Paul is yelling. "Easton! What's wrong with him? What's happening?"

My body jerks and I slip from my chair. My head hits the edge of something solid and everything goes blank.

Paul

STRAIGHT TO VOICEMAIL

"His dad's not here! He's all alone back there after having a *fucking seizure* and you won't let *any* of us fucking see him? I'm his fucking boyfriend, you good for nothing piece of worthless *shit*!"

I've been trying to get someone to answer my motherfucking questions for two shithell hours, but *nothing*.

"Paul, Paul, stop," Huxley urges, whining for me to calm down. She's exhausted like the rest of us. Tyler pretty much fell asleep on Aidan's shoulder ages ago. "The man's just doing his job—"

"I don't give a flying *fuck*. Whatever he's *doing* isn't his job!"

"Paul, seriously stop."

"Sir, please have a seat and calm down, otherwise I'll have to call security." The look on this man's face says he's had enough. I don't blame him. I wouldn't want to deal with a pissed off me either. That's why they should just *let me see my boyfriend* already.

He pinches the bridge of his nose. "I've been here for sixteen straight hours and I refuse to tolerate this. I don't get paid enough for that. Sit and be quiet or leave. I don't care which."

Aidan pipes up from across the waiting room. "That's the nice way of him telling you to eff off."

"Fuck you," I retort.

Aidan rolls his eyes.

Huxley sighs then yawns, leading me back to sit down across from Aidan and Tyler. "Paul, sit. I'm going to get some coffee."

I sit on the edge of my seat and lean my elbows on my knees. "Aidan, what the fuck is going on? Just fucking tell me, dude. I can't deal with this shit. You're not giving me answers, they're not giving me answers." I throw my hands up in defeat. "I feel like I'm literally about to explode. *Please just tell me.*"

Aidan's cheeks puff as he blows out air and readjusts himself in his seat. Tyler stirs and yawns. Aidan apologizes to him and faces me. "Fine, I guess if it's between you getting us kicked out of the hospital and me telling you what's going on, I'm stuck. But like I've told you a million times, this really is East's story to tell. Not mine." He sighs heavily, clearly uncomfortable. "East has MS, multiple sclerosis. It's a disease that attacks the central nervous system like the spinal cord and...the brain."

Excuse me, WHAT? "You've got to be fucking kidding me. He has MS and *never fucking told me?* What the hell! How did I not know? How did I not see?"

"It's not an always thing. Sometimes East is good for months at a time without a relapse or whatever. Other times he gets really tired and misses some class for a day or two. His biggest issue is with his eyes. They go blurry sometimes and he can't see right."

"So, what? He could go blind? Will this kill him?"

Huxley is standing above me, sipping her coffee with one hand on my shoulder reassuringly. She gives it a squeeze in anticipation.

"He could go blind, yes. But only if the disease persists. It attacks the nerves. There's a lot of things that can go wrong. He had a minor issue a couple weeks back, but other than that he's done really well the past year. We don't need to worry though because he's going to be fine."

"How do you know so much?" Huxley asks.

"Easton's my friend and roommate." Aidan looks at her and smiles weakly. "I've known him for a while. Also, I'm a nursing major."

"A couple weeks back? Like when we first started dating? Wait, was that why he canceled plans with me? He said he was dizzy or something, but I thought he just had a headache or whatever."

Aidan shrugs. "Maybe? Probably."

I jump out of my chair and rub my hands viciously over my face. I'm so tired, but I doubt I could sleep right now. My mind is reeling. "What the *fuck*. He kept this from me, that little shit. He *lied* to me!"

"Paul, would you grow the fuck up?" Aidan scoots forward in his chair but doesn't stand. His voice is getting louder now. I'm literally causing the guy who never swears to swear. At least *I've* never heard him swear. "Seriously? This isn't about you! You've known East for, what? A couple months? You don't get to decide how or even *when* he tells you *shit*. That's up to him and him alone. So stop being such a selfish prick and focus on what matters. If you love him, then cut the crap."

I huff and grumble with layers of sarcasm. "If I love him." A statement, not a fucking question.

Tyler raises his eyebrows. "Yes, Paul. Everyone can see it. You clearly care. Don't be so mean because you can't see past your anger."

"Whether or not East should have told you doesn't matter right now," Aidan reiterates. "And anyway, it's something to *talk* about with him, not scream about."

I deflate. I digress. He's right, I guess, and I don't have it in me to argue back anymore. I just want him to be safe, healthy and safe. I just want him in my arms, to hold and protect.

I need to see him!

It's been over three hours of sitting in this hellhole waiting room. Actually, scratch that, if a portal to hell opened up, then I'd rather sit there than here. I can't stand the sight of *Kevin the Receptionist's* face.

How did we get here? How? My time with Easton since that clusterfuck of a V-day party has been top tier, quality time well spent. Sure, it hasn't always been sunshine and fucking flowers, but I wouldn't trade it for anything. I can't for the life of me think of a good moment for him to tell me about his…condition.

Son of a *bitch* I had a full-fledged panic attack meltdown in front of him. I told him about my sexual assault and he couldn't find it in his cold dead heart to tell me about this shit? Sorry, no, that's not fair. His heart isn't dead. It just doesn't give enough of a shit about its *fucking boyfriend*.

Shit. That's not fair either. *I don't know!* I feel like I'm going crazy right now.

I love the hell out of him. I do, but he clearly doesn't love me. How could he? I opened up to him. I told him *everything*. He told me nothing. I guess…he didn't have to. I just wish he trusted me enough to tell me he's *sick*. What…did I do wrong?

I never should have moved here.

Tyler's voice interrupts my spiraling inner monologue. "Have you heard from his dad?" he asks Aidan.

Aidan nods. "Yeah, he's on the way. Should be here in…thirty minutes or so."

And now I have to deal with his *dad*? This is bullshit.

"I'm going for a walk."

No one says anything as the sliding glass doors open and the hint of Southern spring humidity invades my senses.

* * *

I'm not sure how long I'm gone, and my phone died. I don't give a fuck anyway. I probably walked around the entire hospital five times before I decided to go back inside.

I walk through the sliding glass doors and everyone is standing around, clearly not waiting for me. There's a man talking to a doctor that I can only assume is Easton's dad.

I don't want to do this, not here, not under these circumstances. If ever.

"We'll let you know if we see any more issues," the doc says. "You may see him soon, but no one else. We don't want to cause Easton any more distress. He needs his rest."

"Thank you, Dr. Shinabarger." The man shakes the doc's hand and Dr. Shinabarger leaves.

Huxley sees me and her face turns sour. "Where the hell have you been? I've called like a billion times."

"Phone died." I shrug. I've had some time to think and I've come up blank. I just want to see Easton and go to bed.

"Easton's been trying to call you."

"Wait, what?" I pull my phone out and try to turn it on…again. Nothing happens. "*Fuck!*"

"You must be Paul?" The man, Easton's dad, steps a little closer to me. Everyone is standing around in a circle but making sure to keep their distance…from me. I need to get my anger in check before I do something I'll regret. This is *not* how I wanted to meet his dad.

"Sir." I nod curtly.

He smiles, but it's faint. "It's wonderful to finally meet you. I'm Nick, Easton's dad." He looks like he wants to shake my hand but then thinks better of it and keeps to himself. "It is nice to meet you, though I'm sure East would have liked it under better circumstances."

I nod again.

"He's going to be fine. He—" Nick starts, but I cut him off because what the fuck!

"He's clearly not fucking *fine*." I scoff and roll my eyes. "Sir."

Guess I should still be polite. Don't want to burn that bridge before it's ever been built.

He rubs his hands together. "We've known about his MS since he was sixteen. But he *is* fine. He just overexerted himself and his body reacted. The doctors here have spoken with his primary doctors back home and are helping to give him the best care they can."

"I'm sure," I deadpan.

Easton's dad smiles at me again, but it doesn't reach his eyes. "He wants to talk to you."

This sets me off. I motion toward *Kevin the Receptionist*. "I've been trying to fucking do that, but they won't *let me* —"

"Paul," Huxley interjects.

" — and my phone is dead."

Huxley unlocks her phone. "Here, use mine. I'll call him now."

She hands me her phone and I step away from the group. It doesn't finish a full ring before the line connects. "Huxley, did you find —"

"It's me," I nearly whisper. I thought hearing his voice would make me feel better, I thought it would help calm my fucking nerves, but it just doesn't. I feel like my insides are going to implode.

He sighs, "Paul."

"Yeah." I grit my teeth. There is so much I want to say. I want to make sure he's okay. I want to fucking *lay into him*. I want to tell him nothing else matters because I…love him. But I don't. I don't know how to do any of it over the phone when he's probably two doors down.

"Paul, I'm so sorry —"

"Are you okay?"

"Yeah," he says. "Yeah, I'm okay."

"Good, 'cause you scared the fuck out of me, Easton."

"I'm so, so sorry! I wanted to tell you. I—"

"You fucking lied to me," I nearly yell.

Easton's dad steps over. "If you can't talk to my son calmly, then I suggest you hang up and deal with this when you're not worked up."

"Sorry, sir," I say and take a breath before I turn from him to talk to Easton again. "I trusted you with my *life*. But you couldn't trust me, could you?"

"I trust you, Paul. I just..." He sounds weak. He needs to rest. I should do this later, but I don't know if later is ever going to come. "You don't deserve to deal with this. You don't deserve to take on all my...baggage."

Fuck all trying to keep my cool. Nah, he doesn't get to say shit like that to me. To *me*. "Baggage? Wow. Having baggage is such a fucking *burden*, huh?" I mock. "You kept this *big bad secret* from me and decided, on your own, that I didn't deserve to know! That wasn't your call to make! Easton, I fucking lo—" I cut myself off and rub the back of my neck nervously. I can't tell him that. Not here, not like this.

I'm agitated, pacing. I can't get my mind to *shut up*!

I pull the phone away from my mouth and yell, "FUCK!" then put it back to my ear. His dad moves in again, and I nod. "Sorry, sorry." I attempt to settle my breathing and soften my tone. It takes everything I have left inside me. "No, you don't get to tell me what I can and cannot take. That's *my* decision when you tell me like you should have."

"You're right. Of course you're right. I'm sorry." He sounds so hurt, so broken. I can tell he's crying and it's breaking me in two.

I shake my head. "I can't do this."

He sniffs. "Wh-what?"

"Paul, don't." Huxley steps closer and puts her hand on my forearm, tears spilling down her cheeks.

I shrug her off. "I'm sorry this happened to you, Easton. I am. If I could take your disease away from you, I would. But you fucking lied. You kept that from me. I can't—"

"Who, who told you?" he whispers.

My mouth drops to the floor. *That's* what he's worried about? He's worried about who spilled his fucking secret? "Are you kidding me right now, Easton? What *told me* was when you had a *fucking seizure* because we've been doing too much this week for your body to handle. If you would have told me, we could have avoided this whole shit show."

"I'm sorry. I—"

"Maybe we'd be better off alone." I didn't mean to say it. I swear I didn't. It just came out. My mouth said it before my mind could think it through. "Shit, Easton, I—"

"I can't believe you just said that."

The line goes dead.

I try calling him back.

Nothing.

I try again.

Nothing.

I try again.

Straight to voicemail.

I stand there, flabbergasted by my behavior. Mutilated by my actions. Shook because of how we got here. And it's all my fault. I fucked up, but his message is clear.

"Let's go home," I say, voice breaking. Hands balled up at my sides, fingernails digging into my palm, drawing blood.

"Are you sure?" Huxley asks from behind me.

I hand her back her phone and nod. "Yeah. It's over."

Easton

I'M SCARED

"You not going to eat your cake?" Dad asks from across the table.

"Huh? Oh, sorry, yeah." I snap back to reality. Eyes jumping from my slice of red cake up to Dad's concerned gaze.

I'm sitting at the dining room table back home. It feels like forever ago that I was last here. The decor is the same as when I left, the same as when Mom left too. I think it's the last remnant of when things were good between them that Dad can't let go of, and I'm sort of glad he didn't.

"You okay?" Dad asks, and he does this little sigh at the end.

"Yeah," I lie, and I think they all know it. Even Boone's sitting in the corner, his little nut-brown eyes judging me.

Things just haven't been right since the beach.

It's not the seizure. I feel much better, and there's nothing really lingering from it. I wasn't even concussed from hitting my head. Everything cleared up the next morning, except the fact that it happened, which keeps running through my head alongside how much I don't deserve Paul. It scared the hell out of me. I didn't know what was happening, and then I couldn't control my body anymore. I can't even explain how it felt, the loss of control, it was…horrifying. I was totally helpless, and I'd put that on my friends.

"You know I can see right through all that, right?" Dad

smirks. "I'm sort of your old man."

"Me too." Sam raises her hand with a knowing glare.

"Yeah, yeah," I sigh. "I...I just feel stupid."

Dad cocks his head.

"Could've told you that years ago." Sam sticks out her tongue and pats Denver on the head. I think he likes her more than me now.

Dad gives her a look, but it lets me laugh a little. She might be older than me, but we're both children at heart when we're in the same room. Not sure that'll ever change, don't really want it to.

"Yeah." I shrug it off, trying to keep a smile on my face. "I mean, just being so helpless. It feels wrong. And I don't know if I can face Paul again after that."

"Face him?" Dad looks confused.

I feel dirty, so dirty.

He was so open to me. He told me his problems, the demons in his past and in his head. Paul bared his soul to me and did what he needed to make things right, to make them work, to help himself and to be there for me.

What did I do? I hid.

And what's worse? I knew I should tell him. I knew he'd find out one day, but I was scared. Now he knows, and I'm scared to face him. I made it all about me, and what I said on the phone...it was so stupid. He trusted me, but I couldn't trust him enough to tell him everything. I even told him he could trust me, that I'd be there for him no matter what. And I meant it. I did, but I wasn't willing to let him do the same.

And what he said on the phone, it was just...cruel. It felt like the old Paul. The man I remember before he opened up to me, when I couldn't stand him. That abrasive and mean person, but I also know him better than that. But does that mean I can excuse it, that it's okay?

I don't know.

And I don't want to be the boyfriend he has to worry about. If I'm honest, part of me wasn't sure he'd want me anymore if he knew. Who wants a partner you know probably isn't going to live as long as you, or you know is going to need extra help in the future?

I think I was wrong though. He keeps texting and trying to call, but I haven't answered yet. I just can't get myself to do it. This isn't how I wanted him to find out. It's not the way I wanted it to go, and now I'm mortified.

"Yeah. He didn't know that I'm...sick," I tell Dad and Sam. "He had no idea."

"Huh?" Sam nearly gasps.

Instead of answering, I shove my fork into the cake and take a bite. It's my favorite, red velvet. I focus on its sweetness a moment before answering. Mom used to make these for me before I came out, when she was actually a mom. Now Sam does.

"I hadn't told him yet." I sling my head back in self-disgust. "I know I should have. I know that now, but I just felt like he'd not want me anymore if he knew, you know? Like I'd be a burden."

"If he loves you, you won't be a burden, Easton," Dad says slowly.

"But that's how I *feel*."

The table goes quiet. There's no answer to that. It's something I have to deal with and I know it.

"Have you talked to him since...you know," Sam breaks the silence.

I shrug and shake my head.

"Why not?" She doesn't stop.

"I already said I feel stupid." I'm tired of talking about it. I just want to drop it. "And he doesn't deserve to be stuck with me. I'm fucked up."

"Language," Dad warns. He's not a stickler for language unless it's the big ones, but I should have known better.

"Sorry." I lower my head. Boone comes over and rears up, resting his paws on my knee. I rub his head and neck.

"Don't think like that, bud," he continues. "You're not...messed up. We all have problems. But that's what relationships are. You see past them to the person they are inside, to the person you need in your life. You're not your disease. You deserve to love and *be* loved, too, bud."

"I know." I don't look up. I know I should answer Paul's texts and calls, but I can't get myself to do it. Because he's proven what I knew all along. I don't deserve him.

Paul

I'M NOT HAVING FUN

"...and I just...don't remember what happened afterwards. I just kinda blacked out or something." I finish telling Dr. Orleen about everything that happened the past week. It took up most of my time with her, but I tried not to leave anything out. It's been over forty-eight hours since I said the words that have haunted me in my time away from Easton. And relaying them all back to the doc? Pure torture. I fucked up so badly. "I'm worried there's something wrong with me. Huxley has bipolar. Do..." I look down at my hands. "Do you think I do too?"

"I do not. Though I cannot talk about Huxley's condition, I can say that I am very familiar with Bipolar Type 2 Disorder and I do not think you fit into this box." She likes to talk about her damn boxes, that's for fucking sure. "However, I do believe you had a fit of rage or a rage blackout in which you experienced an extreme, almost primitive anger, followed by unconsciousness of the psyche. Some might try to classify it as Borderline Personality Disorder or even Intermittent Explosive Disorder. Neither of which do I think you have.

"Listen, Paul." She places her notebook and pen aside and takes off her glasses to lean forward in her chair. "You have been through a lot in your life and you have experienced more than most would in a lifetime within only a couple of decades of your short existence. And even still, you have been through so much these past few years, months, weeks. You met a boy, fell in love, and then felt lied to and betrayed. You are *not* broken, Paul. Even if you did have any of the previously mentioned disorders, you are *not* broken. Knowledge is power, and knowing and learning these things about yourself only aid in, as you've said, 'evolving into your best self.' I can see how much your actions are affecting you. Though we should not excuse your behavior, I think patience is key here. Patience and understanding, action and acceptance."

"Yeah." I nod vigorously. "Yeah, you're right. I just...feel so much shame for what I've done. What I've said. Even for the things that have happened to me that are out of my control. I feel like I'm going *insane* and I don't know how to stop it, let alone fucking control it."

I pause a moment while I fidget with my fingernails in my lap. I don't know how to put into words how I feel. I love words, but they escape me right now.

"I-I just... I've always felt so out of control, ya know, with my emotions... But I suppressed them. For years. Now that they're out for a stroll, they're running fucking rampant and I-I don't know what the *hell* I'm doing." I throw my head into my hands and double over. I'm not going to cry. I'm not. But this is all so hard, too much. "It's moments like these I wish I was a smoker or a drinker. Dealing with reality without a coping mechanism like this isn't fun. I'm not having fun," I mutter into my hands, then sit up. "Sorry. I'm being dramatic."

"Not dramatic, passionate," Dr. Orleen clarifies, leaning back.

"Yeah, I guess."

"Our time is almost up, but before you go I have three bits of homework for you. Firstly, I want you to do some research, Paul. I feel it will be important for you to learn and understand what angry means. Start with the basics and work your way up from there. There are many facets to anger in and of itself, but there are many ways to overcome and release it. In sessions to come we will explore those ways. For now, research."

She leans forward, her notepad abandoned.

"Secondly, I want you to think about making amends. You have expressed your love for Easton and Huxley, and I do believe, based on your analysis, they feel the same. As troubled as your past is, your future is a blank canvas waiting for your masterful artistry to grace it. You've expressed many times how important your relationship with your siblings is to you. Might I make a suggestion?"

I think I already know where this is going, but I don't say anything. I just nod.

"Go see your brother, Jace. No, I don't mean call or text or even Facetime. I mean go to Kansas City and speak with him face-to-face. It is my belief that such an act would bring you the results you've expressed that you desire.

"And lastly, write. Not journal entries, but *words*. Write about all your thoughts and feelings in as much detail as you can muster. Use the anxiety log we've spoken about in sessions past. Let your words flow from you however they may, however they see fit. Let yourself be a vessel to these words, and maybe, just maybe, you'll find they have a place together with your canvas. Think you can do those three things?"

I nod. "Yes. I'll try my best, yes."

Easton

JUST A DREAM

He texted. Again.

> **PAUL:** *i can't even begin to explain to you the remorse i feel for my words and my actions. i have some work to do to make it up to you, easton. and i want to. i don't know how, but i want to. i will*

> **PAUL:** *i saw dr. orleen yesterday. i'm trying, easton. i really am trying*

But I can't. I just can't get myself to respond. Instead I switch my read receipts off, take a deep breath, and turn my phone off.

The music is too loud in here. I know they're going for cool old bar by the lake vibe, but we're not at the beach, or a lake really. It's more a pond in the middle of University City across from campus. It's not that bad though. There's even a sidewalk tracing the edge of the pond that they try to call a boardwalk. The smell of beer mixes with the fish odor hanging in the air, but I keep hearing Paul's angry words repeating in my head.

Maybe we'd be better off alone.

"You good?" Aidan cranes his neck over the table.

I break from my stupor. "Oh yeah. I'm good."

"Look like you zoned out there for a minute," Cam says, slouched back against his chair.

I know it was an intervention, bringing me here, but I didn't fight it. It's best I don't stay in the dorm all day, cooped up in that tiny space, letting all my thoughts build up around me. Aidan didn't even give me a chance to allow it. The moment classes were over he dragged me from the dorm and we've been out ever since. First it was the mall over in Concord — he even let me stop in the western store to browse the boots, but I didn't get anything — then we met up with Cam and rode some electric go-karts. And now we're here at Boardwalk Billy's.

"Maybe." I shrug. "A little."

My phone buzzes on the table again, but I refuse to look at it. I know who it is. I close my eyes and take a breath.

"Are you just going to ignore him?" Aidan asks. "I mean I know you are, but why?"

"He's an asshole," I let it pour out of my mouth. It's not even a lie. He is. It just so happens that he's my favorite asshole, which is making this all really difficult.

"You know how Paul is, Easton." Aidan shakes his head and huffs. "Yeah, he shouldn't have blown up, but he's been through a lot too."

"I know, but..." I'm about to tell Aidan how I don't deserve Paul, how I messed up and wasn't truthful to him, but then it hits me. "Wait, you don't even like Paul."

Cam recoils like he's confused. "Yeah, I thought you hated —"

"Shut up, Cam." Aidan kicks him under the table and a small grin eclipses his face as his eyes lock on me. "We got off to a rocky start, and yeah he can be difficult...but..."

His words trail off and his mouth scrunches together while his eyes search me for what to say next.

"He's good for you." Aidan's entire body shakes and he sticks out his tongue like he's gagging. "I can't believe I just said that."

"Me neither," Cam laughs.

"But yeah, you two are good together." Aidan takes it a step further and it starts a smile on my face that I'm quick to wipe away.

"Are we? I didn't trust him. I thought I did. I really thought I did, but I hid my sickness from him. I hid it, like it would have changed something," I remind them. It's the big blight on our relationship, and it's on me. And as much as I want to talk to Paul, as much as I want to feel his hands cupping my back, and his cheek on mine, I can't. I can't do that to him. "He deserves someone who trusts him completely."

"You were scared though." It's Cameron, which I totally wasn't expecting. I like him and all, but usually he doesn't get involved in this, even when it's my Grindr "dates" that Aidan hates so much. "Yeah, you screwed up."

"Thanks." I glare at him, but it makes me laugh.

"You're welcome." Cam bows. "He screwed up too. We all do. I once tried to get some wine by getting in the back of some stranger's car with my BFF back home and got robbed. So yeah, we all screw up. But… Uh…"

"Were you going somewhere with that?" Aidan is eyeing Cam like he's insane.

"I think…" Cam skews his lips. "Oh yeah, that doesn't mean you give up though. No one's perfect, East. But you clearly care about him. Otherwise you would've already moved on, ya know?"

"So you're saying you got in strangers' cars again for wine after that?" I scrunch my brow and, for a moment, forget about all the shit that's happening to me.

"No." Cam laughs. "Of course not."

"So basically that part didn't apply at all." Aidan lifts his eyebrows and grins at me as if to say *I don't know this person.* "But still, he does have a point. You can't just say I effed up, so now it's over. You care about him, and he obviously cares about you. I mean you showed me the texts."

I huff and nod. Maybe they're right. Maybe they are. But I

don't think I can do that. I'll just hurt him again. Or me.

But still, I pick up my phone and excuse myself to go to the bathroom. I was right, it was him. And...I think he wrote me a poem.

PAUL: i called you thrice,

staring at my broken face in the bathroom mirror

as the tears that rolled down my cheeks

shattered the bowl of my porcelain sink

from the weight of my heavy heart.

but it's nothing...

...to keep on playing the music loudly in the back of your mind,

avoiding what you know.

avoiding me to cause a scene, to cause a scene in my dreams

of a story that once was, that will never be

again...left with my thoughts.

no. no, please

confront me, babe,

confront us, babe,

so we can be together again, babe.

my mouth is always running...away from the thought that initiated this very moment,

the very moment you were gone,

gone from me like the light of the sea when the sun set in your eyes

the very moment i was alone...

...and here I am suffering as if i'm confused about how i feel about life, yet i know exactly how i feel about you.

from watching raindrops in my dreams to catching them on the sheets of my cold and empty bed as tears spill out,

out of...time.

that one time where you once begged me to lay my head next to you

has me tormented in the center of the earth's calmest

hurricane.

> *i should have cherished it more*
> *now that you're gone,*
> *which is ironic because i have destroyed everything about us in*
one swift blow
> *cause what i did to you was vicious.*
> *as i try to be strong, every item that glistens in the sun on the*
sea
> *reminds me of what we were supposed to become.*
> *ashes in the burning sands*
> *glass between my hands*
> *and i am swirling red wine that tastes like the blood of my lost*
love story because...
> *because i didn't understand.*
> *i had high hopes for us.*
> *whispering your name thrice in my sleep,*
> *staring at my broken face in the bathroom mirror*
> *as the tears that rolled down my cheeks*
> *shattered the bowl of my porcelain sink*
> *from the weight of my heavy heart.*
> *but it's nothing...*
> *because our love story was only in our dreams.*
> *PAUL: easton, please don't let our love story be only in my*
dreams.

I brace my head against the wall in the bathroom stall and breathe away the tears. Fuck me. I don't want him to be just a dream, a thing of my past. But what else can it be?

Paul

FUCKING MONSTER

The last time I stepped foot in Missouri was the day after classes ended this past December, four months ago. I packed everything I owned into my car and hightailed it out, never looking back. So returning here to the source of all the pain and anguish I've been through hasn't exactly put me in the best headspace. I've been antsy all day and I can't sit still. Huxley stopped asking what was wrong hours ago. I think she gets it; she gets me. She's been such a good friend as I've tried to keep my mind from spiraling.

When I brought this whole trip idea up to her she was reluctant at first. She said I might be making a rash decision, but when I told her I needed my family with me, she was on board. I thank God for her and Easton and Dr. Orleen because I would not be able to do any of this without them. Even if Easton won't answer any of my texts right now. He's the whole reason I'm even doing this, and although I'm nervous, I'm grateful to him.

Easton thinks he doesn't deserve me, I'm sure of it, but…it's I who don't deserve him. I've been awful, and it's time I cut my own bullshit. I just gotta do the work, right? I gotta work this shit out with my family in order to heal, in order to move on, right?

Jace still hasn't responded, but I think he forgot that I can see his location on SnapChat. I haven't really needed to check it until now though. He's going to be pissed when we just show up tomorrow. He'll get over it because I'm not leaving this fucking state without fixing this shit. He's my brother and used to be my best friend. I need him and I miss him and the rest of my siblings, but I'm starting with him.

Oh God, please give me strength to deal with this bullshit.

We've been in Kansas City for about an hour now and we are walking around the Country Club Plaza — it's like a high-end outdoor shopping and restaurant area — while I show her all the amazing fountains scattered throughout. Maybe we'll do some shopping. I don't know, anything to take my mind off the endless possibilities that tomorrow could bring.

"Ya know, Kansas City has more than 200 fountains both big and small. The art and architecture of it all is why I loved growing up here. The Midwest sucks, but KCMO is really pretty. Just wait until we go to the Nelson-Atkins Museum."

"Oh yay! I love a good museum." Huxley morphs into London Tipton again.

"Actually let's head there now and then we can grab some — " But I stop short because my phone just went off. It could be Jace. It could be Easton.

But it's just Instagram. Shit.

I've texted Jace nearly ten times and nothing. I texted Easton more than that. I don't care if I look like a bitch, I want my man back. I want my brother back too and I'll do whatever I gotta do to make it happen. Jace honestly can't be that pissed at me, but then again, I wouldn't know because I left and he never responded. I shoot off another text.

"Nothing?" Huxley asks, squeezing my arm and snapping me out of my head before I spiral again.

I pocket my phone. "Nah. Nothing. He's still at his house though. Not too far from here actually," I say, leading us down the sidewalk.

"What the hell *are* you gonna do about that, anyway? Just

show up and hope it's all brotherly love and Care Bear rainbows?" Huxley asks.

"Uh, yes?" I shrug. "That's all I've got."

"You sure? You don't sound too sure, bestie."

"I don't know, Huxley. I mean I know I left, but other than that, I can't think of any other reason for him to be mad at me. He's..." I stop to consider it. "He's my brother, my best friend. I never meant to leave him or any of them behind."

"I know, babe. But you gotta prepare yourself for anything. Just know that there's a possibility he's gonna slam the door in your face and call the cops or something. I don't know." Huxley Davenport, everyone! Ever the optimist, Giver of Pep Talks.

I roll my eyes. "Yeah, I know. But I gotta try."

"And E?"

I can't even speak on that one, so I just shake my head and change topics. "We're almost there."

We cross the street and veer left to a small pathway. A sign that says *Nelson-Atkins Museum* greets us as we walk under a copse of trees. The small path opens up to a much larger path lined perfectly with more trees, but we don't go that way. I want her to take it in all its glory. I lead her forward until we hit the lawn. Huxley's jaw drops.

The main lawn is at *least* a quarter mile long as it leads up the hill to a large building reminiscent of the Lincoln Memorial, only bigger. Its massive pillars replicate etchings from some ancient world long since passed. Scattered throughout the lawn are giant-sized badminton birdie sculptures.

"Holy *shit!*" Huxley says.

"Toldja," I say.

We walk around the museum grounds looking at all the sculptures. Huxley looks right at home with all the art. It's kinda precious.

"Is that a labyrinth?!" Huxley scrunches her eyes.

"Yep—"

"Come on! Let's go!" Huxley grabs my hand and pulls me along like a little kid in a candy store.

"Okay, okay." I belly laugh.

We go through the all-glass labyrinth twice, and then race each other out of the entrance. Huxley pushes me into the grass and jumps on top of me and we roll around and land on our backs. My head on her stomach as we laugh like kids on the playground.

Once we sober slightly, we lie there looking up at the cloudless sky.

"Thanks for coming with me. It's weird being back, but I'm glad you're here with me."

"It's cool to see your world," Huxley says. "Well, your world before me. And Easton because we both know eventually you're going to get back together. *We're* your world now, bitch," Huxley states.

"Wouldn't have it any other way."

We're quiet for a moment.

"I used to spend a lot of time here studying for classes. I would lay a blanket next to one of the birdie statues and spend my afternoons reading or contemplating how to deal with my parents. My dad was…awful. But he still paid for everything and gave me a monthly allowance. I didn't know how I could ever get out from under his thumb. My mom didn't do shit, like, literally nothing. And that is just as bad to me."

"Do you think she knew?" Huxley asks.

"Not at first, no. But there was no way she didn't eventually. How she stayed with that fucking monster, I'll never know."

"I'm sorry, babe."

"It's okay." I reach up and twirl my fingers around Huxley's curls. "I'll never be able to repay you for your help, Hux."

"It's not necessary, Paul. I want what's best for you—

Wait…" Huxley props herself up on her elbow and looks at me in bewilderment. "You just called me Hux! You never use nicknames."

"Guess that means you're kinda growing on me then."

Huxley hits me and lays back down. "'Bout fucking time." Then she falls silent for a moment. "Devina and I broke up."

I bolt upright.

"Wait, what? Why?"

Huxley sits up too and shrugs. "We just wanted different things. Mostly I wasn't in love with her. So we ended it."

"Oh shit, Hux. I'm sorry!" I say.

"It's okay. I promise I'm okay. It's for the best."

"Okay. If you say so." I move to pull her in for a hug. "But you know you can always talk to me."

"Yeah, I know—"

"Paul?"

I snap my head around as I let Huxley go to see who just called me. The only other people who know me in Kansas City are…

"Holy shit, Jace!" I can't believe we ran into him. I thought he was still at his place, last I checked. But I guess it's been a minute since I did, and *whoa* he's changed. He's still his skinny self, but it looks like he has more of a runner's body now. He's wearing running clothes, so he obviously is…well, on a run. His hair is grown out and he has it up in a bun, doesn't have his beard anymore, and he's really tan. We used to look almost exactly alike. Not anymore since I've beefed up. Same eyes though. We've always had the same eyes.

"What the flying fuck are you doing here, Paul? I thought you left!" Jace takes out his AirPods and puts them away.

"Well, shit. Good to see you too, asshole."

"Oh, *I'm* the asshole? Fuck you very much, shithead. Go back to wherever the hell you came from," Jace says with a dismissive wave of his hand, then puts his AirPods back in his ear. He's not running away from this shit even if I wasn't planning on doing this today. I thought I'd have more time, but whatever. Let's get into it, I'm feeling like Petty Betty.

"Technically, I'm from here." I chase after him.

"Fuck you," Jace yells back.

"What the fuck is your problem, dude?" I put my hand on his shoulder and pull him around to face me. He scowls at me, takes out his AirPods again and pockets them. "Look," I continue, "I'm sorry I left, but I had to get out of here. You don't know what *really* happened."

He looks taken aback. I know that look in his eye and whatever he's about to say is gonna be some shit. I brace myself.

"He started drinking again. Only it was worse because he...he hit them. He hit Dani and Felix during his worst moments. But if we're *truth-telling*, you wouldn't have known even if you were here because you left long before leaving Missouri, you selfish-ass bitch." Jace's voice goes softer, but the hurt pours out. "And you weren't here to help me get them out of that shit. A lot has happened in the past eight months, Paul. Fuck you for thinking you were special enough to—"

No, no, no. This can't be happening. I wasn't expecting all that. I had no idea. I've done nothing but text him constantly, trying to get him to talk to me. He could have told me!

"I left because I confronted Mom about what Dad did to me. He didn't just molest me, dude. It was so much worse than you know. So yeah, I was dealing with my own shit, bro! I texted you so many times, but *you* never respond! So how the *hell* was I supposed to—"

"YOU FUCKING WOULDN'T BECAUSE YOU LEFT!"

"Okay, okay. I think we need to take this somewhere else. People are looking," Huxley says, stepping between us and holding up a placating hand. I didn't realize how close we were until that moment. We're literally screaming in each other's faces.

"Who the fuck are you?" Jace swipes her hand away a little too violently.

I step forward into his space again and grunt through gritted teeth, "Touch her again and I'll fuck you up, I swear on my life, dude."

We stare each other down for what feels like an hour before Jace finally relents. He rounds on Huxley as his attitude deflates, and smiles weakly. "My apologies, ma'am."

"Ew," is all Huxley says.

I snap my fingers in his face, getting his attention. "*By the way*, I'm not done with you yet, Jace."

"You wanna do this now?" His focus returns to me. "Fine. We can do this now. I don't live far and I don't have to get Felix and Dani until three."

"Wait, why…why are you picking them up?"

He just stares at me.

"Do they live with you?"

"Yeah, dipshit. I couldn't leave them with Mom and Dad, so I brought them to live with me. I literally just goddamn said I got them out. Good to know you still don't listen to shit I say."

Jace checks his Apple Watch and I spare a glance at Huxley. Huxley's eyes go wide as she shrugs.

Jace finishes what he's doing and looks up. He rolls his eyes and storms off. Guess I forgot dramatic flare runs in the family.

He stops, looks up to the sky with his hands on his hips then turns back. "Coming? We don't live that far from here."

* * *

"So, you've been living in North Carolina this whole time?"

"Yep, pretty much." I nod.

I explained everything to him. Literally everything from my

sexual assaults and therapy to me and Easton to school and work. I must say that, as pissed as he was, it didn't take long for us to fall back into being brothers again. Just a quick little fight and make-up sesh. And oh my holy hell did I miss him.

He points between Huxley and me. "And y'all are roommates?"

"And BFFs, but yes," Huxley unnecessarily chimes in.

I roll my eyes.

"Well, it's nice to officially meet you, Huxley." He holds out his hand over the kitchen island. Huxley takes it...sheepishly? I've never seen her do anything *sheepishly* since I've known her. What is she doing? "Sorry you had to catch me in the middle of my run."

"No apologies necessary," she says, blushing a shade I've never seen on her either. Guess her "ew" comment earlier no longer stands. And OMG they're still holding hands.

"What the hell is going on here?"

Jace drops his hand and addresses me, his eyes never leaving Huxley's. "Just being friendly, baby bro." He turns to me and smiles.

"I hate everything." I huff and toss my head back and blink up at the ceiling. I run my hands down my face. "*Anyway*, when did you go back for Felix and Dani?" I ask. Dani is our little sister, she's fourteen. Felix is the baby, he's eight. "I'm honestly shocked Mom and Dad let you take them."

"It wasn't much of a fight. There was a lot of yelling on their parts, that's for fucking sure, but I told them exactly how I would call the cops and tell them all about what Dad has done to three out of his five children if they tried to stop me. I told Mom everything in front of Dad, actually. Dad was pissed. He ran and locked himself in their bedroom. Mom cried and went to the kitchen. I for real wanted to burn the house down with them in it. They just...gave up." He shrugs. "So I packed up the kids and left. They haven't seen them since."

"Fucking *hell*, Jace. I'm so sorry. But you shoulda told me."

"And what? You woulda come back? Ha, doubtful." He pulls an apple out of the fridge.

"Fuck you. I may hate Mom and Dad, but I care about y'all. I've been nothing but worried since I left. And leaving wasn't exactly easy either. You're my damn family, Jace."

"It is what it is, Paulie." He shrugs and I wince, but he doesn't notice. Dr. Orleen has helped me a lot, but that nickname still stings. Huxley looks at me. I breathe deeply and I look at the floor, picking at my fingernails. She places her hand on my forearm, grounding me.

How can he be so pissed and still just brush this shit off like it's not a big deal when all it is is a big deal to me? It's been on repeat in my mind as much as I've had *Schitt's Creek* on repeat. Maybe I've just been making too big a deal out of it? Maybe it's not as bad as I made it out to be? Or maybe Jace is avoiding and deflecting and gaslighting. I'll fuck him up if he is.

But he's not even paying attention to us, so maybe not? He finishes off his water bottle and grabs a knife to cut up his apple.

"Where y'all staying?" Jace asks in between bites.

"Crossroads Hotel."

"Nah. Save your money. Stay here. Someone can stay in Felix's room. He can sleep in my room, and someone else can sleep on the pullout."

"Fab! I'll take the bedroom." Huxley claps.

"Guess that means I'm taking the sofa." I narrow my eyes at Huxley even though I'm smiling. I'm honestly so glad she's here. Even if she's flirting with my brother, she's smiling right back.

"Okay, listen, I need to go get the kids. Y'all make yourselves comfortable, or do y'all need a ride back to the hotel to hand in your keys?"

"Wait, that's it? All's forgiven?"

"Not entirely. You still need to get past Dani. She's the most pissed. Felix will be happy to see you though." Jace looks down and gives a considerate grin. "He asks about you all the time. Trevor is in Denver working for some tech company. He doesn't really know about all of this."

"And you?"

"I'm still pissed at you, dude, but I get it. I was just mad my..." He pauses and huffs. "I'm hurt you left me to deal with all this shit alone. Trevor's been gone, and I may be older, but not by much. I coulda used your help, bro. But really, I get it. We actually have a good life here now. They've both been through hell. We all have, and things were hard at first, but the kids are happy and safe and that's all I care about. And you seem happy. Even if you're a dickwad for saying what you said to your boyfriend. Anyway, yeah, we're good."

I breathe a sigh of relief. "That was easier than I thought, actually."

"Like I said, you gotta get past Dani. Raising a teenager is the worst, dude. My condolences in advance."

Huxley leans forward against the kitchen island on her elbows, chin in her hands. "So tell us, Jace. What is it that you do?"

Oh, for fuck's sake.

Easton

DO I?

The red glow of the streetlight is blurred by the droplets tracing paths down my windshield before the wipers sweep the water away and it clears. I'm not even sure where I'm at exactly. I don't care. I just want to be alone.

But I also don't want to be alone.

It doesn't make any sense, but what about life does? It sure isn't fair, that's for certain. I wish it was, but it isn't. That doesn't stop me from envying those who know what they want and go after it. The type of person who sees potential, even in themselves, and reaches for it. Who doesn't allow those voices in their head to pull them backward. The type of person who doesn't let their body, no matter how broken, have the last say.

How do they do it?

The light changes and I press the accelerator. Rain pelts the glass harder as I take off down a tiny street between old buildings and powerlines. The clouds seem low, casting an oppressive dullness over me, releasing my tears.

I swear that every time I get anywhere close to happiness, anywhere near feeling worth someone else's gaze, I do something that proves that side of my brain I hate right. I don't want it to be right, but it is. It's like I'm hardwired to make life difficult, to make the wrong choices, to hurt people and to be hurt. I have to stop doing that to people, but does that mean there will always be something missing inside me?

I know what I want, what I need to fill that space, but I can't. How's the saying go? "If you love someone let them go," right? Well, I love him. I've loved him for a long time I think. I just haven't had the courage to admit it to myself, never mind tell him. And now I never will. I've ignored him for days now. I've been cruel. I've let him pour his heart out and left it to sit in the digital eternity of my phone. I can't fix that now. It's too late. I don't...

My music from the playlist he sent me dims and my phone rings. I glance down quick enough to see who's calling. It's Samantha. I reject the call, again. I don't want to talk about it. I know she's going to bring *him* up. I just can't do it right now.

Instead I take the next right onto a road that looks sort of familiar, but I'm not sure why. I don't come this way often and I'm still not certain where I'm at. I just don't want to be at the dorm, and I need to avoid campus. The last thing I need is to run into *him*, so a run wasn't an option even if it weren't raining. And I don't want to bother Aidan with all my moping. He's dealt with it enough, like a champ actually, but he deserves a break...from me. Hell, I wish *I* could take a break from me.

How I wish I could jump back ten years. To that time when I wasn't sick, when boys were the last thing on my mind...and I had a mom. To that time when I just lived. Back when things were simple and a smile didn't need a reason. Why did I ever want to grow up?

Wait. I know why this road looks familiar.

Trees cross overhead and old mill houses pass by on the right. I squint through the rain trailing my windows. I can see the brick buildings coming up on the left and then the cute little white coffee shop. The same one I took Paul to for trivia.

A smile cracks the downward turn of my lips as flashes of

that evening play like a movie in my mind. The excitement in his eyes when the *Schitt's Creek* round started. The way I lit up when he held my hand. The smell of his body—leather and sage—and taste of his lips when he kissed me in the car. The smile on his face.

I want him so badly. But I don't deserve him.

Do I?

Paul

FAMILY

LILY: Heard you're back in town. Want new ink?
    PAUL: wtf! how did you know that?
    PAUL: i've been here for, like, three hours
    LILY: I have sources.
    PAUL: i'm gonna kill him
    LILY: So???
    PAUL: free this evening?
    LILY: 10pm. After close.
    PAUL: bet

* * *

Oh my holy *shit*, I'm so nervous. Jace is one thing, but Dani *and* Felix. Gah, I've been such an awful brother to them. This is my chance, though, to make it up to them and create a relationship void of the monsters that are our parents.

Here goes everything.

I knock on the door.

"Maybe it's too early for dinner. Maybe we should have waited." I'm freaking out. Literally freaking the fuck out.

Huxley's beside me, on her phone, completely unbothered and obviously not paying attention to me being on the verge of a meltdown.

We hung out at the hotel lobby for an hour so Huxley could "freshen up" in the bathroom under the guise of wanting to give Jace enough time to pick up the kids, and then took an Uber here. I've almost thought I was going to vomit three, no, seven times. Well, I guess now eight.

"Paul, you're freaking out. It'll be *fine*."

"Oh fuck me. Fuck *me*."

Jace opens the door and Huxley sings, "G'eveniiiiing," though she's soon interrupted by a childish screech.

"PAUL! Paul, Paul, Paul!" Felix yells from the living room and runs into my arms the second I cross the threshold. "Paul, you're here! I missed you so much!"

"Hey there, buddy! I missed you too." I pick him up in my arms and spin him around. Holy shit he's gotten big. When did that happen? I mean, he's eight, so he's not a baby, but he's always been small for his age. Now he's up to my chest. His hair is really curly on top but shaved on the sides and he shares my freckles. "How ya been?"

"Good! My new school is so awesome! I've made so many friends, but I only have two best friends. Hayley and Bruno. They're my favorite people in the *whole* world. Well, except for you and Jace and Dani and Trevor! Oh, and I won first prize on my science experiment. I really like science! Want to see?"

"Hell yeah, dude. Show me."

"Maybe later, Felix. We gotta get to dinner, remember?" Dani comes up behind him and messes up his hair.

"Oh yeah. Sorry. Later, okay, Paul?"

I smile and mess up his hair again. "Yeah, buddy. Later." I look up at Dani and holy shit she's grown up so much too. I'm immediately wary because I know exactly what's about to happen. I could fight her on this, but instead, I decide on diplomacy. "Hey, Dani."

"Hey, Paul. It's good to see you."

Dani looks like the rest of us, but more…average? Not that there's anything wrong with that. She just doesn't look like she cares much about her appearance. It's kinda refreshing. Her dark hair is up in a high pony that would make Ariana proud. She's in ripped denim, Converse, and a crop top. "You too, sis. Listen, I'm sorry I—"

"It's chill, Paulie. Don't stress it. It's not your fault Mom and Dad are bitches."

"Hey! Language!" Jace scolds her, coming out of his bedroom.

"What? They are."

"Yeah, they're assholes. But so was I." I pull her into a hug, and she lets me. "I didn't know Dad would start drinking again and…do what he did."

Dani gives me a half-assed hug, then steps back and puts her hands in her back pockets, looking at her feet. "No one knew. It's fine. Just leave it alone, please."

Fuck she's going to need therapy. I'll have to talk to Jace about that before we leave. Maybe she could do something virtual with Dr. Orleen.

Dani looks back up at me and smiles, then plops herself back on the couch with her Nintendo Switch.

I blink away my shookethness.

"Damn, that's it? I thought you were gonna rake his ass over the coals!" Jace says.

Dani shrugs. "Thought about it, but I'm hungry. And I wanna finish this level before we go."

"Teenagers." Jace rolls his eyes. "I was looking forward to that."

Speaking of *Jace*, I roll my eyes too. "Since when are you and Lily BFFs?" I round on him.

Jace bursts out laughing and grabs a bottle of water out of the fridge. "Figured she'd text you. We dated for a couple weeks a while back. Didn't work out, but we stayed friends. She keeps trying to 'ink me'" — he uses air quotes — "but I keep telling her no. Then she asked what I was doing tonight and I mentioned you're here, and she tried again. Not happening, dude."

Huxley clears her throat behind me and I look back.

"Dani, Felix, I want you to meet someone very special to me. This is my best friend in the whole wide world, Huxley. Huxley, this is my little sister and brother, Dani and Felix."

"Hi, Huxley!" Felix runs into her arms, going for a bear hug.

"Hey. Jace told us all about you, Hux," Dani says without looking away from her game. She even went in for the nickname.

"You did?" I turn to face Jace with Felix's arms still wrapped around Huxley like he doesn't want to let go.

Jace puts up his hands in surrender and leans back against the counter. "Listen, these two ask a lot of questions! Especially Felix after I told him you were here."

"Yeah," Felix chimes in and looks up at Huxley. "So you're my brother's BFF?"

"Hell yeah! The best of friends."

"Not his girlfriend?" he asks, confused.

Huxley bursts out laughing then sobers immediately. "No, sweetie. Your brother has a boyfriend."

"Is he here? I want to meet him!"

I wish he was here, and I can only hope he'll still be my boyfriend after all this. "No, buddy, he's not. He's back in North Carolina where we live."

"Oh. Okay." He finally lets go of Huxley and comes over to me. "Do you love him?"

And oh how that makes me smile. "I do. Very much."

"I want a boyfriend, but Jace won't let me."

My eyes go wide and I look at Jace. He shrugs with a smirk, drinking his water.

"You do?" I ask him.

"Yep! Girls are fine, like a friend. Like you and Huxley! But boys are *so* much cuter." He drags out the so and he's so damn proud of it. I envy him. I didn't have that when I was growing up. The light in his eyes is enough to regenerate my cold gay heart. I hope he never loses that.

"Hey, what did we say about dating though?" Jace interjects. Ever the authoritative figure.

Felix's face drops, then he rolls his eyes. "Not until I'm fifteen. I know, I know." He throws himself onto the couch next to Dani to watch her play her game. Guess the conversation is over then.

I chuckle, watching them. There's a bit of an awkward silence because I'm not sure what to do. Then Jace grabs his keys. "Who's ready for dinner?"

"Me," we all say in a united chorus.

* * *

After dinner, we settle into the living room to play board games. Dani is kicking all of our asses, Felix is so happy and hyper and won't stop touching me or sitting in my lap, but I don't mind. Jace and Huxley keep making eyes at each other and I already know where her mind is at. His too. Good thing they're sleeping in separate rooms. I've been pretty quiet all evening as I soak in what little time we have together before Hux and I leave tomorrow afternoon.

We play two rounds of Monopoly — Dani won once, Felix and I the other — before I leave to meet up with Lily. I figured Huxley would come with me, but she decided to stay and hang out after Felix begged her to play *Super Mario Kart* with him.

Jace let me borrow his car and it's nice as shit. He works remotely for some company doing coding or whatever. I didn't really pay attention when he was telling us about it. He and Trevor were always into tech stuff.

I park his car on the street and meet Lily at the door. She locks it behind us and flips the sign to "Closed".

I pull her into a hug. "It's so good to see you, girl!"

She smiles and smacks my chest when we separate. "You betta not got more tats since you left. I'm still pissed you got one wi'out me, bitch." She scoffs and leads us back to her booth.

"It was just one. Calm down. You're lucky I haven't gotten more since I've been gone."

"I'll Liam Neeson yo' ass so fast if you eva do. You're my work of art…in progress." She winks.

I just laugh. She's wild, but I wouldn't put it past her.

"So, wha'll it be? Finally gon' let me do tha' ches' piece I been dyin' for? Or another sleeve?"

"Ha." I chuckle. "Hell no."

"So then wha'?" She starts cleaning her gun and switching out the needle. "Wha' an' where?"

My heart beats harder as I say, "I was thinking a rose."

"You an' your damn flowers."

"Hey, I'm delicate and sensitive like a flower, okay?"

"Tha's fo' damn sure." Lily takes out her black ink. "An' where?"

I show her and she motions for me to sit while she draws it up.

I sit back in the tattoo chair with my arms above my head for a pillow. "Roses are red, violets are blue…"

"Shu' the fuck up or Imma stick-'n'-poke you," Lily finishes my poem.

I burst out laughing! I will never get a stick-and-poke. Nope.

Lily swivels around in her chair to show me the drawing and places it in position on my hand. I like it. I really, really like it. And I think Easton will too, if he'll see me again. "I love it."

"Dope."

"Fuck this is going to hurt." I breathe. "Okay, okay. Let's do it!" I hype myself up as Lily gets to work.

Paul

BYE, PAULIE

It's three p.m. and we're at the airport and I'm not ready to say goodbye. These past two days have flown by. Huxley bid her farewells and went to get us checked in so that I could have some time with Jace, Dani, and Felix.

"Well, I guess this is it," Jace says like he's the patriarch of the family, ushering his child off to college. It's not far off, I guess.

I don't know what to say. I don't know how to do this. I wish I could stay, but my life isn't here anymore. "Yeah, it's—"

"I promise I'll respond this time," Jace interrupts me eagerly. He clears his throat. "We should Facetime on Sundays. Make it a thing."

Damn it all to hell, I'm *not* going to cry. "I'd love that."

Felix wraps his arms around my waist and squeezes as hard as he can. "I'm going to miss you, big brother."

Okay, maybe I am going to cry. "Imma miss you too, little squirt." My voice hitches.

"Yeah. Bye, Paul. It was really good of you to come." Dani drops her gaze and wipes at her face. I grab her shoulder and pull her into me. This time, she clings on for dear life.

"Thanks for coming. Thanks for trying," Jace says. Looking everywhere else except at me.

"You're family. You don't have to thank me." After Dani releases me, I hug Jace tight. He sniffs and I pull away to address

Felix. I kneel down so he's above me. "Hey, buddy. Maybe we could talk Jacey Poo into making a trip over to North Carolina to visit, huh? You can come too, Dani. I'd love to have you all there."

"I'm actually going to be spending the summer with Trevor. Sorry."

"It's okay." And I stand and hug her again. "That'll be good for you."

"Yes, yes, yes!" Felix's face lights up like a Christmas tree while he jumps around. He turns from me to Jace. "Oh please, Jace! Can we?"

"Once school is out and after Dani leaves, you betcha." He looks at the window where Huxley is standing, pretending not to watch.

"Maybe for Pride?" I offer. "Would be cool to take my baby brother to his first Pride."

"What's Pride?" Felix's face scrunches up and I chuckle.

"We'll talk about that later, but I think that's a great idea. I'll work out the details with Huxley," Jace says. Though that last part is unnecessary. Why can't he work them out with *me*?

I shake my head, but I'm smiling. Apparently smiling is my new thing. Good thing for braces and whitening strips. "I cannot even believe you two. You *had* to move in on my best friend?" I punch his shoulder playfully.

He shrugs, his face flush. "When ya know, ya know. Ya know?"

"I hate you."

"Love you too, brother."

"Yeah, whatever. Love you, man." I ruffle Felix's hair. He hates it. It's funny. "Take care of yourself."

"You too. Bye, Paul," Jace says.

"Bye. Love you," Dani says.

"Bye, Paulie," Felix says.

"Bye. Love y'all," I say. I turn and make the hardest walk of my life.

Paulie. Huh…it sounds nice coming from Felix.

Easton

DOES THAT CHANGE ANYTHING?

PAUL: g'morning

PAUL: no, you're not going to fucking ghost me, easton. i won't accept that, you incomprehensible fucking fucktrumpet bastard. that's not how our story ends!

PAUL: i'm sorry for calling you names

PAUL: you're everyfuckingthing to me, easton! EVERYTHING. you light the world just by your very existence. and i...i need you

PAUL: babe, please talk to me

His texts are killing me. He won't stop. I need him to just stop. I need him to give up. He thinks I'm someone worth being with, but I'm not, and he'll be better off when he realizes that.

"Him again?" Aidan asks.

"What gave it away?" I huff and let my hand and phone flop dramatically to my bed.

"Wild guess," Aidan giggles. I wish I felt like giggling. "You want Chinese?"

It's the most random thing, and before I can rebound, Aidan starts talking again.

"He still writing you poems? Ty never writes me poems. Actually, I'm not sure I want him to."

I'm lying on my bed facing away from him, and I tilt my head back to see him. He's sitting cross-legged on his bed as he rambles. I manage a laugh. I'm pretty sure he's being sarcastic.

"You don't want him to?" I scrunch my brow.

"I've helped him with enough papers to know better." Aidan smiles at me.

"And no," I finally answer his question.

"Huh?"

"No, he hasn't sent any more poems." I deflate a little.

It's the war in my head. The battle that wages in my chest where I'm poised as both aggressor and defender. I want him to stop. I want him to see that I'm not worth it and that he should leave me alone and let me go. I want him to stop texting and saying all the beautiful, often "fuck"-laced things that weaken my heart's defenses.

But I also don't.

I don't want him to stop texting. I don't want him to stop saying the things that light up the black spots in my chest. Why does this have to be so damn hard?

"Ah," Aidan says before throwing his feet off the edge of the bed and letting them dangle freely. "You want to talk about it?"

"About what?" I give him a crazy look. He hates—or well, hated, or maybe still does actually—Paul.

"About Paul. I know, the two of us haven't been each other's biggest fans." He rolls his eyes and grins. "But you're my friend, and your stupid ass is obsessed with him whether I like it or not. Ugh, you're such a bottom—"

"And you're not?" A massive smile shoots across my face. The look I get back says he knows exactly what he's doing. He got the smile he wanted, and yeah, it feels good to smile.

"Not the point. This isn't about me. This is about you." Aidan laughs. "So…wanna talk?"

I consider Aidan's proposal for a moment. He's my best friend. I know I can talk to him. I really do, but I don't know. I just don't want to talk about it right now. If I could get Paul out of my mind, if I could forget even for a second that he exists, I would choose not to even think about him right now, but that doesn't seem to be an option.

"Nah." I shrug. It's in that exact moment that I want to, that I want to tell him how badly I miss Paul, how much I want to just sit next to him and hear him talk about some big crazily cool thing in that way only he does, how I hate myself for not telling him earlier that I was sick, how selfish I was, and how much I want to answer Paul's texts. But I don't. I just...can't. Saying it all out loud would be worse.

He looks at me for a second, seeming to analyze me, to look into my mind if he could, before saying a word.

"You sure?" Aidan asks.

"Ye..." I stop. Why do I stop? Now he'll definitely not let it go. But I guess I don't really want him to either.

"You know," Aidan sighs. "Believe it or not Ty and I didn't just end up together and everything was rainbows and unicorns. We almost didn't make it, and looking back, that would have sucked."

"I know." I roll my eyes and turn over to see him. I've heard their story. It's what movies are made of, I swear, but it's not the time.

"Of course you know. I'm not telling it again. I'm just saying, sometimes we mess up, and maybe you messed up?" Aidan's staring me right in the eye.

"Well thank you for the *subtle* advice." I huff and throw my hands back on the bed. Why does he have to be right? For a solid minute I don't know what to say. My mind is blasting with all the ways I want Paul and all the reasons I don't deserve him. But finally I take control.

"I love him," I blurt out. I haven't said that out loud before. It feels good, right? But somehow scary too. Shit, it's so scary.

"I know you do, East." Aidan grins.

"I...want to be with him, but I feel like I messed things up too badly for us to..." I look at the floor and shrug, "ya know, work anymore."

"But you love him."

He's right. But does that change anything? I guess...it could.

"I do," I reply.

"So go be with him! Talk to him. Do anything! You can't know unless you work it out. Together. He's shown you that he still loves you. It's your turn. Don't wait too long before you actually do lose him. Okay?"

I grin and nod. He's not wrong.

"Now, do you want Chinese or not?" Aidan gets up. "I'm calling it in."

"Yeah. My usual."

ONE LAST TRY

Today is April 14, Easton's twentieth birthday. Today is also the day I'm going to win him back. And I have a plan. It's a good plan…I think.

The walk down Easton's hall feels like some *American Horror Story: Hotel* type shit. There's no one around. No sound coming from anyone's room. I've been here a million times, but I've never noticed that there are no windows to let the daylight in and I swear the shitty fluorescents are playing tricks on my mind.

I thought this was a good idea, but now I'm second-guessing everything. I don't even know if he's here right now. I mean, I have his schedule memorized, but he could be out running or eating or working. Shit, he could be working. He might not even be in town. Or his dad is in town and they're out shopping or something for his birthday. I don't know. Holy shit, he could be sleeping and I'm going to wake him up with my stupid antics and he's going to be pissed off *even more* and it's all over.

Oh God. Please help me.

After putting one foot in front of the other—I don't even remember putting on shoes, oh fuck, how did I get here?—I somehow end up in front of Easton's door, food, drinks, and gift in hand.

Here goes everything.

I pull up Apple Music on my phone, find "This I Promise You" by *NSYNC, and...press...play.

The music is quiet at first, so I turn up my volume as Justin Timberlake lends us his '90s ad lib vocals. He gets through the first verse and chorus before a door at the other end of the hall opens. I don't look and the person doesn't say anything. Another door opens that isn't Easton's. Damn I'm about to make a fool out of myself in front of the whole damn floor.

JC Chasez starts the second verse and I finally hear something behind Easton's door. I step back and wait for the bomb to drop. JC starts the chorus again and then the bridge when the door opens and Easton's finally standing before me. The dramatic instrumental begins and Easton is about to say something when I hold up my finger.

I mouth, *Not yet.*

He squints and closes his mouth.

Justin's falsetto comes through my phone speaker and I join in to finish up the rest of the song.

Then, silence. I'm standing in the middle of the hall looking at Easton, and he's leaning his head against his door looking at me. I can't read his expression as he nervously runs his top teeth along his bottom lip and my heart kicks into overdrive. I should probably say something before this gets more awkward. Our audience demands entertainment and I'm going to give them just that.

"I brought lunch. It's your favorite," I say and hold up the bag of sub sandwiches to show him.

"Paul—"

"Have you eaten?"

"Uh, no."

"Good. Good."

"Paul—"

"Happy Birthday, Easton," I interrupt him again.

"Thank you." He gives me an aggravated grin and opens his mouth again. "Paul—"

"I love you."

"Wha-what?" His eyes go wide.

"Easton," I start but realize I need my hands to get through what I'm about to say, so I set everything on the floor by his door. "Listen, Easton. Okay, um. Okay, it's like, before…everything. Before you and I were just wandering around aimlessly, confused. I didn't know who I was, what my purpose was, what I wanted, or where I was going."

He squints again and folds his arms. Shit. Did I just lose him? *Get your shit together, Paul.*

"But when I saw you, when I looked into your beautiful honey-chocolate-with-flecks-of-gold eyes for the first time, like, really saw them at that party when you were a mess and completely shit-faced, everything just…clicked."

Actually it was probably the goose incident that did it for me now that I'm saying it out loud. Oh well. I'm not backtracking now because he relaxes a little, but I still can't read him.

So I continue, "All of a sudden, I knew. I knew exactly what I wanted. I knew exactly where I was going. I knew exactly what I needed to do." I take a chance and step closer to him. He doesn't back away, but his arms are still folded, tense. "It's you, okay? It's you, Easton. It's always been you. And I'm… I am in love with you. You are my light. My *world*. Love should be a never-ending hope. Hope for you. Hope for us."

I chance taking another step forward.

"I fucked up, Easton. I was scared and I felt betrayed and lied to. But I lashed out hardcore, and when I called you back and you didn't answer I thought…" I close my eyes and shake my head. I can't even think about it now. No. Nope. I look at him again, my eyes tearing. "I couldn't bear losing you. I was *terrified* it was the last time I'd get to see your face. Your beautiful face. I was scared, but I only want to see you happy and healthy. I want to love you for time and all eternity, I am certain of that. You are my future. I've never been so sure of anything in my entire life. You are my true love. You are my everlasting love. I. Love. You."

Easton licks his lips and looks down the hall. I want to look too, but I keep my eyes locked on him. He returns his gaze to me.

"I can't—" he tries, but I'm not having it. I came here to win him back and I need more than *I can't*.

"What are you so afraid of?"

"You!" he blurts out. "I'm afraid of you!" His arms unfold and gesture toward me.

I guess I did get him to loosen up a bit after all?

"You..." He bites his lip and looks down at his feet. "I hated you when I first met you. God, I hated you." Easton shakes his head and huffs, looking at the floor and then back at me. "But I couldn't stop thinking about you. For some reason I knew I could love you. But I didn't *want* to. God knows I didn't. But I knew I could, and that scared the ever-loving hell out of me. I was scared because of what loving you would mean. It would mean I'd hurt you. Not because I couldn't love you but because I could and my body hates me. It's literally falling apart inside. I've seen what it can do, and I didn't want that for you. But in you I found the love I needed, the love I've always wanted, the love I'd been searching for and craving."

He stops and looks me in the eye and smirks. "And you were *such a dick*! But then...you weren't. Why could you not just have been a dick? Instead, you're the man of my dreams. You're literally everything I've ever wanted and I don't feel like I deserve you. Not with my behavior, how I ignored you, and definitely not because I kept my...disease from you. Like, why?"

"Not to diminish your fears or anything, but if you're scared to love me then that's a pretty damn good fear to have," I deadpan. "Like, I'm sorry, but it is."

Easton rolls his eyes, but there's a hint of a smile there. "Paul, stop with the jokes and answer my question. Why?"

"Why what?" I ask tentatively. I'm slightly confused, but I don't want to piss him off.

"Why do you keep trying? You've been texting me nonstop for days, but... Why won't you stop after what I did?"

"What *you* did? Easton, come *on*! Who even fucking cares anymore! Fine, sure, okay, we've both made mistakes, we've both fucked up. Since the literal beginning, since we first met, everything *about* us has been all fuck-ups, mistakes, lies, what-the-hell-ever, you name it. We're both broken, dude. But if we're broken, then I don't want to be fixed if it means we get to be together. You're it for me, babe. I *told* you I don't care what life throws at us, I want to be by your side every step of the *fucking* way!

"So you have MS. That's okay. I want to be there. To help you. I choose you, all of you. But *you* have to choose me too. My heart is wide open to you. I know it's a risk. I know we're young, but *I don't fucking care*. You are more than worth it. But *you have to choose me too.* I've got problems galore, but I also have sandwiches and starry-night dates and all the fucking dick you want whenever you want it, dude."

"AYEEEEE!" someone hollers down the hall.

We both laugh and blush and he's all peachy and cute and I want to take him right here, right now. "I'll do whatever you want, Easton. Just...pick me too."

"Paul, I—"

"And obviously if you need more time, take it." I take a step back. "Take all the time you need. There's literally no pressure to make a decision right now. I mean our sandwiches are getting cold and these people might need an answer or they'll riot, but I can wait. I can—"

"PAUL!" Easton takes a big step toward me, his hand on my

forearm. "Stop interrupting me! If you would shut up for just two goddamn seconds, then I could tell you that *I love you* too."

Well, there I go again squealing. I rush him in milliseconds and pick him up into a hug to the sound of whistling and applause. I never anticipated an audience, but I couldn't imagine a moment more perfect than this.

I spin him around and laugh. I've never been happier in my entire life. Then we're kissing and kissing and I hear murmurs and doors close and by the time we come down from our high, we're alone in the hallway.

"You love me?" I ask with a toothy smile.

Easton rolls his eyes. "Yes. Yes, I love you, dork. But it's not going to be easy, Paul. MS is…unpredictable. Please know that—"

"It's okay." I nod then kiss him again. "I'm all in."

He smiles and kisses me back.

"Okay, okay." I pull away from him, but only slightly. "Then I just have one more question."

"What?"

"Food or sex?" I squint. It's gotta be one, right? "'Cause I'm ready to dick you the fuck down right now."

"You sure you…um…should?"

"This I promise you, Belle, I'm good. Swear." But I need to be sure he is too. "Are you…okay? To have sex, I mean? I don't want to overexert you."

I brush his hair out of his eyes. Little dude is due for a haircut soon.

"It's not that bad." He kisses me again, then pulls back and asks, "Can I?"

"Yes, yes! One thousand times yes!" I'm jumping up and down like a giddy little kid. I did it. It worked! And he said he loves me back. Holy hell, he loves me. I pin him against the wall and kiss him. No tongue. Just lips. It's sweet and simple and so perfect.

I could get lost in him. I could crawl into his love and wrap it around me like a blanket on a rainy day. He is home. No matter where he's at, he's home to me.

"I love you," I whisper into his mouth. "I love you so much."

"I love you too, Paul."

I stop and pull back to look into his eyes. He looks hurt that I broke contact.

"No. No 'too'. Saying 'too' sounds like you're only saying it because I said it and I don't want that. I only want you to say it if you mean it."

"I mean it, babe. I promise I mean it. I love you."

I'm all teeth and red face when I kiss him again. This time I snake my arms around his back, slow and deliberate, and pull him close. His arms move around my neck so there's nothing but our clothes between us.

Eventually we part and I can barely breathe. "Can I take you to my place? Huxley won't be back until tomorrow and I don't want anyone walking in on us."

"Where's Huxley?"

"Visiting her sister. I prepared for this. I knew you'd say yes." And I give him my evil grin and wiggle my eyebrows.

"Oh really?" He smiles.

"Really." I squeeze him.

"You're an asshole, you know that, right?" Easton laughs.

"Oh, speaking of assholes. Can we please go? Like, now?"

"I'll pack a bag." We untangle and I lean down to grab the food and gift.

* * *

Easton decides to eat later 'cause he's worried about bottoming after just eating a footlong sandwich. Totally fair. We can nuke them in the microwave later. Can't have anything getting in the way of what is about to ensue.

Easton drops his bag at the foot of my bed as I lean against the doorframe. He looks back at me. "What?"

"The things I'm about to do to that ass will be sinful."

He sits on the edge of the bed and leans back on his hands. "Only if I let you."

"Can I?" I ask.

He smiles. "Yeah, babe. You can."

"Come here." I hold out my hand and he takes it as I guide him into the bathroom.

"Shower sex?" he questions.

That thought crossed my mind too. I've been toying with whether this is a good idea or not because of what happened to me. But fuck it, I want to push that all behind me forever. I want to replace all my bad experiences with Easton. Always Easton. I want all spaces to be safe as long as Easton is there with me. "Wait, East, I want to tell you something."

He frowns, looking worried, so I continue quickly.

"I saw Dr. Orleen when we were split up, and she told me…she said I should see my family. Like, in person." I lean against the doorframe.

"Oh. Are you going to do it?"

"I already have."

Easton's eyebrows raise and he tilts his head in question.

"After everything…happened between us, I flew out there and resolved things with them." I push myself off the doorframe. "It was really hard honestly. Jace and I were shouting in each other's faces at first. In public. Huxley had to step in."

"Oh my God…" The genuine concern on Easton's face softens my heart in that way only he can do.

"But we talked it through, ya know? I mean we really talked it out, and everything's okay now. With Jace, with Dani and Felix. Well, not everything because Huxley moved in on my brother. But everything else…that's all because of you. I—"

"Wait…Huxley and your *brother*?" Easton looks stunned but he's grinning.

"Right! Was not expecting that. It's cute, I guess, but that's not important. I don't know if I woulda had the courage to do that if I didn't think I'd lose you without resolving those issues. After the way I treated you. So I had to do the work to make sure it won't happen again."

Easton's smile is filled with compassion and love. "Can't believe you did that just because of me."

I reach out to him and he takes my hand, standing from the bed. "I'd do anything for you, babe." I cup his jaw and kiss him with all the love I feel. He has to know what a fucking difference he's made in my life. I'm hoping this will start to show him.

"Come on." I break our kiss, and lead him into the bathroom. I sit on the edge of the toilet with him above me as I fiddle with the hem of his shirt. "You won't be needing this."

"No?" He tilts his head in question.

"No." I trace my fingers along his skin, upward with his shirt hooked under my thumbs. He lifts his arms as I help him out of it, and I throw his shirt in the laundry hamper.

I hook my finger into his waistline. "These too."

He unbuttons his jeans while I tug them off. He lifts one foot, then the other.

"Socks," is all I say. He places his left foot on my thigh and I make slow work of taking it off. After his socks are off, he just stands there before me in his boxer briefs. I kiss his belly button. Then his hip. Then his belly button again, then his other hip. His fingers are in my short hair.

"I love you, Easton Nicholas Belle." I rest my forehead against his abdomen. "I have been in love with you for quite some time now."

"I love you, Paul Donovan Acre. I've loved you since that fucking goose alla – "

"Since the goose?" I look up at him. "Really?"

"Yeah. Really. Those running shorts were too perfect." He rolls his eyes.

"I knew it! Guess I should find that goose and thank it, huh?"

"You sure you want to die?" Easton's shaking his head.

"Fair. Not today." It's a good point. "No more geese."

"And you knew at the party?" he asks, sitting on my lap and straddling me.

"That's when it clicked, yeah. But I think I loved you since the goose too. Whatever cologne you were wearing or body wash or something. I don't know, but it was divine and even though I hated your bitch ass, it was still a nice ass that smelled good, and it stuck with me."

"You like my ass?"

I move my locked hands from his lower back to grab his hips. "More than you know." I look up at him and there's something in his eyes that looks wrong, off. "What is it, babe?"

"Paul, why do you love me? I mean, I know you do. I can feel it. I can see it. But, like, why? I just can't shake the feeling that this is too…perfect? Too good to be true. I don't know."

"Easton." I brush a rogue strand of hair out of his eyes. "I love you because of everything that you are, everything that you stand for. I love you for all the superficial frilly stuff, sure, but it's more than that. Your heart is pure. Your mind is good. Your *soul*, gah! Your soul is my favorite thing about you, Easton. I love you because of *everything* that you are. All of it."

A single tear falls from his eye and I reach up to wipe it away. He nods. "Yeah. Yeah, okay. I love you, Paul. Thank you."

"You don't have to thank me for loving you. But you're welcome all the same."

"Still."

"Still." And then we're kissing. Sweet and simple into deep and longing. I lean forward to balance his weight, then stand. I walk over to the vanity and set him down on the sink. His hands are taking off my shirt, then my hands are removing my pants. My hands are my eyes as they learn every inch of his skin. They find every freckle and lock the information away into my memory.

He's still in his underwear and it just feels off-balance.

"Imma start the shower." I tell him, and then look down at his briefs. "You, get naked."

"Deal."

I find the perfect temp and flip the nozzle to go full on Hilary Duff and let the water fall like rain.

I grab Easton's hand and pull him into the glass encasement with me. The hot water washes over us as two become one. Mouths on each other. Hands memorizing new and exciting terrain. I don't know where I start and he ends.

"I want you," he says.

"You have me," I say.

"Touch me."

"As you wish."

"Can I?" he asks.

"Yes," I respond, and the next thing I know is him on his knees with my hands in his hair. I put my back to the water so he won't choke on it while I thrust into his mouth slowly, cautiously. He uses his tongue masterfully. He's wet and wanting and I swear I could live forever in this moment.

Time doesn't exist.

I cup his chin in my hand and guide him to stand. His tongue is back in my mouth. I can taste myself on him.

My turn.

I move to my knees and turn him around to face the back mosaic. His elbows are up against the wall and he rests his forehead on his forearm.

I motion for him to spread his legs and he abides, arching his back as a gift to me.

He's smooth with minimal hair and it's driving me out of my mind. I bite and lick and suck and tease his glutes until he's moaning my name and begging for my tongue. I smile devilishly and give him what he wants. He greets my tongue with a pulse of pleasure and I swear on my own fucking grave that I have never tasted anything sweeter.

As I work, my hands roam up his calves, thighs, ass, lower back, and I pull him further into my face. My hands are back on his thighs as they snake around to his tight stomach and down around his hips, where I hug him into my face even more.

Time eclipses this moment as I can feel him near the edge.

No.

Not yet.

I stand and turn him to face me.

"Wash up. Meet me in bed."

He bites his lip and nods.

Less than five minutes later, as I'm propped up against the headboard he exits the bathroom.

"Ready?" I ask.

"Paul, I don't know how much more I can take. I've never…" He searches for the words to say, his face reddened and beautiful. "…felt like this before."

I scoot to the edge of the bed and he walks to stand between my knees. I like this position. I may be the top, but him standing over me is incredibly sexy and empowering.

"Still afraid to love me?" I joke.

"If what you did in there is part of your love, then fear doesn't exist anymore."

I grab him gently and begin stroking him.

"Holy shit." He places his hands on my shoulders and throws his head back.

"Can I?" I ask.

"Yes, Paul."

I take him in my mouth and finish the race to make him hard again. But it's not enough.

"Why'd you stop?"

"Come here," I say as I lie flat on the bed and tell him to straddle my face. I've never been a fan of sixty-nining, but with Easton nothing is off limits.

He knows what I want and gives it to me. We take turns sucking and moaning, and moaning and sucking until—

"Paul, stop. I'm close."

I hum and lick my way to my other favorite spot between his legs and keep going.

His moans and whimpers fill my bedroom walls. I hope the walls take pictures so our love can be remembered long after we pass. Long after our love story is complete and we are nothing but a memory. Long after the world ends and the universe takes back what it so freely gave.

"Easton—"

"I know. Condoms?" he says. It's like he's reading my mind.

"On it." He falls off of me and on to the bed as I go to my bedside table and pull out what I'm looking for. I sit against the headboard again to roll on the condom. He moves to straddle my hips, above me right where he belongs.

I take the lube out of my side table drawer and get us both ready.

I kiss him as he lowers his hips. It's slow at first as he lets his body relax around me.

"Slow, Easton. Don't rush it." I lightly run my fingers down his back while I lick his nipple. I want to touch him everywhere, I want him to know that I love every inch of his perfect being. "There ya go, baby. Relax. Give in."

"Ah, *fuuuuuck*," he moans down at me, his hands on the headboard balancing himself.

I start moving slowly. Out, in, out, in. My hands cupping his ass.

He meets me for a kiss. We're chest to chest and I hug his waist and I work him into a fit of euphoric pleasure.

"I love you so much, Paul," he whispers into my mouth.

"I love you, Easton," I answer back. He moans as I leave my mark just above his collarbone.

"Holy…fuck. I've never…felt… Oh my God," he manages to moan in between thrusts. I match his words with action and, once again, I'm grateful for my gym therapy because I never want this to end even though my abs are on fire.

"Lay down on your stomach," I instruct, exiting him and lightly tapping his ass.

But then, there he is, all sprawled out before me and I can't help but think how lucky I am to have a love like this. Not just his body but him. To have an equal to share in *actual* pleasure. Too many times I've been taken advantage of sexually and I'm finally in a place to be able to trade the horrific memories of my past with precious moments like these.

"You okay?" Easton has a pillow under his chest with his arms wrapped around it.

"You've helped fix me, Easton. Of course I'm okay. Sure, there will be some bad days to come. But knowing I have you makes everything seem less…well, just less. Are *you* okay?"

He nods into the pillow. "I meant it when I said I've never felt like this. You make me feel wanted and worthy. Nothing compares to you, babe."

I hum and I crawl to him and kiss him. I climb on top and press my body against his back. My lips against his ear. "You are worthy, Easton Belle, of the most perfect love imaginable. And if you'll let me, I will do my best to give it to you."

"Of course."

"Thank you for choosing me."

He breathes deep as I kiss down his back and find my favorite spot again. He moans his reply as I get him ready. It doesn't take long before I'm back inside and making him sing.

Seconds, minutes, hours, days, weeks, months, years pass as we lose ourselves in each other. I don't know where he starts and where I end. I move and he screams out. I moan and he moves.

I'm in a pushup position with him squirming under me. His face in the pillow, teeth clutching its case.

He moans, "Paul…I'm…gonna come."

I breathe, "Come for me, baby."

"Oh God," he says.

"Holy fuck."

"I'm coming."

He arches his back to allow me to dig deeper, harder. I lace my fingers into his as we clutch the sheets together. I don't stop even after we finish together in a bubble of elite, luxurious bliss. He's shuddering as I take my time slowing down and we both decrescendo from on high.

I roll onto my back and throw the full condom aside. We are definitely going to have to shower again. But that can wait.

I just remembered he never opened his gift!

"Birthday gift time." I catch my breath and get up to retrieve it.

"Haven't you given me enough today?" He's eyeing me down as I walk back.

"It's barely…" I look at the clock. "Holy shit it's after six p.m." I'm back on the bed holding his present out to him. "It's definitely later than I thought, but there's still food and gifts and cuddles, maybe a nap. Perhaps even a round two to look forward to."

"You spoil me."

"I love you."

"I love *you*," he says and plants a kiss on my lips.

"Open, open."

Easton fusses with the bag and removes the tissue paper. He reaches in and pulls it out.

"It's...your *LAKERS* shirt. But—"

"It's yours now. I figured it's the token of when things started to get better between us, and you looked so much better in it than I ever did. So I want you to have it."

His mouth is open in awe, his eyes wide. He fingers the fabric and handles it like it's the crown jewel.

"Oh, there's also some rings and necklaces I thought would look cute on you, too. You have, like, zero jewelry. If you don't like them we can take them back and get something else."

He reaches back into the bag and takes out the jewelry. "No, it's perfect." He leans over and kisses me. "I love it."

"I love *you*." I tell him, and I mean it.

Easton

YOU'RE NOT GOING TO BELIEVE WHERE I'M AT

I wake to Riley Green's voice blaring from my phone. I quickly silence it. I don't want to wake Paul. He's so peaceful right now.

Sleep looks good on him. I yawn as quietly as I can, then trace the freckles running over his cheeks and across his nose, counting each one. I can just make out the movement of his eyes under his closed eyelids. Wonder if he's dreaming of me... I know I was dreaming of him.

It was like a slideshow of memories, some that we haven't even made yet, rolling through my head. The night out in the country in the back of his rented truck, the fire in his eyes after he ran into me when the goose attacked him, the glee in his face when he stomped everyone in the last round of trivia, rolling on the sand together. Only the good parts, they're the only parts that matter.

And then there was a sunset on the top of a mountain I've never visited, with his arm wrapped around me and my head on his shoulder, a kiss under fireworks on the Fourth of July, him on one knee and tears rolling down my face, black tuxes and *I do*'s.

I sigh as my eyes travel to his naturally dark pink lips. They're parted just a little. I want to lean in and kiss him, but it'd be cruel to wake him, especially if he's so asleep my ringer didn't do it already.

Who was calling anyway?

I grab my phone off the little wooden table. Aidan. AIDAN! Oh no! What time is it?

9:03 p.m.

Shit! We're supposed to be at the theater in, like, ten minutes! He is, or maybe isn't now, taking me to see the new Godzilla movie for my birthday.

Please don't be mad, Aidan.

EASTON: Sry! OMW. You're not going to believe where I'm at! We can miss the previews.

Now for the big question. Do I wake him before I go or leave him undisturbed? He's so adorable like this, and adorable isn't usually his look. I could leave a note, then send him a text to wake up to later, but it seems wrong to just leave after the evening we had, especially after finally telling him I love him.

I sigh and shake my head. I have to hear it one more time.

I scoot closer, pressing my bare skin against him and wrapping my arm over his waist. I run my fingers through his beard and cup his jaw. His eyes flutter open, and even in the darkness of the room that seafoam shines through. My breath catches and I smile.

"Hey, babe," I whisper.

"Belle." Paul stretches his arms and yawns, and as he does, I notice new ink on his hand. At least I think it's new. No, I know it is. There isn't a mark on his body I haven't seen. I pull his hand down to look at it.

"Did you just get this?" I ask. "I don't remember this one."

"Uh-huh." He weaves his fingers between mine. "I got it in your honor while I was in Kansas City. Do you like it?"

I try to talk, but my words catch in my throat. I stare at the beautiful art just below his thumb, now permanently part of him, like he's permanently part of me. "You seriously got a tattoo for me?"

"Look." He holds my hand like he would if we were walking outside. "It's like I'm giving you a rose. And it reminds me of you."

"Yeah?" I ask. "How?"

"'Cause you're so beautiful and sweet." He slithers his arms under mine and wraps himself around me. "Well, sweet *sometimes*."

"Hey!" I try to wiggle free but he holds me tighter, laughing. I couldn't be happier. "Uh…wow! I can't believe you did that. I don't even know what to say."

He kisses me gently and I melt a little. "You don't have to say anything. I wanted you with me always. Even when you're in class or…fuck, in the bathroom, I don't know. But"—I can't help but laugh—"you're still with me."

I put my forehead to his. "You're the best. You're the only one I'll ever want."

God I don't want to leave. I don't want to say I have to go, but Aidan is going to kill me if I don't. "I can't believe I have to say this now, but I gotta go." Immediately his brow scrunches and his smile dims. No. Don't do that! "I had plans with A. I'm supposed to be there already. I'm sorry!"

"No, it's okay." The smile comes back. He even giggles a little. "Go have fun with Aidan."

"Sorry, but thanks," I say.

"Stop saying you're sorry."

"Okay, sorry." I do it again.

Paul rolls his eyes and leans in and kisses me gently. I kiss him back, wanting more, but I know if I let him dig deeper into my lips I won't be leaving any time soon. I let the kiss end, as the memory of the way he made love to me bursts into my mind. I swallow back the ecstasy of those moments and smile.

"What?" Paul questions.

"Nothing. Just you."

"O-kay." He squints. I'll let him wonder.

"I really got to go." But I *so* don't want to.

I kiss him one more time, then slide out the bed naked. Immediately I feel cold, but I don't feel exposed like I usually would. I'm comfortable even though I know his eyes are on me, and he even confirms it.

"Dayum, Belle. Cakes for days," Paul catcalls me, and honestly I love it. I've always thought I never had an ass, but he makes me feel like I'm Cardi B or something.

I give him a little shake before getting dressed. The covers rustle and a moment later he's behind me, wrapping his arms around me and kissing my neck again.

"You're beyond beautiful, you know that, right?"

"Stop it." I brush off the compliment.

"Never," he says.

It's the simplest word, but it melts me.

My phone dings and I see Aidan's name pop on the screen. I hope he's not pissed, but honestly, he can get over it. I'm happy, and it's my birthday. Plus, I think he'll be happy for me too. He'll understand.

"I love you, Paul," I whisper with his cheek pressed against my jaw.

Easton

I'LL DO IT, BUT I'M STILL GOING TO COMPLAIN

Well, he did it. He finally did it.

Paul finally convinced me to go to the gym. Apparently, tormenting myself with a morning run every single day isn't enough, even if those have been better lately. We've been taking our Tuesday and Thursday runs together.

"Now we're going to do calf raises." Paul holds out a pair of dumbbells. I take them. They're heavier than I was expecting, but I rebound. "These are easy."

That's exactly what he said about the dumbbell walking lunges, and hell no. My legs feel like putty.

"All you have to do is hold them at your side, like this." Paul lets his arms hang, looking at me. "Just relax them. Then you're going to lift up on your toes and extend your calves. Okay?"

It sure as hell sounds easy.

"Sure," I say.

Paul comes up behind me and places his hands on my waist, for support I guess. I do like he said and try to relax my arms, letting the weight of the little dumbbells pull them toward the floor. Then I lift my heels, pushing with my toes.

"That's not too bad," I tell him.

"Okay, good. Now let's do three sets of ten of those."

"I got this." I shrug and start on the first set.

This isn't bad. Feels pretty good actually. Okay, maybe not good. Okay, no. I'm starting my eighth repetition when I begin to feel a burning in my calf, and now I'm rethinking these.

"Good, take ten," he says, meaning to take a ten-second rest. "You're doing well. Only two more exercises and you'll be done for the day."

He's taken the most keen interest in my health lately. My relapse scared the shit out of him, and of course it didn't help that he didn't have a clue what was happening because I'd been too scared to tell him before. Which in hindsight was so stupid of me. He loves me. He really does, and the last week, being open with him completely—no secrets, nothing held back—has been the best. Even if it did also get me stuck here. Apparently he did a lot of reading on MS while we weren't talking and found out that exercise and working out can help, so naturally, he was adamant about it. I'd been trying to convince myself running was enough.

"Two more? Like different types?" I ask.

"Yeah. We're going to do some deadlifts and squats."

"Squats? Excuse me?" I imagine I look a bit flustered.

"Yeah, you'll be fine." Paul pats my shoulder. He doesn't seem to care if others in the gym see us touch, which is pretty great.

"I hate squats," I tell him.

"Thought you didn't go to the gym." He cocks his head.

"I don't, but I've seen people do those."

"And..." He's eyeing me curiously, like I'm not making sense.

"It looks hard," I complain.

"Well, it is called fucking exercise, not let's have fun." Paul shakes his head, smiling at me.

"God, why me?" I pout. I'm about to complain some more, but he interrupts me.

"Okay, Mr. Complainy Pants, you're well past your

ten-second break." Paul's grinning massively. And did he seriously just call me Mr. Complainy Pants? How old are we? I can't help but smile back though. "I love you, but that means I can't let you slack either. Let's go."

I throw my head back and huff before straightening and lifting back to my toes. One. Two. Three. Okay now it's starting to set in. Four. Five. Ugh. I don't like this anymore. Is there not something easier? Six. Seven. Eight. I'm struggling to complete the ninth one. My legs are getting shaky and ugh it hurts, but Paul gives me a little lift and I make it. Ten!

"I hate you so much right now," I laugh at Paul.

"Ten-second break. You'll get over it tonight." He smiles back with that mischievous grin.

"Oh, will I?" I start to turn, but he tightens his grip on my waist and keeps me in place. Oh. *Remember where you are, Easton.*

"Actually there is something I wanted to talk to you about." He pauses to take a drink. "I want you to meet my family, well, my siblings, out in Kansas City." He looks me in the eye, his brow lifted. "I've been thinking about it a lot. Now that I finally made things right with them, and I want you to meet them. Especially Felix. I showed him a picture of you and he tried to steal it."

"Aw, that's...adorable," I manage to get it out between repetitions. He told me last night that he'd patched things up with them when we were apart, but it didn't get much past that.

"Maybe this summer?" Paul proposes. "Like June?"

"June?" I echo, dropping the bar back on its notches. I shove out a long breath and then breathe in. "That's soon."

"I know, but I want you to meet them." Paul pats my back. "We can fly out and spend a week—"

"You mean drive, right?" I pull into myself. I hate flying.

"No. I mean fly." Paul grins. "We wouldn't have time to drive there and back in one week. I'll have to get the time off work and I'm assuming you'll still have a job then too."

"But you know I hate flying," I remind him.

"No, I know you've never been on a plane."

"Because I hate flying," I remind him.

"How do you know you hate flying if you've never been on an airplane?" He raises his shoulders and gives me a questioning stare.

"I just do. Planes are scary. They crash and everyone dies." I know technically they're safer than driving cars, that statistically you're more likely to get in a car accident than a plane crash, but I don't care. Planes are huge death contraptions.

"Not often," Paul chuckles.

I feel sort of stupid. Like, I know it's one of those fears, those irrational things, but it'd be my luck I'd get on the one plane some mechanic missed a wire shortage on during preflight checks and the engine blows up mid-flight and we end up in pieces in the middle of the desert. Like, I can just feel it.

"Fine, whatever. I'll fly with you to Kansas." I huff. That's *if* we make it.

"Missouri," Paul corrects me.

I always forget about that. Why'd they have to go and split a city with the name of a damn state between two different states?

"I hate you."

"You love me." Paul leans over and kisses my nose.

I try to keep my mad face on, but he pecks my nose again and I can't do it. So I roll my eyes and smile. Who cares if we're in the middle of the gym, I guess.

"There's my Belle. Now," he says, slapping my ass, "let's focus." Paul laughs. He knows exactly what he's doing to me.

"Oh, I'm focusing, just—"

"On this. On your calf raises." He shakes his head, pointing to my calves, but I can see the lightness in his eyes.

"Okay." I huff again, and then I remember the concert I heard about this morning. Chris Housman is coming to town, to the area's only country nightclub, and I want to be there. "So if I'm getting on a plane for you, does that mean you'll go to a concert with me?"

"Maybe…" He squints.

I can hear the caution in his tone.

"Just say yes." I smile.

"What type of concert?" Paul asks, a smile returning to his face. I think he's on to me.

"Country…" I drag it out.

"Oh hell no!" Paul's grinning but shaking his head furiously. "No way!"

"Come on, Paul!" I pout, lips flared and everything as I start to twist around to face him.

"No, nope." He grabs my waist and keeps me from turning.

Dammit. He's too strong to fight against it, so I'm stuck. Guess I'm just going to have to beg.

"Please." I slump my shoulders. "You don't want me to go alone, right?"

"Why not?" Paul shrugs.

"What if someone tries to grab my butt?" I bump my ass back against his crotch.

His voice catches in his throat for a second, and the fact that I can affect him like that sends a thrill up my spine. He regains his composure.

"It's a country concert, who is going to grab your butt?"

"Someone," I dig. It could happen, right? "It's not like there are no country gays. I mean…" I throw my hands out and then point at myself.

"Ugh." He lets his head fall back dramatically. "Fine. Whatever!"

"Thank you!" I scream and jump, before I remember I'm in the middle of a gym with a bunch of straight bros.

Paul shakes his head and huffs, but I can see an underlying

grin. He wouldn't have let me go alone. Even if he wants to act like he would have.

"Alright then. Break's over. Back to work." He claps his hands to hype me up, then tightens his grip to steady me when I begin.

"You know I'm not coming to the gym every day, right?" I remind him. He knows, I've made certain of that, but I like to tell him, because he always does this adorable eye roll.

He does it, just as expected, then blows out a quick breath before relaxing. This really isn't that bad. Yeah, I sort of hate it, not going to lie, but he's here. He cares and wants me here, and why? Because he wants to keep me around, he wants me healthy so that we can spend more time together. How can I hate being here knowing that?

I can't.

But I'm still going to complain.

Paul

A LITTLE BIT COUNTRY

Time truly is a warped sense of being. When you pay attention to it you have all the time in the world. *But* when you're distracted by life? Time escapes in silence, running away without ever looking back and taking everything, save for your plans for tomorrow, your memories of today, yesterday.

The last week and a half went by in a blur. Easton, school, gym, work, therapy, and I've been dying to get another new tattoo. Maybe one with Easton, but given how much he winced when I told him more about getting my rose tat in Kansas City I'm not sure if he'd be down for it.

The weather's getting warmer, and Easton and I lose ourselves in each other every chance we can get. Every night is date night when our homework allows. We usually decide to go out and do something fun, stay in and watch *Sense8* or an indie gay film, or we make love. That's my favorite part, despite the mild panic attack I had the other day right in the middle of sex. Therapy has been great, really great, but that doesn't mean the trauma isn't there anymore. Easton was perfect through it though. He's learned tips from Huxley on how to help me through my panic attacks and I couldn't love him more. Everything with him is perfect.

He's had a couple off days, too. Days he's been "less than"

he normally is. "Less than" because they aren't bad, per se. He's just tired and weak. Aidan was right about him needing to take time to recoup on such days. He gets a lot of headaches and his vision really is affected the most. It's all been pretty mild symptoms compared to spring break. He gets irritable during these moments, but I think he's just scared. Fucking hell I am too, but I try to be strong and patient for him like he is with me.

I've been writing a lot. My classes force me to, but I've nearly filled an entire notebook with poems and spoken-word pieces I wanna perform. Work has been great, really great! I love my job at the bar and the people who work there. They've even started letting me bartend and the money is amazing. I haven't been able to get back up on stage except for one other time. I don't know, I kinda wanna do more with it. I just don't know what yet. Easton inspires me to want to be better.

And I must really love this jackass 'cause he somehow got me to agree to let him drag me to this *country bar* for a *country concert*. And on a Monday! What is it with this city always doing shit on Mondays?

I show my ID at the door and I kinda feel bad because Easton is the one who'd want to drink, not me. Though I'm sure I can sneak him something.

"I already hate this place," I growl.

"Hey!" He elbows me. "What was our one rule?"

"I know, I know. Don't bitch," I say. Why did I agree to this again?

But I smile and grab his hand and he pulls me through the crowd, even though this might not be the best place for it. Fuck if I care. I'll knock a bitch out if anyone says anything slick about me and my man. We are going to enjoy this night even if I didn't want to come.

"Come on, let's get some drinks and find a table," Easton suggests.

"So many people," I say as he continues to pull me through the crowd of bodies. Gah, and the smell of alcohol. It's everywhere. Fucking vom.

We find a table—a big empty high-top overlooking the dance floor and stage—and I go to the bar to order a water and a hard cider. I really don't want him getting drunk, but I also don't have a right to say shit to him about it. He knows his own body, not me. Well, I do know his body...just in other ways.

The first band is set up, but the show doesn't start for another half hour or so. Some dickwad's country twang is blaring through the speakers. Easton's singing along softly as a few couples swing around on the dance floor. I can feel myself scowling, but somehow all this bullshit makes Easton feel at home. I melt a little. I can see the way he's relaxed here and it makes me wonder when was the last time he really relaxed. Like, I'm all city, but there will always be a piece of Easton's heart that's country. If I want to spend my life with him—and I definitely fucking do—then I'm going to have to get used to this, I guess. Kane Brown isn't so bad.

I lean closer to Easton and tap the brim of his cowboy hat. "You do look sort of cute in that." He laughs a little and I really want to kiss him. "Think you're the only guy here in ripped jeans though."

"Probably, and you stick out like a sore thumb."

"Ha. At least I have my bandana. Cowboys wear bandanas around their necks, right?"

He smiles into his cider. "Something like that. Sure."

"Even if I found a single fuck I wouldn't give it. The only thing I like about this place is you." I smile and lean over to kiss him. It's quick, but he still blushes and looks around like we're going to get hate-crimed. "It's okay, Belle. I gotchu."

He just nods and I take his hand under the table. "When's this thing gonna start?"

He checks his phone. "'Bout ten minutes. Do you hate it that much?"

My shoulders droop. I know he really wants to be here and I don't want to disappoint him. I need to suck it up and do this for him.

"I... No. Just not my favorite." I smile. "But you wanted to come. I can deal. Might lose a few brain cells while I'm here, but I'll make it. You can make it up to me later." And I wink.

"Rude!" He grins at me as he takes a generous gulp from his glass bottle. "You just don't appreciate good music."

"Good music? Ha! *Good music*? Oh, don't get me started on that, because that shit is not happening here." I steal another kiss, then whisper in his ear, "Not a fucking chance."

He flips me off and we both laugh.

"Thanks for coming," he whispers back.

It's a simple thing, but I can see how much this means to him.

"Of course, babe."

"And you're right."

"I know," I preen. "Wait, about what?"

"I will make it up to you later." Then he attempts to wink, but both of his eyes close at the same time. He thinks he's doing it correctly, but he never does. I don't have the heart to tell him because it's just too damn adorable. I don't ever want him to change.

But before I can say anything, the music stops and someone comes on stage with a guitar in hand. This is going to be a long night.

Easton

I KNOW I CAN BELIEVE HIM

"You, sir, are supposed to be letting me win."

Paul apparently didn't get the memo. Let the bottom win.

"Uh, you've met me, right?" He's walking back to our seats from the shiny bowling lane, neon lights flashing and glaring across his flowery oversized white button-up and ripped jeans.

"Yeah, so?" I ask, acting as if it doesn't matter.

"You have to *earn* your win. Like, if Huxley didn't force us to be on the same team when we played pool all those weeks ago, you clearly would not have won," he comes back, smiling mischievously. "And don't lie, you like looking at my ass while I kick yours."

"First off, you *sucked* at pool! If it weren't for me we definitely wouldn't have won."

There's a big forty-eight on the far right of the screen by my name. We're starting the eighth frame right now, so I'm not doing too good. Paul's about as good at bowling as he is pool, but his seventy-seven looks a lot better up there.

"Maybe you'll do better the next round then." Paul smirks as I get up.

I find my ball, the lightest one I could find. The way I see it, it's lighter so I can throw it harder. Although if my high school physics class taught me anything, I think my reasoning might be a bit off, but oh well.

I approach the lane and someone, being Paul, whistles. "Nice butt!" I turn and roll my eyes at him, and go back to taking my stance. The music is blaring. It's one of Dua Lipa's hits, "Levitating". Lights flash and crash about the room like a rave. I focus on the lane—maybe I can at least get six. I pull my hand back and then sling it forward, sending the ball careening down the lane, but it's immediately obvious it's not going to knock anything over as it goes flying toward the gutter. Dammit.

I do the walk of shame back. I swear it's always awkward, and it's not just because I'm losing spectacularly. No. It's always weird. I don't know why, but it's like I don't know what to do with myself, and I feel like everyone is watching me. And of course, *he* is, but I like that he is.

"Not bad, not bad." Paul tries to pep me up, clapping.

I give him a strange look while I wait for my ball to come back through the ball machine or whatever it's called.

"Not bad? Are you…blind?" I yell over the music, refraining from using the F-word since I have to scream in here, and well, it's supposed to be a family-friendly zone.

He laughs and walks up behind me, wrapping his arms around my waist. He gives me a little squeeze and it makes it a bit better.

"You're trying, Belle, that's all that matters." Paul melts my heart again. Like, stop it!

My ball pops out of the machine and I grab it up.

"Nah, I want to beat your ass, that's what matters," I spout back, trying to act like I care that much. I don't, well, not really, except it would be cool to beat him and be able to brag about it the rest of the night.

"Have at it." He lets go of me and waves his hand dramatically toward the ten remaining bowling pins, with a gargantuan smile.

I roll my eyes and approach the lane. The light glares across my vision and I feel a tiny pang at the corner of my eye. They really need to calm the hell down on the lighting. Like, really? I refocus, but it's hard to see the pins in the dim lighting. I take my stance and go for it. The ball spins down the lane, and thank God it doesn't go straight for the gutter. I lean in, watching it fly forward, then crash into the pins on the left.

"Three? Really? Just three?" I throw my head back.

My score updates as I walk back, and Paul's already up.

"You're having fun, right?" He comes up before taking his turn.

"Of course I am." The weird part is it's true. This isn't something I'd probably do voluntarily with Aidan or my dad or Samantha, but it's what Paul wanted to do today, so I didn't even question it. Is that weakness? No. Definitely not.

"Okay," though he doesn't sound convinced.

I give him a smile and slap his butt when he starts off. He jumps and shakes his head. It's not his thing. So naturally I've made a habit of it. The good news is that I *can* do that now; he's come a long way. I swear Dr. Orleen is a miracle worker. I'm proud of him.

"Go babe!" I yell as he keeps shaking his head and makes his way to the lane.

When I take a seat I notice the group of old dudes in the lane two over from us. They're staring at me in disgust. Inside, my chest tightens. I don't want trouble, but I'm not letting them ruin this day for me. No matter how small-minded they might be. So I give them a big wave and smile. "Kill 'em with kindness" is what my dad always says, so consider yourselves dead.

Refocusing on Paul, I watch him glide toward the lane and release his ball in a way that looks like art. When I do it, I look like a bumbling idiot. The ball shoots down the lane and smacks the pins, sending every last one to the ground. He spins around, hands in the air.

"Strike!"

"Good job!" I yell. Sucks for me, but I ain't winning anyway.

Two rounds later we wrap up the game with Paul leading 122 to my sixty-seven. It could have been worse, but it also could have been better. I mean we could have used the kiddie guards. That would have gotten me a few extra points.

"Another game or the arcade?" Paul hooks his arm around me and pulls me close.

"Uh, arcade," I say in the most obvious way possible. "I can at least beat you in Skee-Ball, maybe even *Street Fighter*!"

"Oh, I dare you to try."

"Challenge accepted." I throw off my bowling shoes and slip back into my sneakers.

The arcade is in the same building. There's a bowling area, obviously, a massive arcade, laser tag, a mini golf course out back, concessions, and even this big kids' playhouse type of thing. We skip past the food court and enter the land of beeps and pops and screaming children. One of the little monsters nearly clips me coming around the gawky *Jurassic Park* game, and I'm reminded once more why I think I'll never want any of my own.

Maybe I should mention that to Paul. Hell, what if he wants kids? The possibility hadn't crossed my mind before. What if he wants a full house of kids? I'm about to ask, but I stop myself when my game comes into view. Skee-Ball. I used to dominate in this when Dad would take us.

"It's time for you to lose." I stick out my tongue and he shoves me playfully. "Let's not get violent now."

"Violent?" He shakes his head like I offended him, then laughs as I put tokens I bought earlier in each of our machines, lined up side by side.

The balls roll into their little container and I grab the first one.

Paul does the same, and I can see the competition building in his eyes. Please be bad at this, Paul. Please be bad at this!

"You ready?" It's not a timed game, but I act like it is anyway. Maybe that'll throw him off.

"Oh yeah, Belle." He snarls his nose and I just can't.

No distracting me, Paul! Stop it! I focus on the holes and their point values and assess my best route. The goals get smaller the closer they are to the center or the very top, and the points go up. I think I'm going to play it semi-safe.

"Go!" I yell, and without delay I send the first ball flying up the ramp and watch it swoosh near the middle but miss the thirty-point hole I was aiming for. Instead it rolls into the twenty ring. I don't wait for the points to hit the scoreboard before going for my second shot. Thirty this time.

Damn. I go to toss my third ball, but I can't make out the numbers on the goals anymore in my right eye. They're blurred no matter how many times I blink. A dull pang throbs in my forehead and behind my eyes. I shake my head. *Just keep going.* I close the blurred eye, but it throws off my aim. I'm lucky to hit anything. I throw my last and it's the fifth ten in a row.

"What was that about beating me?" Paul rings victorious. "Guess I'm not so bad at these games like you thought. Ha!"

"Ha, yeah. I guess maybe not," I say, all the confidence I had before gone. For a moment I consider acting like nothing's wrong, like I'm not having any problems. There's literally nothing he can do anyway, but hiding it from him again, it hurts. I can't do that. "I swear I'm not being a sore loser here, but my eye is all blurry all of a sudden. I could barely see the board."

"Oh! It's happening again? Do we need to go to the doctor? I can get the car." He's about to rush out the front door but stops to ask a few more wild questions. "Can you walk? Do you need me to carry you?"

"First, calm down. Please. I'm okay," I tell him. Yes, my mind is going a hundred miles an hour. I keep wondering if this will be the time my vision goes away and never comes back, but I know what's happening, so I'm not going to panic. I take a breath and try to smile. "It's just a little thing, like a couple weeks ago—"

"We need to get you to the hospital, Belle! It can't be normal that this is happening so frequently." He starts talking over me, and if it wasn't for him being worried, it'd piss me off.

"No." I stop him, putting my hands on his shoulder. "Stop, babe. It's just a headache and a blurry eye. I'll call the doctor tomorrow. I promise. I've dealt with this before. I'm just stressed with finals coming up or whatever. I'm not going to pass out on you this time. At least I don't think..."

That last part I probably should have left off. I mean if one thing is for certain it's that I don't really know what my body is going to do, but I don't need him panicking and right now, there's no reason to.

"But—"

I put my finger to his lips and smile. "It's okay."

"Uh...okay." Paul's shoulders relax a little and now I have time to think.

And the thoughts flood my mind. I can still "see" but it's just colors in my right eye. Everything is fine in my left eye. But is it going to stay like that? I'm always worried the clarity isn't going to return, that I'm going to be stuck with only one good eye forever. But then what if it happens to my left eye too? I don't want to be blind. I like seeing. I like being able to see Paul's seafoam-green eyes, his bleached-blonde hair and brown beard. I love to take in the pinkness of his lips and the thickness of his thighs and the way his chest flexes. His tattoos. I don't want that to be taken away from me.

"You sure you're okay?" Paul steps closer.

"Sorry." I realize I've drifted away in my head. I say what I'm thinking, even though I know I'm technically okay right now.

"I'm scared, Paul."

His eyes go glassy and he pulls me into a gracious hug. His warmth pulls me closer, and even in this moment when I'm scared of what might be, there's so much comfort in his arms. I never thought that would actually happen, not for me.

"It's okay to be scared, baby." He squeezes me tightly but doesn't say more right away. Then he kisses my cheek and pulls far enough back to look me in the eye under the neon lights. "I'm scared too, but we've got each other, right? I'm going to be here for you no matter what happens, holding your hand all the way through it all. I've got you, Belle. But legit, I don't care if it's Fun Before Finals. I think we should skip trivia tonight. I don't care about any of that. You are what matters. Your health. We should really take it easy. Once finals are over two weeks from now, then things will be less stressful. And if you're feeling up for it we can go to the party Huxley told us about tomorrow night. But we gotta get you in to see the doc just in case."

I nod and he hugs me again, holding me tight. His words run through my mind, covering up all the horrifying things streaming through my head. They're just words, and words mean little coming from most people, but I know I can believe him. He's got me. I know he'll be there for me.

Paul

I'M HOME

I cannot wait until finals are over because this past week of classes and homework and studying as we gear up for them in two weeks has been like living in the absolute depths of hell. Easton's been doing better since yesterday afternoon, and even though he insisted on going to the party tonight, I'm nervous. I really don't want to repeat spring break.

"Wait! What the *hell* are you wearing?" I'm sitting on the couch with Easton asleep on my chest, watching Patrick propose to David, and Huxley walks out of her room dressed like the Scarlet Witch.

She stops. "Uh, a costume. For the *costume* party we're going to?"

"Excuse me, *what*?" I put *Schitt's Creek* on pause as Easton stirs from my hysteria.

"You never mentioned it was a *costume party*. I thought it was just, ya know, a party. A regular old party."

"Uh, I'm almost entirely certain I *might* have."

"I'm going to fight you." I scowl. I don't have a costume! I can't go to a costume party without a damn costume.

She walks over to the living room mirror to put in her earrings. "Why don't you put those charming dramatics to use and go put on the costume I left laying out on my bed for you."

Oh shit. I can *only* imagine what kinda costume she has for me. Beggars can't be choosers, I guess. Only I for real didn't wanna go to this thing in the first place.

"I don't have a costume though," Easton says sleepily. Guess he's awake.

"Yes you do." Huxley turns around to face us. "Aidan says you have a little Spider-Man number in your closet."

Easton scrunches up his face, rubbing his eyes. "That doesn't fit. That was from high school."

"So it'll be a little tight. I doubt Paul will care." Huxley shrugs, makes her way to the refrigerator, and pulls out a Dr. Pepper can. "Shit, I need to Facetime Jace real quick."

"Huxley—"

"No, Paul. No." She slaps the island counter. "This is literally the very first time you have agreed to go out with me and you *both* will be putting on your costumes and going to this damn party. I'm pulling a selfish. You're going. We're young and sexy as fuck and we're going to flaunt our assets for the world to see. The semester is almost over, *RENT* is only a week away, and I'm stressed. We're all going. Deal with it."

"What do you mean 'flaunt our assets'? Huxley?!"

* * *

"I hate you. I hate you so fucking much. You're gonna get it, Huxley. I swear you are." I grab her arm and whisper into her ear as we ascend the stairs to the house party. Easton's in his Spider-Man costume—minus the mask since it's, and I quote, "hot as Satan's balls"—and it's definitely small on him. I don't mind though. It leaves nothing to the imagination and all I can think about is the jock strap he's wearing under it...and nothing else.

Aidan's Man in the Mask from *The Strangers* and he looks awesome. Aidan's friend Cameron is a vampire, cloaked in a crimson robe. But me? I look ridiculous. I'm wearing the skimpiest maid costume Huxley could find on Amazon. So this was all premeditated. Yeah, well, two can play that game because I'm thinking about all the ways I could hide her body.

"Paul, you have literally never looked sexier. So you're welcome," she not-so-whispers back.

"That's what I told him. But he won't believe me," Easton adds. "I mean, look at those thighs! And your tattoos? I'm *dying*."

"See?" Huxley says smugly. "Toldja."

"It's literally riding up in the back. Everyone is going to get a look at my literal asshole tonight."

"It's a good ass though." Easton smiles.

"Now you know what it's like to be a woman." Huxley smirks.

"I didn't realize you had so many tattoos, Paul," Aidan comments. But yes he did. He saw me at the beach.

So glad everyone can have a laugh at my expense. Ha ha.

"Oh, he does. He even has one on his —"

"I hate every single one of you," I yell over him.

"Can't hate me. We just met," Cameron pipes up.

"Yeah, and what a great first impression I'm making," I deadpan.

We're in the kitchen while Huxley and Aidan mix drinks. Easton took one shot but decided that's all he's having for the night. We agreed he would take it easy after what happened at the arcade yesterday. I'm playing DD, and good thing too with the amount of alcohol Aidan is pouring everyone.

We all head out back to the pool area. It's the end of April, and North Carolina is going through a heat wave. The partygoers are countering Mother Nature with very little clothing. So I'm right at home.

Insert eye roll here.

Olivia Rodrigo blares through the speakers and Party City colored strobe lights take over my vision as I slip my hand into Easton's.

"Do we have to stay the entire time?" I whine.

"Why?" Easton rolls his eyes, but he's giggling at me.

I take the most obvious glance at his backside. "Have you seen your ass in that costume?"

He always says he doesn't have an ass, but from my point of view, it's the perfect twink bubble butt. All that running has done him good.

Easton smiles weakly at me. "I tried not to look. It's honestly so small. I have a wedgie and I'm wearing a jockstrap. Figure that one out."

"I'd be able to figure it out…with my teeth," I whisper into his ear.

He blushes my favorite shade of peach and hits me in the chest. "Paul, I will *murder* you if I get a boner in this costume right now."

"What are you two talking about?" Huxley comes up behind us and flings her arms over our shoulders. She's so short that her feet practically dangle in order to reach us.

"Oh nothing." I feign innocence. "Having fun yet?"

She scoffs and takes a rather large swig of her most recent drink. "When am I ever *not* having fun?"

"Point." I nod.

"Where's Aidan and Cameron?" Easton asks, looking around.

She doesn't answer as she finishes off her drink, tosses her cup, then grabs Easton's and my hands. "Come on! Let's daaaaance."

"How the hell are you already tipsy?" I ask, but I'm not shocked.

"Come on, come on, come on."

So we do. We go and we dance and dance and it actually feels really good. The semester is almost over and I have my three favorite people here with me—plus Cameron. I couldn't ask for anything better. To be able to let loose all of my stress and fears as I hold Easton close, it finally clicks why people do this. I don't drink, but the energy here, being surrounded by people my age trying to let loose as well…it just makes sense.

I look around and smile. Coming to Charlotte might just have been the best decision of my life.

Everything fades away as I lock eyes with Easton. Their honey-brown majesty takes me away to the farthest corners of the universe where the brightest stars mingle with Easton's red aura with fuzzy pink edges. Nothing else matters.

"I love you, Easton," I mouth.

"And I love you," he responds in kind.

His hands wrap around my neck and he pulls my mouth to his. Our hips swaying to whatever Top 40 is currently playing. His lips greet me with a wet hello as his tongue works in tandem with mine.

A minute later he breaks away to check his phone, and a drunk, wobbly Aidan comes into view.

"¿Jacob te envió un mensaje… Ha," Aidan says, then translates himself for Easton. "Did Jacob text you?" But it sounds more like "di shacoob tess you."

"Yeah, I just got it," Easton chuckles. "Want to go?"

Aidan complains, "This party sucks. Muy cojo."

"What's going on?" I ask.

"Jacob, you remember, from the beach?" Easton stops long enough for me to nod. My memory isn't that bad. "His band is playing at the coffee shop we did trivia at. We should go!"

Huxley comes over with Cameron. "What's happening?"

"Jacob's band is playing at–" Easton starts to explain, but Huxley gives him no room.

"Yes!"

I laugh. "But you don't even know —"

"I don't care. This party is lame. Whatever it is, let's G.T.F. outta here."

"I second that," Cameron says.

So everyone hates this party then? I didn't think it was that bad, damn. But then again, I'm not exactly a party connoisseur.

Plus, I could really use a cinnamon iced coffee.

* * *

We all pile into my car and Easton gives me shitty directions to where Jacob is playing. I wanted to go home and change first, but Huxley said no and Aidan insisted — albeit drunkenly — that we wouldn't have time. At least we'll all look like fools together dressed up for Halloween in April.

I park, but we finish singing One Direction at the top of our lungs before we make our way inside, and it looks like the show has already started.

It's a very different atmosphere from the last time I was here. The lights are low — there are fewer people, but it's still a good turnout — and music blares. Huxley spots Skylar and Imani and screams, which gets my attention, but it's all just garbled noise under the music. Skylar waves us over with the biggest smile. Everyone says their hellos and then Cameron, Easton, and I go to get drinks.

By the time we make it back to the tiny area holding all the concert goers, the openers are finished and it looks like The Nevermores — that's Jacob's band — have taken the stage. It's guitars and drums and more guitars. The first riff breaks and music fills the shop loud enough I'm worried about the windows. They only play a few songs — a couple covers that I don't recognize, mostly rock, and one original. They all sound original to me, and love it! Aidan and Imani sing along while the rest of us just enjoy the show.

After it settles down and the last song ends, the crowd disperses, but we stick around to catch up with Skylar and Imani while Jacob and his band pack everything up. Everyone is making fun of my maid costume again, and I guess I'm the butt of everyone's joke tonight. I don't mind though. I know I only spent one evening with them before, but it's like seeing old friends. Imani introduces her boyfriend, Seth, and Aidan introduces Cameron to everyone, and suddenly I'm kinda sad Tyler's pale self isn't here with us.

The shop is all cleared out by the time Jacob comes back over to the group.

"Hey, everyone! Thanks so much for coming. I hope you liked the show."

We all give him a chorus of congratulations and — from Huxley — bravos.

"Also, I want to introduce y'all to a friend of mine. This is Noah! I've known him for years. Thought he could hang out with us tonight. Dawn said we could all stay and chill for a bit as long as we clean up." He turns back to Noah. "If that's okay with you."

I don't know who this Dawn woman is, but sure.

"Yeah, yeah. I'm cool with that." Noah nods. He's a handsome guy, on the cute side, he looks a little timid, like he's on the brink of breaking out of his shell but hasn't fully gotten there yet. "Nice to meet y'all."

We all take turns introducing ourselves to him and then make our way to a few tables to sit and hang and chat.

We break off in two groups since there are so many of us. Huxley, Skylar, Imani — who I learned tonight is basically Skylar's translator too — and Seth huddle between the new thrillers and new young adult books while Easton, Cameron, Aidan, Jacob, Noah, and I crowd up the space in the used section.

I swear it looks like Cameron and Noah are hardcore flirting. Go Cameron! Even though I literally met them both tonight. I don't know, it's just cute.

Everyone here is coupled up. Sure, Tyler and Jace aren't here physically, but we all have someone, and that's really special to me.

I put my arm over Easton's shoulders and pull him into me. I kiss his temple and tell him I love him. He turns to look at me and gives me a kiss.

"I love you," he whispers, then kisses me again.

"Ew!" Jacob throws a wadded-up napkin at us. "Get a room."

Everyone laughs and we all come back together as a group.

"Ya know," I start but get a little choked up. Everyone is watching me. Easton takes my hand and gives it a squeeze. "Before I moved here I felt like I had nothing, no one. I was lost and angry and…broken. But coming here, I've found a…family. I've found myself. I've found love." My eyes water and I move to dry them. "I found a family in you, Easton, and in Huxley and Aidan. In all of you. A wise woman once told me that waffles and pancakes and syrup can fix anything. You all are my waffles and pancakes and syrup. You all are like Waffle House—"

"*Please* stop with the cheesy metaphors! Waffle House is so dirty. We're better than that!" Huxley interrupts and everyone laughs.

"You know what I mean, bitch. I'm trying to be sentimental."

"Sentiments have never been your brand, bitch." Huxley rolls her eyes.

"Yeah, it's not you," Easton chimes in, and I slap his shoulder playfully.

"It is hard to take you seriously when you're half naked and your ass is hanging out of your bloomers." Huxley wiggles her eyebrows and leers at me seductively. "But I love you anyway."

Everyone laughs again and I throw Jacob's napkin at her.

"I love you too, Huxley."

We cheer and clink plastic cups and everyone breaks out into conversation again.

Cameron whispers something to Noah and they go off on their own. Ooh la la! Is someone making a move?

I take inspiration from Cameron and pull Easton outside with me.

"Everything okay?" he asks once the door closes behind us.

"Yeah. It's perfect."

I pull Spider-Man into me and kiss him. He doesn't part his lips, but just kisses me sweetly. It reminds me of that time back in my apartment when we made up after my anxiety attack. That time he kissed me the exact same way. That time I knew for certain that I was in love with him.

He pulls away with a devilish look on his face, then whispers in my ear, "I want you to fuck me—"

"Oh, I will." I let my lips hang open.

"—wearing this." He places his hand on my chest over the maid costume.

I pull back, eyes wide. He seriously wants me to keep this on while I fuck him? Whoa. I mean, it would be sexy as shit, I guess, but I didn't think Easton would want to get that freaky. I certainly haven't done anything like that before, but I'm totally down. "Wait, what?"

"I want you to wear this while you—"

"Oh, no, I got that. But really?"

He shrugs. "Take me home and find out for yourself."

My groin flares and I grin so hard my face hurts. So I push him up against the wall and kiss him until my lips are numb. Until time doesn't exist.

There was a time before all of this when I thought I wasn't allowed to want love. Or sex. I was so terrified to open up and let anyone in after the abuse I endured. But that's just it, I *endured* it. Continually. I didn't give up no matter how much I truly wanted to. And I'm learning not to let it all define me.

Sure, not every day will be a good day, but not every day will be a bad day either. I have a great support system around me so that I don't have to go through anything alone anymore. I get to choose who I want to be and how I want to live. I get to choose who I want as my family.

I'm not afraid anymore. Because I'm home.

Easton is my home.

Easton

EPILOGE - UNDER THE STARS

It's clearer out tonight than I remember it being last time, and so much warmer. The moon might not be visible, but the katydids and crickets are out in force, filling the air with their chirping while the stars shine overhead.

"Whachya wanna do?" Paul asks, rolling to meet my gaze atop the thick blanket I stole from his closet earlier.

"I don't know." I smile up at him, and he leans down and pecks my lips. "What do you wanna do?"

"You, if you let me."

I hit him and laugh. "No, not like that. I was thinking… We've got all summer to do what—"

"Never a better time than the present." Paul's smile gleams back. He's so full of himself, but I love it.

I roll my eyes and laugh. "True, but I wanted to talk to you about *our* summer. You didn't exactly get off on the best foot with my dad, but I'd really like for you to meet him…again. Like, really meet him, and Sam too. She's been asking when she gets to meet you. Well, so has Dad."

"Your dad's been asking about me?" Paul's surprised, like really surprised. Eyes wide, chin tucked back and all.

"Yeah." I nod.

"Well, shit. I thought I blew that. I mean, I was a total asshole to him, and he saw my whole freak-out." Paul throws his head back. "I'm not going to lie. I knew this was going to come up, and I know I need to actually meet him, but you know how I am with parentals."

"I know, but I really want you to meet him. You'll like him. I swear, he's not like…" I stop short of bringing Paul's dad into the conversation. There's no need to stir that up, but I do want him to get to know my family — well, my dad and sister. I mean he's a part of my family now as far as I'm concerned, so he really needs to. "He's cool."

"I'm sure he is," Paul says.

"Maybe we can go after Pride," I say.

Charlotte Pride is next weekend and we've already decided we're going. Jace and Felix are even flying in to join us. I've been to Pride parades, but only back home, and those can barely be called parades. There were maybe five little floats going down Main Street, and most of the people attending were protesters. I hear the one here in Charlotte is huge and I can't wait to meet his family.

Paul's gaze leaves me, gravitating toward the stars. His lips bunch up then skew. I want to lean over and kiss him, but I don't. He'll have to give in first. The space in between us on this blanket is staying until that happens.

"I will —"

"Yes!" I squeal.

"— on one condition," he finishes and I grunt.

One condition? This better be one of those give-me-a-blowjob-and-I'll-go type of conditions. I'd be down for that.

"We should go to NYC for the Fourth of July. Just us."

"*Only* if you don't make me get on an airplane." I make it very clear. I'm not getting on one of those death traps unless I have to. "Make it a road trip?"

"I can deal with that. And I'd go with you to meet your family either way by the way." Paul grins. I roll my eyes, but then he says something I'm not expecting. "Have you thought about where you're going to live next semester when classes start back?"

Have I? Of course I have, but I'm split on it, and that's why I've not brought it up. I want to stay with him. I want to spend every single night with him, even if he is a human oven. That's what I want, but how can I leave Aidan on his own? He'd have to get a new roommate—again—or let the campus assign one to him. But at the same time if I moved in with Paul I'd save money, and God knows I need that.

"A little bit," I tell him.

"I was thinking maybe you could move in. With us. Huxley and I are keeping the apartment," he tells me.

It's what I was expecting, but I'm not really ready for this conversation.

"Maybe..." I shrink in on myself. "I want to, I do, but what about A?"

"You don't think Aidan would be rooming with Tyler if the roles were reversed?" Paul asks. "For real, serious question."

I don't have to think about it, it's not even a question. He would, and I'd be stupid to think otherwise. He loves Tyler.

I look up at Paul and smile. I love this man. I love him so much, and he's right. I scoot closer so he can wrap his arm around me and pull me in. I sigh. This is what I want.

"You're right." I lean over and brush my cheek against his beard and take in the leather and sage scent of his cologne mixed with the fresh scent of grass and the outdoors. "But maybe we could all find a place together? I can't leave A behind. I just can't."

"Oh! Now there's an idea! We should totally talk to Hux and A about that tomorrow. I'm off work tomorrow night and we can invite A and Tyler over. Make it a game night."

"That'd be great," I say, rolling over on the ground and gazing up at the stars.

"What is it?" Paul's staring at me, boring into my soul like he does.

I keep going between him and the stars, shifting my focus between his breath and the crickets or the seldom soft hoot of an owl. I don't say anything right away. Instead I keep looking to the midnight sky.

The stars are gorgeous. I love the way they hang above us like little glittery nightlights, how they move slowly, almost imperceptibly across the sky, looking so close to the Earth, but in reality they're millions and millions of miles away, out of reach. And maybe, just maybe, there's another giant ball of rock orbiting one of them with another boy lying next to his favorite person looking at the stars, seeing ours and thinking the same thing. But as fascinating as that is, as much as the thought thrills me, nothing amazes me like the guy lying next to me.

"Everything," I tell him. "The stars. The moon—"

"The moon? It's not even up," he interrupts, joking. And I want to slap him, but instead I smile.

"I was trying to be romantic, thank you very much."

"Fail," Paul blurts and kisses me on the cheek.

"Eh," I grunt and shift to face him. He slips his arms around me and pulls me closer. "But in all seriousness, this is perfect. All of it. You're perfect."

"Perfect definitely isn't something I'd call myself, I'd—"

I put my finger against his lips to stop him.

"You're perfect for me, to me. I don't need you to be literal perfection. That'd be boring," I tell him. It's the little—and big— imperfections that make him Paul, that make him unique. Even the bad and the unfair and all the shitty things that made him into the person he is today. I wish I could have spared him from all of that, all the horrors he had to endure. The crazy part is that would probably mean this moment never would have happened, that I never would have met his beautiful soul. And maybe... I don't really want to think about it, but maybe I'd never be loved the way he loves me, but I'd still do it if it meant sparing him from that, because he deserves better. But that's a myth, a fantasy, something I can't give him. So he gets me instead.

I keep telling myself that's not selfish. Because maybe I do deserve this. Maybe I do deserve to be loved, to be happy and satisfied. To be me.

I still question why I hid my sickness from him. I mean, I know it was fear. Fear that he'd not want me, that I'd be a burden, but it was so stupid. *I* was so stupid. And now I can finally see it.

My sickness doesn't define me, it never did. It doesn't make me unworthy of his love. It doesn't make me less than, a thing to be used and thrown aside. I don't have to fight for love. I let my negative feelings consume not only my physical being but my mind. I let them degrade me and convinced myself that was what I deserved. But no. I think, just maybe, I'm worth more. Because he sees me. He saw *me* before I ever did.

"Holy shit. I love you, Easton Nicholas Belle. I love you so much." Paul inches closer and our lips become one.

My eyes close and the taste of his mouth blends with all my other senses, caught up in this rapture of chirps and the gentle touch of the wind on my cheek, the cherry sweetness of his kiss. Our lips part, but my mouth hangs open a little while longer while I process it all.

I'm loved. I'm loved for who I am, not for what I can give, and in spite of all the shit that pulls me down. He loves me. He truly loves me. I never thought I'd believe that, but I do. I know it. And he's helped me learn how to love myself too.

"Then show me." I flash a grin and practically jump him.

It's just him and me. No one else. No bugs or birds, no stars or sky, no ground beneath us. We're floating in each other's touch, cradled by sweating arms and euphoric motions that swirl in my mind, losing ourselves in each other's love.

By the time we come down from it all, we're naked and breathing hard. I fall on my back and stare into his beautiful seafoam-green eyes. They shine under the stars as he looks at me, as he sees me, the person I am, the person he wants. And I see the person I want too.

"I love you, Paul Donovan Acre," I breathe, leaning in to peck his lips again. I sigh happily and smirk at him. "And just in case you were wondering, my ring size is seven."

ACKNOWLEDGEMENTS

Writing a book isn't the easiest feat one can attempt, but thankfully with some help it's actually a lot of fun. Without each other, we wouldn't have been able to do what we've done. It was truly a joint effort. We're both so grateful to have collaborated with each other, and for Kalob having this crazy idea that we should in the first place. We're also eternally thankful to everyone who has been involved in the process, from the initial first draft, to the multiple edits, and even the massive changes that made this story what it is now. If y'all would have read the initial draft, y'all would have been so mad at us (read: Kalob, y'all would have been so mad at Kalob). Just like our beta readers were.

A big shout out goes to our beta readers Jordan Webb, Ian Day-Oshita, and Renee Thiringer. Y'all were an integral part in shaping this story, and redirecting it in the direction it really needed to go.

Thank you to Jennifer Upright and Gavin Evans for their help with the book's back cover synopsis, our least favorite part of writing. Truly.

Thank you to Roni Duran, Renee Thiringer (again), Jaida McDonald, Tyler Welton-Stewart, Rachel Witte, Megan Nichols, and Laura Zimmerman (even though you're moving away - Jordon) for your advice and emotional support during all the ups and downs of writing.

It's also a great honor to get to work with other amazing creatives to prepare and develop different parts of our finished book:

Thank you to Sabina Laura (Jordon's favorite poet) for graciously allowing us to use another of her poems! You're amazing.

Now for that cover! Thank you so much to Myriam Stasbourg, known on Instagram as @peaches.obviously, for designing such a breathtaking cover that really captures the way Easton and Paul adore each other. It was truly a dream to have worked with you, and we really can't thank you enough!

As always, thank you to our amazing editor, Christie Stratos. You are amazing, and everyone who reads this book should be thanking you!

ABOUT
JORDON GREENE

Jordon grew up in a small southern town in the foothills of the Appalachian Mountains just south of Boone, North Carolina. He is an alumni of the University of North Carolina at Charlotte with a B.S. in Political Science and now works at the nation's largest privately owned shoe retailer as a full-stack web developer. While not writing, Jordon spends most his time entertaining his cat babies, Genji & Mercy, watching Schitt's Creek and Queer Eye re-runs, and probably overthinking something simple. He lives in Kannapolis, NC.

VISIT JORDON ONLINE AT
www.JordonGreene.com

ABOUT
KALOB DANIEL

Kalob Daniel is a gay author and avid bookstagramer. He has a degree in interior design and currently lives in Kansas City, Missouri, where he watches re-runs of Schitt's Creek and Superstore insistently with his shihpoo, Jefferson. When he's not writing, he's reading queer books. He loves anything gay and fantasy or contemporary. Some of his favorite books include *Wolfsong*, *The Song of Achilles*, and *So This Is Ever After*. He is also the author of the *A Faerie Tale* series. Kalob has visited 49 out of the 50 states, and he does great impersonations of Donald Duck and Kermit the Frog.

VISIT KALOB ONLINE AT

www.KalobDaniel.com

CPSIA information can be obtained
at www.ICGtesting.com
Printed in the USA
LVHW032117181022
731001LV00003B/32